TO
SHAPE
A
DRAGON'S
BREATH

TO SHAPE A DRAGON'S BREATH

THE FIRST BOOK OF
NAMPESHIWEISIT

MONIQUILL BLACKGOOSE

NEW YORK

2023 Del Rey Trade Paperback Edition

Copyright © 2023 by Monique Poirier

Published in the United States by Del Rey, an imprint of Random House,
a division of Penguin Random House LLC, New York.

Del Rey and the Circle colophon are registered trademarks of
Penguin Random House LLC.

Library of Congress Cataloging-in-Publication Data
Names: Blackgoose, Moniquill, author.
Title: To shape a dragon's breath / Moniquill Blackgoose.
Description: Del Rey trade paperback edition. |
New York : Del Rey Books, 2023.
Identifiers: LCCN 2022016061 (print) | LCCN 2022016062 (ebook) |
ISBN 9780593498286 (trade paperback; acid-free paper) |
ISBN 9780593498293 (ebook)
Subjects: LCGFT: Fantasy fiction. | Novels.
Classification: LCC PS3602.L3252947 T6 2023 (print) |
LCC PS3602.L3252947 (ebook) | DDC 813/.6—dc23//eng/20220708
LC record available at https://lccn.loc.gov/2022016061
LC ebook record available at https://lccn.loc.gov/2022016062

Printed in the United States of America on acid-free paper

randomhousebooks.com

6 8 9 7 5

Book design by Alexis Capitini

Map and periodical chart illustration by Francesca Baerald

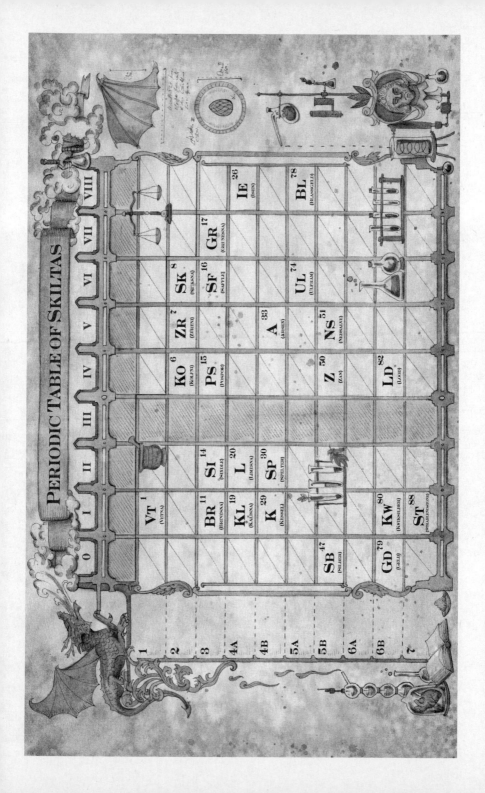

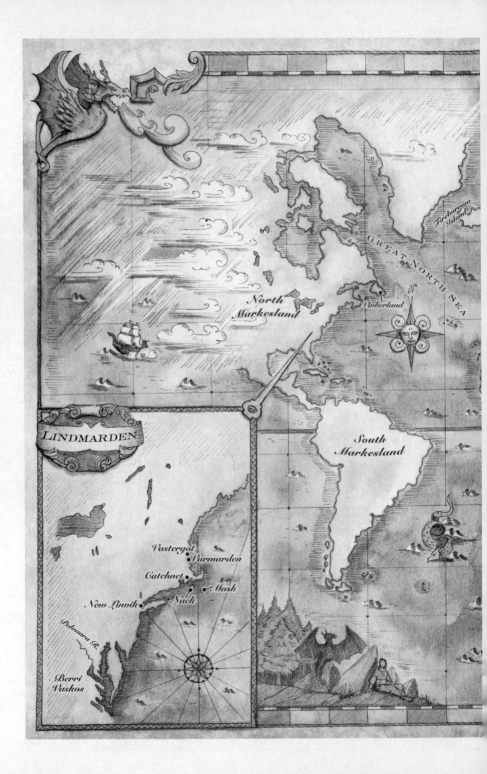

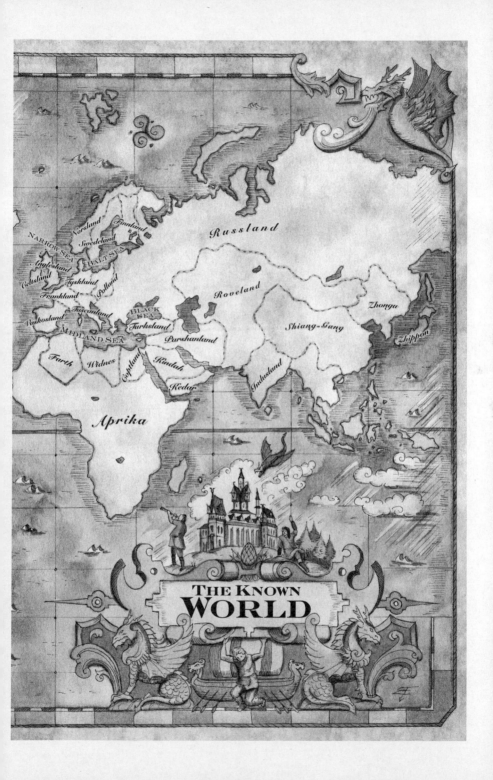

THE KNOWN
WORLD

PRONUNCIATION GUIDE

Akashneisit	ah-KASH-nay-ih-SIT
Akashnet	a-KASH-net
al-jabr	al-JAH-brr
Anequs	ahn-eh-KOOS
Anglish	AN-glish
Aponakwe	app-on-ACK-way
Aponakwesdottir	app-on-ACK-ways-dot-ter
Ashaquiat	ash-AH-quee-at
ather	AH-ther
bjalladreki	BYA-la-DRAY-kee
Chagoma	sha-GO-mah
Chequnnap	che-KOON-app
Eiriksthede	EYE-riks-THEED
Ekaitz	eh-KITES

erelore . . . . EHR-lore

falterdrache . . . . FALL-ter-drack

Fyra . . . . FIE-ruh

Hekua . . . . HECK-oo-ah

Henkjan . . . . HENK-yahn

Ivar Stafn . . . . EYE-var STAFF-in

jarl . . . . YARL

Johan Einarsson . . . . YO-hahn EYN-ar-son

Jule . . . . YOOL

Karina Kuiper . . . . ca-REE-nah KY-per

Kasaqua . . . . ka-SAH-kwah

kesseldrache . . . . KESS-el-drack

Kuhaukis . . . . koo-HOW-kiss

Leiknir Joervarsson . . . . . LEEK-near YORE-var-son

lichtbild . . . . LICHT-build

lichtbildmacher . . . . LICHT-build-mak-ker

machinakraft . . . . MAHK-een-ah-craft

Mamisashquee . . . . MAH-mee-SASH-kwee

Marta Hagan . . . . MAR-tah HAY-gan

Masquapaug . . . . MASS-kwah-pog

Masquasup . . . . MASS-kwah-sup

Masquisit . . . . MASS-kwis-it

Maswachuisit . . . . mass-wah-CHOO-ih-sit

meddyglyn . . . . MED-DY-glin

Menukkis . . . . men-OO-kiss

Mequeche . . . . meh-KWESH

Minanneka . . . . MEEN-ah-NECK-ah

Mishona . . . . mi-SHONE-ah

Motuckquas . . . . MOH-tuck-kwas

mupauanakausonat . . moo-pow-AHN-a-COW-so-naht

musquetu . . . . moos-KET-oo

Nampeshiwe . . . . nahm-PESH-ih-WAY

Nampeshiweisit . . . . . . nahm-PESH-ih-WAY-ih-sit

Naquipaug . . . . NAH-kwi-pog

Naquisit . . . . NAH-kwi-sit

Naregannisit . . . . nah-re-GAN-ih-sit

na'samp . . . . nah-SAHMP

Nepinnae . . . . neh-PIN-ay

Nikkomo . . . . ni-KO-mo

Niquiat . . . . NICK-ee-aht

Noskeekwash . . . . nos-KEEK-wash

Ommishqua . . . . om-MISH-kwah

Peyaunatam . . . . pay-OW-nah-tam

sachem . . . . SAY-chem

Sakewa . . . . sah-KAY-wah

Sander Jansen . . . . SAND-er YAHN-sen

Seseque . . . . seh-SEH-kway

Shanuckee . . . . SHA-noo-kee

Shiang-Gang . . . . SHEE-ang-gang

Shulefrau Verbindung . . SHOOL-frow ver-BIND-ung

Sigoskwe . . . . sih-GOSE-kway

silberdrache . . . . SIL-burr-drack

Sjokliffheim . . . . SYO-cliff-hime

skiltakraft . . . . SKILL-ta-craft

Strida . . . . STREE-dah

Tanaquish . . . . TAN-ah-kwish

Theod Knecht . . . . THEE-ode NECKT

thynge . . . . THING-ah; THING-eh

Valkyrja . . . . val-KEER-ya

Valkyrjafax . . . . val-KEER-ya-fax

Valkyrjafaxnacht . . . . val-KEER-ya-fax-nockt

Vaskosish . . . . vas-KOH-sish

Vastergot . . . . VAS-ter-gaht

velikolepni . . . . vell-ih-KOH-lep-nee

Wampsikuk . . . . WAMP-see-kuk

Witskraf . . . . WITZ-craft

Wompinottomak . . . . WOMP-ih-NOT-oh-mak

Wunnepan . . . . WUN-eh-pan

Wuskuwhani . . . . whu-SKOO-WAH-nee

Zhina . . . . ZHEE-nah

Zhippon . . . . ZHIP-on

Zhongu . . . . ZHON-goo

TO
SHAPE
A
DRAGON'S
BREATH

FIRST, THERE WAS THE EVENING BEFORE THE MORNING

I was gathering mussels on Slipstone Island when I saw the dragon.

I'd never seen a proper dragon before, but there was no mistaking it for anything else. It had come walking out of the scraggy stand of pine trees at the base of the temple mound and was standing on the rocky hillside, looking out to sea.

It was red and gold and glorious with the evening sun behind it, like a hillside in autumn. From nose to tail it was twice as long as my canoe, and from wing tip to wing tip three times as long. It had a crown of antlers that must have come to thirty points or more. It stretched its wings, and the sun came through them, showing the scarlet net of its bloodworks. It had a long, sinuous body, like an otter or a fisher. Its neck double-curved like a heron's. Its mane was bloodred, each spiky feather tipped with black, and it had black markings on its eyes and muzzle and along the rims of its deerlike ears.

For a very long time, it did nothing. It sat poised in the sun with its wings outstretched while I stared, hardly able to breathe. We hadn't had dragons on Masquapaug since the great dying. Anglish and Vaskosish dragons in Catchnet didn't count; they'd come later. This was a . . . Nampeshiwe. That was the word for it. The kind of dragon that *belonged* here.

A seagull screamed, and a pair of them wheeled down to land on my abandoned basket of mussels. I turned to shoo them away, and when I turned back, the dragon was looking at me.

Its eyes were sorrow. Golden, and keenly intelligent, and holding a sadness so howlingly deep that I felt my throat tightening. The dragon looked over its shoulder, back into the trees. Back to where the ruined temple was. It seemed to sigh heavily as it looked at me again.

The dragon turned and leaped off the hillside, falling effortlessly into flight with a few flaps of its enormous wings, gliding away over the surface of the ocean. Eastward, into the darkness of twilight.

In the distance behind me, I heard Sigoskwe call my name.

"Anequs! Anequs, what are you doing?"

A minute later I heard his footsteps thumping on the wet sand.

"What happened?" he asked, panting, as I finally turned to look at him. "What'd you see?"

"A dragon," I said faintly. "Up on the hill there." I gestured with a nod to where the dragon had been. "It flew away."

"What kind of a dragon? Anglish or Vaskosish? Who was riding it?" Sigoskwe asked.

"No. Not an Anglish dragon. A . . . real one. A Nampeshiwe. Nobody was riding it."

Sigoskwe looked up at me and crossed his arms.

"Nampeshiwe aren't a thing anymore."

I shook my head and looked back across the water, where the dragon had gone. Slipstone Island was the easternmost island; there was nothing past it but bits of wet rock fit for seals and then miles and miles of ocean. Where could it possibly be going?

"You're not kidding, are you?" Sigoskwe asked after a long silence.

"No," I said, shaking my head. "I saw it."

"Did you see it or did you *see it* see it? Like a vision or something?" He seemed very excited at the idea that it might have been a vision. Having a big sister who had visions would be something worth talking about.

"I think it was real?" I said, no longer certain. "I've never had visions before . . ."

"We've got to tell Grandma. It's probably important either way, right?"

"Yes, it probably is," I said, dragging my eyes away from the waves. "Did you fill your basket?"

"A while ago. I found half a dozen spotted crabs, too."

"If you found spotted crabs, you've been wading out too far."

"You don't have to have any crab if you don't want any," he said with a shrug. "And it's not even cold."

"It's not June yet," I said, folding my arms. "If you got caught in a riptide and dragged out to the seal rocks, what would I tell Mother?"

Sigoskwe just shrugged again, looking down at his feet, making a little hill of sand with his toe.

I hauled my basket up onto my hip and threw the strap over my shoulder as we started back to where we'd left the canoe. After we had walked a few minutes, Sigoskwe's hand slipped into mine. I wondered if he was thinking about dragons, too.

Grandma said that there'd been thousands of them, back before the great dying. Back then there'd been a city on Masquapaug as great as Vastergot or New Linvik. Back then, the temple on the mound on Slipstone Island hadn't been a ruin.

But then the plague came, and there weren't enough people and dragons to dance away the storms of autumn, and year by year the city had been washed away into the ocean. The Anglish had come, and the Vaskosish after them, and they'd made war on anyone who was in the way of them building their own cities.

Now Masquapaug was part of New Anglesland. Anglishmen came to collect taxes and do folkscoring, and anyone who didn't do what they said got shot or thrown in jail. It hadn't happened yet to Masquapaug, but Naquipaug stood as a stark reminder of how useless resistance was.

I smelled corn cakes frying before we came up over the hill to the house, and I could hear Sakewa and some other girls singing a clapping song. Sigoskwe ran ahead to meet them, and Mother was in the doorway with him by the time I caught up.

"I was getting worried about you two," she said. "Is there something especially interesting on Slipstone Island today?"

"Anequs saw a dragon! A proper one, not an Anglish one! A Nampeshiwe!" Sigoskwe blurted before I had a chance to say it myself. Sakewa and her friends stopped singing and clapping and stared at him. Mother looked at Sigoskwe, then looked at me, her face grave.

"Did you really, Anequs? You're not playing some kind of game?"

"I'm not, I promise," I said, swallowing hard. "It was a Nampeshiwe. A red-and-gold one, with great gnarled antlers and black marks on its face. Like the painting on that shield that the sachem has. And its eyes were so *sad*, Mother, I can't—"

"Anequs," I heard Grandma say from inside, "come and sit by the fire, and tell us this story the way that a story should be told."

Grandma was sitting by the fire, stitching oyster-shell beads onto the yoke of a dress, running her fingers along the line she'd already embroidered and using the tip of her thumb to measure out the space for the next one. Mother ushered Sigoskwe and Sakewa inside after me. Sakewa's friends must have gone home, which wasn't much more than shouting distance away. They'd probably be telling their families what Sigoskwe had said. Mother set the two of them to shucking mussels while I described the dragon.

"It will have been old, to have so many points on its antlers," Grandma said evenly, after I'd stopped speaking. "A dragon from somewhere on the mainland, maybe someplace west of the sunset even. I wonder if it lost its lands to Anglishmen, like us. You say it had no rider?"

"No, there was no one. Just the dragon, looking so sad."

"A dragon that old, maybe its companion died," Grandma said with a long, slow sigh. "In stories, a Nampeshiwe often dies of grief when its Nampeshiweisit dies. You say it flew east? To the ocean?"

"Yes," I said, feeling my throat tighten and my eyes water. "Into the dark."

"You won't see it again, probably," Grandma said, closing her eyes and shaking her head. "Probably it's gone to chase lands east of the sunrise."

There was something in the pit of my stomach when Grandma said that, cold and hard like a stone. It was the same way I'd felt when Mother had told me that Grandpa had died.

"You're the one who saw the dragon, Anequs," Grandma said. "Whether it was real or a vision, you should climb the mound on Slipstone Island and offer tobacco and juniper at the temple."

"I'll go at first light," I said, canting my head.

"*My* grandmother told me," Grandma said, "that when she was a girl, the way that dragons came to love people was that people spoke and sang to their eggs, and that dragons hatched already loving someone. In the days when she was a girl, and there were a dozen dragons in her meetinghouse, they'd lay their eggs there to hatch and be named and be welcomed into the people. Whether it was a vision or something real, it's certainly something that you saw. You saw it alone, so you should go alone to offer thanks for the vision, and then come back and tell us what it's shown you."

"We should send Niquiat a telegram about Anequs seeing a dragon," Sigoskwe said.

Mother sighed and glanced over to Niquiat's empty pallet. He'd sent money, last time he'd written, but that had been more than a month ago. Just before Father had gone to sea.

I felt a prickle on the back of my neck and concentrated on

shucking the mussels, ignoring Sigoskwe and Sakewa chattering about how it would be better to go back to the island tonight, or how we should go to the telegraph office immediately or something. How something needed doing right away. I was two years a woman, and old enough to know that sometimes things had to be waited on, so I kept my mouth shut.

But I knew that I wouldn't be sleeping that night.

THEN THERE WAS THE MORNING AFTER THE EVENING

I lay awake all night, staring at the roof thatch and thinking about dragons. I got up before dawn, as soon as pale blue light began to creep under the door, while everyone else was still asleep. Sakewa was curled up next to Grandma, Sigoskwe on his own pallet near the door, Mother snoring softly behind her curtain. Opposite me, Niquiat's pallet lay empty, like the hollow where a tooth had fallen out.

Niquiat was living in Vastergot, working in a cannery.

Father had cried about it when Niquiat had left. About Niquiat not going on his first whaling voyage. About how Niquiat would never spear a whale and never get a tattoo for it. Father wouldn't buy anything with the money Niquiat sent us. He'd thrown the first envelope full of money onto the ground and spat at it when he'd opened the letter.

Mother had gathered it up again, once Father had walked away.

Our family usually only got money—Anglish money, anyway,

which was the only kind that mattered—in November, when Father came back from whaling and got his share of the haul. It used to be we'd go just once a year to Catchnet to buy salt pork and sugar and cloth and things. But Niquiat was sending money every couple of months now, and Mother and I had already been to Catchnet three times this year to shop for sundries. We had tea and coffee and kerosene and calico to share with our neighbors, and we wouldn't have had them otherwise.

But we didn't have Niquiat.

I gathered juniper and tobacco into an otterskin bag, along with a big quahog shell and a flint and striker. I had a little wheel-lighter that ran on kerosene, but that was an Anglish thing, and it felt wrong for what I was going to do.

The sky was turning from pink to gold when I put my canoe into the water. I could hear the shorebirds calling, and the lapping of the water on the hollow sides, and nothing else. My paddle cut easily through the little wavelets of the sheltered cove between Slipstone Island and Masquapaug, and my canoe slipped through the water like a seal.

Far away on the horizon, a steamship belched out a gray cloud.

I dragged the canoe past the strand line before starting up the path toward the mound. It seemed impossible that people had built this, that there had ever been enough people on Masquapaug to accomplish it, but nature didn't carve in shapes the way people did. The mound was perfectly round, and there was a spiral path, like a whelk's shell, that led to the top. There was a flat place there, with four granite pillars carved and inlaid with quahog shell and oyster shell. If you started in the east and walked south and west and north, the pictures told the story of how Masquasup the Giant had thrown Masquapaug up from the bottom of the sea on the first morning after the sun caught fire. There was a great round stone in the middle of the pillars, like a millstone, blackened with a thousand years' worth of fires.

When I came to the crest of the mound and looked between

the pillars, I couldn't see the stone at all. Something had been built right on top of it.

There, sitting on a bed of rotting seaweed that steamed lightly in the cool air, was an egg.

It was like a seagull egg, speckled dark brown on lighter brown, smooth and oblong and slightly pointed at one end. It was as big as a good blue squash. I forgot all about having come here to offer tobacco and juniper for a moment, stepped forward and knelt down, sitting on my heels to gaze at it. A dragon egg. I don't know how long I sat there staring at it before I reached out a hand and touched it to see if it was real.

It was warm to the touch, and something inside flickered. It was like feeling a moth on the other side of a leaf, but it didn't just flicker against my hand, it flickered against every part of me, against my breath and my thoughts and my spirit.

"Hello," I said, my voice barely above a whisper, "I'm Anequs. I'm going to bring you to Masquapaug, where our people live."

I said it because it was the right thing to say. I didn't know how I knew that. It only occurred to me later that I'd said the words in Masquisit, not in Anglish.

I left tobacco and juniper burning in the hollow where the egg had been. I took off my calico blouse and made a sling from it, walking back down the mound bare-chested, like an old woman or a little girl. The morning air was cold on my skin, but that didn't seem important. While I walked, I told the egg a story. The only story that seemed to be worthy of telling.

THIS IS THE STORY THAT ANEQUS TOLD

In the first days, when the first people lived, Nampeshiwe's Mother was an enemy of people. Nampeshiwe's Mother lived on the island in Great Sweet Pond, and she would hide herself among the reeds and drag people beneath the waters and eat them. Nampeshiwe's Mother would fly over the villages of the first people and loose the shapeless medicine of her breath on crops and homes, burning them to ashes. Many brave heroes tried to hunt and kill Nampeshiwe's Mother, but she was too strong. She was a spirit-creature from the time before the sun caught fire, faster than Eagle and stealthier than Puma and mightier than Whale. No hero could defeat her.

But then Crow, who came flying to Masquapaug from the lands west of the sunset, taught the first people how to dance. Nampeshiwe's Mother came to watch their dances. Nampeshiwe's Mother said to the people, "Your dancing is beautiful. You must teach me your dancing. I would know how it is done."

And the people said to Nampeshiwe's Mother, "We have

learned our dancing from Crow, who brought us fire and corn. You must ask Crow to teach you to dance."

And Nampeshiwe's Mother said to the people, "Crow will not speak to me, because of the wars fought in the time before the sun caught fire. You must teach me your dancing."

And the people said to Nampeshiwe's Mother, "You have killed and eaten many of our people. You have burned our crops and our homes to ash. We will not teach you how to dance."

And Nampeshiwe's Mother said to the people, "I have a little child who has never yet seen light or breathed air, and has done you no wrong. Will you teach my child to dance?"

And the people spoke long among one another. After the fullness of the turning of the moon, they said to Nampeshiwe's Mother, "If you send your child to live among us and learn our ways, we will teach your child to dance."

And Nampeshiwe's Mother brought her egg to them and placed it in the center of their village, saying, "I trust you with the life of my child. If you bring any harm to my child, I will devour every one of you, and burn all of your works, and dig the ashes into the soil, and tear apart this land until nothing of it remains. I will make Masquasup sorrowful that ever he pulled it from the bottom of the sea."

But the people did not fear, because Crow told them the way to sing and speak and dance before the egg, and when in its time it finally hatched, the creature that came forth was very different from its mother.

It said, "My name is Nampeshiwe," and it looked upon the first people and saw a young man and said to him, "Will you teach me how to dance?"

And the young man said, "I will teach you how to dance, and be called Nampeshiweisit—the one who is of Nampeshiwe."

And Crow spoke to Nampeshiwe's Mother and said, "Your time in this world is done, Mother of Nampeshiwe. Will you come with me to the land west of the sunset with the rest of our kin?"

And Nampeshiwe's Mother, seeing that her child would be content, agreed and did not menace the first people again.

THE EGG WAS BROUGHT TO MASQUAPAUG

Sachem Tanaquish was at the house when I returned. He was sitting outside with Mother and Grandma, and they were all drinking coffee out of Mother's good pottery. The sachem stood up when he saw me coming, then Mother stood as well and put her hand on Grandma's shoulder.

The sachem was only just younger than Grandma, and his face and neck and arms were covered in tattoos from his days as a whaler. He wasn't withered, the way old men sometimes were. It wasn't terribly unusual that the sachem should be at my house; he was a good friend of Grandma's, and he visited all around the village for coffee and stories and news. But we all knew that this wasn't a social call. My eyes darted to Sakewa, sitting on the ground near Mother's chair. She must have been the one who went and told him what was going on. She looked away from me and sniffed, playing with one of her braids.

"Sachem," I said, as soon as I was near enough for it to be polite.

"Your family was just telling me that you've had a vision, Anequs," he said, a thread of urgency in his voice, "and I can see that you're carrying—"

"It's an egg," I said, carefully lifting the sling's weight from the back of my neck, letting the sides of my blouse fall away to reveal my burden. It was heavy enough that it stopped my hands from trembling, but I had to fight the impulse to pull it close to my body and refuse to give it up to him.

Sachem Tanaquish took the egg into his hands as gently as he would have taken a newborn baby. I looked at my feet while I untied the sleeves of my blouse from each other and put it back on.

"We'll have to have a meeting," the sachem said softly, still looking at the egg. "We'll have to have a *dance*. I never thought I'd see a Nampeshiwe. I thought their time was over."

The egg was taken to the meetinghouse, which was the right thing to do with it. It was laid on a cushion of sealskins, and everyone in the village came to see it. I had to tell the story of how I'd seen the dragon and what it had looked like over and over, until my voice started failing, and then the sachem brought me sassafras tea with rum and honey to bring it back again. Elders came and touched my hands and patted me on the shoulders and said it was a blessing.

By the middle of the day, a feast had been assembled from things people had brought to share. Savory corn cakes with smoked eel, and sweet corn cakes with strawberries and blueberries. Na'samp with honey, and rosehip syrup, and cranberry jam. Someone decided to light the cooking pit, and a couple of roasted turkeys slowly appeared, and succotash and greens, and mussels and oysters and fish.

In the middle of the afternoon, my cousin Mishona came with the other drumsingers. A circle was drawn, with the egg at its center where there would normally have been a fire. The four points were marked and blessed. Tobacco was offered. The dancing began.

I'd never been especially good at dancing. I wasn't *bad* at it, but

I wasn't good, either. Not like Mishona or Kiquoit or even like Mother. I could keep a rhythm, but I'd never become part of the music like others did.

But something flickered in me when the drummers started. Something in the palms of my hands and the hollows of my eyelids. Something in my heartbeat hitched and moved in time with the drum's rhythm. I looked at the egg sitting on its nest of skins, and it seemed almost like it was glowing, as golden as the sun. Like it was pulsing with the drum's heartbeat rhythm. One of the singers began a deep, resonating chant, and three women joined him to pick up the melody of the song, and my feet started moving without my even having to think about it. Kick hop, kick hop, spin, spin, change, spin, kick hop, kick hop, heel, toe, heel, toe, and I could *fly*.

I danced until all of the stars came out.

No one wanted to leave the egg, but people began to return to their homes by ones and twos all the same. Sometime just after sunrise, I did as well. Before I left the meetinghouse, I walked to the egg and laid a hand on it. I knew that people were watching, but that didn't seem to matter. The words came effortlessly, in Masquisit, in an accent as old as my grandmother's grandmother's.

"These are your people, and this is your village," I said. "This is your home."

The egg pulsed under my hand, as if in answer. It understood.

I found my bed and sank into it and didn't get up again until the next morning.

ON MASQUAPAUG IT HATCHED

From the end of May and all through June, the entire village revolved around the meetinghouse and the dragon egg inside it. Everyone spent as much time as they reasonably could there, while still getting done what was absolutely necessary. Blueberries and strawberries had to be picked and put by while they were ripe, crops had to be sown, fishing had to be done, and chickens had to be fed and all that, but apart from things that had to be done elsewhere, people stayed in and around the meetinghouse. Corn was ground there, and mending and sewing were done there, and meals were made and eaten there. Every night people gathered around the egg to tell stories.

There were a dozen elders, Grandma and Sachem Tanaquish included, who didn't really leave the egg's side. Everyone else brought them meals and saw to things that needed doing. The elders spoke Masquisit to the egg, and sang it old, old songs. Me and Hekua and all our friends read pennik novels and magazines from

Catchnet to it. Sigoskwe and the other boys told it sea stories. Sakewa and her friends sang it clapping songs. Mishona's mother and her sister, who were from Naquipaug, both knew some Vaskosish. They had a lot of laughing and faltering conversations with each other in front of the egg. Everyone was in agreement that we should show it everything that there was of the Masquisit.

Younger people in the village mostly spoke Anglish. I was better at Anglish than Masquisit; Grandma spoke it sometimes, and Mother, so I understood it and could usually make myself understood when I had to speak it to elders who didn't speak any Anglish at all. But Father, whose people were from Naquipaug, could only speak Anglish. My friends and I commonly spoke Anglish to one another because everyone knew that Hekua only spoke Anglish, and it was rude to make much of it.

One day, about a week into July, the egg hatched.

It wasn't a sudden affair. It began during a song the elders were singing, when a thin, whistling cry from inside the egg answered their rhythm. A small hole appeared the next morning. By afternoon, everyone in the village had stopped whatever they'd been doing to come and watch as the little dragon scratched and pecked a line around the middle of the egg. Hekua's mother, who was a midwife, got everyone to start singing songs for laboring women because it seemed right. The drum pulsed out a deep, even rhythm, and the air was thick and close with tobacco and juniper and the heat and breath of so many people.

I was granted a seat very near the egg, mainly on Grandma's insistence. I had been the one to see the dragon and bring the egg to the village, after all, and Grandma wanted me to describe what was happening.

The shell fell into halves around sunset, and a bedraggled little creature pushed them apart, clawed feet kicking the larger half away. It lay on its back with its head cradled in the top half for a long moment, panting, then rolled onto its belly and shook the shell off.

Overall it was about the size of a marten, dull yellow and speckled brown and black across its back. Its wings, as it stretched them out and flicked off bits of slime, proved much smaller than its mother's had been. They didn't look at all suited for the task of getting it into the air. Its head was overlarge for its body, and so were its feet. It had no sign of antlers or feathers. It looked as soft and bald as a baby songbird.

The little creature looked around, stumbling in a circle like a fawn finding its feet. Its eyes were enormous and golden, with black markings around them—a thin black line across them, like a baby sandpiper, and a smattering of speckles behind that continued on the backs of its ears. It yawned hugely, displaying a set of very well-developed teeth that resembled nothing so much as those of a skunk pig. The hatchling spun, studying its audience, until it met my gaze.

I *knew*. There was a drumbeat beneath my breastbone, something unfurling inside me. My voice wasn't quite my own when I said, "Her name is Kasaqua."

A slow murmur went through the gathered crowd.

Everyone was watching the dragon, and the dragon was watching me, so everyone was watching me as the dragon stumbled forward and jumped into my lap, nuzzling under my jaw. She was warm, and lighter than I'd have thought, weighing like a hen. Her skin was soft and damp and smelled of eggs that had gone a little bit off. My hand came up to stroke the back of her head as if it were the most natural thing in the world.

"She's *hungry*," I heard myself say.

The roasted turkey appeared then, the platter passed hand over hand through the crowd, which was good because I wasn't sure that I could have gotten to the table.

Kasaqua proceeded to devour the remains of the turkey, including all the bones, and a plateful of steamed mussels including the shells, and three ears of corn with cobs and husks. It was a wonder to watch, because that much food really shouldn't have fit inside her, and a good deal of it wasn't precisely food. Dragons in stories ate things like trees and stones sometimes, but lots of things happened in stories that didn't often happen outside of them. It was different to *see* it.

Once sated, Kasaqua padded back to her nest and nosed around the blankets, selecting a sealskin that especially pleased her and carrying it back with her to my lap, where she turned herself in a circle and lay down in a tight little ball, like a kitten.

Sachem Tanaquish's voice rang out above all the other voices, rich and powerful, "Anequs, daughter of Chagoma and Apon-akwe, has been chosen. She is Nampeshiweisit of Kasaqua, who is a Nampeshiwe of Masquisit."

Kasaqua only flicked an ear at the roar of triumph that rose in the meetinghouse.

NIQUIAT RETURNED WITH NEWS OF THE ANGLISH

The village had become an alien place, no one quite knowing how they were supposed to treat me now. I'd gone from being just Anequs, just a daughter and sister and cousin and all that, to being Nampeshiweisit. As if I'd suddenly started having visions, or had discovered that I was a mupauanakausonat or something. I was a different kind of person, suddenly.

The shapeless medicine of a dragon's breath is change.

Those words appeared again and again in stories about dragons.

It was strange how much Kasaqua felt part of me. I could feel what she felt; I knew when she was curious, or startled, or frightened. I knew when she was hungry or tired. I knew when she liked or disliked something. I *felt* these things as naturally as my own feelings, *knew* them the same way I'd known her name.

I found myself needing a lot of space and time to think and feel without talking to others—just being with her. Kasaqua didn't need much looking after; she begged for food whenever anyone was eating, but she also seemed perfectly capable of feeding herself. She caught minnows and mice, peeled starfish and mussels off the rocks, chased after dragonflies and locusts, ate pine cones and dandelions and whatever else took her fancy . . . I had no doubt that she'd have gotten on fine without me—which made her choosing me mean that much more. She didn't *need* me—she *wanted* me.

I walked all around the village with Kasaqua at my heels or perched on my shoulder, showing her everything that was Masquapaug and introducing her to everyone. I got in my canoe and brought her to Slipstone Island, to the temple mound. I brought her to the ruins on Beachy Hill, and to Great Sweet Pond, and to the island in Great Sweet Pond where Nampeshiwe's Mother was supposed to have lived long ago. I brought her to the place where Great Sweet Pond overflowed and made its way down the rocks to the marsh.

When I arrived back at home from the marsh, Niquiat was there.

He'd sent no word, so I was surprised and delighted to find him sitting by the fire with everyone else, as comfortably and naturally as if he'd never left.

He was taller. I was sure that he was taller, watching him stand up. He was wearing corduroy trousers and a canvas shirt and a flat cap. He'd cut his hair. My throat closed up as he came forward to hug me. He had that cannery smell that some of the men in Catchnet had: fish oil that never really washed out, even after a dozen baths.

"You got bigger, Chipmunk," Niquiat said fondly, laying his chin on the crown of my head for a moment before pulling away. He held me by the shoulders to look at me, and there were tears in his eyes. "My sister, the dragoneer."

"Your sister, the Nampeshiweisit," I corrected him fondly.

He looked down to where Kasaqua was standing at my heel,

her wings folded and her tail wrapped around her feet, watching with an air of reserved judgment that I'd only ever seen before in cats.

"You're going to have to go to a dragon academy," Niquiat said. "I brought the application."

Mother and I put luncheon together while Niquiat explained himself.

"I started looking into how to get an application without actually declaring who needed it since I got your first telegram about there being a dragon egg," Niquiat said between bites of corn cake, "and when I got the second telegram about the dragon picking Anequs, I got on the next train to Catchnet. Stayed the night in a hostel over there, to be on time for the Tuesday morning ferry."

"I don't see why there should be any talk of Anequs going anywhere at all," Grandma said firmly, her mouth drawn in a thin line. "She's only fifteen, and the dragon has only just been born. If such things must ever happen, and I don't know that they must, but *if* they must, then surely they can happen later. What's she going to learn at some Anglish academy? The Anglish don't even know how to dance."

"I think I haven't explained it right," Niquiat said, lowering his eyes respectfully. "There's a ministry for dragons. The Anglish have a ministry for everything. Dragons are supposed to be registered, and dragoneers need to be tested to prove they're competent, because dragons are dangerous. There's going to be trouble with the law if you don't enroll in an academy."

"They can't take anyone from Masquapaug. We signed a treaty," Grandma said, closing her eyes.

"Besides, Grandma, who's going to teach her here?" Niquiat asked. "Do you remember any of the old dragon dances? Does anyone? They've got dragons on the mainland, and a dragon ought to have other dragons to teach it how to be a dragon properly."

"If your father was here—" Mother started, only for Niquiat to turn and snap, "Well, he's *not* here, is he? He's someplace in the middle of the north sea, and he'll go on being there for weeks yet, and he might as well be on the moon for all that we can ask him anything about what he might think. So I don't see why we should consider his feelings."

The silence that followed was thick and sour. I looked helplessly toward Mother, but she was looking studiously away, paying attention to turning the corn cakes as they sizzled in the pan, or at least pretending to. There was a sting of unfairness in that; she should have said something.

"What about my feelings?" I asked, very softly in the silence. Kasaqua was sitting in my lap, drawn tightly on herself, making a noise somewhere between a whine and a growl. I stroked her, hoping it would settle her. Hoping it would settle *me*.

Niquiat sighed, and his voice was soft when he spoke again.

"Everything I've read about dragons since I got the telegram about the egg says that it's important that they start learning witskraft from the moment they're out of the shell. I've been reading everything I can lay my hands on—books and magazine articles and newspaper articles. I brought some with me, if you want to look at them. Every Anglishman and Vaskosman I've talked to says that dragons and their dragoneers go to dragon academies. You need to know al-jabr and anglereckoning and skiltakraft and all that to properly shape a dragon's breath."

"We are not Anglish, and we are not Vaskosish, and their ways do not concern us," Grandma said, her voice quiet but firm. "A Nampeshiwe on Masquapaug does not concern them. We will keep to ourselves and our ways, and the Anglish will keep to theirs. They've agreed to that. They signed a treaty. We pay them taxes and we follow their laws and they leave us alone. That was what we agreed to at the end of the war."

"That's what they said in Naquipaug, and look how that turned out for them," Niquiat said, slapping the table. I tensed at that, shocked that Niquiat would do such a thing in front of Grandma.

Kasaqua scrambled out of my lap and up onto the table. Mother gasped and dropped something; it clattered against the hearthstones, then the smell of burning corn filled the room. Sakewa made a tiny little whining noise, but stifled it immediately.

In the silence that followed, Grandmother said, "Is this what happens to young people when they go among the Anglish, then? They come back and think that this is how one speaks to one's elders?"

There was a long, painful moment before Niquiat said, "I'm sorry, Grandmother. I didn't mean . . . I'm sorry."

It was quiet again, with just the sounds of mother cleaning up the spilled corn.

"We don't want the Anglish to come to us, I know that much," I said into the painful silence. "So it might be better to go to them—to meet them on our own terms. I don't think Niquiat's wrong, exactly, about how it might be good for me—and for Kasaqua—to talk to other people who know more about dragons."

"There's a school right in Varmarden, just a dozen miles southeast of Vastergot, and they give scholarships. They let in a Naquisit student last year, and the newspapers all went mad about it. If they let *him* in, I don't see why they shouldn't let Anequs and her dragon in, too—and it neatly solves the problem of registering the dragon with the ministry and making sure we're not suddenly up to our ears in Anglishmen accusing us of deceit, saying we're hiding a dragon on Masquapaug."

"If the Anglish find out that there's a dragon on Masquapaug, they're going to try and take her," Mother said. "It's what they do. If your father was here, he'd tell you that; he's had more dealing with Anglishmen than any of us."

Niquiat's eyes flashed, but he didn't say anything. When had he become so angry? Was it before he went among the Anglish or after? Was it why he'd left to begin with? I wanted to ask him . . . but not in front of everyone else.

"No one's going to take Kasaqua from me," I said. "I've read novels and articles and things. The Anglish know that once a dragon has chosen a companion that there's no undoing it."

"They might *kill* Kasaqua," Niquiat said grimly. "They kill dragons that don't choose companions, or who choose the wrong sort of companions. They call them feral and put them down like they would any wild animal they see fit to. School begins in September and ends in May, and there's a long recess in December because Anglishmen have one set of winter holidays and Vaskosmen have another. It's not as if she'd be gone forever. It's less time than Father spends away, even."

"Your father isn't away spending time with Anglishmen and learning their bad habits," Grandma said.

"There's lots of Anglish whalers, though," Sigoskwe protested. "I saw them when Father brought me to see his ship!"

"Our people have been hunting whales since long before the pale folk ever came to these shores. It's different," Grandma said tightly, her milky eyes moving quickly from side to side. "It's different."

Seeing Grandma upset—*really* upset—was the worst part about all of this. Grandma was always so steady. It made me feel small and uncertain, a tightness in my throat and a roiling in my belly. Kasaqua made a little noise, but I couldn't tell if she was complaining or concerned. I petted her, but neither of us calmed.

"We can't hide from the Anglish forever, Grandma," Niquiat said. "If Anequs goes to one of their schools and learns how to do Anglish medicine and makes friends with Anglish dragoneers, that can only help Masquapaug. We could have some of them on our side for once, maybe."

"I'm going to fill out the application, at least," I said, trying to make my voice firm. "I don't have to go. I just . . . don't want to miss the chance. We can keep talking about it. I really think we ought to talk with more people about it—Sachem Tanaquish and the other elders and all, I mean. But I'm going to fill out the application. It seems like the right thing to do."

"This is how Masquapaug will die," Grandma said. "Not murdered, like Naquipaug, or smothered, like the Naregannisit and the Akashneisit, but slowly by bleeding away its young people. More and more of you every year. My own grandchildren. I shouldn't have lived long enough to feel this pain."

"I'm not going to stay gone, if I go," I said, my face feeling very hot. "Masquapaug is my home and I don't ever want it to not be my home. But this might be something I have to do, for a while. Kasaqua chose me to be her Nampeshiweisit, so I need to learn how to be that. If this were a story, I might gather up three of my friends and walk to the edge of the sunset to ask Nampeshiwe himself. But this isn't a story."

"The Anglish can't teach you how to be a Nampeshiweisit," Grandma said.

"What if they can, though? Shouldn't I at least find out?" I asked.

"You'll do what you think you should do," Grandma said with a sigh. "Young people always do, in the end. Like your brother did."

I turned to look at Niquiat. He was looking at the floor between his feet, his eyes shining. He got up and walked out without saying anything else, and after a moment of looking from Mother to Grandmother and back, I got up and followed him.

We didn't speak as we walked to the beach, Kasaqua trotting along at my heel with mounting concern about where we were going and why, because she knew that I was upset. Niquiat led us along the path through the dunes and stopped when we came to the shoreline. Slipstone Island was visible against the horizon, and we both stood looking at it in companionable silence for a while.

"Why did you run away?" I asked, after a long time. Niquiat blew a sigh, not looking at me when he spoke.

"I didn't run away. I left because . . . because I don't want this life—being a farmer or a fisherman or a potter or a blacksmith. Father always wanted me to be a whaler, but I never wanted to be one. You'll understand better when you visit the city, I think. Masquapaug is the same as it was a hundred years ago, two hundred years ago, a thousand years ago. I know you've seen automaton horses on Naquipaug, when we go to visit Father's family, but we don't even have that much here. The only tatkraftish thing we have is the telegraph, and that's not something of our own doing. I want to be a machinakrafter, and make engines and machines and automata. I want to bring our people into the modern world. No one here can teach me how to do that, just like no one here can teach you to be a dragoneer. With you, it's that dragons have been gone from us for so long that no one remembers how things were done in the old days. With me . . . Our people never had machinakraft, not really."

"Some elders might say there's a reason for that."

"Some elders were children in the terrible times after the great dying, and never knew a better life than this one," he countered. "Our ancestors built the temple on Slipstone Island, but could our people do such a thing today? We were greater once."

I looked at Kasaqua, who was chasing the froth line down the beach and running from the waves as they lapped in, enjoying herself immensely. A Nampeshiwe, a creature of greatness from a time long past. My companion, who would absolutely change the way we lived on Masquapaug if any of the old stories about dragons were true at all. I was her companion and had no idea whatsoever how to shape her breath.

Niquiat and Kasaqua and I stayed on the beach, not saying much of anything else, until Sakewa came to tell us that dinner was ready.

KASAQUA LOOSED THE SHAPELESS MEDICINE
OF HER BREATH

The ferry only visited Masquapaug on Tuesdays and Fridays, so Niquiat would be home with us at least until Friday morning. On Wednesday, all my siblings joined me in my wanderings with Kasaqua—just now we were on the strip of sandy shoreline west of Beachy Hill. Sakewa and Sigoskwe were close in the same way that Niquiat and I always had been, and they ran ahead of us. Kasaqua was very happy to follow them, possessing the same childish energy—she loved to run and climb and explore. Niquiat and I walked a dozen paces behind them, talking about this and that.

Kasaqua was poking her head into crevices between boulders on the surf line when I became suddenly and acutely aware that *something hurt her face*. She was startled and pained, crying out in protest. I turned in time to see her scrambling backward, a large crab hanging from her lip by one claw. When backing up didn't help at all, Kasaqua . . . opened something inside herself. I felt it, the swell of it like a cresting wave beneath my breastbone, a tightness in my throat. There was a searing flash of light, and she gave a booming cry—a sound bigger and deeper than such a small creature should have been able to make; a thunderclap noise. A gust of wind blew outward from the place she was standing. The air smelled like it did after a huge thunderstorm—strangely pungent, clean and empty, just a bit sweet somehow. When my vision cleared and my ears stopped ringing, I realized that Sakewa was screaming.

The beach in front of Kasaqua was black and smooth, extending for fifteen or twenty feet in a widening fan shape. Sakewa was sitting on the far edge of it, only just beyond the blackened sand. She had an arm thrown up to shield her face, and she was lowering it now that the flash had passed. Sigoskwe was running to her, Niquiat close behind.

Kasaqua was panting, confused, afraid. She was glad to have the crab *gone*, but she didn't know what she'd done. She hadn't known until just now that it was a thing she *could* do. I felt her confusion, as bright and brittle as if it were my own. I looked from Kasaqua to Sakewa and back, and strode over to gather Kasaqua up in my arms. She needed calming. I turned to my siblings, holding Kasaqua, but Sakewa edged away from us to hide behind Niquiat, making a little squealing sound.

Sakewa's arm, forehead, chest, and the fronts of her shins and feet were ruddy and hot like a sunburn. No blisters, but still . . . it was terrifying how close she'd been to Kasaqua's blast. She was crying, saying that she wanted to go home.

Niquiat picked up Sakewa and took her to the water's edge to bathe her burns in the ocean.

I turned, Kasaqua still cradled in the crook of my arm, to examine the blackened patch of beach. It was filmed in soot-blackened glass, as thin and brittle as ice but warm to the touch. It was shaped like a splash of water, a solid sheet of it where Kasaqua had been standing, breaking up into droplets farther out. Where the boulder had been was a pool of black liquid, like pine tar, still hot enough to be bubbling. A wave came rolling up the beach, and it hissed and steamed where it touched the black stain.

"Why did she burn me, Anequs?" Sakewa asked between hiccuping sobs. "I didn't even do anything and dragons are supposed to be people's friends and I was just standing by the rocks—"

"A crab pinched her," I said. "I don't think she knew you were there. I don't think she knew what would happen when she breathed that way, not really. She's just a baby; she didn't mean it."

"Sigoskwe, you'd better go and get Mother," Niquiat said. "And Sachem Tanaquish, too."

Sigoskwe nodded and ran back toward the village.

I sat down in the sand with Kasaqua in my lap, a little way apart from Sakewa and Niquiat because Sakewa didn't want to be close to Kasaqua. I petted her and tried to calm her, because it hadn't really been her fault, but fault or not, my little sister was hurt and frightened and there was no undoing that. Kasaqua was whining softly, hiding her face against my shoulder. She knew something was wrong, and she wanted me to tell her everything was all right.

But everything *wasn't* all right. She'd loosed her breath for only a moment, and there'd been enough power in it to melt sand and boulders into glass. What if she'd done that in the village? What if she'd done it in the meetinghouse with a lot of people around her?

What if Sakewa had been half a yard closer?

Others arrived then—Mother, and Mishona and her mother, and the sachem. They'd heard the booming sound Kasaqua had made all the way back at the village.

Inside of an hour, a gathering was called in the meetinghouse to talk about what should be done. Mother didn't come, staying home with Sakewa to soothe her burns with salve. I was sitting beside Sachem Tanaquish, Kasaqua on my lap. Grandma was at his other side, and the rest of the elders flanked us. It didn't feel like a place where I belonged, here among the elders. I should have been across the way with Niquiat and Sigoskwe. With the rest of the people. I'd never been the kind of person who sat at the head of gatherings before.

"It's not right that Anequs should go from her home, I think we all agree on that," Sachem Tanaquish said, looking very grim. He waited for the general murmur to quiet before he continued. "But we have to ask ourselves this—who among us knows the ways of dragons? Who remembers the dances that the first people taught to Nampeshiwe? We've all seen now what a dragon's breath can do unshaped."

"This is something that we can solve among ourselves," Grandma said with a voice like melted lead. "The Anglish have their ways, and we have our own. They cannot interfere with us— they signed a treaty."

"They do have a treaty with us," Sachem Tanaquish said, putting his hand on Grandma's shoulder, "and that would mean something if they were honorable people. But they had a treaty with the Naquisit, too, until they found coal on Naquipaug."

"A Nampeshiwe is something worth fighting them over!" Mishona's mother said, her voice calm and even, but carrying like a loon's call.

"There is a young man among us who has lived this past year and a half among the Anglish in their city Vastergot, where he's learned something of their ways," the sachem said, gesturing toward Niquiat. "Niquiat, son of Chagoma and Aponakwe, will you speak?"

Niquiat stood, slowly, keeping his gaze respectfully down.

"My family sent me a telegram when the egg was found on Slipstone Island, and I began reading everything I could about dragons and the Anglish way of dragons being among people. By their laws, a dragon must be registered with the Ministry of Dragon Affairs. Dragons' companions are required to attend special academies, to learn anglereckoning and minglinglore and skiltakraft. The Anglish put to death any dragon whose companion isn't competent at skiltakraft—something proven by trial. If they'd do that to their own people, I can't imagine they wouldn't do it to us. They won't like us having a dragon at all."

A lot of people started talking all at once then, and after a minute or two Sachem Tanaquish thumped his staff on the floor. The deer toes fixed to the top rattled, and everyone went quiet again, waiting for his words. Kasaqua could sense the grim and anxious attitude of the meeting; she fidgeted in my lap, rubbing her face against my hands, demanding that I stroke her neck and wings. She was beginning to grow a double row of pinfeathers from the little ridges of skin that started on her brow and extended down her neck and between her shoulder blades. They were prickly under my fingers, and she liked having them scratched.

"If the Anglish want to take from us the first Nampeshiwe to be hatched on Masquapaug in two hundred years and more, they're going to have to fight us," Ashaquiat said with fierce determination. "If they think we'd let them slay a Nampeshiwe—"

"If the Anglish wanted to, they could come with a company of soldiers riding dragons and burn all of Masquapaug and everyone on it to ash. It would be stupid to give them a reason to make this a fight," Niquiat said, staring levelly at Ashaquiat. "Look what they did on Naquipaug, and that was only for the coal mine. What would they do for a dragon? For the promise of a Masquisit Nampeshiwe?"

Ashaquiat looked like he was going to say something, but his mother said something to him, too quietly for the rest of us to hear, and he closed his mouth and just let out an exasperated sigh.

"It would be easy to avoid a fight, at least for now," Niquiat continued. "There's an academy in Varmarden, and last year they accepted a Naquisit student—I don't know who his people are, but apparently there was a lot of trouble about his bonding with a dragon with a moot and everything, until this school enrolled him. I've brought application papers with me. Anequs could present herself and her dragon for consideration, and then they couldn't claim that we're hiding anything."

The sachem turned to look at me, speculation in his eyes. His gaze dropped to Kasaqua, then rose back to meet mine.

"Anequs, what do you think of all this?" he asked.

I thought about the glassy scar on the beach, the melted rocks, Sakewa's burns.

"I think that I have to find someone who can teach me how to shape Kasaqua's breath, because if I don't she'll be a danger to everyone on the island," I said. "I think the Anglish academy might be a place where I can find that kind of teacher. I think it's my duty to Kasaqua and to her mother and to whatever spirits sent her here to be the best Nampeshiweisit that I can be, and that means learning more about dragons. I think that I have to go."

"I see wisdom in these words," the sachem said, thumping his staff on the ground. Silence followed, and he looked around the gathered circle of people to see if anyone had objections to speak.

No one did.

Niquiat went back to Vastergot on Friday morning, taking my completed application with him.

THE STRANGERS CAME, AS THEY OFTEN DO

On the Monday after Niquiat returned to Vastergot, I was sitting with Mother and Sakewa outside the house, weaving cattail mats, Kasaqua sleeping in the sun like a lazy cat.

Kasaqua's sudden attention was the first sign that something was about to happen. She startled awake, and I could feel her excitement buzzing beneath my breastbone. She sprang to her feet, ears forward and wings flared, balancing on her hind legs and tail to crane up and sniff the air. She made a whistling cry so sharp that it hurt my ears.

Another cry answered it from the far distance, something deep and haunting. A dragon sound.

Kasaqua was bounding down the path toward the meetinghouse, looking back over her shoulder at me. I scrambled up to follow her, drawn by her sudden urgency. Mother and Sakewa followed.

The sachem was standing outside of the meetinghouse with a

few other people, gazing up at the sky. We arrived in time to watch the Anglish dragon land.

It was an altogether *larger* creature than Kasaqua's mother had been—stockier and more forwardly built. If Kasaqua's mother could be likened to an otter, this dragon could be likened to a bear. It was green and bronze, and instead of antlers it had a pair of sharp horns that swept back from its brow. This was the sort of creature that had been turned against the Naquisit in 1825, laying waste to entire villages with its breath. The sort that could reduce everything and everyone in its path to ash and wind.

The sort of creature that Kasaqua would become.

The dragon was wearing a complicated-looking arrangement of leather straps across its chest and belly, and as it folded its wings and stood at attention I could see that they supported a kind of saddle, from which an Anglish woman was dismounting.

She was old enough that her hair was white and her face lined, but I'd never been terribly good at judging the age of Anglish people. Her skin was very pink, like boiled bacon, and her white hair was pulled back into a tight knot at the back of her head. She was dressed in gray trousers and a high-collared blue jacket with gold braid at the shoulders and brass buttons all down one side, and every inch of her was starched and pressed and polished. The black leather belt at her waist was closed with a brass buckle.

Two pistols were hanging from it.

Pistols were not allowed on Masquapaug. That was part of the treaty. We could have rifles for hunting, but not pistols. I felt the hairs on the back of my neck stand up at the sight of them.

"Who among you is Anna-kiss?" the woman asked, in a voice that was crisp and precise, with an accent that I couldn't quite place. I felt a hand light on my shoulder, and then on my other shoulder. Mother, and the sachem, lending me strength and sureness I wouldn't have had otherwise.

"You say it Ahn-eh-KOOS, actually. Ma'am," I said, when I found my voice again.

The woman made a gesture as if she were swatting away flies and strutted over to me, folding her arms behind her.

"You're the one who submitted an application to Kuiper's Academy of Natural Philosophy and Skiltakraft in Varmarden?"

"Yes, ma'am."

"I'm Karina Kuiper. I've come to see this dragon of yours."

I let my gaze fall past her, to where Kasaqua had already bounded over to the other dragon and was leaping and prancing all around it, sniffing at its ankles and wingtips and tail. The other dragon maintained a stiff posture, only following Kasaqua with its eyes.

"I've never seen a nackie dragon before, but I've heard there are still a great number of specimens on the western and northern frontiers. What can be expected of her final growth? I don't suppose I could have a look at her sire or dam?" Karina Kuiper asked, looking at Kasaqua critically.

"No, ma'am," I answered, swallowing and trying to keep my voice firm. "I saw her mother, but only briefly. She was six or seven yards long, and at least ten yards from wingtip to wingtip. I know nothing at all about Kasaqua's father."

"A pity, but that's to be expected of savage-borns, I suppose. A decent midsize, then, in all likelihood."

"What sort of dragon is yours, if I may ask, ma'am?"

"Gerhard is a kesseldrache. His ancestry is impeccable."

Something in her tone implied that it was plain that Kasaqua's ancestry was not.

"Do you have any background at all in skiltakraft?" Frau Kuiper asked, turning back to me.

"No, ma'am," I answered. I didn't add that I had only the vaguest idea of what skiltakraft even *was*, and that much only from pennik novels. I knew that it involved drawing figures, and sometimes included strange and rare ingredients. In novels, it shaped a dragon's breath to useful ends, producing all kinds of effects important to the action of the story.

"I didn't suppose you would. Well, you'll have a lot of catching up to do. I do hope you can manage it. Do you read at all?"

"Is that what you Anglish think of us?" Mother said, her hand on my shoulder tightening just a bit. "My daughter can read, and probably in more languages than you. If she couldn't read in Anglish, how could she have even filled out your application?"

"Young Mr. Knecht couldn't read at all when he came to us," Karina Kuiper replied, utterly unmoved by Mother's anger. "It's dismayingly common, for the children of the lower classes, regardless of their provenance. How cheering that it isn't the case for you."

She reached into her jacket and produced a letter, which she held out to me.

"The term begins officially on Monday, the fifth of September, and classes commence the following day. You will report to the school on Friday, the second of September, to meet with your prospective professors and to take some preliminary examinations. We must assess how to place you in your first term of classes. You are a rather exceptional case, you understand. You will, at that time, be interviewed by Captain Johan Einarsson. He is the local representative of the Ministry of Dragon Affairs. Your failure to report this dragon prior to its hatching has already been noted, but we have convinced the ministry that it would be impolitic to meddle in nackie affairs when the young dragoneer in question has already submitted herself to study at a reputable academy."

"I'm accepted, then? On scholarship?" I asked, feeling bewildered.

"Certainly you're accepted, in whatever capacity you might prove most capable," she said, looking at me critically again. "The letter explains what you will need to begin your term. I'll expect to see you and your dragon at nine in the morning on the second of September. Do be prompt in your arrival—it's my understanding that you lot are rather lax in your timekeeping, and that will not be tolerated at the academy."

She mounted her dragon again without further comment, her demeanor inviting no further questions. The dragon took a few prancing steps backward, away from the gathered crowd, and leaped into the air. They were gone before I had time to collect myself, or to even think of what questions I might have asked. Kasaqua was running in circles, looking up and making little protesting cries. The other dragon wasn't supposed to just *leave* like that, without paying any attention to her at all.

Someone was talking to me, but I couldn't hear or understand. Kasaqua came and pressed herself against my leg, but I just kept staring at the letter in my hand.

The shapeless medicine of a dragon's breath is change.

ANEQUS AND KASAQUA WENT AWAY FROM MASQUAPAUG

I read the letter over three times before my mother asked me, gently, what was in it.

Monday, July 18, 1842

Miss Anequs Aponakwesdottir,

We congratulate you on your acceptance to Kuiper's Academy of Natural Philosophy and Skiltakraft. We are glad to inform you that, due to your unique circumstances, you have been awarded a full scholarship for the coming term. You are expected to report to the offices of Karina Kuiper at nine o'clock on the morning of September the second. Prior to this meeting, you will be expected to have situated yourself in the student quarters assigned to you and dressed yourself in uniform; it is recommended that you arrive at the school no later than seven o'clock to be certain of sufficient time to accomplish this task.

You will find below the addresses of establishments associated with the school; provide them your measurements and those of your dragon, and you will be supplied with school uniforms and dragon tack upon your arrival.

In addition, you are permitted to bring personal effects and toiletries, as well as clothing to be worn off school grounds—though your personal possessions should not be in excess of what can be fitted into a standard military sea chest.

Further, your address has been provided to Miss Marta Hagan, a student already enrolled at the academy, who will serve as Shulefrau Verbindung. She will be contacting you at her earliest convenience.

We look forward to seeing you in September, Miss Aponakwesdottir.

Karina Kuiper, Headmistress

"I don't care what they think scholarship means. The Anglish don't give anything away for free. They'll make you pay for it sometime later, and you won't even know what you've agreed to until it's all said and done and you're in their debt," Grandma said when we went home and told her about the letter. "My brother was a debt-thrall for ten years, and he died on an Anglish boat, far from home and family. Their gifts aren't gifts."

I looked to Mother, hoping that she'd have something to say, but Mother was still looking at the letter, her mouth a thin line. With her other hand, she was absently stroking Sakewa's hair. Sakewa's burns had healed to the awful-looking peeling stage, and she kept picking at her skin even though everyone told her not to.

The days seemed to drag after Frau Kuiper's visit, and I found myself wandering from the meetinghouse to the post office and telegraph station, waiting for word from the *Shulefrau Verbindung*— a term I'd never heard and which I did not know the meaning of.

I was coming back from the telegraph office when I heard Mother and Grandma talking.

"It was different with Niquiat," Mother was saying, her voice tight, as if she might start crying. "With a boy, you expect to say goodbye to them. He left too young and he went too far, but I always knew that he'd leave home, to the sea or to a wife or to both. Boys leave home, and you make yourself content with it. But Anequs . . . She's my oldest daughter. She was supposed to keep the house after me. She was supposed to stay home. I wasn't supposed to lose her!"

"She might not be lost to us, Chagoma," Grandma replied, her voice small and uncertain in a way that sounded wrong coming from her. "She doesn't seem . . . Anequs has a sense of place. She might come back to us. Like a whaler."

"What am I going to tell Aponakwe, when we go to meet him at the docks and she's not there? What am I going to say to him? How do I tell him that *another* of our children left me?"

I felt my throat tighten up, and I turned on my heel and walked away. I couldn't walk into that. I heard Kasaqua struggling to keep up with me, her little feet scrabbling on the broken shells that paved the path, but I couldn't seem to slow down until after I'd passed the stone wall at the edge of the cornfield. I sat down in the shadow of the wall and put my elbows on my knees and held my head.

She wasn't wrong. Daughters weren't supposed to leave mothers. That wasn't how it was supposed to be. Still, I was only going on a short journey. Just until December. Just a few months. Not even as long as Father went to the north after the whales every year. It shouldn't have been something that caused such fuss and worry.

I didn't want to go. But I *had* to go. It was what Kasaqua needed me to do.

Kasaqua, knowing that I was close to just sitting here and bawling my eyes out about how unfair all of this was, about how I shouldn't have had to leave home because there should have been other Nampeshiwe and other Nampeshiweisit right here to teach me, crawled into my lap and crooned. I scratched the back of her neck, along the little ridge of budding feathers, and she leaned into it. A pair of tears squeezed themselves out of my eyes and rolled down my cheeks. I wiped them away and took a deep breath, then went down to the beach to gather a basket of mussels. I needed to be doing something, and it might as well be something useful. Kasaqua splashed in the tide pools, prying starfish off the rocks and eating them. Her enthusiasm was infectious, and I felt better by the time my basket was full despite nothing at all having changed about my situation. I stopped at the post office before going home, and there was a letter for me that had come on the morning ferry.

It had three postage stamps, which was a bit excessive, and like the headmistress's letter it was addressed to *Miss Anequs Apon-akwesdottir.*

Wednesday, July 20, 1842

Dear Anequs,

My name is Marta Hagan. I am a student of Kuiper's Academy and I have been asked to serve as Shulefrau Verbindung to you; we will be sharing a room in the coming term. I plan to be in Vastergot on the third and fourth of September, staying at the home of a good friend. We can meet for luncheon on Saturday at Gaststätte Irmtraude, on the corner of High Street and Ingolfsson Way. If this arrangement is in some way unsuitable, please respond as immediately as you are able. I can be contacted at the following address:

> Miss Marta Hagan
> Sjokliffheim
> Estervall, New Anglesland

> I look forward to meeting you!

Best regards,
Marta Hagan

It was dated the twentieth, and today was the twenty-second. I brought the letter home straightaway to show Mother.

"From what Niquiat said, there's a train between the academy and the city proper," Mother said, scowling at the letter. "Does she expect you to have fare both ways, just for a luncheon meeting?"

"I expect she didn't even think of that," I said, scowling, too. "I expect Anglish people just have enough money to take the train anywhere they want, as often as they like."

"Well, we must hope that this school of yours is willing to provide you with train fare. Otherwise you'll just have to explain to them when you arrive on Friday that you've no way to attend a meeting in the city on Saturday."

"We could ask Niquiat," I said. "He always seems to have train fare. Besides, if I'm going to be at the school at seven in the morning on Friday, I'll have to take the Tuesday ferry and stay somewhere in the city until Friday morning. Where else would I stay but with Niquiat?"

Mother only made a dissatisfied sound.

As for my personal effects, there were a number of standard military sea chests in the village—mostly brought back by whalers or bought secondhand in Catchnet. But a sea chest seemed quite excessive. I was in possession of two cotton shifts, two day dresses, two sturdy woolen skirts, three blouses, and a plain but serviceable winter coat. All of it had been Mishona's before it was mine, and would likely be Sakewa's after—young people's clothing got handed down until it was worn past wearing and then taken apart at the seams to make quilts and bags and whatever else. The only really *new* articles I owned were my stays and my boots—and my dancing dress, but there was no reason at all to take that to the academy with me.

I supposed that Anglish people must simply own more things.

I packed a small medicine bundle—pouches of tobacco and juniper and a large quahog shell to burn them in. I didn't know if any occasion would arise where I might need or want to make an offering, but I didn't want to be left without the means to do so.

All of it together, neatly folded, fit into a rucksack and still left room for a couple of pennik novels and my beading and embroidery box. I didn't expect that I'd have much time for amusements at the academy, but having something to keep my hands busy might be useful. Something familiar, to remind me of home.

The ferry departed Masquapaug at nine in the morning on Tuesday, the thirtieth of August.

Women from the islands who went alone to Catchnet often didn't come back. Sometimes, they later turned up drowned, but more often they never turned up again at all. So Mother went with me, and Uncle Mequeche so we'd have a man in our party and so there'd be someone to keep Mother safe on the journey home. It meant three fares, but there was no better way to do it.

The clock tower at the harbor square read just after half past ten when we made land in Catchnet and started walking to the train station. The streets near the harbor were crowded with porters and hawkers. A dray wagon passed us, pulled by a pair of automaton oxen that hissed and steamed. Kasaqua perched on my shoulder, her little claws digging into my shawl, looking all around with great curiosity.

It had been April the last time we'd come to Catchnet, and everything had still been gray. All the streets were paved in cobblestone, and all the walls were whitewashed. It seemed cheerier under August sunshine. Catchnet was a place we only ever visited to buy sundries, and only when Niquiat sent money. In April, we'd been able to buy a whole crate of glass canning jars with tin lids— enough to share with everyone.

The train station was very close to the docks by design, allowing loads of coal mined on Naquipaug to be carted down Ware Street and loaded directly onto train cars to be brought north to Vastergot and south to New Linvik. Naquipaug was being hollowed out one shovelful at a time to power Anglish steamworks.

Kasaqua had never smelled coal before and was very curious about it—she wanted very much to *eat* it.

When we arrived at the station, Uncle Mequeche stood in line to purchase the tickets while my mother and I stood aside and waited.

"Mummy, look, that nackie girl has a baby dragon!" a little boy shouted, and I looked up to see him pointing. The woman whose hand he was holding was trying to drag him away, not looking at us.

"Don't stare at the nackies, darling. Come away."

I'd never actually been on a train before. I'd seen them, but I'd never had a reason to ride one. An Anglish man in something like a soldier's uniform took our tickets and brought us to our seats. He spoke only to my uncle, and he said everything very loudly and slowly. My mother and I were seated beside the window, with Uncle Mequeche beside me. I gasped when the train started to move, and squeezed Kasaqua so tightly that she made a squealing noise in protest, and I had to spend several minutes petting her back into calmness.

Kasaqua and I watched the scenery roll by with dizzying speed. We left Catchnet behind very quickly, and the buildings gave way to fields of yellow wheat and grazing goats and cattle and sheep, broken by short tracts of forest that stood between the fields like narrow walls. I could see in the distance how they'd cut the land apart into little squares. Anglishmen liked straight lines and sharp corners. They built square houses and square fields and square tools. They'd probably have built square boats, if they could have made them float that way.

About three-quarters of an hour later, buildings and roads began to spring up again. From the window, as we came around the curve of Vaster's Hill, the city rose as a glittering collection of brick and stone, steeples and towers and smokestacks reaching into the sky, sprawling out across the horizon with the shining band of the river running into the heart of it. Even this far out, I could already smell the coal smoke.

We arrived at the station and consulted maps to find the main pavilion, where we'd arranged to meet Niquiat. The giant clock above the big map said that it was noon.

"Anequs! Mother!" a voice called, cutting through the crowd.

"Niquiat, over here!" I called back, waving.

Uncle Mequeche hugged Niquiat once he was close enough, then took him by the shoulders and said, "You take good care of your sister, here in this Anglishman's place, you hear me?"

Mother embraced me awkwardly, having to make space for Kasaqua. She took my face in her hands, stroking her thumbs across my cheeks.

"Be safe, and be good, and come home when you can. We'll keep the fire burning for you."

It was the same thing she said to Father before he left on whaling trips, and I felt my eyes sting a little at having it said to me. I wasn't doing anything as dangerous as whaling, after all. I was only in Vastergot. I nodded quickly, ducking away as Mother let me go.

Niquiat embraced Mother and put an envelope into her hand before she and Uncle Mequeche left us to catch the train back to Catchnet. The evening ferry would be leaving for Masquapaug at four in the afternoon. If they missed it, they'd have to take the six o'clock ferry to Naquipaug instead, stay the night with Aunt Shanuckee, and canoe across tomorrow morning.

"What did you just give her?" I asked Niquiat quietly.

"Nothing to worry about, just some money and a letter," Niquiat replied. He scratched the back of his head and said, "Let me carry your bag. You've already got the dragon, you shouldn't have to carry the bag, too."

"Thank you," I said, handing my rucksack over. "I'm glad you're here. I've missed you."

He raised his hand as if he was going to ruffle my hair, but then hesitated. I had it up in braids, like a woman. Not like a little girl anymore.

"Well then," he said, sticking that hand in his pocket instead, "I'll show you where I'm staying."

TO A CITY OF SOOT AND SPARKS

Going to the place Niquiat was staying—he didn't call it "home," and neither did I—involved going to a part of the city near the waterfront, where the buildings were very tall and crowded thickly together. The narrow walkways between them were caked with mud and filth, and there were planks and bricks laid down in the road to step on. I could smell the rancid fish-oil stink of the cannery.

Niquiat's flat was up six flights of creaky stairs in a square brick building with slits for windows. They were covered over in oiled canvas to keep the wind out. It was stifling in the summer heat, and it had to be punishingly cold in winter. Why would anyone ever *pay* to live like this?

"Is this where you've been living the whole time?" I asked on the landing while Niquiat fought with the lock to open his door.

"No. This is the fourth building I've lived in," Niquiat answered. He turned away from me, and I didn't ask if the others had been better or worse than this. He opened the door to reveal a room with four beds and hardly enough space between them to walk. On the bed nearest the door, an Anglish man with one eye was sitting, whittling something with a knife that flashed in the dim light. A little pile of wood shavings was falling to the floor. It was plain that he did this a lot, and didn't bother sweeping afterward, because there were a lot of wood shavings that had been trodden on with dirty feet. He looked up at us as we entered. He was on the older side of middle age, with skin like boiled leather.

"This is my sister Anequs," Niquiat said, standing aside for me to enter. "She's staying with me until Friday. She and her dragon won't make trouble."

"Does Aestergaard know about this?" the man asked, looking back down to the thing he was whittling.

"Aestergaard doesn't need to know about this," Niquiat said tightly. "She's not staying long enough to count as another lodger."

"He'd want another share of rent from you. That's a halfmarka for every day she's here."

"It is."

"I owe Rokiskwe a halfmarka. And you nackies are always so fastidious about your money, aren't you?"

Niquiat reached into his pocket and pulled out a handful of coins, counting out five of them.

"Aestergaard doesn't need to know about my sister staying for a couple of days?" Niquiat asked, pressing the coins into the man's outstretched hand.

"I don't know anything about that," the man answered, looking up at him and smiling. His teeth were yellow brown. He put the coins into his own pocket before going back to his whittling.

"Aestergaard is the landlord," Niquiat explained softly. "That's Tarvo, by the way. No one will bother your things with Tarvo around." Niquiat's voice was studiously casual and just a little louder than it had to be. "It's not as if you have anything valuable that you'd need to worry about anyway. Besides Tarvo and I,

Bjarni and Rokiskwe live here. They'll be at the cannery all day and then at the ale hall half the night. They're quiet when they come in. I've got good roommates at this flat, better than the last place I lived."

I looked around the tiny room, at the four beds and at the back of Tarvo's head.

"There's a washroom at the end of the hall that we share with the other three rooms on this floor. It has running water."

We looked at each other for a long time. Kasaqua fidgeted on my shoulder, wanting to get down, and I stroked her to keep her where she was.

"Thank you for welcoming me into your home," I said, because it was the only polite thing that I could say. Because this place was disgusting, and he knew that I knew, and what else was there to say?

"Home is where you live," Niquiat said. "This is just where I sleep. Now that we've put your things away, you should come and see the workshop and the coffeehouse. That's where I spend most of my time that's not at work, really." He put his arm around my shoulder as he said it and looked squarely at Tarvo.

"If you see the others before I do, Tarvo, you'll tell them about my sister?"

Tarvo nodded.

Niquiat led me back out the way we'd come.

"You don't have to say it, Chipmunk, I know," Niquiat said on the stairs. "Don't come here unless I'm with you. It wouldn't be good for you to be alone here. I'll show you better places to be. But please, don't tell Mother and Father? I'm trying, all right? I'm trying. It's hard to find anyplace that will rent to nackies."

"You could come home," I said.

Niquiat sighed deeply, sounding more weary than anyone as young as him should have sounded.

"No. I can't. You don't understand. You *belong* there, you and Sigoskwe. Maybe Sakewa, too, but she's too young to tell. I'm not like you. I need a world that's moving."

"This can't be where you belong—"

"It's not," he interrupted, "but it's something. It's someplace where the world is changing. Masquapaug is like a bug in a piece of amber, stuck in one time and place."

"Masquapaug is never going to change if all our young people wander away to find work in Vastergot," I said.

Niquiat didn't say anything else for a while. When we were at the bottom of the stairs he said, "I want to show you something, and maybe you'll understand then. I want to introduce you to my friends."

He brought me down a path of winding alleys to a little doorway in a brick wall that looked just like any of the other doorways in all the other brick walls. He opened it to reveal a tinker shop.

There was nothing at all like this back on the island.

The workshop smelled like smithing and coal tar and tatkrafted air. There were two long tables down the middle of the room. One had bits of metal and coils of wire and a half-built monstrosity that looked like a dead crab made of brass. The other held bottles and vials and tins, some with labels, others without. Some of them were faintly glowing. There were a couple of automaton horses, both partly disassembled, standing near the back wall. Somewhere nearby, something pneumatic was pumping away with the hiss of steam and the slide of metal on metal.

Two people were in the shop. A man of middle years was perched like an owl on a tall stool. He was curled over some clockwork thing on the table, gazing at it through a compound lens and poking at it with some wickedly sharp little tools. He was pale, but sunburned across the cheeks and forehead. His hair was brownish, faded to yellow on top, and looked like it hadn't been washed in entirely too long. He had a pair of goggles with smoked glass lenses perched on his forehead, and as I watched he switched the compound lens for the goggles and picked up a device that proved in short order to be a cutting torch. It made a very impressive flash of blue-and-orange sparks as he used it to cut a small piece of steel in half.

At the second table, a young woman was pouring liquid from a narrow glass tube into a bottle with a wide bottom and a narrow top. She was brown-skinned and dark-eyed. She had her hair tied up in a yellow scarf, but what showed at the edge of her hairline was black. She was probably Kindah. She was tall and wide, dressed in a drab green coverall suit and a long leather apron.

Niquiat waited for the man to put down the torch before he said anything.

"Jorgen, Zhina, this is my sister—"

The man looked up, then immediately scrambled off his stool, pointing at me rudely.

"Sweet Fyra's tits, it's a dragon!" he shouted.

"This is my sister Anequs," Niquiat said, sounding a bit exasperated, "and her dragon, Kasaqua."

"Is the dragon old enough to transmute athers?" the girl asked, setting her bottle down carefully and taking a step forward, around the edge of the table. She had a strange accent, a kind of Vaskosish twang that I'd never heard before, and there was something disconcertingly hungry in her dark eyes while she looked right at Kasaqua. I resisted the urge to take a step back.

"I don't know what that means," I answered, when I realized that she'd asked a question.

Niquiat strode over, taking his hat off, and he playfully swatted first the man and then the girl with it.

"Usually, you two, you say 'hello' to someone you've just met," he chided. He turned back to me, smiling. "Anequs, this is Jorgen, and that's Zhina. Jorgen is one of the founding members of this co-op. Zhina's his chief apprentice."

Jorgen seemed to remember himself then, and wiped his hand liberally on the side of his thigh before thrusting it at me. I hesitated for much longer than was probably polite before taking it. He shook it heartily enough to rattle my bones. Kasaqua, affronted, jumped off my shoulder and onto the table. I put a protective hand on her hackles to keep her from going too far.

"Jorgen mostly fixes engines," Niquiat said. "Zhina is studying minglinglore and enginekraft. I hang about and make a nuisance of myself, reading manuals and schematics."

"And building a self-stabilizing reciprocator that's more efficient than anything else I've ever seen," Jorgen said, looking at me in a way that indicated I should be impressed.

"It was efficient for five minutes, before it broke apart," Niquiat said, scratching the back of his neck. "The idea needs a lot more work before I can start producing them and making thousands of marka. Until then, it's the cannery for me."

"When your dragon can transmute athers, I'd be very interested in buying strahlendstone from you," Zhina said. "The only source I have for it right now is almost prohibitively expensive, but I've read that it can be made by dragons in a thaumaturgical process."

"A *what* now? And what's strahlendstone?" I asked.

"The Anglish don't call it thaumaturgy, I don't think," Niquiat said. "They call it witskraft. Anyway, it's the thing you do to shape a dragon's breath and make things out of other things, you know?"

"Strahlendstone is this stuff," Zhina said, selecting a little glass bottle and placing it in front of Kasaqua. The bottle was wider at the bottom than the top, and it seemed to have a piece of metal fixed to its underside. It wouldn't be easy to knock over. Whatever was inside was a greenish white, and it was faintly glowing. Kasaqua's narrow, pointed tongue flicked out to actually taste the glass and perhaps the glowing fluid trapped within it. She was very interested in it, so I moved to pick her up, because eating it would probably be a very bad thing for her to do.

"Careful," Zhina said just as I was scooping Kasaqua out of harm's way. "Strahlendstone's dangerous to touch, like kwiksilber— it can cause bone rot. It has to be stored in transmuted loodglas containers, because the radiant athers can't pass through lood."

"So, wait, in one family you've got a dragoneer *and* a mechanical genius?" Jorgen said, laying his goggles aside, followed by the complicated eyepiece. "Your parents must be very proud."

Niquiat and I looked at each other, and for a moment our pain was exactly the same.

"I come here whenever I can, and work at the cannery for money when I can't find enough work here," Niquiat said, changing the subject. "I'll come back home someday, when I've made enough money to build a machine shop of my own there. But that's probably a long time in coming. This is where I need to be in the meantime, to study."

All I could do was nod.

"Do you know anything at all about enginekraft or thaumaturgy?" Zhina asked.

"Only what I've read in novels and magazines, really," I said.

"From what I've read, the bedrock basis of skiltakraft and minglinglore both are that you can't get something from nothing—" Niquiat began.

"I've got *that* much," I interrupted, rolling my eyes at him. We'd been reading the same sorts of things, after all.

"Usually you get tatkraft out of coal by setting it on fire, which transmutes it into heat that you can use to power other things like steam boilers and whatnot," he said, louder, glaring at me.

"I've understood that bit, yes," I said just as loudly, glaring right back at him because he knew that I knew that.

Niquiat swept aside some assorted metal bits and pieces from the table, and Zhina unrolled a large piece of brown paper with drawing all over it: automaton horse sketches on the edges, and diagrams of how gears fit together, and some kind of engine dominating the middle.

"Automaton horses usually work by having a coal burner and cogs in the belly and back end," Niquiat said, gesturing to one of the drawings, "but we've recently laid hands on a kind of engine core that, if it does what I think, makes a cachet of magnets on a shuttle spin around a coil of copper wire on an isen spindle."

"The junkman we bought it from says it was originally salvage from a shipwreck, which seems about right for how tarnished and rusty it is," Zhina said.

"Best guess is that it's from some Far East place originally," Jorgen said. "Shiang-Gang or Zhongu or Zhippon or someplace like that."

"I can tell you the writing on some of the pieces is Shiangish, because it's like the writing on the cloth imports my father deals in. I don't know how to read it, though," Zhina said. "We've been teasing the thing apart piece by piece. There are skiltas in it."

"If it works the way we think it does, and if we can get it in working order again, there seems to be a spot in the middle of all the skiltas where coal goes in," Niquiat said. "We think it's supposed to transmute the coal right into the orbiting mechanism *without setting it on fire*. That it could produce tatkraft at room temperature, like strahlendstone does, but without the danger of radiant athers."

"Problem being none of us know how to read skiltas," Jorgen said, "and there's precious little to be found on the subject in any of the books we've been able to lay hands on. Not that it would make much difference anyway, even if we could read and draw skiltas, without having a dragon to breathe on them."

"I'm presumably going to be learning skiltakraft, when my lessons start," I said.

"I wouldn't mind having a look at any books they give you on the subject, Chipmunk," Niquiat said with a grin. "If you can figure out how to read the skiltas . . ."

"I'll let you know everything I know as I learn it," I said.

"Will you be at the coffeehouse later, or did you have other evening plans?" Zhina asked, rolling the paper back up. "I'm sure the gang would love to meet your sister and her dragon."

Niquiat glanced at me, then back to Zhina, shrugging.

"Whatever she wants, she's the guest," he said, glancing at me in a way that made it abundantly clear that we'd be going to the coffeehouse. "I was going to bring her by the bookstore on Verner Street before it closes, though, see if we can't find any books on telkraft. She'll need to know al-jabr and anglereckoning to do skiltakraft, after all."

"Good luck in finding useful books, then!" Zhina said cheerfully, looking back to her bottles and jars. "See you at Haddir's if you turn up."

I put Kasaqua back onto my shoulder and followed Niquiat out onto the street.

TO A PLACE OF WARMTH AND STORIES

The bookstore on Verner Street was like the one in Catchnet where we got our pennik novels secondhand: a little shop packed as tightly as it could be with shelves and shelves of books. Some were only a bit used, many halfway to falling apart. I selected *Principles of Telkraft*, *An Introduction to Al-jabr*, and *Anglereckoning*. I also picked up a book called *Dragonreckoning*, because I'd never read any books that were specifically about that subject. I looked for books on skiltakraft, or even on witskraft in general, but there didn't seem to be any.

Niquiat paid for the books without my having to ask, and added another tenpennik for a canvas bag to carry them away in. He pulled his remaining coins out of his pocket and stared at them afterward, looking slightly distressed.

"I'm going to have to go to work tomorrow," he said with a sigh. "The cannery has an open pool of day labor—they pull in the first hundred or so men who turn up every morning. It pays a marka and a half a day, but you only get paid if you stay the entire shift—six in the morning to six at night. If they're full up, I'll have to try the mill. They only pay one marka a day, but they're always in want of pickers and sorters. Let's go to the coffee shop. That's where you should stay while I'm at work. Haddir won't mind you hanging around. The people there are good . . . safe."

Which meant that the people at his flat weren't.

I smelled the coffeehouse before I saw it. The aroma of coffee was pervasive, spilling out into the street and aggressively pressing back the general stink of the cannery district. It was mingled with the smell of boiled sugar and something I couldn't quite put words to—herbal or spicy.

"This is Haddir's," Niquiat said as he opened the door. "There are probably some of my friends hanging around; there usually are."

The coffeehouse was full of people gathered in tight knots of three or four, the general murmur of excited chatter, and the smell of coffee and sugar. It was as warm and friendly a place as anywhere I'd been since leaving Masquapaug that morning. Most of the people were Kindah, and a few were Vaskosish and Anglish. Niquiat and I were the only nackies.

"Dragon!" a pale man standing by the bar yelped, actually going so far as to rudely point at Kasaqua and me. The whole coffeehouse went silent, and then everyone was looking at us.

"My sister Anequs. Her dragon, Kasaqua," Niquiat said, looking right at the man who was pointing. He looked beyond him, to the man standing behind the bar. "Haddir, a pot of coffee for our table, please?"

"Almond milk and orange-blossom water?" the man behind the bar, apparently Haddir, asked without hesitation or apparent surprise.

"Please," Niquiat answered. He glanced around the room, and his eyes lit up when he spotted someone at a table toward the back, beckoning me to follow him.

"Don't mind Lars over there; he only said what all of us were thinking when you walked in," a young man who was already sitting at the table said as Niquiat pulled out a chair for me. "You don't see dragons in the cannery district. I'm Ekaitz, by the way, and Niquiat never mentioned that his sister was so beautiful."

His name and his accent were both quite strongly Vaskosish. I nodded politely at the compliment he'd paid me, but didn't meet his gaze. I didn't feel especially flattered, being told I was beautiful by a stranger I'd met in the cannery district in Vastergot.

"You don't see dragons hanging around with nackies, either, comes to that," the pale, yellow-haired woman beside him said.

"This is Ekaitz and that's Strida, and along with Zhina and Jorgen and I, we make up the entire population of the enginekrafters co-op."

"I'm pleased to meet you," I said, dipping my head. "What's that you're adding to your coffee?"

"They make it differently here," Niquiat explained. "They don't pound it, they run it through a kind of mill until it's fine as dust, and they add a spice that I can't remember the name of—"

"Cardamom," Ekaitz interrupted.

"And then you add sweetened almond milk and orange-blossom water to it. It's very nice."

"That's a lot of books you've got," Strida said, nodding toward the bag that Niquiat was carrying.

"My sister needs to learn anglereckoning and al-jabr before her big examination for dragon school, so we bought everything that old Zurine had on the subject, and another book about dragonish erelore or something. I was looking around for books on machinakraft, but there wasn't anything new."

"You want to know more about dragonreckoning, eh?" Ekaitz asked, draining his cup. "Strida here should tell you the story of Sigur Windtooth. She's a great storyteller."

Strida looked vaguely embarrassed, hiding behind her cup for a moment, but when she put it down her face was composed.

"I like telling stories for nackies; you're always so polite about not interrupting," she said, then cleared her throat and steepled her hands. She closed her eyes and opened them again, looking down at the space between her palms, and something about it felt like a ritual.

THIS IS THE STORY THAT STRIDA TOLD

It was Sigur Windtooth who conquered dragonkind.

In the ancient days when summer seldom came, there was a great warrior-king named Sigur Windtooth who ruled the ancient center of Anglesland. He built a great hall in which to shelter his people against the cold that lay upon the land, to feast them on the cattle and mead he had taken in brave raids upon the soft and cowardly men of the southlands across the narrow sea, and the hall was called Sigur's Fast. But Sigur's Fast was menaced by the great lyndwyrm, a monstrous dragon with a heart made of ice and a mind made of fire. It had claws and teeth as hard as isen, and wings as tough as sinew, and horns as sharp as daggers, and spines as great as spears, and breath as cold as the teeth of winter and as hot as the flames of Lothreid's forge. The lyndwyrm was the child of Enki the mad god, from his love affair with Rune, the unknowable goddess of the narrow sea.

Sigur took twenty of his bravest and fiercest warriors and as-

cended the icy cliff above Sigur's Fast to face the beast in its lair
with sword and spear and bow.

Sigur alone survived to return to his fast, the beast uncon-
quered.

Sigur was a clever man, and he sought the counsel of his
skalds, saying, "The lyndwyrm comes every night to eat of my
cattle and my people, and twenty of my bravest warriors have
been slain, and none can dispatch it. What can I do?"

The skalds asked Sigur how he had slain the wolves, and Sigur
said, "I did not slay the wolves. I beat them and collared them, and
now they hunt beside me as my hounds."

The skalds asked Sigur how he had slain the horses, and Sigur
said, "I did not slay the horses. I bridled them and saddled them,
and now they are my steeds."

The skalds asked Sigur how he had slain the mammoths, and
Sigur said, "I did not slay the mammoths. I bewildered them with
fire, and harnessed them, and turned their might against my enemies, that they be crushed and cowed."

The skalds took Sigur to a secret place where the waters that
Lothreid used to quench blades from his forge ran from the rocks,
and drew for him a skilta—one such as could be woven in those
days that cannot be woven now. It was to be fed on silver and gold
and blood and bone, the caul of a child and the egg of a hen, and
many other things.

"That," said the skalds, "is how you must bridle the lyndwyrm.
You must go to its lair while it is sleeping, and you must draw this
skilta all around it, and when it is finished, you must pluck out
your own eye and feed it to the skilta, and then it will awaken and
the lyndwyrm will be snared."

Sigur Windtooth thanked the skalds for their wisdom and
gathered the things he would need. In the silence of the night he
climbed the icy cliff and hid in wait in the lyndwyrm's lair until the
beast slept. Creeping more quietly than a cat, he made his preparations, drawing the skilta all around the lyndwyrm while it slept,

and as the first light of dawn appeared over the eastern mountains, he cut out his own eye and gave it to the skilta to awaken it. The lyndwyrm woke with a cry, but all its might and guile and rage could not overcome the power of Sigur's skilta. Sigur sang to the great writhing beast, "I am Sigur Windtooth, and you are mine. You are mine as my hounds are mine. You are mine as my horses are mine. You are mine as my mammoths are mine. You are mine, and I name you Dragon!"

But the lyndwyrm was too proud a creature to be conquered. It screamed to him, "I am the child of Enki and Rune. I am fire and I am ice. I cannot be conquered by any mortal creature!"

And the lyndwyrm breathed its icy fiery breath upon itself and crumbled to ash.

Where it had lain, there was only a perfect egg.

Sigur picked up the egg and carried it down the mountain and placed it in the middle of his hall and said, "I have slain the great lyndwyrm, and this is my prize."

And when the egg hatched, the little creature that came out bowed its head to Sigur and was tame under his hands. He bridled it and saddled it and rode it into battle. So Sigur Windtooth tamed dragonkind for man.

ANEQUS WENT TO THE SCHOOL

I slept in Niquiat's bed that night, with Niquiat curled behind me and Kasaqua tucked against my belly. I changed my clothes in the washroom. The running water that Niquiat had told me about was cold and rusty brown. During the night the other men had come in. One of them had been sick on the floor, and no one had cleaned it up.

Niquiat and I left there before the sun was up, and he brought me back to the coffee shop. Haddir brought me a cup of coffee and a plate of little fried cakes with sugar. I told him that I didn't have any money. He told me that it didn't matter, and asked if he could pet Kasaqua, because that was lucky. Kasaqua seemed to like him.

Niquiat's friends came and went. They bought coffee for me, and hand pies, and boiled potatoes, and meaty bones for Kasaqua. I set myself at a table and read, and people would chat with me about telkraft and anglereckoning and al-jabr and dragons. They'd ask about life on the island and what I thought of the city, and ask about things Niquiat and I had done as children. Strida and Ekaitz especially wanted me to share embarrassing stories. Zhina wanted to know everything about Nampeshiwe, and what they'd meant to us on Masquapaug.

I didn't sleep at all on Thursday night. I sat on the floor beside Niquiat's bed, reading by the light of a kerosene lamp, with Kasaqua asleep in my lap. It was strange, how restful her sleep was for me—part of the bond we shared. I put my best dress on at dawn, and Niquiat helped me braid my hair. He came with me to be sure I got to the school safely; his cannery job meant that he didn't worry much about train fare.

The school had its own telegraph. I knew the coordinates for the telegraph office on the island, and now for the one at Niquiat's co-op, too. I knew the letter addresses as well. I wouldn't be entirely out of contact, the way whalers were for months at a time. It only *felt* like I was going away from everyone and everything, friendless and alone into a strange place.

Niquiat and I didn't have much to say to each other on the train ride to Varmarden. I didn't want to say goodbye to him again. We said goodbye to each other too often.

The path from the train station to the school took us down a wide, gravel-paved road through fields of dozy cattle. According to my pocket watch, we arrived at the school half an hour before seven.

Kuiper's Academy was a huge building made of dark beams and smooth plaster, all sharp angles and straight lines, its roof covered in slate tiles. On the left side there was an open archway, like a carriage house. On the right side a tower rose to a flat roof with a fenced walk, like the houses in Catchnet, where people could stand to watch the ships come in. The front door was enormous, painted bright red and protected under its own jutting roof. At the peak of that roof there was a wooden figurehead, like a ship's, in the shape of a roaring dragon. Another building off to

the left of the archway—only half as high as the school itself—
had a number of open arches along its front and smoke curling up
out of its central chimney.

There were a half dozen dragons sleeping or lounging on the
wide lawn that separated the two buildings—the largest one might
have been Frau Kuiper's. Certainly it was a kesseldrache. The
smallest one, a red-and-black dragon, was still the size of a dray
horse.

The book on dragonreckoning had focused on what each sort
of dragon was most suited for, and had included a pencil sketch
of breed type to accompany each entry. A few of the sketch pages
had been neatly excised from the copy I had. From it I'd learned
that kesseldraches and falterdraches were best suited for battle,
and for breaking up lines of cavalry. Silberdraches and velikolepni
were specially bred to perform powerful skiltakraft. Bjalladreki
were very fast fliers and could keep up speed across long distances,
so were best for scouting and as messengers, or for the sport of
racing.

Kasaqua, scrabbling along at my heel, was a great deal smaller
than any of the dragons lying about on the lawn. The dragonreckoning book had nothing at all to say about Nampeshiwe.

One of the dragons saw us coming and rose to its feet, approaching with great interest. It was a breed I didn't know from
the book, light brown with black stripes across its back and wings,
pale on its belly. It was as tall as a pony, but longer from nose to
tail. It yawned hugely and loped forward with a wolfish gait, and
Kasaqua bounded ahead to meet it. They touched noses, much as
cats greeting each other might, and the bigger dragon's tail swept
lazily from side to side.

"You're the one Karina was talking about, aren't you?" a voice
said. I looked up to find a woman standing in the archway, wiping
her hands on her apron. She was Anglish, probably of an age with
Frau Kuiper. She was plump and pink-cheeked, her hair a mix of
brown and gray. Her eyes were very blue, and crinkled at the corners so it looked like she was smiling, even though she wasn't.

"I'd expected a much younger child from the way she spoke, but here you're practically a woman," she said. I frowned at that, because no one back at home would have considered me anything other than a woman; I'd become a woman two years ago when my monthlies had begun. I'd had a New Woman dance, and had begun wearing long skirts and braiding my hair up and everything. I was young still, but I certainly wasn't a *child*.

"Come on inside, then," the woman said after a moment of silence, "before all the other dragons get curious about that hatchling you've got there. Who's this with you?"

"This is my brother Niquiat. He wanted to be sure I got here safely."

"Well, you're here now, so he's fulfilled that duty. Welcome to Kuiper's, dear. I'm sorry that you're not getting the grand welcome that most first-year students get, but needs must and special circumstances and all that. I'm Frau Brinkerhoff, matron of the house—I see to the affairs of students' quartering. Thank you very much, young man, but I assure you that your sister is in capable hands now. You may dismiss yourself."

Niquiat and I looked at each other. Neither of us was satisfied with that dismissal.

Niquiat hugged me, and I didn't want to let him go. I half expected him to say goodbye to me the way Mother had, brushing his thumbs across my cheeks, but he didn't. He only pulled away from me and smiled sadly.

"Be good, Chipmunk. You know where to find me if you need me."

I nodded, not able to speak around the lump in my throat. He handed my rucksack to me. I watched him walk away, back down the road to the train station, leaving me alone among strangers.

"Come along, dear, I'll give you a tour," Frau Brinkerhoff said, drawing me away.

I followed Frau Brinkerhoff inside, Kasaqua at my heels. The door closing behind us made the hairs on the back of my neck stand up, and every part of me was shouting that I didn't belong here, that I should go home. I set my teeth and squared my shoulders, trying to walk tall.

"The other students will be arriving on Monday. Until then it's only you and young Mr. Knecht in residence; you'll be introduced to him after your examinations. Were you able to arrange a meeting with Miss Hagan?"

"She'd like me to join her in the city for luncheon tomorrow, at a place called Gaststätte Irmtraude . . . if there's some way that I can arrange train fare."

"You haven't come with any personal funds?" Frau Brinkerhoff asked, her voice mildly disapproving.

"Anglish money isn't something that my family has in abundance," I said.

She hummed slightly, toneless and calculating, then said, "Well, I'm sure that train fare can be arranged. We will have to discuss your ongoing financial situation with Karina in the coming days, but perhaps some matter of allowance can be arranged. It would reflect badly on the school for anyone to think you a pennikless ragamuffin."

She led me through an interminable series of corridors. There were the kitchens, and there was the library, and off that way were the male students' quarters. I was not to go that way under any circumstances.

"We have not generally had a sufficient number of female students in residence to necessitate full quarters for the young women. As Miss Abbink has completed her education and Miss Linna has elected to seek education elsewhere, Miss Hagan and yourself are the only residents of the suite reserved for our female students," Frau Brinkerhoff said. "Here we are, dear."

She opened a door into a room with two writing desks, four venerable leather chairs around a low table, and a number of bookshelves. There was a door on the far wall, directly opposite the one she'd just opened. The wall to my left was dominated by a wide window with a seat. Near the window, there was a long copper pipe that disappeared at each end into perforated brass panels set into the floor and ceiling respectively. It attached at right angles to a pipe that looped around the room near the floor, caged all around with fancy brass filigree. On the opposite wall, there was a tall standing clock, its pendulum quietly swinging away. To either side of the door at the back of the room, there were beds made up crisply with white linens, and imposing wooden wardrobes—each of which was set with a pair of tall, narrow mirrors.

"You're on the left, dear, I hope you won't mind terribly. Miss Hagan requested the right, and she is senior to you. You'll find your school uniforms in the wardrobe. I'll leave you to dress and smarten yourself up a bit; the bathing chamber is just beyond. Do you know how a pump is operated?"

"Yes, ma'am," I replied with a forced smile. "We have pumps on Masquapaug."

"Oh good, I'm very glad! I'm afraid that you'll find all of us woefully ignorant about the lives of nackies, even after having young Mr. Knecht in attendance, but hopefully you can educate us. Please make yourself comfortable, and when you're ready, meet me in the library. You're to meet with the board prior to your examinations."

She canted her head a bit as she backed out of the room and closed the door behind her, leaving Kasaqua and me alone. I walked toward the left-hand side of the room, gazing out the window. I could see the roof of the other building and the wide field beyond it. Kasaqua leaped off my shoulder, scampering over to jump onto the bed. She walked in a tight circle then lay down, kneading the bed with her front feet like a cat. She was very pleased with its softness.

The first article of clothing, hanging neatly in the wardrobe before a cotton shift, was a corset. It seemed an especially sturdy construction: a double layer of tight-woven canvas with strips of sprung steel girding it from hem to hem and an additional band of twill tape bolstering the narrowest part of the waist. I'd never worn a corset. I'd packed with me two pairs of plain canvas short-stays like the ones I was wearing beneath my calico dress now; they were supported entirely by quilting and cording, lacking whalebones or steels. Often enough on the island, I didn't fret about underpinnings at all, going bare beneath my blouses. But the presence of the corset made it very plain that I was expected to wear it as a part of my uniform, and I pursed my lips slightly as I took off everything I was wearing and brought the shift and a pair of pantalets with me into the washroom. I'd already washed at Niquiat's flat, but the water here looked a good deal cleaner.

The shift I'd selected was a length I was used to, coming down to just below my knees, but the one hanging behind it was oddly short; only hip-length. That made sense a moment later when I realized that in addition to skirts, I'd been provided with two pairs of trousers. In the drawer beneath were a half dozen pairs of black stockings and a pair of black ankle boots—the sort that had to be done up with a buttonhook. The boots had pronounced heels, meant to slide neatly into a stirrup. They made me at least half an inch taller, once I'd put them on, and felt very stiff. They'd never been walked in at all.

The corset felt slightly too small through the waist and squeezed unpleasantly against my lower ribs; the narrowest part was higher than my natural waist. The way it enclosed my hips forced me to stand in a slightly sway-backed manner. I now understood why so many of the women in the watercolor plates in fashion magazines looked as if they were leaning slightly forward and sticking their rear ends out. I was very glad I'd had the presence of mind to put my boots on before lacing myself in, because I was no longer able to bend at the waist. I paused to admire the effect in the mirror. I wasn't anything like as wasp-shaped as the ladies in fashion magazines, but the corset did do . . . something. I looked older, wearing it, and somehow unfamiliar to myself in a way that made me frown.

I inspected the rest of the clothing I'd been provided. There were two plain high-collared white shirts with horn buttons, two gray ankle-length skirts with petticoats, two pairs of high-waisted gray trousers, all tailored such that they wouldn't have fit me unless I was wearing the corset. Also one waistcoat, dark blue with narrow gray stripes, and one dark blue tailcoat with very square shoulders. Everything was sharp and polished, starched and pressed. I decided to err on the side of Anglish feminine attire and selected a skirt and petticoat rather than a pair of trousers, which was just as well since I'd chosen the long shift and already had my boots on. Order of dressing was going to matter a great deal more with these clothes than the clothes I was accustomed to. Kasaqua bounded off the bed and padded over to me as I was buttoning up my jacket, and I absently made to bend down and pet her, only to find myself wholly unable. I was too tightly trussed in layers of canvas and cotton and wool. I looked up to take in the overall effect in the mirror, to be sure that I was perfectly presentable.

I found that I didn't know the woman who was looking back at me.

This was some other Anequs; an Anequs dressed up like an Anglish woman. I felt faintly ridiculous, and my looped braids looked . . . out of place, somehow. But I didn't have time to rearrange my hair, and I found that I didn't want to. It was the last part of my assembly that recalled the island.

I took a deep breath to fortify myself and turned away from the mirror, off to present myself for examination.

AND FOUND A COLD WELCOME THERE

Frau Brinkerhoff looked at me critically when I walked into the library with Kasaqua at heel, as if she was trying to find some flaw.

"You're earlier than expected, but that can only be to your advantage," she said after a long pause. "Yes, I think I can send you in."

The room beyond the library was wide one way and narrow the other, dominated by a huge wooden table. There was one chair on the side I approached. There were a half dozen people sitting on the other, lit from behind by a bank of windows that took up most of the far wall. Frau Kuiper was centermost, and the only person that I recognized.

"Presented for consideration is one Miss Anequs Aponakwesdottir, of Masquapaug," Frau Brinkerhoff said from behind me before walking around the table to take a seat at the other side, "and her dragon, Kasaqua."

"Welcome to Kuiper's Academy of Natural Philosophy and

Skiltakraft, Miss Aponakwesdottir. Please take a seat," Frau Kuiper said. I did so, arranging Kasaqua in my lap. Frau Kuiper indicated the man seated to her left and said, "This is Captain Johan Einarsson, the representative for the Ministry of Dragon Affairs here at the academy. He makes sure that all of the laws and ordinances concerning the husbandry of dragons are being correctly observed."

He was a severe-looking man, whip-thin, his skin pale as tallow. He was wearing a woolen jacket so black that it seemed to absorb the light. On the right breast, embroidered in red thread, was a dragon. It was standing on two legs, wings outstretched, forelegs clawing at the air.

"You will tell us the circumstances which led you to possess this dragon," Captain Einarsson demanded, staring at me in very obvious disapproval. Frau Kuiper opened her mouth to say something, but I spoke first.

"I don't *possess* her, sir; it's not as if she's a thing I own."

"You will answer the questions that are asked of you without impudence—" he snapped, but Frau Kuiper interrupted him in a voice that commanded silence.

"Captain, I *had* intended to introduce the remainder of the staff to Miss Aponakwesdottir before beginning our questions."

They stared at each other for a moment, and I was suddenly aware that I'd walked into the middle of a well-established rivalry.

"I defer to your will, Frau Kuiper," he finally said.

"Thank you, Captain Einarsson," she said with a tight smile before nodding toward the rest of the row of professors.

"Professor Mesman teaches dragon husbandry."

He was a small, fastidious-looking Anglishman with sharp, dark eyes.

"Professor Ezel teaches skiltakraft."

A tall, square-faced Anglishman with yellow hair, balding at the crown, he looked especially displeased, as if he had somewhere more important to be.

"Professor Ibarra teaches erelore, folklore, and wordlore."

A short, paunchy Vaskosish man with gray hair.

"And Professor Nazari teaches anglereckoning and al-jabr."

A thin Kindah man with a black beard that came to a point.

"Frau Brinkerhoff is our housematron. Professor Ulfar, who teaches natural philosophy and minglinglore, could not be here for this meeting."

I repeated the names over in my head, matching them to the faces, entirely missing what Frau Brinkerhoff was saying to Frau Kuiper and hoping that it wasn't terribly important.

"And now that formalities are attended to, I trust we may resume with matters of pressing concern to the ministry?" Captain Einarsson said.

"You're entirely at liberty, Captain," Frau Kuiper said with a serene smile that didn't reach her eyes.

"I repeat my question," the captain said, pinning me with his gaze. "How did you come to possess this dragon?"

"I'm not quite sure what you're asking," I faltered. "Kasaqua was hatched on Masquapaug. Her mother laid her egg in the ruins of the temple on Slipstone Island, and we brought it to our meetinghouse to be hatched among people. She chose me to be her companion—her dragoneer."

"Why was no one in authority contacted and informed of the presence of a dragon egg on Mask Island?" the captain pressed.

"Who are we supposed to have told, exactly?" I asked.

"Dragon eggs are to be registered with the Ministry of Dragon Affairs. You failed to report the presence of an egg, or the egg's hatching and subsequent bonding, to your local representative."

"We don't have a local representative, not that I know of. No Anglish people live on Masquapaug. It's only we Masquisit, and Mr. Aroztegui, who runs the telegraph and post office. We've never had anything to do with you, except for the taxmen, and they only come once a year after the whalers return. Are you thinking of Naquipaug, perhaps?"

"All of the outlying islands on the east coast fall under the jurisdiction of Lindmarden, as per the treaty of New Linvik, and local governances are required to report to—"

"I'm sure Sachem Tanaquish and the other elders would have said something if they'd known that we were supposed to have done something that we didn't do. Begging your pardon, Captain, sir, I don't see how it matters anyway. I'm already here, and Kasaqua's here with me, and she's the only dragon on Masquapaug."

"There's no need to become emotional," he said severely. "The ministry's concern is this dragon's origin. What is her parentage, and how did her egg come to be laid on your island?"

"Her mother laid it there."

"And where had she come from to do so?" he asked, slowly, as if he thought me stupid.

"Someplace west. We don't know where. She was riderless, and she flew on eastward. My grandmother thinks that her companion must have died, and that she flew out to sea in grief."

"Which is terribly convenient, as origins go. A dragon of that breed appearing from the west can only have come from someplace beyond the western frontier, in lands currently held by western nackies."

"The Shawan-wa, Captain, and their associates the May-mee, the Pote-wadmee, the Wendat, and the Odwa who together make the Wapash-Neepee Rikesband," Professor Ibarra said. "They've nothing whatever to do with nackies. I believe we've had this discussion before, concerning the matter of Mr. Knecht—"

"Nothing like the same thing at all!" the captain interrupted hotly. "*That* dragon's egg was registered, and its parentage accounted for. It was only by misfortune that it was not appropriately bonded with its intended dragoneer. This is a far more troubling situation. If we're dealing with feral dragons—"

"The girl and her dragon are *here*, and the dragon is clearly not feral," Frau Kuiper said, glancing at Kasaqua as she sat quietly in my lap. "We've got the situation well in hand."

"I do think that the captain is right to be concerned about the sudden appearance of dragons where there previously have been none, Frau Kuiper," one of the Anglishmen said. Second from the left. Ezel.

"If the captain thinks that this situation is serious enough for him to bring it before a moot, then he's within his rights to do so," Frau Kuiper said firmly. "In the moment, the girl has given her account of the provenance of this dragon, which is clearly bonded with her. I see no reason to believe that this account is not factual, given the extreme unlikelihood that a dragon of that breed could have been acquired by any citizen's household without it coming to the attention of the ministry. It is a fact well established that a broody dragon, unconfined, is often very fickle about where she chooses to lay—it's perfectly plausible that some feral from the far west or north might have chosen to lay on one of the outlying islands, which are so thinly peopled that the creature might well have mistaken them as uninhabited. There are other items to be attended to, not the least of which is the examination of this girl's academic knowledge. I remind you, Professor Ezel, that classes begin on Tuesday."

"As you have been reminding me with constancy for the past two weeks, Frau Kuiper. I am well aware. I simply feel that it's within our collective best interest to fully examine the situation, given that this is the second time in as many years that we find a wild nackie standing before us—"

"Captain Einarsson, I believe that this portion of the meeting can be concluded," Frau Kuiper said. "Take us to the moot about it or don't, as you see fit. Professor Ezel, your examination of the child will proceed after she has been examined by Professors Ibarra and Nazari. All but Professor Ibarra can be dismissed for the moment. Captain Einarsson, I'd like to ask you to join me in my office for a moment."

Frau Kuiper stood, and then all of the other professors stood as well and filed out behind her as she left. Professor Ibarra was still sitting at the table opposite me, arranging pieces of paper in a leather folio. He looked at me appraisingly, but not unkindly.

"It's my understanding that you've had no formal education at all, is that correct, miss?" he asked.

"Not formal in the Anglish sense, no," I said.

"But you *are* able to read and write?"

"Yes."

"Excellent," he said with a smile that wasn't precisely warm. "I intend to assess your language skills and general knowledge of wordlore, correct use of the Anglish language to convey meaning; folklore, the study of stories; and erelore, the study of eretide."

He took out a stack of paper and slid it across the table to me, and from the bag sitting at his feet he produced an inkwell and a tin-nibbed pen. I sighed inwardly. I'd been hoping for a quill. There was never enough play in the spread of a tin nib, and writing with one invariably made my handwriting blobby and awful.

The first line asked for my name and the date. I wrote my name as Anequs. I had no idea why they kept tacking "Aponakwesdottir" onto my name, but I wasn't going to encourage it.

The first question was:

Write down a story with a beginning, a middle, and an end.

I puzzled at it for a moment, then looked up to where Professor Ibarra was sitting opposite me, his dark eyes keen and his expression expectant.

I wrote down the story of how Nampeshiwe came among the people on Masquapaug—the same one I'd told as I'd carried Kasaqua's egg back home. I covered the front of the paper and carefully moved it aside. The second piece of paper had another question written at the top of it:

In what year did Stafn Whitebeard discover Nack Island? Describe his journey.

I looked at what I'd already written, and then looked to Professor Ibarra.

"I need another piece of paper, please. I haven't finished the story I'm writing."

"It requires more than one page?"

"Yes."

"Very interesting indeed," he said, raising his eyebrows, turning the paper to look at what I'd written. He got up and walked away. I hoped it was to get me more paper. In the meantime, I wrote on the second page:

By Anglish reckoning, Stafn Whitebeard came to Naquipaug in the year 1626. I know nothing else about him.

Professor Ibarra returned with a whole stack of crisp, grayish paper for me to continue writing on. There were five more pages of questions, and by the time I'd finished answering them, I had twelve sheets of paper laid out in front of me.

"Thank you very much for your time and cooperation, Miss Aponakwesdottir."

"That's not my name. My name is Anequs. Aponakwe is my father, but my name isn't Aponakwesdottir. We don't reckon names in the way you do. Please just call me Anequs," I said, closing my eyes.

"Very well, then, Miss Anequs. Professor Nazari will see you next. I suggest you get up and stretch your legs a bit while you're waiting."

He gathered up everything I'd written and took it with him, leaving the table clear except for the pen and ink and stack of gray paper. I walked around the room three times after he'd gone, not certain if I was allowed to go anywhere else. Kasaqua would have liked very much to leave the room and go back outside. She hopped onto the windowsill, and I stepped up behind her. From the wide bank of windows, I could see part of the jutting red roof above the main entrance and the gravel path that led away to the train station.

A few minutes later, Professor Nazari walked in with another stack of papers. He moved in a very quick, precise manner—almost birdlike. When he smiled, he showed all of his teeth.

"Good morning, lovely to meet you," he said in a very thick Kindah accent. "I am Professor Nazari, and I will teach you all the parts of telkraft while you are here."

He slid the papers across the desk to me and leaned back in his chair, stroking his beard.

His questions were the kind of thing I'd been reading about for the past few days. The first page was nothing but sums and scoring, the second some simple anglereckoning; working out the areas of circles and triangles, the angles that made odd shapes, that kind of thing. The third page had some al-jabr, solving problems with unknown quantities. It wasn't until I got to the fourth page that I encountered something that I had no idea how to do, so I wrote that. It took far less time to complete than Professor Ibarra's examination had. As I completed each page, Professor Nazari practically snatched it off the table and began looking over it. His look of surprised pleasure made me feel strange . . . proud and angry at once.

"Excellent, excellent," he said, grinning. "I'll be able to put you directly into the normal first-year class, yes. Very good. Very good. You needn't continue, I know everything that I need to know. Lovely to meet you, good day, I look forward to seeing you in class. Professor Ezel will see you next, I'm very sorry."

He put his hand forward for me to shake, and I took it with some hesitation because none of the other people here had done that yet. His handshake was short and crisp.

I didn't have time to walk around the room before Professor Ezel appeared. He'd evidently been waiting in the next room for Professor Nazari to finish with me, as there wasn't even enough time for the door to close between Nazari leaving and Ezel entering. He strode in with the air of an annoyed cat, sitting down heavily.

"I will say this to you once, girl," he said, before I'd even had a chance to sit down again. "Skiltakraft is exact. Your hand and eye must be steady and in perfect accordance. Mistakes are unacceptable. A hastily drawn skilta, a smudged skilta, a sloppy or inexact skilta—these things will result in failure, and failure can result in death. There is no room for mistakes in skiltakraft. It is done correctly, or it isn't. If you do it incorrectly, there are consequences."

"Yes, sir," I said, sitting, staring at him. "I understand."

"You will complete these questions. I very much doubt that you're any more ready for my instruction than the other one was, but this is what Frau Kuiper desires."

He pulled out a pocket watch and looked at the time. He was still looking at it when he said, "Begin."

The first question was:

List the twenty-four known athers in order by their number of motes.

I wrote:

I have no idea what that means.

The second page said:

Draw the figures for Kolfni, Vetna, Zurfni, Stiksna, Pospor, and Saffle. Number the motes.

I wrote:

I have no idea what that means.

The examination continued in that fashion for twenty pages.

When I handed my completed examination back across the table, he raised his eyebrows and looked at his watch again, scribbling something onto the paper with a red wax pencil. He began to read my answers, and then he laughed. It was a cold, hollow, nasty laugh.

Professor Ezel set a book on the table before me; on the cover was written *A Primary Introduction to Skiltakraft*. He said, "Have that read, in its entirety, by the time you show your face in my laboratory on Tuesday morning."

He got up and walked away without saying anything else to me. I was happy to see him go.

THOUGH IT WAS NOT A PLACE WITHOUT INTEREST

I was left alone for the fullness of five minutes after Professor Ezel left, and I spent most of it playing with Kasaqua. During the previous examinations she'd fallen asleep in a rectangular patch of sunlight that came through the windows, but she was more than happy for my attention. I was throwing a piece of crumpled paper around for her to chase when Frau Kuiper appeared in the doorway. I didn't know how long she'd been standing there when I saw her, but she was smiling fondly.

"Your examination with Professor Ulfar will take place in his laboratory, for reasons that should soon become abundantly clear. Please follow me, and I'll introduce you."

Professor Ulfar's laboratory was down a flight of stairs and on the other side of the wide open hall that Frau Brinkerhoff had told me was the dining room. The laboratory was less *empty* than other rooms I'd been in so far. At the front of the room was a huge expanse of black slate with notes written on it in chalk, and between that and the door we entered through were six round tables, each surrounded by five chairs. Around both sides of the room were shelves littered with an assortment of things that put me in mind of Niquiat's co-op—intricate glassware, charts and graphs, stones and bones and feathers, jars with dead animals in them.

The man sitting at the far end of the room was plainly Anglish, older than the other professors, more Frau Kuiper's age. His gray hair was slightly disarranged, as if he ran his hands through it frequently. He had bushy gray eyebrows and though his mustache entirely covered his mouth, I could tell that he was smiling. He was dressed in a blue jacket with brass buttons all down one side and a number of colorful medals and ribbons across the left breast. He nodded as Frau Kuiper and I entered, and I heard a clockwork sound. The man emerged from behind the desk, but he didn't stand up to do so.

The chair he was sitting on was made of polished brass, and stood on six multi-jointed legs that splayed out to either side, like a crab's. The arms of the chair formed a wide arc, and I could see an array of little switches and buttons within easy reach of his hands. Even as I watched, his hand moved deftly over them, fingers flicking in an obviously practiced rhythm.

The chair walked like an ant, moving three of its legs at a time. He came forward between the rows of desks, smiling warmly, looking from Frau Kuiper to me.

"And this will be young Miss Anequs, I presume?"

"Yes, sir. Pleased to meet you. You're Professor Ulfar?"

"Indeed. I'm so glad to finally meet you. I've been hearing talk about you all day."

I couldn't stop looking at the chair, and at his hands as he controlled it. The dead-crab thing at the co-op might have been a piece of machinery like this, or at least part of one . . .

"I lost the use of my legs in the battle of Polvaara," Professor Ulfar said, catching my attention back. "Fell from flight, broke my back. I don't recommend it. Always remain securely fastened to your dragon's harness."

"I'll remember that, sir," I said, lowering my eyes respectfully.

"I'll be getting back to my office," Frau Kuiper said. "After you've finished your examination with Professor Ulfar, please report back to Frau Brinkerhoff in the library."

"Yes, ma'am," I said, nodding.

"Now tell me, child," Professor Ulfar asked after Frau Kuiper had left, "what do you know about natural philosophy? And please, take a seat; there's no need to keep standing."

I was surprised that he didn't just slide a packet of papers in front of me like all the other professors had. I sat down at the nearest table, looking at him uncertainly.

"Very little, I'm afraid," I said.

"It's likely that you know more than you think. There are five basic principles to natural philosophy. First, through observations of the natural world, determine the nature of the phenomenon that is being explored. Having done this, develop one or more vermutun—educated guesses—to explain the phenomenon. Then, devise a versuch—a plan of action—to test the vermutun. If it can't be tested, it is not a valid vermutun. Examine the results of your tests and determine to what degree the results fit the predictions of the vermutun. Finally, modify the vermutun, repeat the versuch, and continue in this fashion until a conclusion can be reached."

"All right . . ." I said. "So . . . what is it that you want me to do exactly?"

"Yours are a farming people, are they not?"

"Yes, sir."

"Let us suppose that you have a patch of land where a crop isn't doing well. What would you do?"

"I'd look at the soil and see if there's something wrong with it, if it's too sandy or pale or something. I'd look at how sunlight moved across the land through the day. I'd look at what we were

trying to grow and what we'd tried to grow there before—
arrowroot should follow corn, and onions should follow arrowroot, and squashes or melons should follow onions, and sunflowers
should follow squashes, and so on. Sometimes you plant things
together because they help each other. Squashes have big leaves
that shade the ground so they keep corn from getting too dry, and
beans like something to climb and cornstalks serve well. If the
soil was too sandy, I'd add seaweed and dead fish and autumn
leaves to it. If the soil was too thick with clay, I'd add sand. If the
soil is too salty, there isn't much to be done about that. You can
only plant something like beach plums there."

"Good, good, a very rational answer!" he said, grinning. "Now,
how do you know this?"

"I learned it from my parents and grandparents and aunts and
uncles," I said, eyebrows going together.

"All right, and how do you suppose *they* know it?"

"They'd have learned it the same way, but I see what you're
getting at. I suppose someone long ago must have just noticed
these things were true by observing and trying things."

"Excellent. Now suppose you were given a new crop, something you've never planted before. How would you know where
to plant it?"

"Well, I'd ask whoever had given it to me about the best way to
grow it, but if they didn't answer me for some reason, I suppose
I'd try growing it in a lot of different places and see where it did
best? If it was like something I already had—if it was a new breed
of melon or something—I'd try treating it like a melon I already
knew first."

"Good, good! You seem to have an excellent grasp of rational
thinking. Now let's suppose that you were given a bag of white
powder and were told that it makes beans grow very well when
tilled into the soil. How would you find out if this is true?"

"I'd till some into the soil of one bean field and not on another, plant both with the same beans, and wait to see which beans

prospered. I'd also ask whoever was giving it to me what it was and where it had come from."

"That would be a versuch, based on the vermutun that the unknown compound positively affects the growth of beans."

"You're saying a lot of words that I've never heard before, but you seem to mostly be talking about things that I understand well enough."

"In the ancient world, Tyskland was the seat of all art and philosophy. That's why so many of the words we use in natural philosophy are Tysklandish in origin. All the names of the athers, for example, and the word 'ather' itself."

"So I'm going to have to learn to speak Tysklandish?"

"Well, that certainly wouldn't hurt," he said with a bark of laughter. "It's taught by many of the better primary schools, but it's hardly required."

"If it's what others have done, I probably should do it. I'm sure there are books in the library that could help me."

Professor Ulfar smiled hugely, offering me a hand to shake.

"You will make a fine scholar, Miss Anequs. Now, I do believe that you should proceed to the library. It's very nearly noon, and I'm certain that Frau Brinkerhoff will be arranging a luncheon for you and Mr. Knecht, as you are the only students presently in residence. I look forward to having you in my class. Good day."

I smiled at him as I left. He was the first professor that I'd felt inclined to smile at.

SHE MET SOME INTRIGUING PEOPLE

I went back to the library, but Frau Brinkerhoff wasn't there. The vast room was empty except for a young woman who was standing beside one shelf, holding an armful of books and putting them away.

She was beautiful.

Her skin was a dark, glowing brown, striking against the starched whiteness of her collar. She wasn't wearing the same kind of uniform that I was; her dress was gray, and she had a white apron over it. Her mouth was wide, her cheeks high and her chin narrow. She looked at me as I walked over. Her eyes had the subtle angled cleverness of a fox's, just higher at the outer corner than the inner. Something in those eyes faded a little even as I watched, disappointment creeping in.

"Miss?" the girl asked. "Did you need something?"

"I'm sorry. I was told to come here and wait for Frau Brinkerhoff . . . I'm Anequs, by the way."

"I know who you are, miss. Everyone here knows who you are."

She bit her lip then, as if she'd just said something wrong.

"I'm afraid you have me at a loss, then, because I don't know who you are."

The girl's eyebrows went up and her eyes went wide, every part of her tense.

"I'm Liberty, miss, and I apologize for any impertinence."

"Why do you keep calling me miss?" I asked.

"Because you're a student, miss. You're above my station."

"I've just gotten here today; I shouldn't be above anyone's station. And you don't have to call me miss. My name is Anequs. If *you're* not a student, are you . . . a professor?" She seemed quite young to be a professor.

Liberty laughed, covering her hand with her mouth.

"No, miss," she said. "I'm a *maid.*"

Housemaids were something of an abstract concept to me; they often appeared in pennik novels, but I'd never met one in life. In novels they often confided in one another about secrets of the household.

"I'm sorry," Liberty said, "but if there's nothing else that you needed, I've got to get these books put away and get back to my duties. It wouldn't do to have anyone think I've been dawdling."

"Oh, I'm sorry, I wouldn't want you to get into trouble on my account. It was lovely to meet you, though."

"The same, miss!" she said with a pleasant smile, putting the last of the books onto the shelf and scurrying away.

I stood there watching where she'd gone for a long moment before Kasaqua started batting at the edge of my skirt. I played with her a bit, and when she was tired enough to stretch and laze in a patch of sunshine, I set myself to the task of reading the book that Professor Ezel had given me. I skimmed through the introduction quickly, and began with the first proper chapter, titled "The Principles of Athers."

*All things in existence are composed of base components, or
"athers." Hans Muench discovered the basic principle of athers,
and their orderly arrangement, in the year 1784.*

*Twenty-four athers are known, though many more are theo-
rized, because athers behave in an orderly manner. The most important ather in skiltakraft is Kolfni, represented by "K" on the chart,
most commonly present in its natural form as coal and charcoal. It
attaches itself readily with the simplest element, Vetna, "V," to
form long chains of motes that store large amounts of tatkraft—
the functional essence that enables all living processes. Critically
important to the shaping of natural objects—things that are or
were living—are the athers Kolfni, Vetna, Zurfni, Stiksna, Pospor,
and Saffle. Other critically important athers to skiltakraft are Isen,
Geld, Lood, Silber, Kwiksilber, Kessel, and Zan. When you have
learned these athers, their principles and properties, their placement
on the chart and why they are placed thusly, you will possess the
understanding needed to successfully create skiltas.*

On the following page there was a chart, oblong boxes arranged in a grid six high by eighteen wide. In twenty-four of the
boxes, there were detailed diagrams and neat rows of text describing the weights and properties of the athers. The remainder of
the boxes were empty. I couldn't see any particular pattern or
sense to it.

Before I could read further, the door opposite opened. Frau
Brinkerhoff entered the library with a young man following her.

He was dressed in the same uniform I was wearing, with trousers in place of skirts. His skin was much the same shade as my
own, his dark hair cut short and waxed into place. He was tall and
slim, and had a very Naquisit look—narrow-faced and sharp-
nosed, with warm brown eyes. He could have been one of my
cousins on my father's side.

"Miss Anequs Aponakwesdottir, this is Mr. Theod Knecht,"
Frau Brinkerhoff said, standing aside for him to step forward. I
dipped my head politely in greeting. He bowed at the waist in the

kind of strictly formal Anglish fashion that I'd only ever seen in watercolor plates.

"Very pleased to meet you, Miss Aponakwesdottir."

"I'm very pleased to meet you as well," I said, smiling as much as I could muster, "though that isn't my name. Please, call me Anequs."

He looked mildly surprised and looked to Frau Brinkerhoff as if for permission. She only smiled and said, "If you'll follow me, luncheon for the two of you has been arranged in the dining hall. Afterward, Mr. Knecht will escort you to the dragonhall to show you the facility and introduce you to his dragon. Mr. Knecht has distinguished himself, in his time at the academy, in his dedication to dragon husbandry."

Theod looked mildly embarrassed at the praise, but said nothing. I took up my book and followed them.

Frau Brinkerhoff seated us and dismissed herself. The dining hall seemed very empty with just the two of us in it. A woman in a gray dress exactly like the one Liberty had been wearing came in with a tray, and we were given fried sausages and pickled cabbage and boiled potatoes, with short beer to drink. Kasaqua padded around my feet, looking up at me expectantly, thumping her tail against the floor. No one had brought anything for her to eat, so I gave her one of my sausages.

"You can't do that!" Theod said, looking positively alarmed. "It's not proper for dragons to be fed at the table. They're fed in the dragonhall, even when they're little and can still live indoors. Don't ever let anyone see you feeding your dragon from your own plate. They'll accuse you of training bad behavior into your dragon and call you a savage."

"It's rude to eat in front of someone else who's hungry," I said, "and I expect they'll call me a savage no matter what I do."

"They might, but that's no reason to give them cause. I apologize; that was an awful way for me to have begun a conversation. Would you care to tell me about yourself, Miss . . . Anequs?"

"Just Anequs, thank you, not miss. And I'm not sure what you want to hear, exactly, so it might help if you asked me questions. I've gotten very used to answering questions lately."

"Well . . . all I really know is that you're from Masquapaug. What does your family do?"

"My father's a whaler, and my mother keeps the house and farm with us," I said. "I have an older brother and a younger brother and a younger sister. Niquiat is seventeen; he lives in Vastergot. He works at the cannery, and at a tinker shop; he's studying clockworks and engines and things. Sigoskwe is ten, and Sakewa is eight. I can go on to my aunts and uncles and cousins, if you want. My cousin Mishona is a drumsinger—the Anglish might consider her a scholar of erelore? I'm really quite ordinary, or I was until Kasaqua chose me. What about you? Who are *your* people?"

"I don't have any people," Theod said. "I'm an orphan."

There was a cool silence after that, and I felt very wrong-footed. I looked down at my food. I hadn't had anything to eat all day, but it didn't seem especially appetizing. I tried to eat it anyway, to avoid being rude. After a moment I asked, "Would you like to tell me the story of how your dragon chose you?"

"Oh, you didn't read it in the newspaper?" he said, something positively nasty creeping into his voice, his eyes going flinty.

"No, I didn't," I said slowly. "We don't get newspapers on Masquapaug."

He looked at me then as if he wasn't quite sure whether to believe me or not. He sighed and set his jaw before finally saying, "I might as well get this out of the way then and give you a factual account of my life and the provenance of my dragon, before you have a chance to form a misguidedly good opinion of me. Everyone else already knows it, which is why no one else speaks to me. I am the offspring of *murderers*."

I swallowed thickly, not at all liking the direction this conversation had taken.

"My father was hanged on April the twenty-third, 1825, for the part that he played in the Nack Island uprising," Theod continued. "My mother was sent to New Linvik Prison and was hanged five months later, on September the seventeenth, on the morning after I was born."

I covered my mouth with my hand, eyes widening at how unfathomably awful that was.

"I'm so sorry," I said, when I was able to take my hand away. I was a bit stunned that he'd just *say* such a thing to me, when I was practically a stranger. Father's father and older brother had been killed in the Naquipaug massacre. We didn't talk much about what had happened on Naquipaug in 1825. His pain and his mourning weren't something he wanted to burden his children with. He spoke about it with Mother, and with the sachem, and probably with a lot of other people, but we'd only spoken about it once— a quiet and formal conversation on the day after my New Woman dance. He'd gone on a walk with me to the point of Beachy Hill, where we could look at the coast of Naquipaug away on the horizon, and he'd told me the story of that night. I'd felt humbled and honored at the time, to be thought old enough to know such things.

"My grandfather and my uncle were killed in the Naquipaug massacre," I said. "Father was at sea, when it happened, or he might have died on that night, too."

Theod's voice was empty of emotion as he went on.

"I was brought up in the New Linvik Orphanage, and when I was six years old I was given as a ward of service to the household of Isbrand Mahler. I was taught a variety of useful skills, and I might have been allowed to become a footman if the incident with the hatching hadn't occurred. My dragon, Copper, is an akhari—a Kindah breed. Herr Mahler acquired his egg from a dealer out of Berri Vaskos at no small expense. They are a notoriously fickle breed, and prone to becoming feral if not very firmly managed. He was meant to choose one of the Mahler sons; both were presented at his hatching. Copper attacked and bit the eldest Mahler boy and escaped the presentation room. He made his way, by the service halls, to the scullery. I was washing dishes for the cook at the time, because the scullery maid was ill and the second kitchen maid flatly refused to do it. The animal's mind was made up by the time anyone of any importance knew what had happened; he'd chosen me."

"A dragon does not choose lightly or without reason," I said. Theod only sighed.

"Herr Mahler took me to the High Moot over it. It was quite sensational, for a time. The prevailing opinion was that Copper should have been put to death, as if he'd gone feral, and that I should have been held accountable for the cost of his egg and enthralled to make up the debt."

"But you hadn't done anything wrong! And to kill a dragon just because—"

"I was very lucky that a lawyer chose to take up my cause for the publicity," Theod continued, talking over anything I'd been about to say. "A long legal battle ensued, and Frau Kuiper came forward with an offer of scholarship. She paid for the cost of Copper's egg and took over my wardship. She could have made me a thrall, for that debt, but she chose not to. In the eyes of the law, I'm a ward of the school, and not personally responsible for my actions or those of my dragon—as if I were a child, or addleminded. In order to be released from wardship, I have to prove myself a worthy scholar and pass the skiltakraft examination, and that's not likely to occur. We may be of the same species of mankind, Miss Anequs, but our circumstances are not especially similar."

I'd hoped that the only other nackie student here would be a friend, a comrade among strangers—but it was plain that Theod, for whatever reason, had already decided that he and I didn't share common cause.

Theod looked down at his plate, then pushed it away. He glanced at my largely untouched plate, took a long breath, and said, "If you're not going to eat any more, we might as well make our way to the dragonhall. I'm supposed to introduce you to the professors' dragons, as well as to Copper, and show you the facility. Dragons are permitted to remain by their dragoneers' sides until such time as they exceed a height of three feet at the shoulder or a length of five feet from hackle to haunch. After that, sense demands that they be stabled in an accommodation suited to their size."

I found myself staring at him, dumbfounded at such a cold and sudden change of subject.

"Theod," I began.

But he looked at me with sharp, hard eyes and said, "Anequs. I will show you the dragonhall now."

The words I'd been about to say died in my mouth. Theod rose, pushing his chair in, leaving his uneaten food on the table.

What could I do but the same?

I followed him outside.

AND LEARNED ABOUT ANGLISH WAYS

The dragonhall was the second building, the one shaped like an overturned boat with arched doors along the front. Theod took something out of his jacket pocket that turned out to be a little brass whistle, on which he played three sharp notes. The same brown striped dragon that I'd seen that morning came loping out from one of the arches along the hall, and upon seeing Theod it bounded over, head down and rear end in the air, tail raised and lashing back and forth happily. I saw Theod smile for the first time, but he stopped smiling when he looked back at me.

"This is Copper," Theod said. "He's only just been moved to the dragonhall last month because he's getting too big for standard doorways, and he's still a bit sulky about it."

Kasaqua had already broken from my heel and padded over to Copper, making a little trilling noise at him. He lowered his head to touch his nose with hers, then they both dropped into that head-down-tail-up posture and fell to prancing around each other. Her absolute enthusiasm for meeting another dragon that *acted* like another dragon (as Frau Kuiper's dragon had not) was infectious, and I found myself giggling.

Their introduction was going far better than my own with Theod had.

"What does it mean for a dragon to be moved into the dragon-hall?" I asked.

"Each dragon's got an assigned stall where they'll receive their meals. Once a dragon is too big to be indoors without being an absolute menace, they'll spend any time they're not at your side in their stalls. They mind it quite a lot at first, but they get used to it. Dragons spend a good bit of their time sleeping, after all, so as long as they're warm and comfortable and you're not too far off, they don't grumble much. Let me introduce you to the others. You've met Gerhard, yes? Frau Kuiper's dragon?"

"She was riding him when she came to the island," I said as I followed Theod through the nearest archway. The inside of the building was huge and mostly hollow, with great wooden dividers that separated the space into two rows of cells with a long corridor down the middle. Each cell had a door made of crisscrossed strips of wood, allowing a clear view inside while the doors were closed. In the first cell, Gerhard was curled up with his massive head resting on his crossed forelegs. He regarded us with one sleepy golden eye, which closed again as we passed.

In the next cell, a somewhat smaller dragon lay on its back, belly up and legs splayed. It was a shade of green that reflected blue, like the head of a drake mallard, and had a thorny crown of bone-white quills.

"That's Professor Ibarra's dragon, Abiadura. She's an arin, the Vaskosish equivalent of a bjalladreki. Don't wake her, she'll be mad about it."

The dragon in the next cell was red and black, with a pair of recurved black horns. It was worrying at a bone big enough that it had to be a cow's leg. It flicked a wing open as we passed by the front of the cell, and I saw that it had great black patches on a red field, like a butterfly's wing.

"That's Kostbar, a falterdrache, Professor Mesman's dragon. He's usually good-tempered."

In the cell after that, a brown-and-gold dragon was lying with its back to us. I couldn't see its head at all, but it seemed to have very long, narrow wings.

"Professor Nazari's dragon, Zati, a Kindah jirada. She can stay on the wing all day and night, if it's asked of her. I've heard a rumor that Professor Nazari wants to try breeding her with Copper, when he's old enough."

All of the other cells—something like seventy or eighty of them—appeared to be empty save one at the very end. In that cell a huge white-and-gray dragon with pale eyes stared at us with keen interest. Its mouth was partly open, its black tongue flicking out between glittering fangs.

"That dragon belongs to Captain Einarsson," Theod said. "I recommend never getting any closer than this. She hates everyone but him and has actually *bitten* Hallmaster Henkjan. She's a silberdrache, a notoriously ferocious breed. That's all the dragons that are currently in residence. The rest of the students will be arriving on Monday, but they can introduce their own dragons if they feel so inclined. We've got space for a hundred and twenty dragons, in this hall."

"Professors Ezel and Ulfar don't have dragons?"

"Professor Ezel has never been a dragoneer, and I wouldn't mention Professor Ulfar's lack of a dragon—it's something of a sore point. His dragon was killed in the siege of the Polvaara. He was a much-decorated captain of the dragonthede, before he was wounded."

"Oh—thank you for telling me. I'd hate to have brought up something painful out of ignorance," I said. I tried to catch Theod's gaze, but he was very pointedly not looking at me.

"I believe that I'm supposed to direct you back to Frau Brinker-hoff, having completed your introduction to the dragonhall. Though if you'd rather return to your room to get your affairs settled, I don't think anyone would find it remiss. I've got quite a lot of reading to do before the first day of classes, so if you'll excuse me . . . I'm pleased to have made your acquaintance, Miss Anequs."

He did not sound pleased at all.

I followed him back outside, not entirely sure what to do with myself. He played the same notes on his whistle, and Copper, who had been chasing Kasaqua across the field, stopped and came promptly to his heel. Kasaqua took a few more moments to realize that she was no longer being chased and made a discordant cry of protest, but when she understood that the game was over, she quietly padded back to me and immediately demanded to be picked up. Theod was already walking Copper back into the drag-onhall, leaving Kasaqua and me standing alone.

Frau Brinkerhoff's office hadn't been one of the locations on the tour she'd given me, but she had mentioned that all of the professors' offices, save Professor Ulfar's, were on the third floor. It was easy enough to find hers once I'd arrived there; all of the doors were closed and had little brass plaques nailed to them with the names of professors engraved on them. Frau Brinkerhoff's office was farthest from the stairs, to the left. Frau Kuiper's was directly adjacent, behind a double-wide door at the end of the hall. I took a deep breath before knocking.

"Come in," I heard her call from inside.

Frau Brinkerhoff was sitting at a writing desk, a pen still in her hand, when she raised her head to look at me.

"Miss Anequs," she said mildly, "I trust you had a pleasant luncheon with Mr. Knecht. Is there something I can help you with?"

"Mr. Knecht was of the impression that he was to direct me back to you after he'd finished introducing me to the dragonhall.

Also, if I'm to appear at the luncheon that Miss Hagan sought to arrange tomorrow, I need some means of securing train fare."

"Oh, of course, dear! It had entirely slipped my mind."

She produced a ring of keys from her pocket and used one of them to open a desk drawer.

She proceeded to hand me three five-marka coins.

Niquiat made one and a half marka for a full shift at the cannery. Father brought home five hundred marka after spending seven months at sea. I was being handed fifteen marka for having done nothing, as if it weren't of any consequence whatsoever.

"Frau Kuiper and I have agreed that an allowance of five marka per week is reasonable. This is meant to last until the first of October. I will tell you something in confidence; Frau Kuiper means this to be something of a test, a measure of how well you're able to manage money. If you while it away on fancies, you cannot expect to be given more. Do you understand?"

"Yes, ma'am," I said.

"Do you have any experience at all in managing money of your own?"

"I'm not certain what you mean by money of my *own*, precisely?" I said. "I'm my mother's oldest daughter, and it's been expected my whole life that I'd manage the household in her stead someday, and I've been taught what I need to know to do that. We . . . My father is a whaler. He comes home to us in November with five hundred marka. That money has to be made to last for a year."

Frau Brinkerhoff looked mildly surprised.

"Well, we were certainly aware that you've been accustomed to making do with little. A well-bred Anglish girl of your age is not, generally, expected to manage funds of that sort. Such matters are generally taken care of by the heads of household and by the professionals they hire. Perhaps we've underestimated your experience. We shall see. If there's nothing else?"

"No, ma'am. If it suits you, I believe I shall retire to my room for the evening to"—how had Theod phrased it?—"get my affairs settled."

"Of course," Frau Brinkerhoff said with a gentle smile. "I'll have a maid inform you when supper is being served."

I spent the remainder of the afternoon reading in my room. When the pendulum clock rang six in the evening, a woman in a gray dress—sadly, not Liberty—knocked to inform me that the evening meal was being served in the dining hall. Theod was not in evidence, and I found myself quite alone in a room that was meant to be full of people. The meal this time was soup and bread. The soup had beets and potatoes and not enough salt, and I couldn't discern much else about it. There wasn't anything at all for me to feed Kasaqua, so having eaten my soup I went out to the dragonhall, where Theod had said dragons were fed. A man in brown coveralls presented me with a tin pail containing some sort of mashed vegetables covered in raw blood, with pieces of bloody meat and bone on top. Kasaqua was terribly pleased with it.

It was growing dark when I returned to my room. There was a kerosene lamp on the table beside my bed, and I only hesitated for a moment before lighting it. No one here seemed to lack for funds. The lamp cast a little pool of light, the edges of which were eaten up by the largeness of the room.

I was happy to get out of my uniform and put on my dressing gown, but it was very hard to find a comfortable way to be in the bed; it was softer and deeper than I was used to. The sheets were crisp to the point of irritating, and the pillow smelled overwhelmingly of lavender. Kasaqua curled herself into a ball on the corner of the bed near my feet and seemed entirely unbothered. Her breathing, and the occasional grumbling complaints about my fidgeting, were the only sounds. The room seemed *painfully* empty, vast and dark beyond the lamp's circle of light.

This didn't feel like a place where people lived. Niquiat's flat had been disgusting, but at least it had felt alive. This school felt deserted, and cold despite the thick coverlet. I'd never been as alone as I was now.

It took a very long time to fall asleep.

ANEQUS SOWED THE SEEDS OF FRIENDSHIP

The following morning, I was awakened by another maid and told that breakfast was available in the dining hall. I faltered for a moment about how to dress, whether I should wear my school uniform, but decided against it. If I was going to be traveling into the city, I wanted to be in something a bit more . . . maneuverable. If my luncheon with Marta finished early enough, I might drop into Haddir's to see Niquiat and his friends, and it wouldn't do to have my new uniform smelling of Kindah coffee. It occurred to me that I knew nothing of how one went about laundering clothes here; I'd have to ask Frau Brinkerhoff when I next saw her.

Breakfast was two soft-boiled eggs, two slices of dark toast with butter, and overdone coffee. It had clearly been waiting for me for some time when I arrived, because everything was unpleasantly cool. I was, again, wholly alone in the vast dining hall.

With Kasaqua at my heels and five of my fifteen marka in my

pocket, I set out for the train station. When I arrived, I found
Liberty sitting on the isen scrollwork bench on the platform. She
wasn't wearing the gray dress and white apron that I'd already
come to associate with maids, but a serviceable dress of dark
green calico with a floral print. It was, in fact, cut very like the
dress I was wearing.

"Good morning!" I said brightly as I approached. "I hadn't
expected to have company on my journey into the city."

Liberty looked positively startled to see me, rising to her feet
and making an aborted little curtsy.

"Pleasure to see you looking so well, miss," she said quickly.
"Frau Brinkerhoff is kind enough to arrange for each of us on the
staff to have six hours away from our duties each week. I generally
use the time to travel into the city to shop for necessities."

"I have a luncheon meeting with Miss Marta Hagan; she and I
are going to be rooming together in the coming term. Do you
mind terribly if I sit with you?"

Liberty looked around, as if I'd said something quite scandalous.

"It wouldn't be . . . Miss, you're a *student*. I'm a *maid*. It would
reflect poorly on you to be too familiar with me."

"There's no one here and now for me to put on pretenses for,
Liberty," I said, gazing around at the general emptiness. "And that
aside, I might be a student, but I'm also a whaler's daughter from
Masquapaug. So if it doesn't offend you personally, I'd very much
like to have someone to talk to on the way into the city." I sat
down, and a moment later Liberty sat down stiffly beside me.
Kasaqua sniffed at the edge of Liberty's skirt, then rubbed herself
affectionately against her ankles. Liberty was looking down at her
in stunned silence.

"What brought you to the academy?" I asked, hoping to start
some kind of conversation.

"I'm indentured, miss," Liberty said, looking away from
Kasaqua to gaze off into the middle distance. "A thrall."

"Indentured?" I asked, feeling appalled at the revelation. I wondered if there were other indentured servants at the school. I'd known that the Anglish kept debt-thralls, but it hadn't occurred to me that the academy might be holding thralls. I wondered who'd cooked the food I'd rudely squandered at yesterday's luncheon with Theod, and whether they were free to come or go as they pleased.

Grandma's brother had been indentured for years—a debt-thrall. I'd never known him; he died before I was born.

"I was in the wardship of the Vastergot Society for Friendless Girls, who trained me up as a maid of all work," Liberty said. "Housematron Brinkerhoff was gracious enough to seek my service and pay the price of my patronage. I'm legally obliged to serve the academy until my debt to them is paid; a percentage is taken from my wages."

"I'm sorry," I said. "I didn't know."

"It's not as bad as all that; I was given a choice about whether to come work here or stay at the society. And it's a terribly interesting kind of place to work, getting to see all the dragons. It's not the sort of thing that you have any cause to worry about, anyway, miss. The students, in the correct course of affairs, have between little and nothing to do with the serving staff."

"I don't really care about the correct course of affairs," I said.

"You ought to," Liberty said, then sucked air through her teeth. "I'm sorry, miss, that was an impertinent thing to say."

"Don't worry about that," I said. "I'm not . . . You won't be in trouble because of anything you say to me. Everyone here is so terribly cold and formal—I don't think that Mr. Knecht liked me at all; our first conversation went very badly. I've no one to *talk* to here, Liberty."

"I'm sure that will change once you've been introduced to other students, miss," Liberty said. "You and Miss Hagan are sure to become good friends, and she's more the sort of person that you should properly be associating with, miss."

The train came, and we got on. Liberty sat first and I, quite stubbornly, sat beside her. Kasaqua stood on the seat opposite, balanced on her hind legs with her foreclaw braced on the window casement, watching the scenery as we passed.

"What are you doing tomorrow?" I asked after our fares had been collected.

"In the morning I typically start off my share of the white linens that need boiling and soaking. The other maids go to the temple of Fyra on Sunday morning for two hours, after the breakfast cleaning has been finished. I don't . . . I'm not a follower of Fyra. I most usually use the time to set my affairs in order for the week and catch up on anything that's fallen behind. Tomorrow, I plan to do some mending. When the other maids return from the temple, I do whatever the senior maids want me to do. If anyone reports to the matron that I've been shirking or dawdling, she'll withhold my pay."

"Can I come and sit with you for a while after breakfast?" I asked, and Liberty looked at me like I was stark raving mad. "I'll help with whatever needs helping—"

"You most certainly will *not*, miss," she said. "If it came to be known that I'd allowed a student to do work that was meant for me, I'd be sent packing back to the Society for Friendless Girls the same day."

"I wouldn't—" I began.

"Students are allowed above and below stairs as they please, miss," Liberty interrupted. "If you want to spend a part of your Sunday sitting downstairs with the help, it's not in my power to stop you."

"But it would make you unhappy," I said.

"Don't mean to be unkind, miss," Liberty said softly. "You seem like a very nice young woman, and if our circumstances were different I'd certainly have been happy to make your acquaintance. But as things are, any discourse between us is likely to cause trouble for both of us."

"I wouldn't want you to be in trouble on my account," I said, sighing softly.

"Well . . ." She seemed to consider for a long moment, then said, "If you asked me personally to assist you with something, that wouldn't be remiss. If you had emergency mending that needed doing or something like that. If you summoned me up to the ladies' quarters to do something, I'd be expected to attend to that before doing anything that the senior maids asked me to do. We're here to serve the students first, miss."

"Well then, if that's the case . . . I may have a sudden emergency tomorrow morning sometime after breakfast," I said with a smile, and was delighted when she smiled back.

We arrived at the station in Vastergot very shortly after, and Liberty thanked me for the pleasant conversation and wished me a good luncheon with Marta. It felt like something of a victory, having convinced Liberty that I was worth befriending.

SHE HAD AN ILLUMINATING CONVERSATION

The station was at the northmost end of High Street, so it wasn't at all difficult for me to find the corner of High Street and Ingolfsson Way. I spotted the dragon before I spotted the girl.

It was the size of a yearling deer, and of much the same conformation. It was lanky, with undersize wings, and it trotted along gamely, sniffing the air. It wasn't the same breed as any that I'd seen at the school, though it bore some passing similarity to Professor Ibarra's dragon. This dragon had a crown of brown-and-white-striped quills, the ones nearest to its face webbed like a fish's fins. It was a ruddy brown color overall, fading to gray on its belly and beneath its wings, with brilliant sea-green eyes. The webs around its face were mottled with green markings, too. It was wearing a leather harness with satchels at the sides, but it didn't seem to have any kind of saddle.

The girl walking beside it was skinny and lanky in the same way as her dragon, but she moved with a studied grace that made her seem almost birdlike. She was about my age, or maybe a little older, with skin as pale as the inside of a shell and hair the color of dry corn husks. The dragon stopped still and made a trilling noise, looking right at me—or rather at Kasaqua. The girl looked at the dragon, then at me, and started to wave enthusiastically. I went to meet her. As I came close, I saw that her eyes were brown, and she had a profusion of freckles across the middle of her face.

"Hello! You've *got* to be Anakis, haven't you? I'm Marta, and it's a pleasure to meet you!"

"Uh . . . yes. I'm Anequs, of Masquapaug."

Marta bowed and smoothed her skirt, smiling as if she expected something.

I was wearing my best calico dress; a lovely print with tiny yellow flowers and leaves in neat rows on a cream field. It had white beads embroidered on the collar. I had my whitest knee socks, and my boots were brightly polished with seal oil. I had my hair done up in neat braids. This was how one dressed to come among Anglish people. No one on Masquapaug ever dressed like the girls in the fashion magazines that I thumbed through every time we visited Catchnet.

But Marta did.

She was wearing a blue dress with a white lace collar. Her skirt had the kind of fullness that only came from corded petticoats. She had her hair in perfect curls, dressed with blue ribbons. She was carrying a little embroidered handbag that matched her dress.

I suddenly felt very plain, and wished I'd decided to wear my uniform. It wasn't fashionable the way Marta's dress was, but it was at least smart in an Anglish way.

"What sort of dragon is yours, if I might ask? I've never seen the like. It's so little! I don't think Magnus was *ever* that little!"

"She's a Nampeshiwe, and she only just hatched at the beginning of July," I said. "And yours is . . . ?"

"Oh, I'm terribly rude! This is Magnus," she said, looking

fondly down at him, running a hand delicately over his mane of quills. He was looking at Kasaqua with patient interest. "He's a bjalladreki, one of Fossmar's get, out of Hjalla."

I nodded politely, because Marta seemed very proud of that, though I didn't understand the significance.

"I was so very pleased when Frau Kuiper sent me a telegram regarding your attendance at the academy this year; I was worried that I'd be the only girl in attendance! I was one of three last year, but Emmeline married and Kerstin went abroad. There's a general preference for hatchlings to go to boys, you understand."

"I'm not sure that I do," I said, frowning. "But you Anglish seem to do lots of things very differently than we do them on the island."

"Let's get a table and sit down to have a really proper chat. Have you dined at Gaststätte Irmtraude before? This time of year they make the most wonderful plum tart."

"I've actually never been to Vastergot before, so I've never had the opportunity to dine here."

"Well, then, I'm so very glad to introduce you to the experience! Lisbet and I often dine here for luncheon, when we've come to browse the High Street shops. That's Lisbet Jansen, a dear friend of mine; I'm presently staying at her home here in the city. Papa's been away on business, and it was more convenient that I come and visit with Lisbet just before the start of the term. Her younger brother, Sander, is going to be attending Kuiper's this year. I'll be sure that you're introduced on Monday, because they're relations of Frau Brinkerhoff, the matron of the house—and she's likely to try and introduce him to anyone that she can command for a few minutes because the poor dear is simple and will need all the social help he can get. Are you staying here in the city?"

"Actually, I was asked to situate myself at the academy on Friday. I've had to take a number of examinations to determine my placement in classes during the first term."

"That's odd," Marta said with a pause. "But, then, I'm sure

your acquisition of a dragon was rather different than the norm. Where were you schooled before you were accepted to Kuiper's? They couldn't simply send your records?"

"We don't have schools on the island in the sense that you have schools," I answered. "At least not if schools are anything like what I've come to understand from reading pennik novels."

A waiter came with a pot of coffee and two cards describing the offerings of the afternoon, and left again without saying anything. Marta began helping herself, so I did the same.

"But who taught you how to read and do telkraft, and erelore and folklore and all of that?" Marta asked.

"My family?" I said, wondering what she meant. "We didn't have to sit down and copy things out of books for hours. Is that a thing that actually happens, or is that just something that happens in stories?"

"Oh, that's a thing that happens, believe me," Marta said with a weary sigh. "In the usual course of things, a young lady is attended at home by her governess until she's twelve, and then she attends a primary school until she's sixteen to learn the social graces—dancing and pleasant conversation, letter-writing, and accomplishments like watercolor painting and music. The more proper sort of lady attends a secondary school to learn folklore and erelore and Tysklandish and such things until she's twenty, or until she marries. You and I have rather replaced that last step, trading secondary school for dragoneering, but the principle is much the same. Now, I understand that most girls of the country sort are educated at home until they marry; they'd have little use for the sort of things a lady learns in secondary school. But who taught you al-jabr and anglereckoning and things like that? Surely not your parents—"

"I had very little knowledge of anglereckoning or al-jabr until just a few days ago," I said. "My brother helped me find some volumes on the subject, and I did very little from Tuesday to Friday except read them."

The waiter came back again, and I hadn't even glanced at the list of offerings. Marta announced that she'd have Wurzelsalat and Weichkäse, with Pflaumentorte to follow. Not having any idea what that meant, except that the words sounded Tysklandish, I said I'd have the same.

"Oh, you've been in the city since Tuesday?" Marta asked. "I do wish I'd known; I could have arranged for us to dine properly at Lisbet's home! Where have you been staying, before situating yourself at school?"

"With my brother Niquiat," I said. "He rents a flat in the cannery district."

Marta paled a bit and put down the cup she'd been about to sip from.

"That . . . can't have been the most ideal situation. It's my understanding that the cannery district is . . ." She made a slightly pained face. "Well, I've never been."

"The ferry from Catchnet only travels to Masquapaug on Tuesday and Friday. If I want to get to the mainland any other day of the week, I have to paddle across the strait and take the ferry from Naquipaug," I said by way of explanation. "I came on Tuesday, and stayed with Niquiat on Wednesday and Thursday, and arrived at the academy yesterday. I've already been examined regarding my skills in telkraft; Professor Nazari actually seemed quite pleased."

"Well, then, I suppose you're a prodigy of sorts," Marta said with a musical little laugh. "I've always had trouble with telkraft, but a good understanding of physical telkraft is essential to skiltakraft, and skiltakraft is an absolute necessity if one wishes to be a dragoneer. The Ministry of Dragon Affairs won't approve the licensure of any dragoneer who hasn't proven themselves proficient."

"And what happens to dragoneers that they don't approve for licensure?" I asked.

Marta looked mildly surprised, then said, "Would-be dragoneers who don't prove themselves equal to the task can't be allowed free custody of their dragons, of course. Dragons that are tame can sometimes be kept in wild animal collections and used for breeding, but most usually they're destroyed."

"Destroyed, because a dragoneer isn't proficient enough in skiltakraft? Even if the dragon is tame?" I asked, appalled at the notion. Kasaqua whined, alarmed at my sudden distress.

I must have made a face, because Marta quickly said, "Oh, Anequs, please don't think that it happens very often! When it must happen, it's considered a terrible shame and a great waste. Besides, I'm very sure that you'll prove equal to skiltakraft, especially if you're such a quick study at telkraft. You've nothing at all to worry about, I'm sure."

She was entirely wrong about that; I had quite a lot to worry about. I understood now why that Einarsson fellow from the ministry had asked me how I'd come to possess Kasaqua. The Anglish treated dragons as if they were dogs.

"Dragons are *sacred* to my people," I said, trying to understand how she could so casually talk of dragons being put to death. "Being chosen by one is an incomparable honor that changes one's life forever. The word for 'dragoneer' in Masquisit is 'Nampeshiweisit.' It means 'person who belongs to a dragon'— just like Naquisit means 'person who belongs to Naquipaug,' and Masquisit means 'person who belongs to Masquapaug.' I don't think that 'dragoneer' means the same thing at all, from what I've seen. I don't think that your people understand dragons."

Marta looked stricken for a moment, and her dragon rose to his feet. Then she took a breath and seemed to compose herself. After a moment, her dragon lay back down, and she spoke.

"Well, I can certainly see why Frau Kuiper solicited my assistance in making you aware of civilized customs, as it's obvious that you have little experience with polite society. Primitive superstition and folklore aside, dragons are beasts—as much as dogs or horses are. I very dearly love Magnus, and I'm sure that every dragoneer would say the same of their dragon, but I hold no particular illusions about him. He's an animal of a witskrafty nature. If he weren't bonded with me, or some other dragoneer of firm resolve, he would be vicious and dangerous. There are still truly wild dragons in the remote mountains of Tyskland and Vaskosland, and they still menace shepherds and even kill and eat mountaineers and explorers from time to time. It's my understanding that there are wild dragons in the interior of Markesland as well, along the western and northern frontiers, and that they're as much a menace to settlers as wolves and great cats are."

"The dragons—and the wolves and great cats—were all here long before people were. My people have always endeavored to be good neighbors to them, and if your people find them menacing, then I can only presume that you haven't taken the same care," I said. "My grandmother didn't think that there was anything worth knowing that I could learn by coming here, and I'm beginning to wonder if she wasn't right."

"If you're not interested in being a dragoneer, then why did you sit before an egg?" she asked.

"I am Nampeshiweisit because Kasaqua chose me," I said.

"Well, it's not as if hatchling dragons really know who they're choosing or why," Marta said, reaching to scratch Magnus behind the ear. "They're put in front of the candidates they've been appointed to, and they choose one. Else they don't, in which case they're feral, and must be either captive or destroyed."

"Among my people," I said, trying very hard not to be angry, "a dragon's egg is brought into the village and surrounded by everyone. We talk and sing and tell stories to it until it hatches. I've gotten the impression that it's rather different among your people."

"In polite society, an aspiring dragoneer's parents arrange to purchase an egg from its dam's dragoneer shortly after it's laid. For dragons with quality bloodlines, the arrangements are often made years in advance—and the Ministry of Dragon Affairs is informed of every step in the process. Eggs are registered individually to their prospective dragoneers, and the outcome of the hatching reported and documented. When Magnus's egg was delivered to our home, I was required to lay hands on it each day and to sit by it for several hours reading aloud, to make an impression upon the hatchling as it developed. When he hatched, his bonding with me proceeded without complication."

"So the hatchling isn't really offered a choice . . ." I said.

"Well, it's common enough that a hatchling be presented equally to a group of siblings in the same household," Marta said thoughtfully, "but that invites potential complications—like what happened with Mr. Knecht. It's much safer for there to be only one intended dragoneer placed before an egg."

I might have said something else, but the waiter arrived, carrying a tray. Marta was suddenly all genteel smile and grace again, thanking him as he set dishes before each of us.

Wurzelsalat and Weichkäse was evidently a dish of thinly sliced turnips, beets, and carrots in a vinegary sauce served with soft white cheese. I began eating without being specifically invited to, and Marta looked at me as if she thought I'd done something rude, but after a moment she did the same. She looked thoughtful, glancing at me between bites. Then I saw her eyes shift focus, looking past me. They grew wide, and she drew a sharp breath.

"Don't turn and look, but I've just seen Niklas and Dagny Sørensen come in. If we're very lucky, they'll come over and ask me to introduce you. Dagny is two years my senior and is the undisputed fürstin of our generation of Vastergot society. She knows everyone who's anyone. Her opinion of you will dictate which events you're invited to and which you're shut out of. I was privileged to be invited to a garden party at the Sørensen estate over the summer, and it was of the utmost elegance. Her brother Niklas is a student at Kuiper's. Niklas is *dreadfully* handsome, and I've heard it from Lisbet Jansen who heard it from Saskia Britsch who heard it from Dagny herself that Niklas has more than once inquired after *me*. If they do come over, you simply *must* let me do most of the talking. You're so free with your words and thoughts, you're certain to say something socially ruinous."

Given that introductory warning, I rather hoped that the Sørensens would keep well away from us. But they didn't.

AND WAS PRESENTED TO HER SOCIAL BETTERS

There was a third member of the Sørensens' party, walking a half step behind Dagny and Niklas—another young man. Both young men were accompanied by dragons. Dagny was plainly in the lead as she came toward us, moving with mincing little steps that made her look like a shorebird floating across water. She was first to speak.

"Marta, darling, how lovely to see you. I'd heard that you were in the city, but I haven't had time to pay calls. Would you be so kind as to allow us to join you? And who*ever* is this?"

"Oh, please, do come sit," Marta said. "Miss Dagny Sørensen, Mr. Niklas Sørensen, Mr. Ivar Stafn, I present to you Miss Anequs Aponakwesdottir, lately of Mask Island. Anequs will be joining us at Kuiper's Academy this term."

I smiled pleasantly, trying to ignore the fact that Marta had introduced me by a name that was not mine. Both Niklas and Dagny had very pale skin and reddish-brown hair. Ivar was pale-haired and pale-eyed. He smiled at me, and there was something profoundly *wrong* about his smile. Kasaqua, who'd been sitting at my feet while Marta and I talked and ate, stood up and tensed—as if she thought she might have to run or fight.

Niklas pulled out a chair and motioned for Dagny to sit, then Ivar and Niklas both sat. The table now seemed intolerably crowded, and I was obliged to shift my chair closer to Marta's.

"Marta Hagan, a pleasure to see you," Ivar said, looking at her and then at me. His gaze flicked up and down, lingering on Kasaqua. She was looking anxiously from me to the two dragons that had just arrived. She wanted very much to approach them herself in the dragonish way; I knew it in the same way that I knew when she was hungry. I beckoned her up onto my lap, which seemed to comfort her a bit.

"Do tell me what breed of dragon that is?" Ivar asked. "I've never seen its equal. Wherever did you get it?"

"Kasaqua is a Nampeshiwe," I said, stroking her, trying to convey calm and the need for stillness. "Yours is a bjalladreki?"

He stared at me for a moment, raising his eyebrows, and glanced first at Niklas and then at Marta. Marta seemed to communicate something to him in their shared glance, but I hadn't the slightest notion what.

"Sigrod is Llorunder's get, his third out of Ellisif. I can see that you're familiar with Miss Hagan's very charming little example of the breed," he said, nodding toward Magnus. I noticed, peripherally, that Magnus had all of his quills on end and was staring very directly at Ivar's dragon. Niklas's dragon was a bjalladreki as well, and having three of them at such close quarters allowed me to examine the breed in a detail that I hadn't been able to before. Ivar's dragon was the largest of the three, and broadest across the chest. Niklas's dragon was smaller than Sigrod but larger than Magnus, and more gray than either of the others. The quills of its crown were especially long and finely formed, their banding more subtle and dappled, and they were each tipped in brilliant white. Magnus looked rangy compared to the other two, plainly more juvenile in conformation and demeanor.

I wondered what Kasaqua would look like as she grew.

"I've never met a nackie before," Niklas said, smiling broadly and genuinely, catching my attention back. "I've tried to make Knecht's acquaintance, but he's such a closed-off fellow; I haven't been able to get two words from him. He's hardly a proper nackie anyway, brought up as he was in civilization. You're from Mask Island? You *must* tell me all about it! I've read that you organize your society in such a way that no one possesses anything individually, is that true? Everything among you is communally shared, as if you were all of you virgins of Fyra living in a sacred grove?"

"I . . . don't think that I understand the question?" I said, looking to Marta, who was smiling genially and looking at no one but Niklas.

"I've read Nordlund's accounts of his time on Nack Island from 1746 through 1750," Niklas said by way of explanation. "He reports that your people have no sense of property at all; that you don't accumulate wealth and pass it down to your heirs."

"We don't hoard things, if that's what you mean," I said, keeping my voice studiously even. "Those of us who have give to those of us who don't, because we care for one another. We do *own* things. My books and clothes and tools and things are my personal property, until I give them away because they'll be of more use to someone else. As for passing things down to heirs . . . In the general course of things, a mother passes her homestead to her eldest daughter, or whichever of her daughters seems most suited if the eldest isn't."

"The communistic way of living is sensible when an entire people live hand-to-mouth in relatively equal poverty, as among thralls and the deferential pious," Ivar said. "All reputable scholars are in agreement about the inherent nature of the species of humanity natural to the shores of the new world. They wholly lack ambition and desire for personal or social betterment. They are very like bees or wasps: content in their small industries if left undisturbed, but violently resentful to any interference, even that which directly benefits them. They are naturally short-tempered, violent, stubborn, and vengeful—ruled in physical and mental capacities by an excess of bile. They lack the natural industry, intelligence, and desire for improvement that the gods in their wisdom have deigned to impart upon peoples of the white northlands. It is only right and just that the enlightened and advanced species of mankind should supplant those that are backward and primitive.

"Our antecedents, the fierce Norsmen, would have murdered the lot of them or taken them as thralls. But we as a society have elected that we are above such barbarity. It should be very interesting to see the results of the little *versuch* that Fraus Kuiper and Brinkerhoff are running at the academy. Can savages become truly educated and civilized? Have they any place in a modern society? Tell me, Miss Aponakwesdottir, have you read *The Species of Mankind—A Treatise of Natural Philosophy* by Maurits-Jan van den Ouden? Or, perhaps I precede myself. *Can* you read?"

I blinked at him at least twice, then looked to Marta, to be sure that she'd heard the same words that I had. She looked distinctly uncomfortable, a sickly sort of smile plastered on her face. She did not, however, look shocked or appalled.

"I'm sorry, I'm not very well versed in the subtle intricacies of Anglish conversation, so I've probably misunderstood you entirely," I said, trying very hard to keep my voice clear and even. "Did you *intend* to imply that I'm incapable of reading?"

"Well, it is to be presumed," he said. "Your people had no knowledge of written language before it was introduced to them by scholars traveling in the shipthede of my ancestor Stafn White-beard."

"How many languages do you speak, Mr. Stafn?" I asked, narrowing my eyes a bit. "Hauen Ken? Teag kukquenauehik?"

"Your knowledge of a primitive tongue does not impress me, Miss Aponakwesdottir—"

"Ivar, you're being a bore," Niklas said. "I'm sure that Dagny and Marta don't want to hear about all your studies of phylogeny, and it's clear that you're just showing off your scholarship on the subject at this point. Of course the poor dear hasn't read van den Ouden, and probably not much of anything else. Gentlemen of quality do not discuss such matters before ladies, nor do they blatantly compare themselves to their inferiors in an attempt to look self-important."

Ivar did not look at all pleased with Niklas's comment, but Dagny spoke before he had a chance to reply.

"In any case, I do believe we've spent enough time visiting," she said with a knowing little smirk. "I'm absolutely famished. Shall we get a table of our own while we wait for Mother?"

"I do believe that's a good idea, Dagny. Marta, always a pleasure to see you, and lovely to have made your acquaintance, Miss Aponakwesdottir. Perhaps we can continue our conversation some other time, at the academy, and you can tell me more about the way your people live."

"Perhaps," I said. "Though I expect that I'll have to spend the better part of my time in study."

Niklas laughed politely, then stood and offered his arm to Dagny. The three of them walked away, Ivar glancing over his shoulder at me for a moment before disappearing from view. I looked back at Marta, who had let her pleasant facade drop entirely and was scowling into her coffee.

"Ivar Stafn is the most insufferable man in the world, I swear, apart from his father."

"You didn't say a single word in my defense," I said, and Marta looked plainly shocked at the suggestion that she should have.

"It wouldn't have been . . . Niklas and Dagny . . . I was in no position . . ."

"Is it that you agree with the things he was saying? Is that what you think of me, Marta? Of my people?"

"I don't . . ."

"Come to think of it, what's your opinion of Theod? You spent an entire year sharing classes with him, didn't you?"

"I know almost nothing about Theod," Marta confessed, "except that he seems a very diligent scholar. He's quite standoffish and spends most of his time in the library or the dragonhall. I don't know if he has any friends. He's never said more than half a dozen words to me."

"And me?"

"You seem a very decent sort," she said, looking down. She looked up again, her eyes brimming with tears. "I confess to having no practical knowledge of your people. I haven't read that Nordlund book, even. My governess was more interested in seeing that I become a young lady of accomplishment than a scholar. I'm afraid I'm not very well read."

If she actually started crying, I was going to get up and walk away. I had absolutely no patience left to comfort her.

"Marta, I'm very tired now, and I don't feel like talking anymore—about myself, or my people, or anything," I said. "I'm going to go back to the academy. Do you need any money for the luncheon?"

"But the Pflaumentorte hasn't even arrived! I'm sorry that I put you in a position to be accosted by Mr. Stafn, but—"

"I'll see you on Monday, Marta," I said, and rose and walked away before she could say anything to stop me, shifting Kasaqua from my lap to my shoulder as I did. She was positively elated at finally moving again; she hadn't enjoyed the luncheon, either.

ANEQUS MADE A FRIEND

I returned to the academy and went directly to my room and lay
on my bed, staring at the ceiling. I very desperately wanted to go
home. I was not welcomed or wanted here, and everyone I'd
met was quite eager to think the absolute worst of me. Even
Theod seemed in some way prejudiced against me.

I wanted to gather mussels with Sigoskwe, and braid Sakewa's
hair, and take my canoe out to the seal rocks to sit and gaze out
over the ocean in the perfect quiet. I wanted to sit with my mother
and eat a bowl of her sobaheg and tell her all about my several
disastrous days among the Anglish.

I wanted to see my father.

I went to my wardrobe and opened the drawer where I'd
tucked my medicine bundle. I pressed my face into the pouches
of tobacco and juniper, taking in their scent. I stood there for
what was probably a long time, grounding myself as best I could.

I washed, and changed into my dressing gown. Kasaqua, sensing my despondent mood, hopped onto the bed and cuddled close to me, tucking herself right under my chin and crooning softly. She smelled like home as much as the tobacco and juniper did. I fell asleep with tears in my eyes.

I rose on Sunday morning in a more timely fashion than I had on Saturday, and I was already dressed and ready by the time the maid came to tell me that breakfast was being served. I proceeded to the dragonhall after breakfast to see that Kasaqua got her morning meal, and then returned to my room and dutifully waited half an hour for Liberty to be well finished with the breakfast cleaning before summoning her. It wasn't at all difficult to find another of the maids, or to spin a story about having a sewing emergency and having heard that Liberty was especially good with a needle. The maid whose name I didn't catch said she'd find Liberty and send her up presently.

She arrived at my room fifteen minutes later, carrying a large basket on her arm. She was still as beautiful as I remembered.

"What seems to be the trouble, miss?" she asked.

I put on a very earnest voice, batted my eyelashes at her, and said, "I seem to have somehow split the seam right up the back of my waistcoat, and classes start tomorrow, and I'm *ever* so ashamed of having done it that I dare not tell Fraus Kuiper or Brinkerhoff. Please, please fix it?"

"Don't make me laugh, or someone will come and see what we're up to!" Liberty said with a grin, looking both ways down the corridor.

I beckoned her inside and shut the door behind her. She gazed around the room in open appraisal.

"I've never actually been all the way up to the ladies' quarters before," she said. "Only upstairs maids are permitted to enter the students' quarters. I do hope you don't mind, but I've brought mending to do while we talk."

"Oh, I don't mind at all," I said. "In fact, I've got some embroidery I could be working on. I think I'd feel awkward without having something to keep my hands busy. What makes an upstairs maid different from any other sort of maid?" I asked.

"Order of charge," she said, setting her basket down on the table. She looked at me expectantly for a moment, and I inclined my head toward one of the overstuffed chairs to indicate that she should have a seat, which she did. I joined her, sitting opposite. Kasaqua jumped onto a third chair and spent a few moments kneading it before turning a circle and lying down with her feet tucked underneath her.

"Order of charge?" I asked.

"Frau Brinkerhoff is the housematron and also serves as personal lady's maid to Frau Kuiper. Just below her are the chambermaids, who clean the professors' quarters, then the upstairs maids who clean the students' quarters, then the downstairs maids who clean the laboratories and class halls and corridors and all, then the scullery and laundry maids at the very bottom of the ranks. The kitchen maids are their own thede; they report directly to the cook. The young men at the dragonhall are a different thede altogether, reporting to Hallmaster Henkjan, but I think he reports to Frau Brinkerhoff."

"And you are . . ."

"A laundry maid," Liberty said. "Though I do more sewing than washing, lately."

"The Anglish seem to be very keen on ordered ranks, from what I've seen so far," I said. "I'm not at all sure what my own rank *is*."

"Well, as far as I'm concerned, you're a student and a dragoneer. Usually that would mean you're a child of some wealthy landowner or other, but you're obviously an exception to that rule."

"Are most of the other students here my age?" I asked. "I'm afraid no one has told me much at all about the other students, only that I'll be sharing a room with Miss Hagan."

"Well, that would depend on how old you are, I suppose, since you haven't told me that," Liberty said with a wry smile.

"Oh, I'm fifteen!" I said, laughing a little. "I'll be sixteen on the twenty-first of January."

"Then yes, you're about the age that most first-year students are," she said. "Dragons have a strong preference for young people, and the best time to arrange a bonding is when the prospective dragoneer is between fourteen and eighteen years of age—so most first-year students are between fourteen and fifteen. Anyone older than that usually has some unusual circumstance, like an attempted bonding that failed, though it's terribly rude to ask. I've never heard of anyone older than twenty bonding successfully, except in sagas and things."

"Is it terribly rude for me to ask how old you are? I know that Anglish girls in pennik novels often dance around the subject, but I've always found that quite mystifying."

"I'm sixteen," she said, laughing in turn. I'd thought her older, seventeen or eighteen perhaps, because she reminded me of Mishona; she had the same kind of innate *grace* about her.

"I'll be seventeen at the end of May," she continued. "Miss Hagan, by the way, is also sixteen—though I don't know where her birthday falls in the year, I'm afraid. You won't want to ask her because she *would* think it rude. It's something to do with social rankings among the high-and-mighties; I don't really know the details. I understand that social rank occupies quite a lot of the students' time—who knows whom and who's seen speaking to whom. But never mind all that; what's it like on that island of yours? I've never been anywhere but Vastergot."

"I miss it very much," I said. "There's only something like a thousand people there, when the whalers are home, and everyone knows everyone else. I think I've met more strangers in the last week than I've met in my entire life previously."

"What would you have done there, if you hadn't become a dragoneer?"

"I'd have gone on living as I was, in my mother's house. We keep a farmstead, and fish, and gather mussels and clams. September and October are always very busy, harvesting corn and winter squashes and putting them by, gathering nuts in the forest—it's the best hunting time for deer and turkey and skunk pig, because they're all laying on fat for the winter. My father's a whaler; he'll be back from the north in November. We have a feast and a dance about it, when the whalers return. My father's family from Naquipaug comes to it, most years."

"It must be nice to live in a place with so many people . . . like yourself. Even when I lived with my parents, there weren't many black families in the mill district. I remember people being unfriendly to us."

"You're the only black person I've ever really met. There are some black whalers who ship with my father's line, but I've never had any occasion to say more than 'hello' to any of them. If it's not rude to ask . . . how did you lose your family?"

"It's been a long time since anyone asked me that," Liberty said, meeting my eyes for a moment before she looked back to her stitching. Her hands went still for a moment when she said, "My parents were thralls in Berri Vaskos—the Vaskosish word for it is 'eslavo,' and it's a bit different than being a debt-thrall; there's no way to pay oneself out. A person who's eslavo is born into it and is one until they die, and their children are eslavo, too. The only way they can stop being eslavo is if they're turned out by their masters, or if they run away. My parents escaped to New Anglesland because they'd heard that thralldom was outlawed here. I suppose I've still got family back where they came from, because I'd hear my mother and father talk about the people they'd had to leave behind sometimes, but I don't know anything at all about any of them. I was born here. My father worked in a mill, and my mother was a seamstress. My father died in a fire at the mill when I was six. My mother died of a kind of fever that swept through the mill district when I was ten. I tried to get work for myself, but after two weeks the landlady turned me out and sent me to the Society for Friendless Girls, and I've already told you how that ended up."

"I'm sorry," I said, having nothing else to say.

It was quiet for a moment, then Liberty glanced over to Kasaqua and said, "Your dragon is a dear little thing. Never seen that sort before. She's some kind of nackie breed, I've heard?"

"She's a Nampeshiwe—the kind of dragon that used to live here long before the Anglish came. They were all lost in the great dying."

"The nackies in the west have dragons, but that's not a word I've heard for them. The . . . what're they called . . . the Shawna or something? They've got a breed of dragon called a mishy-ginny-bick or something like. They give the settlers on the western frontier no end of trouble. Captain Einarsson's forever on about it, and how the nackies out there are a menace. He's been in a horrible temper ever since he heard about you and your coming here. Can't see why, since you seem perfectly nice. I've never actually met a nackie, before you. I mean, I knew about Mr. Knecht, but he and I have never had a reason to talk to each other."

I rather wondered whether Mr. Knecht ever spoke to anyone at all without being pressed to it, but I put that thought aside.

"I met with Marta Hagan yesterday," I said, "and I'm not at all sure that she and I will be friends. I think she expected me to be more like the classmates she had last year. She was excited to have a second girl as a classmate until she realized that I wasn't . . . a girl like her? If that makes sense?"

"It does," Liberty said. "This is my third year working at the academy, and there've only been four girls the whole time. Miss Dynah Wozniakowa was in her final year when I arrived—"

"That's another thing that no one has been particularly clear about. How many years is one expected to be at the academy for? Sorry, it's rude of me to interrupt."

"No, no, it's fine!" Liberty said. "In the typical course of events, a student spends four years at the academy—but I've heard of students being in their fifth and sixth year, and sometimes students leave to attend other schools elsewhere, and I'm not sure how that works. You'd do better to ask other students, I think, or maybe professors. Anyway, when I first came, Miss Wozniakowa was rooming with Miss Emmeline Abbink, and they were the only two young ladies in residence. Miss Wozniakowa completed her education, and Miss Abbink would have been quite alone if Miss Kerstin Linna and Miss Marta Hagan hadn't begun attendance."

"Marta mentioned Emmeline and Kerstin, and that neither of them is in attendance this year. She mentioned that there's a preference among the Anglish for dragons' eggs to go to boys?"

"Oh, yes, of course," Liberty said. "Dragoneering here in New Anglesland began as the exclusive purview of dragonthede and the jarl's guard—fighting men. There are tales about war maidens in folklore, but war maidens have rather fallen out of favor—Frau Kuiper notwithstanding."

"Frau Kuiper is a war maiden?" I asked, surprised at that revelation. Maybe I ought not have been. She had come to Masquapaug on an absolute bear of a dragon, after all, with a brace of pistols on her belt.

"You don't *know*?" Liberty asked, leaning forward and grinning as if she was about to tell me the most wonderful gossip. "Forty-five years ago, girls were not *permitted* to seek positions as dragoneers, not unless they were the daughters of jarls—and even then it was always one of those dainty racing breeds, nothing like a kesseldrache. The Anglesland-Vaskosland War was just beginning then. Frau Kuiper disguised herself as a man and enlisted in the dragonthede to be allowed to stand before an egg—it's one of the only ways that young men who aren't from wealthy families have a chance at dragoneering. Gerhard chose her at his hatching, but her secret was discovered six weeks later. She was brought before the High Moot with charges of deceit! The moot found that if she could prove herself equal to the other soldiers, she should be allowed to stand and fly among them, like a war maiden of old. She highly distinguished herself at the siege of the Polvaara. There's a painting of Fyra and her Valkyrja hanging in the High King's Open Gallery that depicts High Queen Sæfinna as Fyra and Frau Kuiper as the Valkyre at her right hand, bearing a cup and a sword. Frau Brinkerhoff has a framed print of it in her office. The whole thing is a bit sensational, even still. There are sagas about dragons choosing war maidens and jarls' daughters, always very romantic and dramatic—but it's not even legal, in Old Anglesland, for a woman less than a jarl's daughter to be deliberately placed before a dragon's egg. It's something that the woman and her family can be taken to the moot over. Back in Old Anglesland, the young Frau Kuiper would probably have been hanged as a liar."

"I hadn't been aware that it was at all uncommon for women to be dragoneers," I said, horrified at the idea that a woman might be hanged just for having been chosen by a dragon. But then, I'd already learned that the Anglish might put a dragon to death for not choosing the right person, so maybe it shouldn't have surprised me that they'd kill people just as freely.

They'd hanged Theod's parents, after all.

"What does it mean among your people, for a woman to be a dragoneer?" Liberty asked after a thoughtful moment.

"The word isn't even 'dragoneer'; it's 'Nampeshiweisit.' I've gathered that Nampeshiweisit and dragoneer mean *entirely* different things regarding a person's relationship to their dragon. It doesn't matter, especially, that I'm a woman. In stories, Nampeshiweisit can be any sort of person. The hero Requeiska, who rode the dragon Nonoma, was a mupauanakausonat—"

"A what?" Liberty interrupted.

"I don't know that there's an Anglish word for it. It *literally* means 'someone who does the work of a caterpillar.' But really, it means . . . a little girl who grows up to be a man, or a little boy who grows up to be a woman. Or . . . someone mistaken in childhood for the sex opposite their true one? It's hard to say in Anglish. It can also mean someone who's not precisely a man or a woman—someone with two spirits, or with a trickster spirit that can change from man to woman and back. My great auntie Mamisashquee is a mupauanakausonat. Everyone thought she was a boy when she was a child."

Liberty's eyes got very wide, and she quickly glanced around as if to make sure that no one could have overheard us. Then she leaned close to me and said, "You'll get yourself in the worst kind of trouble even talking about things like that, miss. The Anglish word for a man who passes himself as a woman is 'baeddel,' and you must never ever say it, because it is the vilest of curses. If a man calls another man a baeddel, that's just cause for the insulted man to challenge the other one to a holmgang—"

"A what?" I asked.

"A fight to the death!"

"I've read about that kind of thing in novels, but I didn't think it actually happened!" I said, appalled.

"It doesn't happen often, not anymore—people just take one another to the moot these days—but there's no law against it. In places like the cannery and mill districts, if there's a drunken brawl that goes too far and someone is killed, all the fellows involved just insist to the thanegards that a holmgang was declared and no one's taken to the moot for murder over it."

"That sounds absolutely beastly," I said, making a face. "Anglish people just . . . murder one another in the street?"

"Well, I've heard it said, anyway. I don't personally know any examples. But the virgins of Fyra plaster all of the mill district with leaflets speaking against it. They're particularly scathing in their assessments of black men, and studiously petition the thane to bar black folk from living in the city at all. They say we're all unmanageably influenced by the Vaskosish, since practically all of us are thralls that've fled Berri Vaskos, or the children of such."

"I'll confess to knowing even less about Vaskosish ways than I do about Anglish ones," I said.

"Everything I know is secondhand. My parents both spoke Vaskosish, but they were very adamant about me being a citizen of Lindmarden and speaking Anglish. I really only know enough Vaskosish to haggle and to curse. They never had anything good at all to say about Berri Vaskos, for obvious reasons, but all the Vaskosish people I've met in Lindmarden seem good sorts. Mama told me that it's because they're the ones with the sense to have left Berri Vaskos."

"I'm afraid I wouldn't know; I've barely met anyone at all from Berri Vaskos. There's a young man at my brother's tinker co-op, but I haven't spoken to him about whether he's from Berri Vaskos or was born here. The only conversations I've had with him have been about my brother, and tinker works, and dragons."

"I know some Vaskosish folklore; stories that my mother told me," Liberty said.

"I'd love to hear a Vaskosish story, if you're willing to tell one," I said. "I'll trade you a nackie story for it, if you like."

"Now that's an offer I'll take you up on!" Liberty said with a grin. "This one was my favorite as a child."

She didn't put down her sewing while she spoke; she simply closed her eyes for a moment and then opened them and began speaking, continuing to sew all the while.

THIS IS THE STORY THAT LIBERTY TOLD

Once, long ago, in Ostagavia there was a kind king with a wicked son. A sorgina—a witskrafter—lived in his lands, and often he would send messengers to her home in the hills with gifts of white flour and fine cloth and southern wine. He would seek her counsel on this matter and that, and she would give it, and all was well in the kingdom. By and by, though, the kind king grew old and died, and his wicked son became king after him. He declared that all gifts to the old sorgina be stopped, and when she rebuked his stinginess, he declared that she be banished into the mountains. Upon hearing this, the old sorgina spat on the ground and cursed the young king that his only child, a beautiful daughter who had just flowered into womanhood, should be married to a slave. Then she took up her broom and leaped to the roof of her house, whereupon she whistled a jaunty tune, and presently a great red dragon flew down from the sky. She climbed upon its back and flew away toward the mountains.

The wicked young king flew into a rage upon learning of the witch's curse, and had his daughter sent to live among the virgins of the sacred grove deep in the forest, at the foot of the mountains—for they worship Fyra in Vaskosland, but they call her Athna there. Anyway, she was sent into the forest so that no man should ever look upon her until she was summoned home to marry a young man of the king's choosing. His poor wife, pining for the loss of her only child, soon fell ill and died.

Now, the wicked young king was very greedy, and he raised taxes on his people such that the poor could hardly buy bread or cloth, and even the rich were forced to diminish their slaves because they couldn't afford their keeping.

One such slave turned out into the world was a young man of fourteen years named Iñaki.

Iñaki's master, who wasn't an unkind man, provided him with a loaf of stale bread and a sack and wished him his luck upon the road. Iñaki thought that he should travel to the great city of Aux and there find some work, or else he would surely starve.

Iñaki had walked many miles on the road toward Aux when he met a black girl scarcely older than himself, with a baby carried on her back. She was begging at the roadside and she said to him, "Dear young man, my master has turned me and my child out, could you spare a loaf of bread?"

And Iñaki, who was a kind young man, thought that this poor girl was in a worse way than he was, and though he was hungry, he fetched up his loaf of bread and gave it to her. He said, "I wish that I could offer you better than stale bread, Sister, but my master has also turned me out to seek my own keeping on the road. I wish you and your child the best of luck."

She said to him, "You're a kind young man, and you deserve a good fortune. If you follow that path there, it will lead you to a spring where grows a certain tree. There's a tree maiden living in it, and her true name is Haritza. Tell her that Ahizpa sent you and see what she has to say."

He thanked the girl for the advice, and proceeded to the spring where grew an enormous oak tree, and he said, "Haritza, Haritza! Ahizpa has sent me to see what you have to say!"

Out from the tree came a beautiful maiden, and she said, "If Ahizpa has sent you, you must have done her a kindness. Take this oaken cup—it will always be filled with good water to drink."

Iñaki put the cup to his lips and found it to be filled with the purest spring water, and drinking it made him feel quite refreshed. He thanked the maiden, who went back into the tree. Iñaki put the cup into his sack and continued his way down the road.

After he'd walked many more miles, he came upon another woman who was begging, blacker and more wretched than the first, a scrap of red fabric tied across her eyes to show she was blind. She said to him, "Whoever comes, please, my master has turned me out, and I am so thirsty. Could you go to yon well and pull me a drink? I fear that in my blindness I would fall in and drown."

And Iñaki, who was a kind young man, thought that this woman was in a worse way than he was, and he said, "I can do better than that, Mother—I can give you this cup, which will always have sweet water in it, so that you will always have water to drink."

She said to him, "You're a kind young man and you deserve a good fortune. If you follow that path there, it will lead you to a spring where grows a certain tree. There's a tree maiden living in it, and her true name is Gaztaina. Tell her that Ama sent you and see what she has to say."

He thanked the woman for the advice, and proceeded to the spring where grew an enormous chestnut tree, and he said, "Gaztaina, Gaztaina! Ama has sent me to see what you have to say!"

Out from the tree came a beautiful maiden, and she said, "If Ama has sent you, you must have done her a kindness. Take this chestnut bowl—it will always be filled with roasted chestnuts to eat."

He thanked the maiden, who went back into the tree. Iñaki sat down and had a fine meal of sweet chestnuts, then continued on his way.

After he'd walked many more miles, he came upon an old woman, the blackest and most wretched he could imagine—withered with age, bent-backed and rheumy-eyed. She was begging, and she said to him, "Dear young man, my master has turned me out, and I am too old and too wretched to ever find work again. Could you spare me something to eat, that I might live to beg one day more?"

And Iñaki, who was a kind young man, thought that this old woman was in a worse way than he was, and he said, "I can do better than that—I can give you this bowl, which will always be filled with roasted chestnuts, so you may have something to eat for the rest of your days."

She said to him, "You're a kind young man and deserve a good fortune. If you follow that path there, it will lead you to a spring where grows a certain tree. There's a tree maiden living in it, and her true name is Sagarra. Tell her that Amona sent you and see what she has to say."

He thanked the old woman for the advice, and proceeded to the spring where grew an enormous apple tree, and he said, "Sagarra, Sagarra, Amona has sent me to see what you have to say!"

Out from the tree came a beautiful maiden, and she said, "If Amona has sent you, you must have done her a kindness. Take this golden apple. You may sell it for great fortune in the city of Aux—but, if you're brave you may bring it to the red dragon that lives atop the mountain, who greatly covets gold. He will give you a great boon indeed for a tree maiden's apple."

Iñaki thanked her, and she went back into the tree, and he continued on his way until he came to a crossroads. In one direction lay the hard and rocky path that led to the top of the mountain, in the other the broad and even road that led to the city of

Aux. He had no more food or water, nor any comforts at all but the clothes on his back, only his sack and his golden apple. He knew that it would be very hard to climb to the top of the mountain, and very easy to walk into the city and become a rich man. But he also knew, because he was an attentive young man who had always listened to his mother, that the advice of tree maidens was never to be taken lightly. So with a sigh and a squaring of his shoulders, he started up the mountain path.

At the end of the first day he was cold and hungry. He slept under the shelter of a beech tree and continued on. At the end of the second day he was colder and hungrier. He slept under the shelter of a fir tree and continued on. At the end of the third day he was colder still and hungrier still, with blisters on his feet and scrapes on his knees, and he thought that it was a pity that a golden apple could not be eaten. He slept under the shelter of a pine tree and continued on.

On the fourth day he reached a great cave near the top of the mountain where the great red dragon made its home. Now, this cave was a dragon's cave and thus carved from the stone of the mountain with powerful witskraft. It was bigger within than without, and inside it was all the warmth of summer. There was a clear pond, and rows of apple trees and fig trees and grape vines, and a tidy garden, and a beautiful house. Just beyond the house was a hill made of gold—as tall as the house itself was—and upon it sprawled the great red dragon itself. Sitting at the dragon's right shoulder was an old woman whom he knew at once for a sorgina, and she said, "I have watched your journey, young Iñaki. I appeared to you as the girl with the child, and as the blind woman, and as the old wretch. I see that you have a kind heart and a brave soul. I would have you for an apprentice, and teach you the ways of witskraft, and have you be the rider of my dragon's only child who yet sleeps within its egg."

Iñaki was overjoyed to accept the old sorgina's offer, and to become the young dragon's companion. For seven years he served the sorgina and learned her ways, and at the end of seven years she told him where to find the sacred grove where the king's daughter still dwelled—for in the seven years that Iñaki was learning and the king's daughter was living among the maidens in the grove, her father's kingdom had fallen to ruin in an uprising of slaves, and was thereafter despoiled by many petty wars between great lords to determine who would be the new king of Ostagavia.

Iñaki, who by this time had grown to be a very handsome man, and a clever one, and brave, and kind, flew upon the back of his dragon to the grove and asked to speak with the king's daughter. She had likewise grown very beautiful, and because she was brought up by grove maidens, she was also kind and sure and clever in all the ways of the wild wood. The two were very soon married, of course, and Iñaki and his bride climbed upon his dragon's back and flew to unknown lands far from Ostagavia, where they lived happily for all their days.

THE OTHER STUDENTS ARRIVED

L iberty took her leave just before luncheon, and I spent the remainder of Sunday in the library reading what I could about Tysklandish and skiltakraft. I woke on Monday morning, washed and dressed, and found Frau Brinkerhoff waiting for me in one of the leather chairs by the table.

"Good morning, dear, I'm quite glad to have caught you early," she said, rising. "The rest of the students will be arriving today. Some are already here, with their families. There's an informal smörgåsbord on offer from now until the afternoon, with both breakfast and luncheon foods. Today is an excellent day for you to get to know your fellow students, and for you to become known to them. If you're not opposed, there are in fact some introductions I'd like to make."

If the remainder of the students were at all like Ivar Stafn and Niklas Sørensen, I had no particular desire to either know them or be known by them. But I put on a pleasant smile and followed

Frau Brinkerhoff downstairs, Kasaqua happily bounding half a step behind.

The main hall, when we arrived there, was full of people. All of the professors were there, including Professor Ulfar in his crab-chair. Frau Kuiper was talking to a group of people who must have been the parents of students. Then there were the students and their dragons.

I recognized dragons of every variation that I'd seen in the dragonreckoning book, and a number that I didn't recognize at all. Slender dragons and stocky ones, dragons with narrow wings and wide wings and pointed wings, dragons in every color. Each was sitting or standing or walking at the heel of a young man, somewhere between twenty and thirty of them, all about my age.

Kasaqua made an excited trilling noise while I was still at the foot of the stairs, and a great number of faces—human and dragon alike—turned toward me in unnerving unison. A hush fell over the room.

"Ah, Miss Aponakwesdottir, how good of you to join us," Frau Kuiper said, looking at me for a moment before turning back to the man she'd been talking to. Most of the parents in the room stopped staring, but a good number of the young men continued, whispering to one another.

"Miss Anequs, if you are so inclined I would very much like to introduce you to Frau Jansen and her son, Sander," Frau Brinkerhoff said from my side. "Sander is also joining us for the first time this year, and will be sharing several classes with you."

I nodded, following Frau Brinkerhoff across the room, where a woman was standing with a young man my age. He was as pale as a fish's belly, as if he'd never seen the sun. His hair was dark and curling, his eyes very blue. He had his hands stuffed into his trouser pockets and was looking down at the dragon sitting at his feet—which was looking adoringly up at him with enormous yellow eyes. Kasaqua chirped a greeting that made the dragon look our way. It was only a little bigger than Kasaqua, and it had a very distinctive look. It was very pale all over, wheat-colored above and below with bands of white along its flanks, shading to brilliant gold on its tail and the backs of its wings. It lacked any sort of a mane, but had three sets of little horny nubs on either side of the crown of its head. It had a pair of barbles sweeping back from its nose, another above its eyebrows, and a double pair sprouting from its chin—taken together, I was reminded very strongly of a catfish. I'd seen illustrations of the breed in the book on dragon-reckoning; it was a velikolepni, too young to have grown its distinctive three-tiered crown of golden horns. They had been bred deliberately, by northeastern icefolk in Roveland and Russland, to be very powerful in skiltakraft.

"Frau Jansen, Sander," Frau Brinkerhoff said, canting her head slightly, "this is Anequs Aponakwesdottir, and this is her dragon, Kasaqua. Anequs is also joining us for the first time this year. She and Sander have been placed in a few classes together."

"Anequs and her dragon, Kasaqua," Sander said all in a rush, without looking up. "My name is Sander my dragon is Inga a pleasure to meet you."

"Sander, we *have* talked about making introductions properly," the woman said with a too-perfect smile, putting her hand on the young man's shoulder. He became absolutely rigid, though the expression on his face didn't change at all.

"The Jansens are very close intimates of the school, Miss Anequs," Frau Brinkerhoff said. "Frau Jansen is my niece."

"I'm very pleased to meet you, I'm sure," I said, trying to smile genuinely.

"A pleasure to meet you," Sander said again, still looking at Inga. His gaze flicked sideways, to Kasaqua, and then he said, "A very pretty dragon."

"Thank you. Kasaqua is a Nampeshiwe. Is Inga a velikolepni? I've never seen one, but I've seen illustrations."

"How clever of you to notice, you dear creature!" Sander's mother said, smiling at me as if I were a dog that had just done a trick. She looked at Frau Brinkerhoff and said, "It's so wonderful of you and Karina to take in these savage children and see to their proper education, Elsie. I said so about the first one and I'll say it about this one, too."

I stopped trying to maintain a smile.

Frau Jansen said, "I understand, from various correspondences, that you were born and raised on one of the outlying islands, Nack or Mask or some such place? Vastergot must seem very grand to you, having lived in a little bark house all your life. The lithographs in Emanuel Nordlund's *The Savage Peoples of North Markesland* certainly make it look charming, though."

"I'm from Masquapaug, ma'am," I said. "We live in stone houses with bark roofing over thatch. Bark houses are only used for beach camps, in the summer. I think they might have been used more frequently a long time ago, though—shortly after the great dying—but I'd have to ask my elders. I could send a telegram, I suppose, though I haven't been instructed on the etiquette of correspondence here at school yet."

"You have a telegraph office on your island?" Frau Jansen asked, raising her eyebrows.

"We have for as long as I've been alive. I think they laid the line across the bottom of the sound shortly after the unfortunate events at Naquipaug in the year 1825."

"Hah! Fancy that, savages dabbling about with telegraphs. I'd never have warranted it!" Frau Jansen said, with a false-sounding titter of laughter. "But I suppose that the improvement of your civilization is only the natural outcome of continued exposure to ours, after all. Telegrams!"

"Frau Brinkerhoff, I'm afraid I don't know the rules of social engagement," I said, looking pointedly away from the Jansens. "Is it permissible for me to inquire with the professors about my examinations on Friday?"

"All students will receive their class assignments this afternoon," Frau Brinkerhoff answered.

"Thank you, ma'am," I said, taking that answer to mean that no, it was not.

The room stilled again, and I looked along with everyone else toward the front entrance, where Marta had just floated in with Magnus at her heel. She glanced across the room, smiling like the illustration on the cover of a ladies' magazine, and she nodded when she saw me. I felt a strange mixture of irritation and relief when I realized that she was walking over to us. She wasn't someone I particularly liked, but she was someone that I at least knew.

"Good morning, Frau Jansen, Frau Brinkerhoff, Anequs, Sander," Marta said, nodding at each of us in turn and looking at Frau Brinkerhoff expectantly.

"Frau Jansen, you're well acquainted with Miss Marta Hagan, aren't you?" Frau Brinkerhoff asked. "She and Miss Anequs are rooming together this year."

"Oh, of course. Marta has been staying in our home lately, and is a great friend of my daughter, Lisbet. I'm not sure where my darling has gotten to just now, though."

"Lisbet is with Bergitte at the dragonhall, admiring her brother Hartvig's dragon," Marta supplied. "This is terribly rude, but could I borrow Anequs from your company? I would *so* love to present Anequs to them, before they take their leave for the day."

"If it doesn't offend the present company," Frau Brinkerhoff said, smiling and looking askance at the Jansens.

"No, no, by all means," Frau Jansen said, waving her hand. Marta giggled and linked her arm with mine, drawing me away. It felt overly intimate and rude, and part of me wanted to dig in my heels and refuse to be moved like that, but the more sensible part of me didn't want to be in front of the Jansens anymore, so I allowed Marta to pull me right out the front door.

"Sorry if I've imposed, but you looked like you needed rescuing," Marta apologized once we were outside. "I just knew Frau Brinkerhoff would try to push you into conversation with that Jansen boy. He's simple, the poor thing. He was a very sickly child, subject to the most awful dyspepsia. He was only paired with a dragon as a kindness to his future. As you may recall, I've been staying with his sister, Lisbet, for the past few days; we were chums in primary school. Sander scarcely left his chambers the entire time. Anyway, Lisbet and Bergitte were both recently accepted to Vígsteinnsdottir's Academy for Young Ladies, out in Skaldstead. It's very prestigious. The jarl's niece graduated from it. I've been up to our room, by the way. Are your other things being delivered sometime today?"

"What other things?" I asked, slightly puzzled.

"All of your other things, of course!" Marta said with a faltering smile. "Your soaps and creams and perfumes and hair oils. Your bedding and your curtains, art for your walls . . . I've brought a Victrola that takes wax cylinders, and I'd be happy to play any from your own collection for you."

"Everything I brought with me is either in my wardrobe or my trunk," I said.

Marta's face held an expression of icy incomprehension for a moment, then she plastered on a pleasant smile.

"Well, we each of us make do within our means, I suppose," she said. "Look, there are Lisbet and Bergitte!"

THERE WAS A LOT TO LEARN AT THE ACADEMY

Marta introduced me to Lisbet and Bergitte, and then a while later to Saskia and Annetta. All of them had brothers attending Kuiper's. None of them said anything of substance, but none of them seemed patently awful, either. It was an exercise in empty congeniality. I paid more attention to the varieties of dragons that were being situated in the dragonhall; the dragons paired with the eldest students were all roughly of their adult sizes and conformations, the smallest of them the size of large horses.

A great many more people had arrived when Marta and I returned to the main hall, and everything was very close and crowded. A frankly absurd amount of food had been laid out on the tables that flanked the walls. There was bread and butter, cold sliced beef and turkey, sausages both hot and cold, smoked fish, pickled fish, fish roe, pickled vegetables, a half dozen different sorts of cold salad, boiled potatoes, boiled eggs . . . People seemed to be taking whatever they liked.

The food was unfamiliar, but the service sent a pang of home-sickness through me. It wasn't terribly unlike a feast in the meet-inghouse. I wondered, absently, if the foods on offer had been provided by the guests.

"Look, there's Papa," Marta said, pointing with her fan. "He returned this morning for the start of the term. Let's get our plates and go sit with him. That's Herr Sørensen he's talking to, Niklas and Dagny's father."

I wondered if that meant Dagny was around, and rather hoped that she wasn't. Marta seemed more tolerable when Dagny wasn't present.

Marta's father was a bear of a man with yellow hair and a yellow beard to match. Herr Sørensen was tall and narrow, severe-faced, and apparently uninterested in either of us.

"Papa, Herr Sørensen, this is Anequs Aponakwesdottir, lately of Mask Island. She will be rooming with me in the coming term," Marta said when we were near enough to be heard. She pulled out a chair and sat down without being invited to. I hesitated a moment before doing the same.

"A pleasure to meet you, my dear, a great pleasure," Marta's father said, dipping his head just slightly. "Very heartening to see more young people of your race becoming properly educated, very heartening indeed. Three of my captains are of native heri-tage, and they're some of my most diligent men."

"Uh . . . thank you," I said.

I remained politely silent while I ate, listening to the two gen-tlemen talk about the buying and selling of freight ships. From what I gathered, Marta's father owned a shipping line that im-ported goods from Anglesland and Norsland.

After I spent some time sitting and staring at my empty plate, not really wanting to eat any more but wondering if I shouldn't go and get something else to be polite, Frau Kuiper appeared in the great double door at the far end of the hallway. A hushed feel came over the room, as if she'd been expected.

"We welcome and thank the families of our students, and wish them a prosperous year," Frau Kuiper said. "At this time, students may proceed to Lecture Hall One to receive their class assignments. Families are of course invited to finish luncheon at their leisure."

Marta and I bid goodbye to her father and Herr Sørensen, and I followed her and all the other students, who seemed to have a much better idea of where they were going than I did. The lecture hall turned out to be a sort of stage flanked on three sides by rows of benches that formed tiers. There was an expanse of floor before each row of benches large enough that smaller dragons could comfortably lie down in front of their dragoneers. I sat beside Marta. No one else sat on the bench where we were sitting, which seemed strange, because the room was quite crowded.

On the stage at the bottom of the pit formed by the tiers of benches, Frau Kuiper was sitting behind a desk, a pile of small cards before her.

"She'll call your name," Marta whispered to me. "Go up and take the card from her, then return to your seat. There's no need to say anything."

I was glad that Marta seemed to have some idea of what was going on and had deigned to tell me, because none of this was familiar at all and yet everyone else seemed perfectly aware and at ease, as if they'd done all of this before. Frau Kuiper waited patiently for everyone to take their seats and for a hush to fall in the room before she said, loudly and clearly, "First-year students. Adilsson, Kole."

I watched as a young man rose, descended to the stage, and accepted the card that she handed to him with a polite nod before returning to his seat.

"Anderssen, Frederik," Frau Kuiper said, to much the same effect.

Then, "Aponakwesdottir, Anequs."

I motioned for Kasaqua to stay, and I felt her pang of anxiety as I left her to walk down and take the card. I didn't look at anyone but Frau Kuiper. I could feel everyone staring at me. A murmur went through the crowd of students, and Frau Kuiper loudly cleared her throat. I went back to my seat.

"Bjorn, Edvin," Frau Kuiper said the moment I'd sat down. Kasaqua jumped into my lap. I didn't attempt to stop her; it was a comfort that both of us needed equally.

"What classes are you in?" Marta whispered giddily, nodding toward the card I was holding. The card was printed with narrow letters:

APONAKWESDOTTIR, ANEQUS. FIRST YEAR, AUTUMN.

Natural Philosophy One. Professor Ulfar. Professor
   Ulfar's Laboratory, Monday and Wednesday
   morning.
Anglereckoning Two. Professor Nazari. Lecture Hall
   Two, Monday and Wednesday afternoon.
Skiltakraft One. Professor Ezel. Skiltakraft Laboratory,
   Tuesday and Thursday morning.
Directed Study: Erelore. Professor Ibarra. Library,
   Tuesday and Thursday afternoon.
Dragon Husbandry One. Professor Mesman. Flight
   Field, Friday morning.
Directed Study: Folklore. Professor Ibarra. Library,
   Friday afternoon.

"Oh, you've gotten passed through Anglereckoning One!" Marta whispered, sounding positively jealous. "You must have done *very* well on your examination."

"What's a directed study?"

"It means you'll be meeting personally with the professor, for specific instruction."

"It means that I *didn't* do well on those examinations," I translated.

"Well, yes," Marta said, "but that doesn't mean anything. I

don't think anyone expected you to excel at folklore, not having had a civilized upbringing."

"Frau Kuiper was surprised to learn that I could read at all. But I know that I did horribly on my skiltakraft examination, so why don't I have a directed study in that?"

"Professor Ezel probably refused. He's an absolute beast, so consider yourself lucky."

"I don't think Professor Ezel approves of me," I said. "He seemed particularly displeased when Frau Kuiper introduced me to the professors on Friday."

"Professor Ezel doesn't approve of anyone," she replied. "He spent his youth becoming a master of skiltakraft, and then no dragon would have him, and he's never stopped being bitter about it. Everyone knows."

I was wholly unsurprised that dragons at large would balk at the thought of Professor Ezel as a companion.

There were twenty-eight first-year students in total, and the only one whose name I recognized was Sander Jansen. Frau Kuiper went on to the second-year students—I recognized Theod, and Marta, and Niklas and Ivar. Marta returned to her seat, card in hand, smiling.

"You and I are going to be in anglereckoning together," she whispered, "and I've gotten passed to Wordlore Three, which is lovely, because Professor Ibarra is something of a bore. I'm very glad that I did so much reading in the past spring term; the weather was awful. It helped my grades on last spring's final examinations immensely."

I hadn't been introduced to any of the young men in the third and fourth year classes. After one hundred and four students in total had been called, Frau Kuiper dismissed us, telling us that we were all at liberty for the remainder of the day. Dinner would be served in the dining hall at six o'clock in the evening, and dragons would be fed at seven o'clock in the dragonhall. Not knowing what else to do, I followed Marta back to our shared room.

Her half of the room had been transformed.

I hadn't thought that there was anything particularly wanting about the window dressings, but Marta had seen fit to replace the crisp white curtains with heavy drapes of blue taffeta, tied back with tassels. She'd also replaced her coverlet with a blue-and-gold one, and had a whole stack of gold cushions artfully arranged near the head of the bed. It hadn't occurred to me that I could or should bring my own bedding when I'd left Masquapaug, but putting a layer of cattail mats and a bear pelt on the too-soft mattress would certainly have made it more comfortable.

Against the wall opposite her writing desk, Marta had somehow produced a little table that looked to be made from brass scrollwork and panes of glass. A large gold-framed mirror hung on the wall behind it, and all manner of little bottles and jars were neatly lined up on its surface. A sea chest was sitting at the foot of her bed, a lacy cloth laid out over the top of it, and a wide, shallow bowl full of dried flowers sat on top. To the right-hand side of her bed she'd laid out an oblong brown-and-gold rug, which Magnus immediately made for upon entering the room, walking directly to it, turning in two tight circles, and lying down. She'd hung a number of small watercolor paintings in little gold frames on the wall, and on her writing desk there was a framed lichtbild of a much younger version of Marta's father, standing beside a woman who looked very like Marta.

The bookshelf on her side of the room had a row of books on it now, held up at one end with a little bronze dragon.

"I hope you won't think it impertinent," Marta said, walking over to her little brass table and taking off her gloves, "but I believe we were quite wrong-footed when we met on Saturday . . . though you do seem to be generally unfamiliar with Anglish modes of polite behavior."

"I know practically nothing of what your people consider proper," I confessed, watching as Kasaqua padded over to Marta's trunk and sniffed at the bowl of flowers. She considered trying a mouthful because they smelled interesting, and I looked at her sternly and tried to convey that she should not.

"I imagine, then, that this will be of great help to you," Marta said, scanning over her shelf of books and selecting one to hand to me. The cover read: *Sævinsdottir's Guide to Social Grace and Perfect Comportment.*

"My mother gave it to me when I was twelve," Marta said with a brittle smile. "It's most delightfully instructive."

"Thank you," I said, staring down at the book in my hand. It was heavier than the pennik novels I was used to, bound in a hard cover and painted gold along the edges of the pages.

"I intend to spend a part of the afternoon writing a few letters," Marta said, sounding apologetic. "Last year, the first-year students gathered in the common room to become acquainted with one another. I'm sure that if you inquired with Frau Brinkerhoff, she could arrange a suitable chaperone for you."

Considering that Frau Brinkerhoff had introduced me to the Jansens, I wasn't eager to submit myself to her social pairings again.

"If it's all the same to you, I think I'll read until dinner," I said, smiling. "I'd like to have some idea what I'm doing before I attempt conversation and make a fool of myself."

Marta smiled brilliantly at me, and we retreated to our respective writing desks.

THOUGH SHE FOUND HER TEACHERS WANTING

I had never read as tedious and absurd a book as *Sævinsdottir's Guide to Social Grace and Perfect Comportment*.

There were rules about whom to speak to, and when, and about what subjects. It seemed that the only reason to speak, in polite Anglish society, was to please and praise others. There were a hundred different rules governing the conduct of ladies in the company of gentlemen, and a lot of confusing rules about how to address one's social betters and social inferiors. All of it seemed to be the height of nonsense, having nothing to do with actual polite and respectful behavior and everything to do with complicating one's life and hobbling one's ability to communicate.

I sat with Marta at dinner. She told me that we, as the only girls in the school, had the prerogative to command a table of our own and that young men could not join us at it unless expressly invited. I learned from her that breakfast was served at seven o'clock, the morning session of classes ran from eight o'clock to ten o'clock, luncheon was served at noon, the afternoon session ran from one o'clock to three o'clock, dinner was served at six o'clock, and dragons were fed in the dragonhall at seven o'clock. All of the meals were served in a smörgåsbord style because it was the most practical way to feed a hundred or more people.

Marta suggested that we go together into Vastergot on Saturday morning, that I might do some shopping "to improve my part of the room." Apparently, there were particular shops that she wanted to take me to.

I didn't mention that I had only thirteen marka to last until October, and that I fully intended to spend it on train fare and postage, because her book had said that it was rude to discuss money.

The following morning, I had my first class at Kuiper's Academy: skiltakraft—the thing I'd come here to learn.

Professor Ezel's laboratory, like Professor Ulfar's, held a dozen tables in two columns of six with a narrow aisle between them. Unlike Professor Ulfar's, it was otherwise completely empty. There were no drapes of any kind on the windows, and the morning light filled the room harshly. Professor Ezel was seated at a long, narrow desk at the front of the room, lit from behind and looking especially angular. On the far wall was a single tall cabinet—presently closed. There was a chalkboard to the left of his desk and a wide expanse of bare stone floor. There were two small items laid on the tables before each chair. I wasn't able to get close enough to examine them before Professor Ezel started speaking.

"You will sit at the back of the room, with Mr. Jansen," he said sharply, glancing to the left. Sander Jansen was seated at the rearmost table, with Inga curled at his feet. I moved to sit beside him, placing Kasaqua on the floor, where she promptly padded over to touch her nose with Inga's. Inga seemed less enthused with the interaction than Kasaqua was.

There was a sharp noise. Professor Ezel had struck his desk with something—a wooden ruler.

"The two of you are being included in this class at the behest of Frau Kuiper, and for no other reason. You will not speak unless you are spoken to. I don't give half a damn how many questions you have, I am not going to coddle you and slow down the progress of all the other students. You'll keep up or you won't. You are each being *tolerated* in this class. I don't expect either of you to gain much of anything from it."

I narrowed my eyes at the professor, but said nothing.

While we both had a set of the unfamiliar tools, Sander had a number of other items laid out in front of him. A cube of metal about two inches across with a different number of little dome-shaped depressions on each side of it, a summer mink tail, a river stone, a lump of clay, an inkwell, and a neat stack of paper.

I hadn't brought anything with me. No one had told me that I'd be expected to. There were so many infuriating little presuppositions that everyone made—things that they all knew and expected without it being expressly stated—and no one bothered to explain them to me, who had no way of knowing them.

The two tools that were laid in front of me were a mapwright's compass and a half circle of stamped metal with measure marks along the curved side. It had a set of small stamped holes near the edge of the flat side.

Other students and their dragons began to file in, passing by Sander and me with little more than a glance. Professor Ezel didn't say anything to them about where to sit; they were allowed to sit wherever they liked. Every one of them was carrying a small bag or satchel, and upon sitting down produced paper and pen and ink from it—though none of them set out anything like Sander's collection of oddments.

Professor Ezel took a watch from his pocket and looked at it, then without a word stood and walked down the narrow aisle between the desks to lock the laboratory door. That was positively alarming; knowing that we were locked in, that it would be impossible to simply get up and walk away. Professor Ezel walked back up the aisle and stood before his desk, turning to face us.

"Anyone who does not arrive at my class in a timely fashion will be barred entrance," he said. "Those who are absent more than three times during the term will be expelled from this class—which most often results in expulsion from this academy at large, because satisfactory mastery of skiltakraft is the keymost skill associated with dragoneering, along with dragon husbandry. All assignments will be turned in exactly when they are asked for; any assignments not turned in when they are due will receive no credit. I do not offer extensions, and I do not accept excuses. Those who cannot excel here should prepare to find some other institution of learning."

Many of the other students were writing. Lacking paper or pen, I simply folded my hands and paid close attention. Professor Ezel moved to stand beside the chalkboard, his hands folded behind his back.

"It is well documented that a dragon's breath, unaltered, reduces all things that it touches to their most fundamental stable components—primarily vetna and kolfni. By the design of the gods or of nature, it is fortunate that neither vetna nor kolfni are disastrously reactive in air—though concentrated vetna can ignite violently if produced near a source of flame. It is absolutely imperative that each of you learn the skills needed to contain your dragon's breath in an orderly manner and transform its raw power to useful ends."

He turned to face the chalkboard and drew a circle, beginning at the top and drawing a smooth line counterclockwise. Something about that felt just slightly *off*; a circle ought to have started at the right-hand quarter—the east—and moved south-west-north.

"It is of critical importance that the borders of any skilta be sharply defined, to contain the powers that are being manipulated. A circle—or more precisely a sphere of which a circle is a cross-section—is the most resilient form that such borders can be made to take. A skilta drawn without a containing circle may loose any athers formed by it in any direction. I'm sure that any of you will understand the potential disaster that could create. Let us presume that the input is salt, and that we wish to separate it into its constituent athers. Who can tell me what the atheric constituents of salt are?"

Several of the young men seated ahead of me raised their hands, and Professor Ezel indicated one of them with a nod. He said, "Salt is composed of brinesna and grunesna in equal portions, sir."

"Correct, Mr. Fafnirson," Professor Ezel said with another nod. He drew two figures on the board, one to either side of the circle. They looked like many-pointed stars—the same kinds of figures that I'd seen in the skiltakraft book he'd given me to read.

"Brinesna," he said, indicating the figure to the right of the circle, "is, in its pure atheric form, a soft gray metal that quickly rots into a white rust if exposed to air. If atheric brinesna is exposed to water, however, it will react with great violence. It will produce jets of vetna that propel it at great speed across the water's surface. The vetna may, under certain conditions, burst into open flame, and the mass of brinesna itself may burst into many small, burning pieces. It is therefore imperative that the brinesna be deposited into an airtight container—ideally one made of loodglas. Meanwhile, grunesna in its pure atheric form is a green-colored poisonous air—one that will cause watering of the eyes and blistering of the skin. Exposure to air of grunesna can very quickly render you blind, and at sufficient concentrations it will choke you to death in minutes. It is even more imperative that the grunesna be contained if we seek to divide salt into its constituent athers. The fundamental purpose of a skilta is to direct and channel the power of a dragon's breath—to break down the chosen inputs into their simplest forms and recombine those forms into the desired complex outputs, containing any harmful products and by-products of the process."

He turned to the chalkboard once more and drew a number of

dots inside the margins of the circle, then connected them with an unbroken line to form a figure like a many-pointed star. Two of the points were extended, moving just beyond the borders of the circle.

"In this skilta, the input—salt—would be placed at the center and would be the focus of the dragon's breath. The lines channel and direct the power of the dragon's breath, and these extended points of deposition let the finished products exit the circle— either into the open air or into prepared containers. In more complex skiltas, the component athers might not be harvested, but instead utilized to build more complex forms."

He stepped to the right, drawing another circle on the blank part of the board. This one was much more complicated, an arrangement of circles within circles and arrays of little stars converging on a single point. It took him the better part of five minutes to complete it, during which we all sat in utter silence and watched him.

Kasaqua was very, very bored.

He finished the skilta with a decisive tap of the chalk at the end of the only point that extended beyond the margin of the circle, then turned to us and said, "Who can tell me what this figure is and what it would do?"

Only two of the other students raised their hands this time; and Professor Ezel selected one.

"It would produce caustic soda, sir," the young man said, his voice just a bit uncertain. "Salt would be placed in the bottom corner of the central triad and broken into its constituents. The grunesna would move through the circle until it was reduced entirely to vetna, then channel into the bottom right corner. The bottom left corner attaches to an array that would draw stiksna from the air. The surrounding shell of figures would combine the brinesna, stiksna, and the vetna into caustic soda, which would be deposited from the point that pierces the circle."

"I can see that you've been a diligent scholar, Mr. Laasko,"

Professor Ezel said. "This is, indeed, a skilta to produce caustic soda from salt and air, by the transformation of grunesna into pure vetna. All athers can be broken into vetna, eventually, by tearing their motes apart. It is much more difficult to force small athers to fuse into larger ones than it is to break large athers into smaller ones."

He turned to the board again, erasing everything he'd drawn. I glanced to the side, to see that Sander had made a copy of each of the figures. I had not.

He turned away from the board, pacing along the front of the room, hands folded behind his back again.

"Hans Muench discovered the basic principle of athers, and their orderly arrangement, in the year 1784. Twenty-four athers are known, though many more are theorized, because athers behave in an orderly manner. The most important ather in skiltakraft is kolfni, represented by 'K' on the chart, most commonly present in its natural form as coal and charcoal. It attaches itself readily with the simplest element, vetna, 'V,' to form long chains of motes that store large amounts of tatkraft—the functional essence that enables all living processes. Critically important to the shaping of natural objects—things that are or were living—are the athers kolfni, vetna, zurfni, stiksna, pospor, and saffle. Other critically important athers to skiltakraft are isen, geld, lood, silber, kwiksilber, kessel, and zan. When you have learned these athers, their principles and properties, their placement on the chart and why they are placed thusly, you will possess the understanding needed to successfully create skilta."

He turned to the board again.

"Vetna is represented by a single point," he said, the chalk clicking sharply as he made a small mark. "Kolfni, which weighs twelve times as much as vetna, is represented as a six-pointed star." He drew a star, drawing it all in a single unbroken line. "Zurfni weighs fourteen times as much as vetna, and is represented by a seven-pointed star. Stiksna is represented by an eight-pointed star, brinesna eleven, sindle fourteen, pospor fifteen, and so forth. Now, we will begin with vetna and move up the table, one ather at a time."

The class continued in much the same vein for an hour, Professor Ezel drawing the symbols for each of twenty-four of the known athers in order, explaining the properties of each.

"You will at this time take a piece of paper and draw each of these figures exactly as I have drawn them. It is imperative that they be drawn in a fluid manner, in a singular and unbroken line. You may begin. I will be moving from desk to desk to check on your progress."

I looked at all the other students, who began immediately to do as they'd been told. I looked at Sander. Sander looked at the empty space in front of me and, without a word, divided his stack of papers in half, putting half of them in front of me. He produced a second pen from his breast pocket, and moved his inkwell so that it sat between us.

"Thank you," I whispered. He nodded, not looking at me, and reached for the metal cube in front of him. He took it in his left hand, running his thumb in a tight circle in one of the hollows as he very quickly began to draw the figures with his right hand, gaze flicking from the chalkboard to his work. He used the half-circular tool to measure out angles to place the motes; I paid close attention to how he was doing it. I'd learned in anglereckoning that a circle was composed of 360 points, so the trick to arranging the motes evenly around the circle was to divide 360 by however many motes needed to be drawn.

At some point, Sander put the cube of metal down and instead picked up the clay, rolling it on the desk until it formed a long thin rope, then gathering it in his hand and beginning again.

He was done drawing his figures long before I was, and his were much neater approximations than mine.

"You will at this time, regardless of your progress, write your name at the top of the paper and leave it on the desk," Professor Ezel said. "You are thereafter dismissed."

I hadn't gotten past the figure of arsen. I glanced up at Professor Ezel, who was looking at me intently. I wrote my name on the paper and offered Sander his pen back.

"Thank you," he said as he took it.

"Would you like to join me for luncheon?" I asked him quietly. He looked up, startled, meeting my eyes for the barest of moments before looking down again.

"I don't speak well and I am poor company," he said, packing away his things.

"I'm sure you're not," I said. "I haven't been introduced to anyone else, and you were very kind just now."

He glanced at me sidelong for a moment, as if he didn't quite trust me, but then gave a small nod.

I'd have to find some way to obtain paper and pens of my own before this class met again.

ANEQUS MADE THE ACQUAINTANCE
OF A PLEASANT CLASSMATE

There were far fewer choices presented for luncheon today than there had been yesterday—soup, bread, cheese, boiled potatoes, and the same short beer that Theod and I had been served during the meal we shared. I was at the dining hall before Sander was, so I located an empty table. I sat idly for a few minutes, wondering if it was rude for me to begin eating before he arrived. Most of the other students in the dining hall were already eating. I tried to pretend that no one was staring at me.

When Sander arrived and sat down, he was carrying something that looked like a book with a tin cover. He put it onto the table and opened it, revealing two panes with wax spread on the inside. Along the binding there was a little pocket, from which he pulled a sort of needle. He handled it like a pen, scratching neat text into the wax and holding it out to show me.

Does it bother you if I write instead of speaking?

"No, not at all," I said, looking back at him. He was looking down at the words he'd written. "Your handwriting is beautiful," I said, following his gaze.

He wrote: *It's had to be. I don't speak well. When I was small, I had a governess who made me write pages for hours every day. Sometimes just rows of lines | | | | | | | | | | that all had to be the same length and the same distance apart or she'd make me do it again. It had to be perfect.*

"That sounds awful," I said.

I'm not simple. Something is wrong with me, but I'm not simple.

"No, it's clear that you're not," I said, smiling, because it was obviously something of a sore point with him. "If it's not rude to ask, what were all those things you had on your desk? I don't know much about skiltakraft, but I don't have any of those kinds of things in supply. Are they things that I'll need eventually?"

I'm a hopeless and incurable fidget. If I don't have something to occupy my hands, I can't even begin to think. I become useless, prone to fits and rages. So I carry things to touch, to occupy my hands.

"Well, that seems to be a tidy solution, then," I said. I glanced at his plate; he hadn't taken soup, bread, or cheese.

"Are you only having potatoes?" I asked.

I have a delicate constitution. Potatoes agree with me. Few things do.

I decided not to pursue that.

"What made you decide to be a dragoneer?" I asked, glancing down at Inga, who was sitting at his feet, leaning away from Kasaqua, who was trying to sniff her.

My father decided that I should be put before a dragon egg because I'm uncommonly good at anglereckoning. He thought skiltakraft might be an acceptable pursuit for me. I quite like Inga.

"You certainly seem much better at skiltakraft than me," I confessed. "Have you been practicing for a long time?"

Not really, but many of the principles of anglereckoning carry over. Knowing what angle to make to have the line come out where you want it to and that. I've always liked to draw the sorts of shapes that are called for in skiltakraft—

The wax tablet had become filled with writing, and in the little space left he wrote, *Just a moment.*

He closed the tablet, laid it flat on the table, and pressed a button on the spine of it.

"Smooth it out," he said, staring at it. I helped myself to my soup while I waited for whatever was going to happen, and after a minute or so he opened the tablet again and, as he'd said, the wax within was entirely smooth and untouched.

"How does that work?" I marveled.

It has copper wires all along the back; they can be made to be hot or cold with witskrafty figures worked into the covers. It runs on a little vial of strahlendstone in the spine that has to be replaced every few months. Dragons' breath went into the making of it.

"My brother would probably be fascinated with this. He's a tinker, working out of a co-op in Vastergot."

I should like to meet him some day, Sander wrote.

"I don't see any reason why you shouldn't," I said. "Marta and I are going into the city on Saturday; you could come with me if you want."

Sander laid down his needle, frowning at me, laying both hands flat on the table and gazing resolutely at the space between them. I felt as if I'd made some kind of awful misstep.

"Is this some matter of Anglish custom I've done completely wrong?" I asked. "Are young women not allowed to make invitations to young men? I don't remember reading that, exactly, but everything in my book of manners always has it the other way around."

He glanced at me briefly, then back at the space between his hands. He drummed his fingers on the table. After a few moments he picked up his tablet and wrote,

You really do mean it, don't you? You're actually inviting me. No one invites me places, I'm terrible company.

"You're not!" I said, giggling. "Besides, I think it's more proper that Marta and I have a young man with us anyway. She's never met my brother, either. Do you know how I'd go about sending letters or telegrams from the school? On the island we have only one post office, and it's also the telegraph office."

There's a mail room on the first floor, on the other side of the entrance hall. You can leave letters in the outbox. If you want to send a telegram, you'll have to find Frau Brinkerhoff. She knows how to operate the machine.

"Do they have postage stamps there?"

If they don't, I can lend you one. What class do you have for your afternoon session?

"Erelore, with Professor Ibarra."

I have natural philosophy. Do you plan to be at dinner?

"Yes. Would you like to meet?"

I'd like that. I'll bring you a postage stamp as well.

"Thank you very much—for that and for your kindness earlier in class. I feel rather out of place here. Everyone seems to understand a lot of things that I don't, because they've been to schools before."

I know how that can be. It's been wonderful talking with you, though. I look forward to seeing you again later.

He looked at the clock against the far wall, and I saw that there only remained twenty minutes until the afternoon session. We both finished our meals with great quickness.

My afternoon class was a directed study of erelore with Professor Ibarra. I was quite surprised, when I arrived at the library, to see Theod already seated at one of the tables opposite the professor.

"Ah, there she is. Young Mr. Knecht and I were worried that you might be late, but as it happens he was merely early. I had originally conceived of this study as being pertinent only to you, Miss Aponakwesdottir, but Frau Kuiper reminded me that Mr. Knecht could also benefit from rudimentary study of both erelore and folklore. So you will be classmates."

Theod looked at me as if it were personally my fault that he'd been asked to be here. I had no idea what he'd have been doing otherwise. I took my seat beside him, and Professor Ibarra began.

"Erelore is the study of eretide: all things that have happened in foregone times and why they happened in that way. I hope, in this study, to bring you to a basic common knowledge of erelore as befits a new secondary school student. If you are diligent in your studies, you may be capable of joining the rest of the first-year students in Erelore Two in the spring term. As most of the learning in Erelore Two relies on knowledge of the eretide of Lindmarden and New Anglesland in particular, that is where our focus shall begin."

He unrolled a map onto the table, a larger one than I'd ever seen, wider across than the span of my arms. It included more of the world than most maps I'd seen as well. On the far eastern edge was the island of Zhippon, then Zhongu and Shiang-Gang. There were no clear borders in the east, and the names of the nations were simply written across the land in large letters. Moving westward, Russland and Roveland in the north had clearer borders, and Indusland in the south. West of that was Turksland, with the Black Sea above and Parshanland below, then the rectangular peninsula of Kedar and Kindah with the Arabish dryland between them. Below the Midland Sea, the north part of Aprika was shown; Coptland in the west, then Widnes, then Farth. Everything west of Russland and north of Turksland was very sharply outlined, each labeled section differently colored. Norsland sidled up against Swedeland and was separated from Finnland by the Balt Sea. Beneath the Balt Sea, Polland, Tyskland, Frankland, and the great stretch of Vaskosland. The southern tip of Vaskosland very nearly touched the northmost part of Farth. Across the Narrow Sea, north of Frankland and west of Tyskland, Anglesland and Celtsland occupied the middle of the map. They were very neatly divided into little parcels of land, each with a multitude of labels. My gaze swept across the Great North Sea, which seemed less wide than it ought to have been, and I saw the east coast of Markesland. The great island of Vinberland in the north, the hook-shaped coast of Lindmarden, with Naquipaug and Masquapaug below. They were labeled "Nack" and "Mask." Vastergot was tucked into the sheltered cove just above the hook, and farther south New Linvik sat behind the jutting crab-claw of Narrow Island. There were other Anglish cities down the coast that I was less familiar with, but a jagged line was drawn across the south part of the map, everything below broadly labeled "Berri Vaskos."

"Thorvald Eiriksson was the first finder of the lands today known as North Markesland. His father, Red Eirik, had come from Norsland with a greatthede of his folk, and had made successful steads on Firebarrow Island and Deepdale Island." Professor Ibarra leaned over the map, drawing an arc with his finger across the top of the Great North Sea—from the southern tip of Norsland to Firebarrow Island to the southern coast of Deepdale Island to Vinberland. "Eiriksson set out from Deepdale Island and crossed the Great North Sea, landing on Vinberland in the year 1574. He returned to Deepdale Island, and a thede of his folk followed his path to establish a steading on Vinberland. In years thence, Eiriksson and members of his thede pathfound along all the shores of the Vinberlandish Greatcove. Fyra Eiriksdottir, youngest sister of Thorvald, made a lifework of sailing the river Runestung inland, and was first to find and map the deep lakes, in the year 1588. *Eiriksdottir's Leid* describes her journey, and the many dealings she had with warsome natives of the white north and the lake shores. You will be reading it this term."

"I know *Eiriksdottir's Leid*," Theod said. "I've had it read to me."

Professor Ibarra looked up, glancing from Theod to me and back. He pursed his lips and looked as if he might say something, but then thought better of it and looked back at the map again.

"In the year 1626, the great seafarer and mapwright Stafn Whitebeard set out from Vinberland on a course southward to map the eastern coast of North Markesland. He discovered the Fishhook Headland, Nack and Mask Islands, Gannet Cove and the many islands therein, Narrow Island, and Narrow Cove. Upon his return journey in the summer of 1628, a great storm came chasing up from the south. Whitebeard and his shipthede sheltered in the lee of the Fishhook Headland, but their ship was greatly damaged upon a stony reef. Lacking time and tools to repair the ship before the coming of winter, Whitebeard and his shipthede instead decided to make landfall and make a winterstead on the mainland. Finding the country pleasant and fruitful, many folk determined to stay, and thus was the founding of Vastergot."

"There was already a city at Vastergot," I said. "I don't know what its name was, but the folk who lived there were the Maswachuisit—the great blue hill people—named for the same hill that's called Vaster's Hill now. They were great friends of the Naquisit and Masquisit before the plague. In Catchnet, the people were called Akashneisit, and all around Gannet Cove there were the Naregannisit. They . . . weren't as great friends of ours."

"Have you read Emanuel Nordlund's *The Savage Peoples of North Markesland*?" Professor Ibarra asked, sounding mildly surprised.

"No, I haven't," I said. "This is all just lore to me. My people know it."

"Now that's *very* interesting . . . Let's put aside this lesson for a moment. I'd like to give both of you some materials; *Whitebeard's Leid* and *Eiriksdottir's Leid* particularly, and Nordlund's accounts. You will both read the first three chapters of each. Miss Aponakwesdottir, you will write an account of the same span of eretide as understood by your people. Mr. Knecht, you will write an account of that span of history from memory before reading, and a summary of the materials after reading."

Professor Ibarra disappeared into the bookshelves for a few minutes and returned with a stack of volumes. I looked at Theod. He looked . . . very displeased.

I sighed and began to read.

AND EXTENDED AN INVITATION

I followed Theod after class. He was making his way to the dragonhall. Kasaqua was very interested in going there, once she realized the direction we were taking.

"Is there something you needed from me, Miss Anequs?" he asked, his gaze kept firmly ahead.

"Frau Brinkerhoff told me that you spend the better part of your time at the dragonhall, when you're not in class."

"I've found that Copper is better company than the majority of the students. Please don't repeat that; it's intolerably rude for me to have said."

"I can't say that I've properly met enough students to have come to a similar conclusion. Sander Jansen seems to be a perfectly amiable young man—though I've also met with Ivar Stafn and Niklas Sørensen, and they were most certainly *not* perfectly amiable. Are they typical of the students here? I could understand you wanting nothing to do with them if most of them are like that."

"Mr. Stafn's opinions are common," Theod said. "His family is very influential, descended from Stafn Whitebeard. His father is thane of Vastergot."

"I'm not sure what that means," I confessed.

"It's an office of governance. The high king rules over all the holds in a kingdom—that's Yngvarr Silvertooth just now, high king of Lindmarden. Each hold is presided over by a jarl. We're in Vaster Hold, which includes the thedes of Vastergot, Varmarden, Skaldstead, Estervall, and Catchnet—along with their outlands. Holds are divided into thedes, each of which is presided over by a thane. Vastergot's thane is Arjan Stafn. Ivar's father."

"I'm still not sure what that means in relation to you and me," I said. "Are his opinions weightier than most?"

"People who would otherwise disagree with him will fall in line to gain his favor," Theod said.

"Then you and I will simply have to prove his opinions wholly unfounded," I said with as much conviction as I could muster. Theod snorted. I glanced at him in annoyance and pressed on.

"I was wondering if I might talk with you about your situation here, since I seem to share at least some part of it. Where do you obtain your school supplies and sundries? I went to class without paper or pens today, not knowing that I'd be expected to have them."

"Fraus Kuiper and Brinkerhoff have always provided me with everything I've needed, often without my asking. I expect they confer directly with the professors. I'm not in the habit of making demands. I simply do what's asked of me to the best of my capacity."

"I hardly think that wishing to know what articles I need and where I may obtain them constitutes 'making demands,' as you put it. I *am* trying to be very game about all of this, for Kasaqua's good and for the good of my family back home, but this isn't something I'd have chosen if there were some other way for me to learn what I must in order to be an effective dragoneer and become legally licensed as such."

He paused and gave me a very strange look then, as if he found me utterly incomprehensible.

"Do you not understand how lucky you are to have been given this opportunity?" he asked. "What do you expect would have happened to you if you hadn't become associated with the school?"

"I expect I'd never have left the island, unless someone took me from it," I said.

"And would that have pleased you, living in poverty and ignorance with no attachment to the modern world?" he asked as we continued on. Copper came and pressed himself up under Theod's hand when we arrived at his stall, demanding to be scratched behind the ears. Kasaqua hopped off my shoulder and onto the gate dividing Copper's stall from the hallway, making a little trilling noise of greeting.

"Theod . . . have you ever met any other nackies before?" I asked, studying his face. He looked pained by the question, turning from me.

"I have been privileged to live among an enlightened people for all of my life. I've been further privileged to be allowed to come and study at this academy. I am uncommonly lucky."

"When was the last time you left the school?" I asked.

"I don't leave the school," he said tightly. "I have no occasion to."

"Would you like to join me this Saturday in Vastergot? I'm going to buy school supplies, and to meet my brother."

"I don't have train fare, nor do I have permission to leave the school grounds."

"I expect that Frau Brinkerhoff could help with both of those facts. Would you come? Sander and Marta are coming, I think. We could make a day of it."

"People will talk," he said, looking at Copper.

"People are always going to talk," I said.

"Yes," he said, after a long silence. "If I'm granted permission and the means to attend, I'll come with you on Saturday."

I was going to make it my business to ensure that Theod was granted permission and train fare.

Theod freed Copper from his confinement, and he and Kasaqua made play of bounding around each other as we left the hall and went to the open field beyond. Theod produced a knotted length of rope from his jacket pocket, which commanded Copper's immediate attention. He threw the rope, and Copper ran after it and brought it back. Kasaqua seemed very interested in the proceedings, but not enough to participate; what would she need a rope for? It was quiet for a while, an oddly companionable silence between us while Copper fetched and carried and Kasaqua chased after butterflies.

"Would you like to join me in the dining hall tonight, for dinner?" I asked. "I seldom see you there."

"I dine quite often with Hallmaster Henkjan. Finding an unoccupied table in the dining hall is usually more trouble than it's worth."

"Marta and I command a table of our own by virtue of our sex," I said. "I had luncheon with Sander today, and I plan on inviting him to dine at our table this evening as well. I can see no reason why you shouldn't be invited, too."

He looked at me then like I was a puzzle that needed solving.

"You *are* very intent on having me along on this journey, aren't you?" he asked.

"Is there a reason I shouldn't be?" I asked.

"Do you imagine that your brother and his associates will be impressed that you've befriended the infamous nackie dragoneer of Kuiper's?" he asked, looking down. "Does he have a collection of newspaper clippings about me?"

I couldn't stop myself from tilting my head at the strange turn the conversation had taken. Kasaqua took notice and came bounding over to see what had confused me.

"I wanted to invite you because I thought you'd enjoy it," I said. "I thought that you'd like to meet my brother, and that he'd like to meet you. It can't possibly be interesting or diverting to never leave the school, and I thought that perhaps you'd like to have some social acquaintances outside of it. Please forgive me, Theod, if I've been terribly in error. Where I'm from, it's customary to introduce a new friend to one's family and associates."

Theod looked at me, meeting my gaze for several long moments before looking away again.

"No, please forgive *me*, Miss Anequs," he said. "I seem to have been in error and I believe I've given you insult in the process."

I had the sudden urge to rise and take his face in my hands, to run my thumbs along his cheekbones the way my mother had at the train station, and a thousand other times to let me know that all was forgiven. But that wasn't an Anglish thing to do, and he wouldn't have understood.

"You're not at all what I expected, Miss Anequs," he said after a long moment. "Of someone brought up on the islands, I mean."

"Dare I ask what you expected of someone raised on the islands?" I asked with a chuckle. Theod wasn't laughing.

"I'm afraid that I've been unfair to you," he said, looking over the field.

"Well," I said, bending down to pick up Kasaqua because she'd started pawing at the hem of my skirt, "it's not too late to start being fairer."

FOUR ACQUAINTANCES DINED TOGETHER

The dining hall was already full when I arrived for dinner, and I joined the table Marta had commanded after filling my plate. The offering tonight was bread and cheese, boiled potatoes, and overdone roast beef with pickled cabbage. I was beginning to see an unpleasant pattern in the meal offerings. Thus far there had been nothing even resembling corn cakes or na'samp, or succotash, or squash of any kind. There was a marked lack of fish or poultry, or vegetables other than cabbage, turnips, and beets. It was *September*—we were flush in the season of apples, chicory, cranberries, bitter greens of all sorts, grapes, pumpkins, shell beans, winter squash . . . to say nothing of the foods of the forest. Back home we'd be harvesting white acorns, rosehips, beach plums, sunchokes, mushrooms . . .

I poked at my boiled potatoes with a fork and sighed.

Sander stepped up to the table with a plate and cup of his own; he was once again only eating potatoes, I noticed.

"May I join you?" he said, all in a rush, not particularly looking at either Marta or me.

"Of course, have a seat," I said. Then, turning to Marta, "I do hope you won't mind. I had luncheon with Sander and invited him to join me for dinner."

Marta had a look of blank-faced incomprehension for a bare moment before plastering it over with a lovely smile. She looked around the room, as if to make sure no one was watching.

"Of course that's all right," she said, edging her chair away just a bit, putting herself opposite Sander and me. "How very lovely to know that you're making social connections."

I had the distinct impression that it was *not* all right that I'd invited Sander to share our table without having consulted Marta first, that I'd made some grievous social misstep or something. But I pressed on regardless.

"I also asked Theod to join me; I wanted to discuss the possibility of the four of us traveling together on Saturday. You wanted to show me some shops, didn't you?"

"I hadn't anticipated your inviting others on the outing," she said, her voice careful and precise.

"Is there a reason I shouldn't have?" I asked.

"Well, it is terribly . . . *unusual* for a lady to make invitations of any kind to a gentleman," she said.

Sander took a little book of stamps out of his jacket pocket and slid it across the table to me.

"Thank you, Sander," I said, putting them into my own pocket. Theod walked in, and I waved at him. He nodded smartly and, after filling his plate, joined our table. Marta looked slightly ill at that, redoubling her surveillance of the room.

"I'm going to write a letter to Niquiat after dinner tonight. If we leave the school after breakfast on Saturday, we should be able to get on the train around nine o'clock in the morning and arrive in Vastergot by half past the hour. I'll have to wait for Niquiat's reply to know what time would be best to meet him."

"You intend for your brother to join us as well?" Marta asked, her smile fading to something of a grimace. "This is *dreadfully* unusual, don't you think?"

"I don't understand what's so unusual about it," I said, looking at her directly, challenging her to tell me precisely what I'd done wrong, because she seemed maddeningly determined not to. "Sander expressed an interest in meeting Niquiat when I told him that he's a tinkerer and machinakrafter, and I thought Theod might like to meet him as well because he has few social connections outside the academy."

"I do believe that I'll have to think a bit before committing to join such a large group on an outing into the city. I had presumed that only you and I would be going, and you surely understand that two ladies stepping out together is a quite different thing than ladies stepping out with gentlemen."

"Well, I'm sure the three of us could manage, if you'd prefer not to join us," I said. That was evidently also an incorrect thing to say, because she looked at me as if I'd just viciously cursed her. I waited for her to say something, and when she didn't, I pressed on.

"I also wanted to revisit a small bookstore that my brother introduced me to—"

Sander wrote something on his tablet and slid it across the table to me.

What sort of bookstore is it? it read. *It's not Boekbinder's is it? No one would call that small.*

"It's a secondhand shop," I said, returning the tablet to him. "I never caught the name of it; the proprietress is an old Vaskosish woman. I purchased several books from her a week ago."

"A secondhand shop?" Marta asked, sounding positively alarmed at the prospect.

Sander wrote something very quickly, and slid the tablet to me again.

Do they have serials?

"I don't know, I wasn't looking for them when I was there. We could certainly look into it."

Marta cleared her throat loudly, and I looked up to find both her and Theod staring at Sander and me. Theod looked somewhat interested, Marta positively cross.

"Oh, I'm sorry, have I been rude?" I asked, looking from one to the other. "I'm not sure what the most apt way to include everyone in the conversation would be, since Sander writes rather than speaking. Perhaps we could pass the tablet around? He asked me if they have serials at the bookshop I'd like to go to."

"You read serials?" Marta asked, turning to Sander. "I wasn't aware."

Sander looked down, going slightly pink across the cheeks. He wrote something on the tablet and slid it across the table to Marta.

"Well . . . yes," she said after reading it, looking at Sander, "but I can see now that the situation is . . . something other than what she led me to believe. What serials do you read?"

He wrote something else, and she read it.

"*Berthold Büchner, Boy Adventurer?*" Marta asked, sounding surprised and delighted. "I've read every single one since they started coming out in the *New Linvik Gazette*! Do you read *Sybille Stosch, A Girl's Own Story* as well? I have it from a reliable source that they're actually by the same author writing under two different false names. I don't suppose you would, it's more of a ladies' circulation, but—"

Sander's face lit up with an absolutely huge grin, and he drummed his hands on the edge of the table for a moment before snatching his tablet back and starting to scrawl furiously on it.

"We don't get periodicals on the island," I said quietly, "but we have a wide collection of pennik novels. What do you like to read, when it's not for school, Theod?"

Theod held a stoically neutral expression, looking down at the food on his plate.

"I don't spend much time reading," he said crisply. "It's not something I excel at."

I suddenly remembered Frau Kuiper's first meeting with me on the island, and how she'd presumed that all of us were wholly illiterate. She'd outright said that Theod was when he'd first come to the school. I felt myself flush, feeling as though I'd made an actual social error.

In the sudden brittle silence, Marta said, "While it broadens the mind to experience new things, I do worry what Papa would think if he learned that I'd stepped out on High Street with . . ." She faltered a moment, looking at Sander and Theod and me before continuing, ". . . such a very eclectic group."

"Your father put you before a dragon egg and sent you to an academy," Theod said, something cool and sharp in his voice. "He certainly knows that you're a dragoneer and not a mere society lady."

Marta looked troubled then, glancing down at Magnus lazing by her feet. He in turn looked adoringly up at her, his tail thumping on the floor. Kasaqua took notice of that, and I petted her into stillness. There seemed to be an expectation that dragons, while indoors, should be as quiet and unobtrusive as practically possible. It felt stifling, and I wondered if that was my own estimation or Kasaqua's.

"I suppose there are certain social equities to be considered," she said after a moment. "Very well; we shall all travel together. I think it would be best if we all wore our school uniforms, though, to put forth a united appearance. We might be rather mismatched, otherwise."

"My uniform is the smartest thing I've got to wear, by Anglish standards of dress," I said.

"I don't own any other clothing at all," Theod said.

"I will confess to rather suspecting as much," Marta said, offering a thin smile, "which is why Sander and I ought to dress in our uniforms in solidarity."

I glanced at Theod, who glanced back at me with a look that said, "You invited this."

The rest of dinner proceeded in relative peace; we talked about our class schedules. Marta and Theod and I all had anglereckoning together. Marta and Theod also shared natural philosophy with Sander, and Sander and I were in skiltakraft and dragon husbandry together.

We remained at the table until the clock chimed to announce that the dinner hour had ended, and proceeded outside to see to the feeding of our dragons.

ANEQUS WAS INFORMED OF SOCIAL CUSTOM

Marta confronted me as soon as we returned to the privacy of our shared room—which I'd rather expected, because while she presented a serene and congenial figure, Magnus seemed terribly fitful and anxious. Once I'd closed the door, she turned on her heel to face me, demanding, "What can you possibly have been thinking, inviting Sander and Theod to join us? Do you have any idea what kind of gossip could arise from us being seen stepping out with—"

"Our classmates?" I interrupted.

"With young men of the wrong sort!" Marta said, glaring at me. "Being in the company of young men without a proper chaperone . . . It has certain social implications! You've put me into a terrible position, I'll have you know. It's one thing for a young woman to oblige herself in the instruction and presentation of a social inferior, but quite another for her to appear in public with young men! I understand that you come from quite base means, and that your people have no society to speak of, but now that you've been elevated—"

"I assure you, Marta, that I don't consider being expected to perform to Anglish standards as any sort of elevation," I said, trying to keep my voice even. I was thoroughly tired of the way everyone, Marta included, seemed to presume that I was an ignorant savage in need of civilizing. "I wouldn't have come here if I didn't have to, but skiltakraft is something I need to learn—not just because licensure requires it, but because Kasaqua's breath has such potential for danger and destruction unless it's shaped. I'm not here for any other reason."

"Do you intend to simply go back to your island, then, once you've completed your education?" Marta asked, looking faintly shocked. As if home wasn't someplace I'd want to be.

"Of course," I said, wondering how such a thing could ever have been in doubt.

"But you have the opportunity to become so much more than just . . . well. Dragoneers hold a particular place in society, and having been chosen by a dragon offers you an opportunity to claim a place among dragoneers. You could increase your station in life if you'd just—"

"I am not at all discontent with 'my station in life' as you put it, and I have no desire whatsoever to become a member of Anglish society," I said. "And if you think so highly of all that nonsense, why did you even become a dragoneer?"

She looked stricken suddenly, and Magnus came to her side, whining softly. She ran her hand over his mane of quills, looking thoughtful.

"When I was a little girl, my mother read me *Fyra's Leid* and *The Tales of Vasilisa*, and I followed all the newspaper and magazine articles about Frau Kuiper's career. My mother's father was a dragoneer. I just . . . Society is going to make its judgments. It's so rare for a woman to become a dragoneer, and the rules for being a dragoneer and a lady at once aren't terribly clear. It's so much safer, socially, to err on the side of correct comportment for a lady of my class—but none of the books of proper behavior have anything to say about a young woman who attends school alongside young men. All that's expected of girls of good breeding is that they marry well, but I've seen how small a woman's world can become, once she marries. Everything is luncheon and tea and dinner parties, moving from one function to another, keeping apprised of the social season and the actions of one's peers. Being a dragoneer . . . Well, it's a *different* sort of way to be, if you understand my meaning. It opens a different branch of society. Also, this is dreadfully romantic, but I've always wanted a love match and, well . . . who would marry a female dragoneer except for love? As a dragoneer, it could even be my prerogative to never marry at all and to pursue a career instead. I don't think Papa would naysay me if I wanted to go into formal racing."

"So you don't really want to be a society lady?" I asked, moving to sit in one of the leather chairs. Kasaqua bounded up into my lap, demanding petting.

Marta sat down opposite me, still looking very troubled.

"The other day, with Dagny Sørensen . . . I know she doesn't really consider me worthy of her social circle, which isn't at all fair because our fathers are of similar means. We went to the same primary school! She's not better than I am, she's just more well connected, owing to her mother's society."

"Why does that matter, though?" I asked. "Why do you even *want* to be included in her social circle?"

"Because it's what every young woman of sufficient means in the city wants, of course! She's the arbiter of who is and is not part of polite society," Marta said. "The prospect of being cut from social gatherings, not being invited to events where one might engage in social congress with one's equals—"

"All this nonsense about social rank," I said, snorting. "It can't possibly matter as much as you think it does. Is Dagny Sørensen your friend, Marta? Would you ever play games or do chores with her, or just sit and talk about this and that?"

"Well, no, that's not the kind of—"

"You've said that Lisbet Jansen is your friend. What does that *mean*, for an Anglish person?"

"We played together as children, attended primary school together. We've shared all our wishes and secrets with each other and we can have frank conversations and discussions with each other. I know that Lisbet would defend me against anyone giving me insult, and she knows I'd do the same for her."

"You wouldn't, however, defend me against those who give me insult. So we're not friends."

"Well . . . no, I suppose we're not," Marta faltered. She had that same big-eyed look of hurt that she'd had at our luncheon meeting.

"In my estimation, Marta, you have not been *at all* friendly to me. You behave as if I'm your obvious social inferior, and you have from the moment we met."

There was something of horror in her eyes when I said that, as if I'd uncovered some terrible secret of hers, but then her face drew up in anger and she said, "It's . . . it's the obligation of people of means and good breeding to endeavor to elevate the people around them, and not to draw attention to their personal shortfalls. You come from a place of poverty—"

"What makes you think that?" I asked.

"Well . . . your mode of dress and speech, your general demeanor—you are positively *vulgar*, Anequs, and you don't appear to have any sense of the appropriate deference and gratitude toward the people who have extended themselves in helping you to better yourself."

"I don't believe that any of the changes that you or others seem to expect of me would be improvements," I said. "I don't think that there's anything wrong with the way that I dress, or speak, or behave. My clothes are clean, and in good repair. I can make myself understood. I am honest, and I endeavor to be kind. I don't speak ill of others regarding things beyond their control, and I don't speak against anyone who hasn't given personal insult to me or my loved ones. I wouldn't consider a person to be my social inferior simply for being *poor*."

The anger in her face faded, and the horror intensified.

"Anequs, I had no idea that you felt—"

"You might've, if you'd asked," I said.

I rose from my seat and crossed the room to my nightstand, retrieving the copy of *Sævinsdottir's Guide to Social Grace and Perfect Comportment* and also my copy of *Principles of Natural Philosophy*. I returned and handed the former to her.

"Thank you for lending me this book, but you may have it back. I don't want it."

She stared up at me with a kind of dismay. Magnus rose to his feet, extended his quills, and actually *chuffed* at me. He'd apparently identified me as the cause of Marta's deep discomfort. Kasaqua reacted, from her perch on the back of the chair, by putting her head down to threaten him with nonexistent antlers.

"I've clearly become too emotional about all of this, and it's upset Magnus," Marta said, closing her eyes and taking a slow breath. "It wouldn't do for him to become keyed up to the point of discharging a breath."

"Is that something that happens often?" I asked, standing to gather Kasaqua in my arms, putting a distance of several steps between her and Magnus. "Kasaqua's done it once, back on Masquapaug."

"That's less shocking than it ought to be, given how forward you are," Marta said, her tone positively *poisonous*. "It is the first and most important duty of any dragoneer to moderate the basest instincts of their dragon. A dragon whose dragoneer cannot control their emotions—who cannot *will* their dragon to contain its breath and discharge it only when instructed—is no better than a feral. A dragon's breath increases in power as it matures. Imagine the rampant destruction that would result from dragons discharging their breath whenever they felt remotely inclined."

"I suppose that would depend largely on what caused them to be so inclined," I said.

"If you cannot control your dragon, she will be destroyed for the common good," Marta said.

"Magnus chuffed at me just now," I said. "And Kasaqua reacted to him, not to you."

Marta stared at me in icy silence for a moment, and I knew that I'd touched upon the reality of things. She wasn't afraid that Kasaqua might loose a breath because *I* was overemotional; she was afraid that Magnus might loose a breath because *she* was.

"I'm going to spend the remainder of the evening reading on the subject of natural philosophy, because that's the class I have in the morning," I said. "If you'd like to talk about that, or about any scholarly subject, I'm willing to. But I really have no interest in pursuing further discussion about the rules of Anglish society and my indifference toward them."

"I am going to take an evening constitutional around the school grounds with Magnus."

"That's probably a good idea," I said. "Have a good walk."

And with that, Marta rose and left, Magnus glaring back over his shoulder at Kasaqua and me from his place at her heel. Kasaqua made a little hissing noise in his direction.

I sat down and began to read, and Kasaqua made herself comfortable again on the back of the chair. After a time, she started making little purring noises of contentment, and I felt myself relax at last.

ANEQUS LEARNED THE PRINCIPLES
OF NATURAL PHILOSOPHY

On Wednesday morning, I attended my first natural philosophy class with Professor Ulfar. I was the first student to arrive, so I chose a seat at one of the two tables nearest the front of the room with an excellent view of the chalkboard. In front of each seat there was a small paper carton with DO NOT OPEN UNTIL INSTRUCTED printed on top. Each carton was accompanied by a small notebook and a pencil.

When free seats at other tables were filled, one of my classmates actually took an empty chair from my table—and the attendant carton and notebook—and brought it to one of the others rather than join me. A second followed his example. When everyone was seated, there were twenty-six students in the class including me.

Professor Ulfar entered the room at one minute past the hour, coming not from the doorway that the rest of us had entered through, but from another at the far end of the room that I hadn't noticed because it was partly obscured by the chalkboard. His mechanical chair made a rhythmic sound as it moved, the feet clicking sharply against the floor tiles. Many of my classmates looked plainly shocked at his appearance, as if they'd never seen him and his chair before this moment. He observed the room, obviously making note of the fact that I was seated at a table by myself.

"Good morning, class!" he said jovially, piloting his chair to stand at the apex of the arc that the tables formed. "I'd like to welcome all of you to first-year instruction in natural philosophy. The first thing I wish to impress upon you is that natural philosophy is *not* a collection of knowledge. Most of you will have come from quite prestigious primary schools—Schmidt, Thengilsson, places like that—where you will have become knowledgeable in the subjects of wordlore, scoring, erelore, folklore, and possibly Tysklandish. In that sort of subject, there's exactly one correct answer to every question, and your place as a student is to be an empty vessel that the professor fills with knowledge. Natural philosophy is not at all that sort of subject. It is a *process* for seeking truth, and relies on the asking of questions and the gathering and weighing of evidence to reach a conclusion. My goal, in this first year of instruction, is to put all of you into the philosophic mindset—to encourage you to ask the right sorts of questions. The second thing I wish to impress upon you is that this class is not competitive, but collaborative. In primary school, I presume that most of you will have been taught that sharing your work and gaining insight from others' answers is cheating. That is not the case in natural philosophy. You will rise or fall together, so it is the responsibility of those who have particular cleverness or insight to make yourself understood by your peers. Natural philosophy is the best understanding of the natural world achieved by all of humankind; when one natural philosopher makes an astounding observation, every natural philosopher benefits. I am thus not the only professor in this room, because I am absolutely certain that each and every one of you knows something, right now, that I don't know. Now, who among you thinks they've got the best penmanship?"

The students looked at one another in confusion before several young men timidly raised their hands. I did not, because I knew that while my handwriting was serviceable, it was not particularly skillful and certainly not the best of this group.

"Right then, everyone who's volunteered, proceed to the chalkboard and write 'My penmanship is excellent,' followed by your full name—this will form our body of evidence."

The young men who'd volunteered did as they were instructed and returned to their desks.

"Now, there are many variables upon which we could judge this body of evidence, ways of sorting. This is because I did not define, before we began, what 'best' meant in relation to this vermutun. Are we collectively judging which example is most beautiful? Most immediately legible? Which was produced the most quickly? It is important, when designing a vermutun, to carefully define all of your terms—what you are measuring, and why—and to single out the variable that you're measuring as much as possible. Now, because I have many years of experience weighing all of the relevant variables, I hope that you will trust my judgment when I declare that, from this body of evidence, Mr. Johansson is the most suitable for the job of writing our collective observations. If you wish to challenge me on this, you are very welcome to, and we will discuss the differences in our observations until we arrive at the truth. Does anyone wish to challenge the best suitability of Mr. Johansson's penmanship?"

This time, no one raised their hand.

"Now, you will notice that in front of each of you there is a small carton. Your collective task today will be to correctly identify every object within every carton in this room. Your source of knowledge will be, exclusively, one another. I will not be answering any questions concerning these objects, as I am a biased source—I put them into the boxes. You must consult your fellow students, and about each object be able to answer the following questions: What is it, what is its typical use, and, importantly, *how do you know*? Further information is always helpful in forming a body of evidence, so other questions to consider: Where might this object have come from, how is it produced and by whom, what has been the use of this object in eretide, what activities are made possible by the existence of the object? I also encourage you to ask questions that I haven't considered! On the first page of your workbook, you will find a complete list of students in this class. I expect every one of you to gain at least a cursory answer about your object from every other classmate, and to note that answer beside their name. Let me be absolutely clear; it is perfectly acceptable to say 'I don't know' regarding any or all of these objects. Admitting ignorance is always preferable to making uneducated guesses—assumptions and baseless assertions are the enemy of natural philosophy. Now, open your cartons and inspect the object inside. You may move freely through the room, seeking observations from each of your classmates."

I opened the carton in front of me and found a small wooden tool; it was forked, with a hole bored through it at the base of the fork. I had no idea what use it might be put to. I stood and proceeded to the table nearest to me, where five young men were sitting, pondering their own objects. They fell silent as I joined them, looking at me uncomfortably.

"I don't know what this is," I said, putting it down on the table in front of me. "I observe that it's made of wood, and is very likely some kind of tool. I come to the latter conclusion because I've worked with wooden tools before."

"That's a lucet," one of the young men seated at the table said. "It's for weaving cords. My governess used to weave lucet while reciting lessons to us."

"Thank you," I said. "What's your name, so I can write that observation beside it in my book?"

"Oh, sorry, I'm Kaspar Overgaard. Your name is Aponakwes-dottir, isn't it?"

"My name is Anequs," I said. "Would you and your fellows like to exchange observations about the things in your cartons?"

"Well, between us we've got a buttonhook, a Kindah coin, a blown-out egg, some kind of measuring tool with a little vial of liquid embedded in it, and a handful of some sort of seeds or grains."

"That's samp corn," I said, looking at the little pile of grain. "Corn that's been soaked in lye water so it sheds its skin. This has been dried again for storing—you make na'samp porridge out of it, or grind it to make flour for corn cakes."

"All right, but how do you know?" one of the other boys asked.

"Because back home I ate it for breakfast practically every morning," I said.

I wrote down the observations that each of the five young men at that table had about each of the objects, and they wrote down mine, and then we parted company and moved to other tables. By the end of class, I'd learned that the measuring stick with the vial of liquid was a carpenter's level. Many of the items seemed to have been specially selected to be unfamiliar to all but a few people in the class. I was the only person in class able to identify a quahog shell and the samp corn. Toward the end of class, Professor Ulfar had us compare our findings and had Mr. Johansson write the agreed-upon facts on the chalkboard. We were instructed to put our objects back into their cartons, and to bring our workbooks to Professor Ulfar's desk before class was dismissed.

I'd spoken more to my classmates, and they to me, than I had in the last few days combined, and it was certainly the most congenial that any of them had been to me. Still, at lunch, I found myself sitting with Marta and Sander and Theod again.

SHE LEARNED ABOUT THE KEEPING OF DRAGONS

Anglereckoning was simple enough, once I understood the principles of it, and between my textbook and the books I'd gotten in Vastergot, I managed it without much trouble. Thursday was a repetition of Tuesday: skiltakraft and erelore.

On Friday morning, after breakfast, I went to learn what dragon husbandry entailed.

The sun had only just gotten high enough to shine onto the field behind the dragonhall, and the grass was still sodden with morning dew, necessitating that I lift my skirt to avoid soaking its hem. I made a mental note to wear my uniform trousers to this class in the future, because they could be tucked neatly into my boots.

There were no desks, only wooden folding chairs arranged in a single long line against the wall of the dragonhall. I saw that each unoccupied chair had a card sitting on it, and as I got closer I saw that the cards were printed with the students' names. At the end of the line of chairs, a table had been erected and brown paper cartons of various sizes were neatly stacked on it.

I found the chair with the "Aponakwesdottir, Anequs" card, neatly situated between Frederik Anderssen and Edvin Bjorn. Neither of them was present yet when I sat.

It was something like fifteen minutes before everyone had arrived, coming in pairs or trios, talking and chatting. Sander came alone, as I had, and waved a hand at me as he passed on the way to his seat. The class seemed to consist of all twenty-eight first-year students, each accompanied by a young dragon. Most of the dragons were walking at heel, but a half dozen young men had their dragons collared and leashed, being dragged by overeager creatures or pulling recalcitrant ones after them. I couldn't fathom how they would need such things, or how the dragons could be made to tolerate them, if they shared the same connection with their dragons that I shared with Kasaqua.

Professor Mesman arrived at five minutes past the hour, leading his butterfly-winged dragon by a brass ring worked into the harness at the dragon's shoulder. Many of the little dragons seemed very excited at the sight of him and wanted to prance over and acquaint themselves, needing to be restrained by their respective dragoneers. Kasaqua, in my lap, required no further instruction than my hand on her flank to still her. I ran my hand through her crest of feathers, which had finally shed their pin-quills and now had much the texture of rooster hackles. They were a ruddy shade of brown that reflected scarlet in the sunlight. Most of the other young dragons on the field were too large already to sit on their companions' laps. Kasaqua wasn't going to be small enough to sit on my lap for much longer, either, at the rate she was growing.

"For those who have not been formally introduced to me, I am Professor Mesman, and this is Kostbar," the professor said crisply, catching my attention back. "Each of you, for better or worse, has already become a dragoneer by the simple fortune of having been chosen by a young dragon upon its hatching. Your bond is unshakable, severable only by death. It is my aim to be entirely certain that you will be competent in the basic care and handling of your charges—that you will be worthy of the bond you have formed."

He took a little brass whistle out of his pocket, the same sort that I'd seen Theod use, and blew three sharp notes on it. Kostbar walked a dozen paces away from him and stood in the center of the field, head up, tail held straight behind him, and wings half-folded. Professor Mesman watched and nodded with satisfaction, folding his hands behind his back and walking backward and forward in front of the row of chairs as he spoke. Kostbar remained completely still.

"The early training of dragons is critical to their happiness and comfort for the rest of their lives. In the natural course of events, your dragon will be your closest companion and confidant every day of your life. He or she will look to you for guidance, reassurance, and comfort. You must be a firm leader and judicious guide, commanding your dragon to obedience. A poorly trained dragon is little better than a feral one, and is a menace to all who encounter it."

He blew the whistle again, different notes this time, and Kostbar sat down and folded his wings, looking at Professor Mesman attentively.

"In this course of instruction, your dragon will learn how to sit and walk at heel—which comes naturally to most hatchlings. It will learn to sit or stand and stay when it is told to. It will learn to come when called. It will learn to retrieve objects, and release them on command. It will learn to stand and present itself for tacking, and to wear its tack without complaint. As your dragons are rapidly growing, you can expect them to move through standard sizes of tack quickly—a hatchling that can wear a set of 00 tack in September is often wearing size 10 or 12 by June. Knowing what an appropriate fit looks like on your dragon is an important aspect of this class. When your dragons reach their adult size and conformation, you will be expected to have them fitted for tailored tack."

He blew the whistle again, and Kostbar lay down, placing his head on his foreclaws. His tail thumped once on the ground, but he was otherwise perfectly still.

"When I call your name, you will rise and receive your dragon's tack, your command whistle, and your textbook. Then you will return to your seat," Professor Mesman said, walking over to the table where all the cartons were stacked and waiting.

When my name was called, I rose and walked past the line of young men.

One of them, I didn't see who, tripped me.

It happened quickly, a sudden tug on the hem of my skirt and a misstep and suddenly I was on my knees and the heels of my hands in the wet grass, Kasaqua making a chattering cry of alarm. Everyone was laughing.

Sander was at my side half a moment later, offering a hand to help me up. His hand was trembling when I took it. When I stood, Professor Mesman was staring at me, his eyes hard and his mouth a thin line.

"I trust that you are quite all right, Miss Aponakwesdottir?"

I felt prickly hot anger on the back of my neck, and scanned the line of boys, trying to determine who had done it. I didn't think at all when I answered, "My name is not Miss Aponakwesdottir. It's Anequs."

The laughter slowly stopped.

"You will come and take your dragon's tack and your command whistle, and you will return to your seat," Professor Mesman said, staring at me with hard, unblinking eyes. "I trust that you'll be more careful of your footing in the future. A training field is no place for a skirt. Mr. Jansen, you will return to your seat until you are called. Your assistance is appreciated and noted."

I marched the rest of the way to the table, shoulders back and chin high, holding the hem of my skirt up off the grass. I took the parcel and book and returned to my seat, keeping a close eye on the feet of the boys that I passed, daring any of them to try it again.

When I sat down, Professor Mesman called Edvin Bjorn. I smoothed my skirt and waited. When everyone had collected their equipment, Professor Mesman resumed his lecture.

"In this term you, as dragoneers, have as much to learn as do your dragons. You will learn about the anatomy and habits of dragons, to help you best understand how to care for and keep your charges. At the moment, all of your dragons are under one year of age, and still quite small in comparison to their eventual size. Contrary to the opinions of those dragoneers bonded to kesseldraches and silberdraches, the power of a dragon's breath does *not* precisely correlate to size—rather, it is the maturity of a dragon that determines its power. It is the wit, will, and skill of the dragon's rider that determine the ultimate efficacy of its breath.

"This course does not focus on the use and shaping of a dragon's breath—that's what you're taking skiltakraft for—but your control of your dragon's breath is critically important to safe husbandry. You will have already become aware, I'm sure, that your dragon's emotions can impact your own, and that the opposite is also true. As a dragoneer, it is of paramount importance that you temper your emotions. If you allow yourself to become excessively emotional, your dragon may be moved to act by discharging its breath at whatever it perceives as the cause of your discomfort. It is almost certain that your dragon will discharge its breath unexpectedly at some point during its first year of life—young dragons are often quite unaware of the power they possess until they use it, especially if they've been hatched into a household that does not host an older dragon. Those of you who descend from dragoneering families have a distinct advantage over your peers in having been regularly exposed to dragons prior to bonding and in having exposed your hatchling to an older dragon that it may model its behavior from. That said, feral dragons *are* typically solitary creatures—natural philosophers have reported that it is as common for a bitch dragon to abandon her eggs to their own devices as it is for her to build a den and nurture her offspring. Even when the latter occurs, she will typically drive the youngster from her territory soon after it becomes capable of flight. The most common cause of death among feral dragons is observed to be competition from other dragons. If you're especially interested in the behavior of feral dragons, I'd suggest asking Professor Ulfar for further information.

"Now, those of you bonded to bjalladreki and other midsize breeds will find that your dragons attain their adult conformation between one and two years of age, where those of you bonded to kesseldraches and other large breeds will be waiting between two and three years for your dragons to take flight. In either case, the proportions of the wings will first reach their adult conformation, and shortly thereafter the dragon will begin producing and storing buoyant athers in the air sacks that branch from the lungs. A dragon's first flight naturally follows very quickly, so it is imperative to you as dragoneers that your dragons be willing and able to take tack when it does. When your dragons are of appropriate size, you will be taught to ride them over ground. A dragon must become accustomed to the feeling of tack as a natural part of their being. A dragon that is not accustomed to carrying a rider, or one that has learned to fly without wearing tack, will be unrideable forever after, no matter how patient and persistent its bonded dragoneer might be."

A young man in the first row raised his hand, and Professor Mesman nodded to him.

"How soon is too soon to start acclimatizing our dragons to carrying weight by packing things into their tack satchels? My father asked me why I haven't been packing my dragon's tack, because he did for his dragon when he was my dragon's age, and they're the same breed."

"It is injudicious to burden a dragon that hasn't attained its adult conformation, because such actions can derange their final growth. During the war, it became common practice to burden certain breeds of dragon early in life with the express intent of causing their leg and wing bones to elongate and strengthen. This has proven, with time, to have been unwise. Many of the beasts thusly burdened now suffer from derangements of the shoulders and wing joints. It is best practice to begin testing your dragon's carrying capacity only after it has had its first natural flight. Until then, any satchels affixed to its tack should be used only to carry lightweight necessities.

"Now, as I was about to continue—our knowledge of the anatomy of dragons comes to us principally from the works of Thyskallian scholar Reinhold Schopenhauer and his great work *Drachenkunst*, in which he painstakingly illustrated his comprehensive dissections of several breeds of dragon. Dragons are a distinct class of life, with no close relations other than the Kindah griffin and the Aprikish hwedo. They are possessed of a series of organs beneath the lungs that are still not fully understood, but it is there that a dragon's breath is generated."

I felt a kind of dull horror at the idea of dragons being dissected; it seemed horribly disrespectful, like the idea of dissecting *people*. Kasaqua sensed my discomfort and made a quiet crooning noise.

"The bones of dragons, like the bones of birds, are hollow but immensely strong. You will probably have noted already how light your dragons are in comparison to other animals of a similar size. This is due in part to their hollow bones, and part due to their production of athers. A dragon, at the age of its first flight, weighs as much upon a scale as it ever will—though most dragons double in size between their second and third years of life. The additional weight of their growth is offset by buoyant athers held within the body. It is imperative that a dragon going into battle be well armored across the chest and belly, because any sufficiently deep wound may puncture one of the organs of transmutation. A dragon with such an injury will fall instantly from the sky. Dragonhide is naturally very resistant to piercing, but a bullet from close range can have devastating effects. Of course, gods willing, most of you will never be called to ride your dragons into battle."

"But isn't there a great call for dragoneers in Runestung Hold, putting down nackie rebellions there?" someone asked. I didn't see who, though I'd have very much liked to.

"I've heard the nackies out there have got dragons of their own, and unknown skiltakraft techniques," someone else added.

"Whether or not you choose to join the dragonthede in this hold or any other is a matter to be discussed with your families. Some breeds are, naturally, more desired by the dragonthede than others. Participation in the dragonthede shall remain voluntary unless King Yngvarr chooses to rally a general army, which does not seem especially likely at this time."

"Is it true that nackie dragons eat people?" someone asked.

Professor Mesman sighed through his nose and replied, "Dragons are uncommonly capable of gaining sustenance from almost any natural matter. Though they generally prefer flesh when it is available to them, they will sustain themselves with plant matter—even wood—and with soft minerals such as coal. They are able to do this because of their unique capacity to transmute all materials into their component athers. During the war, when supply lines were pressed, it was not uncommon for dragons to be fed exclusively the blood, bones, and offal of lame horses mixed with sawdust or hay. A dragon will naturally balk at such an offering unless it is very hungry, but an obedient and well-trained dragon will eat what it is commanded to eat by its dragoneer. It is widely frowned upon to allow dragons to consume corpses, even those of your enemies, but there are times when a desperate dragon or one in a blood rage cannot be prevented from such actions."

"But I heard that the nackies *commonly* feed people to their dragons—"

"Such discussions are beyond the scope of this class," Professor Mesman said sharply. "In fact, I believe our allotted time has come to an end. I expect you all to read the first two chapters of your assigned texts and come to class next week prepared to be tested upon the basic anatomy of dragons. You are dismissed."

It did not escape my notice, as my classmates filed past, that many of them looked back to stare speculatively at Kasaqua and me.

AND ABOUT THE PEOPLE WHO KEPT THEM

I joined Sander for luncheon, as Marta was not in evidence when the two of us arrived from class. He informed me that the young man who'd tripped me was Kole Adilsson, and that he was a beast. There wasn't much to be done about it, so we turned our conversation to the subject of dragon husbandry. When I was finished with luncheon I returned to my room to read. Marta wasn't there, either.

I went to the library and had my folklore study with Professor Ibarra, then stayed in the library until Kasaqua grew restless. I took her out to the field to stretch her legs and hunt crickets. There were other students there, traveling in couples and groups, but none of them paid me any mind. I returned to the dining hall for the dinner hour, and found that there was a line at the communal serving table. Marta was already seated and eating . . . opposite Niklas Sørensen. I would apparently have to find somewhere else to sit this evening, because I did not at all desire another audience with Niklas. I looked around for Sander or Theod, but neither of them seemed to be present. I sighed through my nose and resigned myself to eating alone, and as quickly as possible.

I got in line to get my food. Shortly thereafter, Ivar Stafn stepped into line behind me. His dragon wasn't with him; he was of sufficient size as to be housed in the dragonhall at all times.

"Good evening, Miss Aponakwesdottir," Ivar said, an oily quality in his voice. "It's good to see you looking so well. I've been meaning to have a talk with you, but the opportunity hasn't yet arisen. You aren't in any of my classes."

"I don't think you and I have anything to talk to each other about, Mr. Stafn," I said, not looking at him.

"Oh, but I think we do," he replied, managing to sound both jovial and slightly menacing. "I have many philosophical questions concerning your people, you see. How old are you, precisely? You seem rather young to have been put before a dragon egg. In Norslandish tradition, it isn't permissible to place a dragon egg before a child."

"I'm fifteen," I said. "I haven't been a child for two years now."

"Now *that's* terribly interesting! You were regarded, at thirteen years of age, as a woman? Among civilized races, adulthood is generally marked between sixteen and twenty years of age. Sixteen is the age of majority under the law in Lindmarden, though one must be twenty to own land or participate in governance. At what age do your people typically marry?"

"When my people marry is none of your concern," I said, setting my teeth. "I have no particular desire to speak with you, Mr. Stafn. Please leave me alone."

"Come now, I'm only exercising a natural curiosity into the roots of folkreckoning," he said. "The study of primitive peoples and comparisons between savage races and civilized ones are critical to an understanding of human nature. Now, it's been my understanding from my studies that your race, and savage races in general, come to bearing age much sooner than those of Norslandish stock—and your assertion that you were considered a woman at thirteen years of age would seem to support that. Regarding marriage—"

"I don't know enough about Anglish marriage customs to speak on such matters," I said, cutting him off. "Leave me alone."

"Is it true that it is wholly common for women of your race to engage in carnal congress outside of marriage, and to bear children outside of marriage as well? Is a 'woman' of thirteen considered old enough to engage in such congress, with or without being married?"

I didn't properly mean to do what I did then; it was as if my body moved under its own power. My face felt afire, and I was quite breathless. I turned and slapped Ivar Stafn so hard that his head snapped to the side. In the silence that followed I felt a mounting horror at what I'd done. Everyone else who'd been in line and at nearby tables was staring at us. There was a red mark rising on Ivar's cheek and jaw as he turned back toward me with utter disbelief and rage twisting his face.

"You little *bitch*!" he hissed, raising his hand. I scrambled backward, putting a table between myself and him. Kasaqua leaped onto the table, fluffing all of her feathers to their fullest and spreading her wings, hissing at him with bared teeth. She took a deep breath in, and I felt a kind of brimming sensation under my breastbone, like she was preparing to loose a breath at Ivar. I looked at her and focused all of my will in communicating that *she must not do that.*

"What in Fyra's name is going on here?" someone thundered from the doorway. I turned to see Frau Kuiper standing there, her right hand pulled up to her hip, as if she were reaching for a pistol.

"You can't have missed seeing it," Ivar said hotly, raising his fingers to his scarlet cheek. "This feral little savage *struck me* for no reason at all! I've got a dozen witnesses here in line!"

"Mr. Stafn, Miss Aponakwesdottir, you will both come with me immediately."

I took a deep breath and walked with as much poise as I could muster toward the doorway. Kasaqua followed me, keeping her gaze on Ivar, her tail lashing like an angry cat's. I glanced back over my shoulder to see Marta. She was staring at me, pink-faced, her eyes wide with horror.

I turned away from her, and followed Frau Kuiper.

AND OF AN UNEXPECTED TASK

I had Kasaqua in my lap as I sat with Frau Kuiper's cold, appraising gaze on me, and I tried to calm her—and myself—by running my fingers through her mane of feathers. Ivar was seated beside me, and Kasaqua was glaring at him. She wanted to *bite* him—to grab his hand and shake it like she would a squirrel.

"I was simply trying to make conversation on the topic of natural philosophy and comparative folklore and folkreckoning, and she *struck* me. You can ask anyone who was in the line with us and they'll tell you," Ivar said, turning his head this way and that. "I do believe that she's deranged something in my neck. I may have to see a doctor."

"What do you have to say for yourself about this behavior, Miss Aponakwesdottir?" Frau Kuiper asked.

"That isn't my name," I said tightly. "My name is Anequs, and I'm not going to answer to that surname you've assigned to me. He was asking the most absolutely inappropriate questions of me, ma'am, after I'd asked him several times to leave me alone. He asked my age, and what age women of my race typically marry, and that he'd heard we 'come to bearing age' earlier than Norsfolk. Then he asked about carnal congress. That's when I slapped him."

"Mr. Stafn!" Frau Kuiper said, her gaze flying to Ivar and her mouth hardening into an appalled frown. "A gentleman of character would not ask such things of a lady under any circumstances."

"I was trying to start a conversation about the natural philosophy of eugenics!"

"You weren't," I pressed, staring at him.

"Miss Anequs, a lady of character does not lose her temper," Frau Kuiper said warningly.

"I suppose that I'm not a lady of character then, am I?" I said, glaring at her.

"You see, Frau Kuiper? This kind of savage can't be *tamed*! It's the nature of the nackie species to be inclined to rage and violence. They have no innate desire to be civilized. It's remarkable that something like this hasn't previously happened with Knecht, though I suppose such tendencies might have been trained out of him at a young age. This one was obviously allowed to develop in its natural state for far too long."

"Your words are unbecoming of a gentleman, Mr. Stafn," Frau Kuiper said.

"She *struck* me," Ivar replied stubbornly.

"A man who gives egregious offense to a lady should expect to be slapped, Mr. Stafn."

"She's not a *lady*, ma'am," he said with a scoff. "She's a subject of interest to folkreckoning and kinlore. I understand why you've allowed her and Knecht to play at being students here; Joden knows it's netted you the adulation of the Freemensthede. But there's no point in pretending that a wild savage is equal to a Norswoman and deserving of the same decorum."

"In my academy, Mr. Stafn, you will treat *all* women with equal respect. If you are quite unable to do this, arrangements for your departure from this institution can be made."

"My father, the thane of Vastergot—"

"Has no sway here. This is what is going to happen. You, Mr. Stafn, will proceed to the library. You will write an essay on the subject of appropriate conduct and polite conversation, with particular emphasis on the correct behavior of a gentleman in the company of a lady. The essay will be no less than three pages long, and if I am unsatisfied with the product of your efforts, you will repeat the exercise. You are confined to school grounds for the weekend. Now get out of my sight. Miss Anequs and I have much to discuss."

Ivar stalked out, and the door closed behind him with a deafening click. I remained where I was sitting, alone with Frau Kuiper in her office. On my lap, Kasaqua made an anxious little noise at the back of her throat. Frau Kuiper laced her fingers together, staring at me. I could hear the mechanical workings of the pendulum clock in the corner, and Frau Kuiper breathing wearily through her nose.

"Violent outbursts cannot be tolerated, Miss Anequs," she said after a long pause. "Ivar Stafn may indeed be provocative and objectionable, but we do not answer insult with violence—or in any other way. It is our station as ladies to rise above it."

"I didn't come here to be tormented," I said firmly. Frau Kuiper sighed and rose from her desk, crossing the room to gaze out the window, hands folded behind her back.

"Do you know what Captain Einarsson's recommendation to the ministry was, when he was first made aware of your existence?"

"I'm sure that you're about to tell me," I said. She turned her head to favor me with a withering glare. I held her gaze evenly.

"He recommended that your dragon be put to death, and that if your people offered resistance that the resistance should be put down in much the same manner as the Nack Island uprising."

I sucked a harsh breath through my teeth. I might have been

more shocked if I hadn't already learned that the Anglish made
casual practice of slaughtering dragons that they found inconve-
nient, but it was the idea that the violence visited on Naquipaug
could be visited upon Masquapaug because of Kasaqua that made
me feel suddenly cold. She studied my face for a moment and
turned back to the window.

"I'm sure that someone has, by now, told you of my service in
the dragonthede. I was the first woman to be allowed to serve. I
assure you that my fellow soldiers offered me far greater insult and
pain than a few crass words. I persisted with a smile and sharp-
ened my wits. I became the precedent that has allowed young
women to become dragoneers in Lindmarden."

She turned from the window, looking at me very hard when
she said, "You and Theod must be the precedent for your people.
The Eiriksthede and the Ravens of Joden are more than ready to
declare you all as unmanageable as your distant cousins on the
western frontier. It is my aim to prove that your people can be
successfully integrated into a civilized society. You will do yourself no favors by defying those efforts, Anequs. People like Ivar
Stafn want nothing more than to see the worst in you, and behavior like this confirms all of their basest suppositions."

"I didn't ask to be a precedent. I never wanted to leave Masquapaug. If we had anyone there who could teach me, I'd still be
there. But our dragons died two hundred years ago, and their
dragoneers with them, and the knowledge was lost. I'm here to
help my people, Frau Kuiper. I'm not here to make them more
like yours."

Frau Kuiper shook her head, closing her eyes and sighing wearily.

"You must prove yourself equal to the other students of this
establishment if you wish to be regarded by them as an equal. In
fact, you will have to prove yourself superior in all the ways they
expect you to be inferior, just to be regarded as equal. To some,
you will always be found wanting. But there are people here who

are willing to give you the benefit of the doubt. Don't ruin it for yourself by rash behavior and stubbornness. You are a representative of your people here, whether you want to be or not. Mr. Knecht has long since come to understand that, and he holds the office admirably. You would do well to consult with him."

"Do you need me to write an essay on appropriate behavior, ma'am?" I asked, holding her gaze. "Marta lent me a very instructive book about perfect comportment."

"That won't be necessary," she said. "I doubt very much that an essay would help you."

"Am I confined to school grounds for the weekend? Because if that's the case I'll need to tell Marta and Theod and Sander and my brother Niquiat. We've all made plans to meet in Vastergot tomorrow."

Something softened in Frau Kuiper's face, and she said, "I had heard that you and Mr. Jansen had forged an acquaintanceship. It's very good that he should have friends here. No, you're not confined to grounds. I do believe I've kept you long enough. I suggest that you return to your room; I'll have a meal sent up to you. And do read that book on comportment, dear. You need to know the rules of engagement before you can formulate an effective battle strategy."

I left Frau Kuiper's office feeling as though I'd already won my first battle.

FOUR ACQUAINTANCES WENT TO VASTERGOT

On Saturday morning, I met with the other three members of our little adventuring party in the dining hall. Copper and Magnus were both large enough that we'd had to secure fare to the dragoneers' carriage, which was double-tall and had elevated seating, allowing dragons to lie on the floor beneath. Copper and Magnus occupied the floor below, but Kasaqua and Inga were small enough to occupy the box with us. We chatted on the train about our various classes and our opinions of the professors. Theod was characteristically tight-lipped, staring out the window at the passing scenery and only offering quick, short answers if he was directly addressed.

I'd asked Niquiat to meet me at the station at ten o'clock, if he couldn't reply, and I was happy to see him there waiting for us as the train pulled in.

"Look at *you* in your fine school dress," he said with a bark of laughter as I ran to him and pulled him into a tight hug. When I released him, he looked at me incredulously and poked me in the ribs. "Have you got *armor* on under all that? Do you need a can opener to get in and out of it?"

"A gentleman does not inquire about a lady's underpinnings under any circumstances," I said in a mockingly prim and proper tone. Niquiat laughed, then looked past me to my three companions.

"Oh, yes, introductions and all that. Niquiat, this is Marta Hagan and her dragon, Magnus; Sander Jansen and his dragon, Inga; and Theod Knecht and his dragon, Copper. All of them are my schoolmates."

"Pleased to meet you all," Niquiat said. "If the four of you are going to be off shopping, I'd recommend coming down to the co-op first because you'll have parcels to carry afterward."

"That suits me, if it suits everyone else," I said, looking at the other three for consensus.

"There's no reason to believe that we'll be exposed to anything that would render us less presentable on High Street, is there?" Marta asked with mild concern, smoothing an imagined wrinkle from her skirt.

"I don't intend to take you tramping through the gutter, if that's what you're afraid of," Niquiat said. "Though there's a good bit of soot and grease in the shop, so maybe don't touch anything."

Marta nodded, looking very discomforted, and Magnus pushed his head up under her hand.

The streets got narrower as we headed east from the train station into the heart of the cannery district, and the air took on the familiar rancid fish oil smell. It was a different route than Niquiat had taken me the first time, since we weren't going to his flat, and it involved passing down a main thoroughfare where women were hawking fresh fish and clams and mussels and oysters out of wheelbarrows. We arrived at the tinker shop from an entirely different direction, walking around the side of the building that I'd never seen.

The shop itself was just as I remembered it. Jorgen was even perched in the same place with his mask of magnifying lenses pulled down over his face. Strida was standing at the back, beside a steel barrel full of fire, hammering a piece of metal on an anvil. Zhina had a huge sheet of brown paper laid out on the table, and she was drawing on it with a wax pen. They all stopped to look at us as we entered. Jorgen said, sounding far less genuinely shocked than he had when first introduced to me, "Sweet Fyra's tits, it's *four* dragons!"

"Niquiat said his sister was going to visit," Zhina said with a grin. "He didn't say she was bringing a crowd."

"This is Zhina," Niquiat said, nodding toward her. "That's Strida over there trying to make treasure out of garbage, and Jorgen pulling apart old clockwork toys for spare parts."

"This is Marta Hagan and Magnus, Sander Jansen and Inga, and Theod Knecht and Copper," I said by way of introduction. "My schoolmates."

It wasn't the way that introductions were meant to be done, according to Marta's etiquette manual, but it served. This wasn't the kind of place where rules like that applied.

"You scratching out another set of blueprints for that flying machine that's never going to work?" Niquiat said, looking over Zhina's shoulder.

"Your engine with the self-stabilizing reciprocator would be light enough, if we could figure out how to build a gasbag that wouldn't leak. Then we'd just need to acquire the vetna."

"And if we had a hundred thousand marka—" Niquiat began. Zhina picked up a rolled sheaf of brown paper and batted him over the head with it until he laughed out a plea for mercy.

Sander was looking at the building plans that Zhina had been working on, and his eyebrows were knitted together as he wrote something on his tablet. He slid it toward Zhina, who picked it up and examined its front and back and spine for a moment before even looking at what he'd written, saying, "This is marvelous, where'd you get it?"

"Read it," Sander said firmly, looking down at the needle he was passing from hand to hand.

Zhina looked at the tablet and read aloud, "Water can be transmuted into two parts vetna and one part stiksna, but it has to be very pure water to begin with. We haven't been taught the skilta for it yet but I've read about it."

"We have no space to build any such thing anyway," Niquiat said. "According to that book of yours, it takes fifteen cubed feet of vetna to lift a pound of anything. Even if we build the pilot's station out of wicker and canvas to keep the weight down, *and* get one of my little engines to work without spinning itself apart, *and* we could lay hands on enough strahlendstone to keep one in action and enough loodglas to keep the strahlendstone from poisoning the pilot, it's a matter of practicality. Let's say we could get the entire undercarriage, with engine and passenger and whatever cargo and all that you'd need, down under five hundred pounds. You'd still need seventy-five hundred cubed feet of vetna to lift it."

"So? As a sphere, it would need a crosswidth of less than twenty-five feet to have an inside volume of seventy-five hundred cubed feet. We could build it on the roof or something—"

"And I'm sure the neighbors wouldn't have anything at all to say about it, and we wouldn't have thanegards knocking on our door—"

"Build it on Masquapaug," I said.

Both of them stopped and looked at me.

"That's not a half-bad idea, you know, if you can get your people to agree to it," Zhina said, looking at me with a really disquieting interest, like she was planning on picking me apart. "Rent's got to be better on your little island, hasn't it?"

"Anything we save on rent we lose again shipping in everything we'd need," Niquiat said, dragging his hands through his hair. "We shouldn't be having this fight in front of guests, Zhina. I was only teasing."

Zhina sighed dramatically and went back to drawing her plans. Sander sat down next to her without being invited, examining her work. They entered into a private conversation on his tablet; she took up a sharp little tool from the bench and wrote back to him as he was writing to her, allowing them to carry on in silence.

Marta spent the entirety of our time in the tinker shop standing politely in a corner, careful not to touch anything at all while Magnus wandered around sniffing at everything much the same way Kasaqua had the first time I'd brought her here. Marta was watching Jorgen rather intently, though.

"I had a clockwork train set when I was little," she said, as he picked gears and cogs out of an unrecognizable metal object with a pair of tweezers. "I wonder whatever became of it."

"Unless it's in an attic or something, probably it got passed on from one child to another until it broke and became junk. Which is where we get them," Jorgen replied without looking at her.

"So what is it you're planning to do with yourself once you graduate from that school of yours?" Niquiat asked Theod, trying to make pleasant conversation.

"I don't expect that I ever will graduate. I'm not a quick study," Theod said, straightening his waistcoat. "I'm good with the animals, though. I might have a promising career in dragon husbandry."

From across the room, Strida whistled sharply through her teeth.

"This needs to be allowed to cool slowly," she said, laying her welding mask aside and taking off her thick leather gloves. She'd fashioned a strange shape of isen with a hammer head on either end and a hole through its middle. It was still glowing hot. "Who wants to go to Haddir's with me and get coffee in the meantime?"

At the mention of Haddir's, even Jorgen looked up from what he was doing.

I was more than happy to introduce my new friends to the joys of Kindah coffee.

AND WANDERED FAR AND NEAR

After we left Haddir's, Niquiat brought us to a street vendor, where a Naquisit woman easily as old as Grandma sold corn cakes fried in fish oil. They weren't quite as good as ones fried in seal fat, but they served admirably when spread with smoked eel paste, the perfect combination of sweet-salt-savory. The vendor sold sobaheg and succotash as well, and roasted squash, and roasted hickory nuts with maple syrup, and dried cranberries.

"This is *amazing*," I said around a mouthful of sweet hickory nuts while Kasaqua pranced around my feet begging for a share. "If I never see another soggy mass of pickled cabbage, it will be too soon. They have potatoes and cabbage at the school every single day, and breakfast is always toast and boiled eggs and oat porridge."

The others in the party were all very game about trying the nuts and cranberries. Sander wanted to try a corn cake, but refused eel paste on the grounds that he didn't like pastes or spreads of any sort. Marta expressed concern about the oiliness of the food and how oily foods could ruin one's complexion.

"So this is the kind of thing that you eat on your island?" Theod asked, looking slightly lost.

"More or less," I said, offering him the bag of nuts and cranberries. "If it was morning I'd expect na'samp, which is a sort of porridge made of corn rather than oats. It's a great deal nicer than oat porridge, in my opinion."

"She doesn't sell it, but there's a vendor down near the cannery who does," Niquiat supplied.

"I expected . . ." Theod began uncertainly.

"Parched corn drowning in squirrel fat, whole silverside smelts with heads and tails and all, raw rabbit livers wrapped in ramp leaves, fried deer brains, turkey-foot soup?" Niquiat interrupted. "I laid hands on a used copy of that Nordlund book. It's two-thirds nonsense and one-third horribly out of date. I swear the folks he was staying with were having him on; from the sound of it he'd eat anything that was put in front of him. The only thing he seems to have right at all is the clambake."

Theod went quiet again, frowning.

In the bookstore on Verner Street, Marta and Sander amused themselves by thumbing through the periodicals section. Marta squealed when she found an omnibus edition of some serial that she knew but Sander didn't. They each spent a half dozen marka and left with a canvas bag laden with magazines and paperbounds, which Sander carried.

We passed a hundred storefronts on our journey from Cannery Street to High Street. There was a fish market, and several junk shops, a tobacco seller, and a half dozen grog and ale shops. A man on the corner was hawking scrap metal out of a wheelbarrow. There was a pawnshop and a moneylender that I wouldn't have borrowed from. Where the low quarter began to meet the high, there was a pub where men of various means were blustering at one another over pints of ale, and next to it a coffee shop where women were doing much the same. We passed a leather goods merchant, and a cooper, and a glassblower. On the next street there were shoe shops and milliners and haberdashers. High Street was swept and gleaming, the cobbles polished by the passage of thousands of people. We passed a store for clockwork devices, and a flower shop, and a pastry shop that smelled deliciously of toasted almonds. Beyond that were a salt and spice merchant, and a tea importer, a very serious-looking bank, and finally our apparent destination: a paper-goods store.

The proprietor did a good bit of rude staring at our party—at the dragons, and at Theod and me, and especially at Niquiat. He seemed well acquainted with Marta, however, who was perfectly charming and directed him without hesitation.

I purchased a penknife and a dozen snowy white goose feathers, along with an inkwell and a pint of ink. The ink seemed outlandishly expensive. I knew how to brew ink from oak galls and rusty nails and pine tar, but I didn't have the space or equipment. I purchased two entire reams of loose-leaf paper, and a couple of pasteboard ledger books. Altogether it cost five and a half marka.

It was passing noon when we left the paper-goods store, and Marta made the suggestion that we take a walk through the thane's Free Gardens. Sander seemed keen on the idea, and none of the rest of us had ever been.

"But Anequs had told me that you've lived here in Vastergot for better than a year," Marta said to Niquiat. "You've *never* been to the gardens?"

"Folks from my part of the city aren't especially welcome in places like the gardens. Thanegards tend to stroll up and politely ask what you're doing there and if you'd rather not leave," Niquiat said, smiling thinly. "And I don't usually have such finely dressed company to vouch for me."

"Oh," Marta replied, raising her eyebrows and looking slightly lost for a moment before recovering with a winning smile. "Then it shall be my pleasure to introduce them to you."

Niquiat and I looked at each other, communicating instant accord at the idea that Marta was being slightly ridiculous. I glanced to Theod, but his face offered nothing, as serene and blank as a portrait.

The public gardens turned out to be a series of neat brick paths and little wrought-isen fences winding through short-mown green lawns, edged with flower beds and occasional trees. There was a brick-edged pond with cattails at the margin, and a pair of swans gliding across its surface. There were people of all ages walking in couples and groups, all of them finely dressed. Far off on the green, a little girl in a gingham dress was flying a kite while a woman sitting primly on a blanket looked on. On the far side of the pond, a group of young boys was racing clockwork boats. It was like an image from the end pages of a ladies' magazine.

We spent a few minutes chatting about nothing much of importance, Marta pointing out this or that planted flower arrangement and talking about other outings she'd had. The dragons extended themselves a bit, Copper and Magnus trotting together across the grass, one chasing the other in turns. Kasaqua, meanwhile, was more interested in the pond and particularly in the swans, and I tried to convey to her very sternly that they were *not* to be hunted. Inga stayed at Sander's side, coolly observing everything.

"Emmeline and Kerstin and I used to come here every Saturday last year. Oh, I can't wait to show you how the city decorates for Valkyrjafax! The academy has its own bonfire for Valkyrja-faxnacht itself, of course, but Jarl Joervarsson sees to it that there are candle lanterns for the fullness of the week, and in the evening there are concerts in the open air, and beer and cider vendors— it's all great fun. This past July I was here with Lisbet—"

"Lisbet is my sister," Sander said all in a rush, interrupting Marta. When I looked at him, he'd gone absolutely scarlet across the cheeks and was looking resolutely at the ground. Inga was winding herself around his legs consolingly. Marta looked at Sander with mild concern and seemed to have lost her train of thought entirely. Then she seemed to look past him, and her eyes lit up.

"Why look, it's Dagny Sørensen!" Marta said, gesturing with her fan. "And I do believe that's Joreid Valbrandsdottir with her— *the niece of the jarl.* Come on, I'll make introductions."

We all dutifully followed Marta as she floated over in a perfectly ladylike fashion. Magnus came back to her heel with obvious reluctance when she blew her whistle, and Copper returned to Theod's without him having to blow his.

Dagny Sørensen was wearing a yellow-and-green dress with skirts of practically supernatural volume that made her bell-shaped. She was wearing a wide straw bonnet with yellow chrysanthemums and carrying a lacy parasol, which somewhat balanced the overall effect. Joreid Valbrandsdottir was dressed much the same, her dress cranberry red, her hat slightly ridiculous in its ornamentation. It had a pair of stuffed passenger pigeons on it.

"What an interesting retinue you have today, Miss Hagan," Dagny said at our approach, looking at us with a plainly critical eye, her gaze landing on Niquiat with unhidden disdain.

"Well, my school has been good enough to provide absolutely diverting company," Marta said with an airy giggle. "You've met Miss Anequs, who's rooming with me this year, and of course you know Sander Jansen. This is Theod Knecht, also my schoolmate, and Anequs's brother Niquiat. He introduced us earlier to a divine little shop that sells nackie delicacies, and a perfectly darling Kindah coffeehouse that I'm sure I'd never have found without the recommendation of a local."

"A pleasure, I'm sure," Dagny said in a way that indicated no pleasure whatsoever. "Marta, darling, you will of course recognize Joreid Valbrandsdottir, who is lately returned to Vastergot from a summer holiday in the mountains of southern Tyskland."

"Lovely to make your acquaintances," Miss Valbrandsdottir said, showing her teeth in a way that could only charitably be called a smile. "May Miss Sørensen and I borrow Miss Hagan from you? With her permission, of course."

Marta looked at me with a flash of guilt in her eyes.

"I know it's terribly rude of me to abandon the party, but it's been ever so long since I've actually been able to spend any time with Dagny. You will forgive me if I take my leave and meet you back at school, won't you?"

I could have said something about her leaving me functionally unchaperoned in the company of two young men, since no one in her society would consider Niquiat a veritable chaperone. But I didn't. Marta clearly cared more about forging a friendship with Miss Sørensen and Miss Valbrandsdottir than she did with any of us, and I shouldn't have expected anything else from her.

"I'll see you this evening, then," I said. I didn't smile as I said it. Marta looked fraught and bit her lip and fisted her hands around her fan—but she *did* leave us. Magnus looked back over his shoulder and made a mournful little call, as if to ask us why we weren't all coming.

Sander had apparently been using the time we'd spent standing still to write a note on his tablet, which he pressed into my hands.

Do you think that I offended Marta by interrupting her? I blurt things sometimes, especially if I hear certain words, and I can't help myself.

"Well, it's not as if you said anything objectionable, so I can't see why she should be angry. Besides, I think she's far too taken with Dagny Sørensen to even remember being interrupted," I replied, watching as Dagny leaned in close to Marta to say something.

Sander sighed.

"It's time to go inside," he said clearly, his voice somewhat flat. He scowled, writing on his tablet, *I'm going to sit and read awhile and get my head straight. Please don't mind me.*

Sander claimed a bench near the edge of the pond and sat

down, fishing the serial omnibus from the bag of books. After a few moments of reading he drew his legs up under him, sitting cross-legged on the bench, entirely enraptured and quite plainly gone from us for the time being. He had the mink tail in his left hand and was stroking it absently with his thumb as he read. Inga found a stick to chew on, placing herself at his feet.

Theod and Niquiat and I stayed nearby, standing in the shade of a maple tree with leaves that were just beginning to go scarlet and golden.

"So now that it's just us nackies," Niquiat said, "the two of you want to tell me all about this school and what it's like?"

"It's an excellent academy," Theod said immediately, and I laughed.

"There's Professor Ulfar, who's quite nice," I said. "Professor Ibarra is a bit of a bore and clearly thinks of Theod and me as lackwits, and Professor Ezel is an absolute beast. I'm not sure what to think of Professor Mesman yet, but he didn't do anything at all when someone in my class tripped me—"

"I hope you kicked him in the shin!" Niquiat said, frowning.

"I would have, if I'd seen who did it. I'm still giving Mesman the benefit of the doubt because maybe he didn't see, either—he just went on with class without making a fuss of it. He doesn't seem to have it in for me, at least. Ezel certainly does. And there's this fellow Einarsson from the dragon ministry or whatever—"

"*Captain* Einarsson," Theod said, glaring at me, "of the Ministry of Dragon Affairs. He oversees all permitting and licensing of dragons at the academy and in Vaster Hold at large."

"He's an absolute horror, let me tell you," I finished, glaring right back at Theod for a moment before looking to Niquiat.

"Have you learned anything worth knowing yet, though?" Niquiat asked.

"As much as I hate Professor Ezel, I think there are useful things to be learned in skiltakraft class, and probably in anglereckoning, too. I've got no use at all for the erelore and folklore, though. It's absolutely tedious and enough of it is plainly wrong that I doubt the rest. I'm still not sure what to think of dragon husbandry, as I've only had it the once and we didn't do much in it except receive our dragons' tack. I expect it will matter more when Kasaqua's bigger and can fly."

"Professor Mesman thinks that Copper might be flying by the spring term," Theod said, his eyes softening as he looked to where Copper and Kasaqua were playfully feinting at each other in the grass. Copper moved very much like a wolf, but Kasaqua bounced along like a weasel or an otter.

"If he's flying, maybe you can hitch a lift back to Masquapaug and not have to worry about train fare and ferry fare, eh?" Niquiat said to me, laughing.

"It will be at least a year before Copper would be able to carry two riders, and even then I doubt he could carry both of us and Anequs's dragon, since she'll no doubt be much bigger by then," Theod replied tightly.

"I was only joking; don't take everything so seriously," Niquiat said, shaking his head at Theod. Turning to me, he said, "Been meaning to ask you, Chipmunk, you plan on going back to the island for the whalers' homecoming?"

"Are you going?" I asked, looking at him, trying to gauge his response. He hadn't come home for it last year, or come for Strawberry Thanksgiving or the corn-planting dance.

"I can make sure you've got fare is all I meant," Niquiat said, sucking his teeth. "I wouldn't want you to not be able to for lack of funds."

"You should come, too," I said stubbornly. "For Father. Besides, it's not as if it would be safe for me to make the journey all by myself anyway."

"So bring your schoolboy here," Niquiat said, nodding toward Theod. "I'm sure he'd chaperone you if you asked, and you'd be traveling with two dragons. No one would try anything."

Theod coughed into his fist, looking rather pale.

"I couldn't possibly . . . Frau Kuiper would never allow . . ." he stammered.

"Don't be wicked, Niquiat," I said with a grin. "Yes, I hope that I can go back to welcome the whalers home, but that's two months from now. Who knows what might happen in two months?"

"Let's go drag Sander up from the depths of his book and find something more interesting to do, now that your painted pigeon there has abandoned us to go play with the people of quality."

"What have you got in mind?" I asked. "We could go back to Haddir's . . ."

"We could do that, if you wanted, but there's a pennik opera down in Stoke Square that I haven't taken you to yet. Ekaitz's cousin's band is supposed to be playing tonight."

I looked at Theod and Sander. Neither of them seemed to have a strong opinion, so down to Stoke Square we went. Everyone there was very excited to see the dragons, and the dragons were mostly pleased to be petted and cooed at, with Inga being the most generally reserved and hiding between Sander's legs as much as she could.

The band consisted of a woman playing a strange instrument that looked like a violin with a clockwork crank and a keyboard, a man with a big bass drum, a man with a hand drum, and a woman with a tambourine who moved around the stage in very animated ways as she sang. There was a shout-out and callback section to most of the songs—Niquiat seemed to already know many of the responses, but they were very easy to learn, and by the second or third verse I'd managed to join in with the rest of the crowd. Sander covered his ears and screwed up his face every time there was a shouting part, but he laughed and drummed his hands on the table, clearly having great fun. Theod was a bit more reserved, but after a round of short beer even he was singing along. We ate fried cod and potatoes with much too much salt and vinegar, and Niquiat introduced us to Ekaitz's cousin, who turned out to be the woman playing the strange instrument.

It was past dark when Niquiat walked us all back to the train station. I watched him standing on the platform as the train pulled away, hands shoved in his pockets, and wondered if I could find a way to make these trips into Vastergot a more regular occurrence.

SHE CONVERSED AGAIN WITH LIBERTY

Marta did not return to the school on Saturday evening. Frau Brinkerhoff informed me sometime later that evening that Marta had sent a telegram to explain that she'd been invited to spend the night at the Sørensen townhome and would return on Sunday afternoon. On Sunday morning, I asked one of the kitchen maids to see if Liberty could come up to my room. She gave me a sly look, but Liberty did turn up at my door half an hour later.

"I've talked to the rest of the laundry maids and they think it's *hilarious* that you've got me coming up here to chat over mending, so they're willing to play along," Liberty said as she sat down and got herself situated. "But the kitchen maids think they're better than us, so I'd try not to get their attention, if I were you. They might try and get the lot of us in trouble for the sport of it, if they catch on. You're going to have to learn which of the maids are safe to ask about me."

"I could just ask Frau Brinkerhoff for special permission for you to do your mending up here—"

"Don't you dare!" Liberty interrupted, clearly alarmed. "You'll get me dismissed if you do that. They'll consider me a distraction to your studies and a setback to your becoming a proper drag-oneer!"

I sighed deeply, wondering why everything among the Anglish had to be so terribly complicated, but promised not to speak to any maids other than the ones she named. We spent the rest of the morning chatting about my outing on Saturday, and I told her about Haddir's and Niquiat's workshop and the band we'd seen.

"If you're able to line up a Saturday when I'm free," Liberty said, "I wouldn't mind having you join me in the mill district. You can see the sort of shops I frequent. You'll probably find them more useful than the ones Miss Hagan showed you. There's also a salon that I attend on the first Saturday of each month, put to-gether by women who've moved on from the Society for Friend-less Girls. We help one another to make useful social connections."

"I wouldn't mind meeting more women who are at my own level of society. Would I be the only nackie there?"

"As far as I know, yes—and certainly the only one from the islands. I've no idea how one would go about finding nackie con-nections in the city, I'm afraid."

"When's the next Saturday that you're free?"

"The coming one; I can only take every second one off, but I worked yesterday. It would be best if you simply met me at the train station, and had your brother meet us there as well. No one would need to know that we're traveling together, that way."

"That suits. What should I wear? I know that my uniforms look sharpest on me, by Anglish standards, and it was well enough when I was traveling with four other students, but—"

"But it would rather make you stand out in the mill district. Will your dragon be joining us, or are you going to have her stay here?"

"Why would I leave her?" I asked, taken aback at the suggestion.

"I just know that the other girls did, sometimes, when going into the city; there'd be warnings posted about unattended dragons in the ladies' quarters," Liberty said with a shrug. "Yours is small enough that I can't imagine her being a bother, but your school uniform announces not only that you're a dragoneer, but that you're a student of Kuiper's Academy in particular. That's not necessarily something you want to announce about yourself; it would be seen by some people as an invitation to discuss any number of topics. Better to wear something that's smart and passingly fashionable, but ultimately forgettable. You want your clothes to say precisely *nothing* about you."

"I don't think I have anything that says *nothing* about me," I said. "I've brought two day dresses with me, and you've seen the nicer of them already because it's what I wore to meet Marta last week."

"Well, I'm sure that dress made you stand out on High Street," she said, making a sympathetically pained face, "but it's exactly the sort of thing that anyone might be wearing in the mill district. If you don't mind my being frank, asking as a seamstress, what've you got in the way of underpinnings? I hope it's not just the corset that came with your uniform. Those are made to standard sizes to squash you into the right shape for uniforms that are the same—ready-made and not tailored at all."

"I have three pairs of canvas short stays, which I only sometimes wore on the island; a cotton shift and a dress over it are considered perfectly serviceable there. I always wear stays when I visit Catchnet, though, because not wearing stays invites lewd attention from dockmen."

Liberty nodded and made a humming noise of agreement at that.

"You'll want a practical corset and a corded petticoat to achieve a fashionable silhouette," she said. "Anything less and you'll look *poor*—which is a greater hindrance in some places than others. Short stays were fashionable when high-waisted gowns were, but they're a generation out of favor now. Your day dress has a fashionable waistline, mind you."

"My day dress has a waist where my natural waist is," I said.

"I can introduce you to the corsetiere I see this Saturday, if you'd like."

"I'd like that, but I've got practically nothing in the way of money. I have seven and a half marka left of fifteen that Frau Brinkerhoff gave me last week to last me until the beginning of October, and Niquiat has given me a small sum to help with train fares and such."

"Well, you'd do better with short stays than you would with your uniform corset, under the sort of dress you were wearing last Saturday. We might be able to lay hands on something serviceable for you secondhand, if that doesn't bother you. Would you let me take your measurements?"

"Of course! I'd be glad to have the advice of someone sensible regarding proper dress for the city," I said.

That led to my disappearing into the washroom to return wearing nothing but a shift and pantalets and stockings, standing at attention while Liberty measured me. I'd never had my measurements taken by anyone but my mother, and it hadn't occurred to me what a physical, *intimate* process it was. I was acutely aware of the warmth of her hand as it rested for a moment on the curve of my hip, the gentleness of her fingertips as she measured my throat, her thumb pressed softly against the notch of my collarbone. My heart was racing, and she had to be aware of that. I met her eyes briefly as she measured my bust, and I couldn't help taking a gasping little breath. She looked away quickly, but I didn't fail to notice that her breath had quickened, too.

I realized, as she moved to measure across my back from shoulder to shoulder, that I'd wanted to kiss her. But the moment had passed.

In the end, she'd measured my neckline, bust, waist, and hips, the span of my shoulders, and the distance from my waist to the floor. She jotted down the measurements in a little brown-paper book with a wax pencil that she tucked back into her sewing box when she was finished.

We chatted about this and that until luncheon, and after luncheon I took Kasaqua out to stretch her legs. I saw some other students and their dragons in the field, but no one approached me, which I didn't mind at all. Forgoing human company was preferable to dealing with the likes of Ivar Stafn.

I returned to my room to read in preparation for natural philosophy in the morning. Marta returned late in the afternoon and spent a lot of time talking about what a lovely time she'd had at the Sørensen residence both at dinner and afterward—and how she'd endeavor to secure me an invitation to the next gathering that Dagny held. I made neutral sounds of comprehension throughout; she didn't seem to require any real response from me. She'd probably have been just as happy to recount the event to the walls. I had no particular desire to be invited to Dagny Sørensen's home for any reason whatsoever.

I was quite glad when she declared that she'd be turning in to bed early, and I stayed up for an hour or more past that, reading by kerosene lamp.

AND ASSISTED A FRIEND

On Tuesday, after another frustrating skiltakraft lesson with Professor Ezel, Sander and I arranged to meet at the dragon-hall before proceeding to luncheon. The dragons wouldn't be fed until after luncheon, of course, but the weather was especially nice, and it seemed a good day to encourage our dragons to stretch their legs by playing fetch and carry. At my room I briefly met with Marta, who told me not to bother waiting for her at luncheon because she'd already arranged to sit with Niklas, so I'd have the table to myself "and whomever I'd like to invite." I thanked her for letting me know, deposited my books and notes, and proceeded to the dragonhall. When I arrived at the field, however, it was to a very upsetting scene.

Three older students—no one who shared any classes with me—had surrounded Sander and were shoving him roughly between themselves. They'd gotten his tablet from him somehow, and were taunting him with it, rebuffing all of his attempts to get it back.

The boys' dragons were not in immediate evidence, probably still locked in their individual stalls in the dragonhall. Inga, however, danced and dodged around Sander's feet, making aborted gooselike cries: honks and hisses. It was the most noise I'd ever heard from her, in fact. She was looking not at any of the aggressors, but up at Sander. Sander's face was very red and tear-streaked, and he kept shaking his head, but he made no sound. I stomped straight over to the lot of them and shouted at the top of my voice.

"Stop it this instant!"

They did stop, for a moment, everyone looking at me. Sander took the opportunity to pull back from the trio, scooping Inga up into his arms. He edged around, putting himself behind me. I walked directly to the young man who was holding Sander's tablet and tore it out of his hand. He seemed too shocked by this turn of events to resist me at all.

"What is *wrong* with the lot of you?" I demanded, glaring at each of the three in turn, memorizing their faces. There was silence for a moment as they stared at me and looked at one another, but then the one I'd taken the tablet from started *laughing*.

"Watch out, boys, the nackie's come to make war!" he barked, looking at the other two, who quickly joined in the laughter.

He took a step forward and grabbed my wrist—the hand I was holding Sander's tablet in. I startled and tried to pull back, the tablet falling from my hand to thump on the grass at my feet.

Kasaqua made an enraged cry, sounding more like a screaming bobcat than anything else, and darted forward to bite the young man's ankle. He let go of my wrist and I fell backward, landing hard on my backside. He kicked out at Kasaqua, who made a sharp cry and *was about to loose a breath at him*. I rolled and scrambled forward to bodily grab her and hold her close against me, willing her against such action. It was worse than it had been when Ivar had slapped me. She was confused, angry, and didn't understand why I didn't understand that *we were in a fight*.

Then someone else was shouting: a man.

"What's going on here? Break it up!"

Hallmaster Henkjan appeared, carrying a shovel in a vaguely threatening way. He was an imposing figure of a man, broad and strong in the casually capable way that laboring men inevitably became. He towered over the boys somehow, even though he wasn't particularly tall. He took in the scene in a long, sweeping gaze: Sander's tearstained face, Inga twining herself around and around his feet. Me sitting, curled around Kasaqua, who was not at all keen on being held just now. Sander picked Inga up to calm her. His tablet lay on the ground where I'd dropped it.

"You three need to move along, *now*," Henkjan said to the three older boys, tossing his head toward the dragonhall. "Go tend your dragons."

"It wasn't anything serious," one of the boys—not the one who'd grabbed me—said.

"Get out of my sight, or it will be," the hallmaster insisted, shaking his shovel a bit.

They made more complaining noises as they slowly shuffled off, moving toward the dragonhall. In the meantime, Sander had collected himself enough to pick his tablet up. He set Inga down and offered me a hand up, which I gratefully accepted. I kept Kasaqua tucked against me, though, because I was entirely sure that she'd take off after the group of bullies to continue her challenge if I allowed it.

"You, lad, you should go and clean yourself up a bit. Go to the hall lads' quarters—Theod's in there just now, and he's a good sort," Mr. Henkjan said, looking at Sander. Then, looking at me, he said, "You want to explain what was going on just now? Is your dragon calm?"

"She's not planning to breathe on anyone right now, if that's what you mean," I said, rearranging her a bit in my arms and running my fingers through her feathery mane. "Those three were shoving Sander around between them, and they'd taken his tablet—"

"And you decided to get into the middle of it?"

"Well, *someone* had to put a stop to it."

"Do you understand how much more they'll shame him for having been rescued? By a *girl*, no less? It's the nature of young men to fight, and your playing nursemaid to Mr. Jansen will do him no favors. Bad enough that it's already got round the school that he's the housematron's nephew, and his, well . . . condition. This sort of teasing and roughhousing is just how lads sort themselves; it forces the too-sensitive sorts to toughen up."

"How have those young men gotten to be sixteen and seventeen years old while still behaving like *toddlers* who don't properly understand that other people have thoughts and feelings just the same as their own?" I demanded. "Among my people, a child of six years already understands the importance of treating others as one wishes to be treated, sharing and offering assistance for the common good, and the basic responsibility they have to be decent to other people and to animals and to nature. It is the duty of elders to teach these facts to children. How do those young men have less human feeling than little children?"

"Well, I can't say I knew anything about how you and yours get on with their lives, but Mr. Jansen's not one of you; he's one of them. Mr. Knecht understood that—you probably ought to talk to him about it, how he got on his first year, and how it smoothed itself out in the end. My advice to you is to keep yourself out of it next time you see that sort of thing going on. Meddling will just make it worse."

"What if they'd pressed him to the point that Inga decided she had to discharge a breath in his defense?"

"Then that would be a tragedy, but it's the kind of thing that needs to be sorted while a dragon's still small. His creature, luckily, seems to have a very even temperament. Don't know if I'd say the same of yours—she looks like a fighter. So do you. Shame you're a girl, really."

Before I could think of what to say to such an insult so casually delivered, Henkjan was already walking away. I made a frustrated noise and stalked off in the direction Sander had gone.

The quarters for the men who tended the dragonhall and the school grounds at large hadn't been a part of the tour Frau Brinkerhoff had taken me on—but then, neither had the maids' quarters or the kitchens. It was a small, square building made of gray stone, a little ways down a gravel path from the dragonhall. I found Theod and Sander sitting together on the stone steps that led up to its main entrance. Inga was on Sander's lap, Copper lying at Theod's feet. Sander looked better than he had; he'd obviously washed his face and composed himself somewhat, but was still quite shaken.

"Are you all right?" I asked, finally setting Kasaqua down. She was still cross at having been prevented from violence.

Sander nodded, taking his tablet out and writing something down.

"Henkjan give you an earful for meddling?" Theod asked while Sander was writing.

"Yes, and I've absolutely no idea why. Is anything going to happen to those three? I ought to tell Frau Kuiper—"

"No," Sander said. He was holding out his tablet at me. I took it from him and read, *Thank you very much for your concern, but I'd rather not make more of this than it is. It will be worse for me if I do. I've been dealing with this sort of thing since I was first sent to primary school. I'm used to it. I just need to be more careful about putting myself in harm's way.*

"But you shouldn't have to be used to any such thing!" I insisted, handing him the tablet back.

"You haven't been brought up among young men," Theod said gently, "so you don't understand—"

"I have two brothers," I said. "And cousins, and relations more distant than that. None of them would ever—"

"It's different when you chuck a load of young men all together in close quarters, though," Theod said. "It was the same for me when I first came. Got in half a dozen scuffles and had all manner of mischief done to my things, when I first came, until I decided to just clear out of the boys' quarters altogether and take up residence here."

"You . . . sleep here? With the dragon hall workers?" I asked.

"I'm more like one of them than I'm like the rest of the young men who go to this school, and all of them know it. I was brought up to be a servant, and I've got servant's speech and manners and all. Never went to a primary school, don't have a fancy family with a family name and all the kinds of connections . . . It was easier. And no one stopped me. It's been better, since. They don't feel as inclined to show me my place if they see me where they think I ought to be. I'd rather be around Copper and around the lads than around the rest of the students, anyway."

"That's appalling," I said. "You're expected to do all of the work of a student, so why—"

"Your harping on about this will come back and bite you, if you're not careful," Theod said. "It's exactly the kind of thing that men point at when they say girls aren't suited for schooling."

Sander cleared his throat and pushed the tablet at me again.

I've got my own private room, at Frau Brinkerhoff's request, which I'm grateful for because I don't think I could tolerate the common quarters where students sleep four and six beds to a room—I require a space to be quiet and alone sometimes. But it does set me apart from them, and to be different is to be challenged. I need to prove myself equal to whatever harassment they throw at me, and they'll quickly grow bored and stop.

"I don't comprehend at all how both of you are so calm about this," I said. "I'm going to take a walk with Kasaqua and try to sort myself out. I'll see you at dinner, if I decide not to attend luncheon. At the moment, I'm not at all hungry."

I handed Sander his tablet back and turned from them, beckoning Kasaqua after me.

SHE VISITED ENTIRELY DIFFERENT PARTS OF VASTERGOT

We didn't speak about the events at the dragonhall again. Wednesday and Thursday proceeded as usual. Marta had plans to visit with Lisbet over the weekend, and both she and Sander departed following the afternoon class session on Friday.

The next day was Liberty's Saturday off. We met at the train station, and I told her about the disastrous events earlier in the week as we rode. Kasaqua stood on the seat with her forefeet pressed against the window, seeming generally restless.

"I expect the cause of it is young men being raised apart from the tempering effects of girls and women," Liberty said. "It's not at all uncommon for boys of well-off families to be sent to primary school when they're five or six years old, and thereafter to be raised together rather like little soldiers—entirely by male teachers and headmasters—only seeing their families at special occasions."

"How can they stand to be apart from their children so much? Mothers particularly?" I asked, baffled at the obvious inhumanity of it.

"Much is made of mothers pining for their little sons when it's time for them to go to school, but among the toffs they hardly spend time with their children anyway; they're raised by nurses and governesses and such, and sent away to school until they're old enough to join adult society. I don't have any brothers, so I don't know firsthand, but there is a prevailing attitude that boys raised by women are made soft and unmanly by it."

"Well, whatever they're doing seems to turn out absolutely *awful* young men," I said, frowning. "And it can't *entirely* be a departure from softening female influence, because whalers and deepwater fishermen and merchant sailors all seem to manage well enough being on ships for six and eight months at a time with no women."

"Well, unless you've been out at sea with them, you can hardly speak about whether there's such behavior or not," Liberty said pragmatically. "How old are young men when they go to sea, with your people?"

"A young man is generally sixteen or so when he's taken on his first whaling voyage, or on a merchant trip across the ocean—lots of young men who are interested in sailing careers join their fathers or uncles or cousins on merchant trips when they're younger, though. Short journeys, between Vastergot and New Linvik and such, that happen in days instead of months—and even then they'd be with close family. No one would ever think of sending children away anywhere with *strangers*," I said.

"At what age do young men typically leave home to pursue a career and start their own household and such?"

"I'm . . . not sure that I understand the question? A young man goes on living in his mother's house until he marries, then he lives with his wife's family."

"What if a man never marries?" Liberty asked.

"Well, he might just go on living in his mother's house, then living with whichever sister the house passed on to."

"And he wouldn't be shamed by that?" Liberty asked, looking very interested now. "An Anglish man, unless he's the oldest son and due to inherit the estate, is expected to leave home to pursue a career of some kind by the time he's twenty or so. Any man who doesn't . . . Well, it's unfashionable, to say the least. Unmanly. Such a man is usually presumed to have some terrible failing."

"The more I learn about how the Anglish conduct their lives, the more baffling I find them," I said, sighing deeply. "I'm very glad to have someone who's willing to talk sensibly about all of this; Marta would never have given me a straight answer like that, or speculated at all about why those young men would behave so cruelly."

"I think you ought not judge the Anglish as a whole by the actions of the very rich and socially well connected; they're a different breed. I only know so much about them because we were trained in how to serve them, at the Society for Friendless Girls."

"You might be right about that," I said, considering. "The folks at my brother's co-op seemed nice enough, and the people at Haddir's—"

Which led to us discussing coffee shops and tea rooms for the remainder of the ride. We didn't get off at the Vastergot station I was used to, where I'd met Niquiat that first day. We rode one stop past it and got off at the stop called Mill that was farther north and farther inland, upriver from the cannery district and the docks. Liberty seemed to have an excellent idea of where she was going, though, so I followed her lead, and after passing through a few narrow streets we came upon a thoroughfare that was lined on both sides with shops that seemed far more modest than the ones Marta had shown me on High Street, but neater and more polished than the sort in the cannery district.

"I'm going to introduce you to Jenni; she's a dressmaker who also came from the Society for Friendless Girls, though she's been out of indenture for years and years now. If anyone can outfit you smartly on a tight budget, it will be her."

The particular shop she took me to was one of a row of narrow storefronts sharing a single brick edifice; there were residences above. The sign over the door had gold lettering on green declaring *Jenni Viddarsdottir, Dressmaker—Fittings and Alterations, Millinery, Effects, Sundries.*

When we entered, my first impression was of carefully controlled excess—more things fitted inside than really ought to have, made possible by clever arrangement. There were racks of dresses on hangers, bolts of fabric arranged by color and pattern on shelves lining the walls, hanging displays of brooches and hair ornaments, buckles and ribbons, all of it a riot of color. The back part of the room was dominated by a wide table that had rules and curves and measure-markers and bits of paper, all laid out in a neat and orderly but somewhat incomprehensible way. Behind it was standing a black woman, probably between thirty and forty years of age, wearing a very smart dress of russet calico. The bodice was closely fitted and tapered to a point at the front waist, accented by a sort of crossed sash of black-and-gold satin ribbon. The effect was mirrored by a similar sash at the throat. The same ribbon decorated the hem of each tier of the very full, round skirt.

"Oh, Liberty!" she said, looking up as we entered and offering a warm smile. "So good to see you! Who's your friend?"

"Jenni, I'd love to introduce you to Miss Anequs—"

"Is that a *dragon*?" she asked, eyes widening as they fixed on Kasaqua, who was comfortably balanced on my shoulder and gazing around at all the colorful fabrics with interest.

"Yes, ma'am," I said, stepping forward to allow her a better view. Kasaqua took it as an invitation to leap down onto the table. She moved with great care, not disarranging anything on the table's surface.

"You must be a student of the academy, then," Jenni said,

looking back at me thoughtfully. "What's brought both of you in today?"

"Anequs is in need of a proper corset. She only has short stays because they're still fashionable among people of Mask Island, but since she's living here in the city . . . I've already taken a full set of her measurements, back at the school."

I felt myself flush just a bit at the memory of Liberty taking my measurements.

"Ah, I see," Jenni said. She looked me up and down, taking in my attire with casual but not unkind judgment. "It looks to me like the island fashion is more traditional. A generation ago, the fashionable line was a high waist—just below the bust—with scoop necklines and off-the-shoulder sleeves. Short stays were very much in fashion then, to match the outline. Now the fashionable waist is much lower, in a more natural position, and the *really* fashionable thing is to have as full a skirt as can be managed— that's where the corded petticoats come in, lending volume without bulk. Are you looking for a petticoat as well as a corset? I can see that you've just got a shift and stays under that dress—"

"I'm afraid I'm on rather short funds, ma'am," I confessed.

"Well, that's less a worry than it might have been once," she said, offering a smile. "Fabric was dearer during the war with Berri Vaskos, Anglish pride demanding that nothing be purchased that was of Vaskosish origin; cotton was *very* unfashionable until quite recently. At the end of the war, trade was reopened, and now calico can be had for quite reasonable prices. Linen and silk and fine wool are still preferred, though, if you can afford them, and being able to afford them is a way of showing off. No one with good manners will judge you for wearing calico, these days."

Jenni consulted Liberty's notes on my measurements for a few moments, then turned to the wall behind the table, which housed a large assortment of cardboard cartons. She selected a corded petticoat from a hanging stand and a long, narrow box from the shelf and set both down on the table, lifting the box's lid to reveal a rolled-up corset, which she unfurled onto the table-top.

It was of much lighter construction than the one that had been provided with my school uniform. It was made of cotton duck within and printed calico without, corded and quilted at the bust and hip panels, boned on either side of the laces and in channels along the sides. It had laces both at the front and the back, which meant it would be easier to put on without assistance. Jenni directed me to a private corner created by the strategic placement of a set of shelves and a folding screen, where I stripped to my chemise and put the new corset on. It fit me much more naturally than the school corset, the narrowest part falling well below my ribs to fit snugly but not at all uncomfortably at the soft part of my belly. It pulled my waist in just a bit, and the two sets of lacing allowed me to mold the garment closely to my natural shape. It smoothed me and pushed my bust upward and inward a little, but when I looked at myself in the standing mirror, I didn't have the same upsetting feeling of un-self that I'd first had in my school uniform. I was quite able to bend from side to side and to stretch my arms over my head without displacing anything, but I wasn't able to bend double to touch my toes as I might have in my short stays. When I put on the corded petticoat and my dress over it . . . well, *yes*. My island dress, which had been sewn by Mishona's mother with calico bought on my father's whaling money, was suddenly the kind of thing I might have seen in a magazine. I stepped out from behind the screen, and both women turned to look at me; they'd been chatting quietly before.

Something lit up in Liberty's face when she saw the complete effect, and I felt suddenly giddy. Kasaqua chose that moment to make a chirring cry, leaping off the table to trot over and sniff at my hem, making a circle around me, then demanding to be picked up. There was enough flexibility in the waist of this corset that I was able to do so when she jumped up.

"That looks *lovely* on you," Liberty said a moment later. "The school uniforms are smart, but the skirts are too narrow, the jackets too square-shouldered. They're very like soldiers' uniforms in their design, in fact, and look frankly masculine because of it. Especially the version with trousers."

I found myself quite flustered at the way Liberty's eyes lit up when she was looking at me.

I paid for the corset and petticoat, which together cost me only five marka. It seemed a much lower price than it ought to have been, but I wasn't in a position to argue about it. We proceeded from Jenni's shop to a tea room that Liberty frequented, where we spent the remainder of the afternoon chatting companionably.

We returned to the school in time for dinner, parting company at the train station and walking separately, to avoid the appearance of having spent the day together. It was as lovely a Saturday as I'd had in quite a long time.

A SOCIAL COMPLICATION AROSE

I didn't meet with Liberty on Sunday morning, because she had things to catch up on for having had a day off Saturday. I used the morning to write letters; one to Mother back home and one to Niquiat. I took Kasaqua out for some vigorous exercise and saw to her feeding. I completed suggested drills in skilta drawing from one of the texts I'd found in the library.

It was between three and four o'clock in the afternoon when someone knocked on the door, and I opened it to reveal Frau Brinkerhoff and Marta—Marta looked terribly fraught, and Frau Brinkerhoff grave.

"Have you seen the Saturday edition of the *Vastergot Weekly Review*?" Marta demanded as soon as she was fully inside.

"Should I have?" I asked, suddenly very worried, because whatever was wrong was important enough for Frau Brinkerhoff to have involved herself. I'd come to expect Marta as prone to flights of strong emotion, but not Frau Brinkerhoff.

"Herr Stafn wrote an editorial," Frau Brinkerhoff said. "Frau Kuiper would like you to come to her office to discuss the ramifications. Miss Hagan, your presence will not be required. I suggest that you remain here and collect yourself a bit. Thank you very much for bringing this to our attention."

When Frau Brinkerhoff and I arrived at Frau Kuiper's office, Theod was already there. Frau Kuiper was seated at her desk, looking at a newspaper.

"Ah, there you are, Miss Aponakwesdottir," Frau Kuiper said as I entered. "There's been an unfortunate development; do take a seat."

I did, and Frau Brinkerhoff moved to stand behind Frau Kuiper, one hand moving to rest on Frau Kuiper's shoulder. It was a familiar gesture, one of solidarity. It hadn't occurred to me until then that Frau Kuiper and Frau Brinkerhoff might actually be friends.

Frau Kuiper, without preamble, began to read aloud. I glanced at Theod—the reading was probably for his benefit, and it was good of her not to make comment upon it.

A MATTER OF CONCERN TO THE CITIZENS OF VASTERGOT, AND THE CONTINUED WELL-BEING OF THE CIVILIZED PEOPLES OF LINDMARDEN—BY ARJAN STAFN, THANE OF VASTERGOT

As I'm sure many of the readers of this periodical are aware, there exists—just beyond the city limits—an academy of skiltakraft and natural philosophy, with its own attached dragonhall, founded some twenty years ago by decorated war heroine Karina Kuiper and still under her direction. Until recently, it was an institution of the highest degree, training young dragoneers who have gone on to such meritable position as guards of the jarl. However, a deeply troubling trend has taken root which undermines the good name that the academy had previously established.

As many readers will recall, last year a case was brought before the High Moot of New Linvik by Herr Isbrand Mahler concerning the theft of a dragonet. In a great miscarriage of justice, the feral animal was neither destroyed nor released to the custody of the New Linvik Collection of Wild Beasts. Rather, the thief—a common houseboy of nackie descent—was allowed to retain his ill-gotten prize and was put into the wardship of Karina Kuiper, as a versuch in the public interest to determine whether or not the nackie race can be civilized. What many readers may not be aware of is that, this August, a similar case presented itself. Through means not entirely understood, a nackie girl living on Mask Island acquired a dragonet. Frau Kuiper, upon learning of this, plied her influence with Jarl Joervarsson against common sense and decency and took wardship of the girl and her dragon as well.

There are now two nackie youths in attendance at Kuiper's academy, being treated for all intents and purposes as legitimate students—despite neither of them having any previous formal education.

It is well-known that Karina Kuiper's sole source of personal income is her military pension—she herself is of smallfolkish birth, though one who has proven herself of great distinction in her service to the crown. Still, as military pensions are paid by property taxes upon the gentry, it is a matter of public concern when a pension is being squandered. The administration of an academy is funded primarily by the tuition of its students. It is a matter of concern to those paying tuition how such moneys are being spent. Frau Karina Kuiper is, at present, hosting and educating two nackies at the expense of others. My own son is a student of Kuiper's Academy, which is why this concerns me so gravely.

My twice-great grandfather, Stafn Whitebeard, first came to these shores in the year 1626. He is credited with the discovery of Nack Island, and with the discovery of Lindmarden in general. His trusted younger son, Vaster Stafn—my great-grandfather—was the first jarl of the steading that would become Vastergot. Whitebeard's elder son went on to found New Linvik, the current seat of our high king. Both steadings, in their infancy, experienced significant trouble with savages endemic to this land. In prudence, forethought, virtue, and skill, the people of Anglesland—and in fact all people of Norslandish descent—are demonstrably superior to the barbarians they encountered here. They possess no greater organization than the bestial pack or tribe, scrabbling together a meager existence, making no progress or innovation, doing nothing to improve the lands on which they settle, accumulating no wealth, and generally existing without ambition to personal betterment. They are a wholly different species of humanity, more akin to the black people of Aprika or the far-eastern Shiang-Gang than to civilized peoples of the ancient world.

On the mainland, the natural course of human progress has led to the extermination of packs of natives, just as it has led to the extermination of feral dragons, bears, wolves, and great cats—all are nuisances to the progress of cities and the safety of citizens. Those few individuals of the nackie species who remain do so as part of the least desirable class; they are given to drunkenness, violence, criminal activity of all kinds, and sexual immorality. It is a travesty to civilization that enclaves of these savages have been allowed to continue their existence unchecked on the outlying islands. The great tragedy that befell the peaceful settlement on Nack Island in April of 1825 should have proven beyond all doubt that this species of humanity is not suitable for assimilation into a civilized society.

And now, they are being allowed the command of dragons.

The savage peoples are still very common on the western frontier, and because they are in command of a savage breed of dragon, their loathsome presence has greatly impeded the progress of settlements north of the Runestung or west of Enki's Lake. What good can come of the introduction of dragons to the savage peoples of the outlying islands?

If these facts are as concerning to the reader as they are to me, I implore the reader to seek counsel with their local representatives to the jarl. Careful consideration should be given to the wisdom and virtue of our leaders by all of those who choose them. Too long has too free a rein been given to the Freemensthede—and the outcome of the next althynge may shape the society that we and our children live in for many years to come.

Upon finishing the article and laying down the paper, Frau Kuiper sighed deeply.

"Neither of you has done anything to provoke this," she said after a moment. She said it as if she were reminding herself, rather than reassuring us. "It is, however, a matter that we must swiftly attend to. I will be arranging for each of you to be interviewed by an editorialist, and formal portraits of each of you with your dragons will be taken by a lichtbildmacher. I expect both of you to be compliant with these efforts. Your futures depend on your good reception by the public at large. It would be unwise for either of you to leave campus, especially to be seen in the city, until we've settled this. I fear that there are members of the Eiriksthede or the Ravens of Joden who would attempt to do harm to you or your dragons, if the opportunity to do so presented itself. The

Ravens are a minority, but they're growing very bold indeed if an article like this can be published in the *Vastergot Weekly Review*."

"Yes, ma'am. Of course, ma'am," Theod said.

Frau Kuiper looked at me, her eyes hard as isen. Behind her, Frau Brinkerhoff offered a warning look.

"I'm willing to be interviewed, but I'm not going to tell lies," I said. "I'll answer truthfully whatever is asked of me."

"Which is about what I expected," Frau Kuiper said with another sigh. "I'll be sending telegrams this morning. The lichtbild-macher might even be arranged for later today, if I can manage it. I'll expect you both to be smartly dressed." She looked at me critically. I was wearing one of my calico day dresses.

"Mr. Knecht, your dragon is large enough to bear your weight for a short time, is he not? A few lichtbilds of you riding him might be in order, to show that he is at your command. Meanwhile, Anequs, yours is still small enough to be quite the pet, so a more domestic scene would be appropriate. Perhaps in the library, with a book on your lap to show how studious you are, and your dragon in repose at your feet. Both of you should return to your rooms. I'll arrange to have something brought to you for dinner, and something for your dragon, Miss Aponakwesdottir. I'm going to send some telegrams. You will remain in your rooms until further notice. It's the most practical way to keep you out of trouble with the other students," Frau Kuiper said firmly. "Further, I will be making a formal address to the student body. I have no doubt that a number of our students come from families that support the Eiriksthede. I need to find out who they are before an unfortunate incident occurs. We do not need to repeat the event you experienced with Mr. Stafn, Miss Aponakwesdottir."

"Yes, ma'am," I said, holding her gaze evenly. "Are we to be absent from our classes tomorrow as well, ma'am? Will you inform our professors?"

"Yes, yes, of course. I've got to begin making arrangements. You are both dismissed. Mr. Knecht, I expect you'll be called to the dragonhall as soon as I can lay hands on a competent lichtbild-macher. Try to smarten yourself up a bit in the meantime."

"Yes, ma'am," Theod said, standing and offering a short bow.

Frau Brinkerhoff smiled sadly. "You're both good children with good hearts, and you don't deserve the hardships that have been laid on you. But I'm sure you'll both come shining through all of it."

"I'm sure I will, ma'am," I said, holding her gaze. "I never had doubts about that."

The small, nervous smile she offered me as she excused herself told me that she was nowhere near so confident of the outcome.

ANEQUS AND MARTA ROUNDLY DISCUSSED POLITICS

Marta was pink-faced and fraught when I returned to the room, sitting at her writing desk, furiously marking something down. As soon as I'd closed the door, she looked at me and declared, "I shall send a telegram to Papa and make him write an essay for the *Estervall Gazette* about how diligent and knowledgeable your people are. He's forever saying kind things about the captains of his fleet, and three of them are nackies. One even came to our Jule party last year, with his wife and son. You absolutely *must* come to a social function at Sjokliffheim sometime soon; you could make so many connections with people of quality who could be called upon to speak to your good character."

"Thank you, Marta. That's very kind," I said, sighing. I collapsed into one of the chairs that flanked the low table at the front of our room. "But I'm honestly not sure if that would help or hinder our cause at this point. I don't know anything about the Freemensthede or the Eiriksthede or what periodicals each reads.

I do know that there are people who are very steadfastly against me for the high crime of being a nackie, but I don't know who they are or if it's worthwhile to try and sway their opinions."

"It's all a lot of nonsense to do with who gets to be jarl and who gets to be thane and all that," Marta said, coming to sit in the chair opposite me. "My father isn't a formal member of either party, but he tends to look more favorably on the Freemensthede. If he were a staunch supporter of the Eiriksthede, he'd never have let me become a dragoneer. According to the Eiriksthede, everything was much nicer before the Vaskoslandish war, and we didn't come out on the better side of that and ought to have fought harder for lands south of the Polvaara. They think we all ought to try to be more like the old country—Anglesland or Norsland or both. I haven't ever paid much attention to this sort of thing because it's . . . Well, extraordinary interest in politics is not an attractive quality in a lady, and I'm already a dragoneer, so I don't need another line of fault standing between me and a good marriage, now do I?"

"I wouldn't begin to know," I said. "But I can tell you that everything I know about jarls and kings has been gleaned from context in the backgrounds of novels, and a bit in my erelore and folklore lessons. I'm not entirely sure what a jarl or a thane is or does, really, or how it affects the rest of us."

"A jarl is the ruler of a hold," Marta said. "He has a chamber of representatives, thanes, who speak for the thedes of the hold. At a local thynge, the thanes propose changes to laws and taxes and all that nonsense, and the jarl either approves or disapproves, and that's how laws are made. If the thanes agree that the jarl isn't behaving in the interest of his people, they can dissent against him and rally an althynge, and choose a new jarl. There's an althynge every nine years regardless of whether one is rallied or not. If a jarl's done his job properly, he usually goes on being jarl, and jarls' sons often become jarls themselves; there's a long tradition of that kind of thing. The jarls report to the high king—right

now, that's King Yngvarr. He can overrule any laws presented by
the jarls, if he decides to, and he can rally general armies and
things like that."

"And who gets to decide who the thanes are?" I asked.

"Oh, they're chosen by the landowners," Marta said. "The
smallfolk—anyone who doesn't own land—are represented by a
torgar, someone they choose to oversee common folks' sorts of
problems. The torgar reports to his local thane. The Freemensthede is very keen on the appointment of torgars, and on torgars'
rights to challenge thanes."

"I don't think we have a torgar responsible for the islands. No
one's ever come to Masquapaug to ask any of us about our opinions on who should represent our thede, at least. How would I go
about finding out who does, if anyone?"

"I wouldn't begin to know," Marta said. "That's a bit too deep
into the sea of politics for me, I'm afraid, but I'm sure Frau Kuiper could tell you."

"When I first came here, Captain Einarsson wanted to know
why I hadn't reported Kasaqua to the local representative of the
ministry . . . but we don't have any such thing on Masquapaug. As
far as I can tell, we don't have any representation of any kind at
all."

"That might well be the case," Marta said uncertainly. "All of
the outlying islands became an incorporated territory of Lindmarden after the nackie wars of seventeen . . . something or other.
Oh, I really ought to know this one, but I'm useless at facts and
figures."

"It was 1757," I said with a sigh. "I had to write an essay about
it for Professor Ibarra. There was open battle for much of the
1750s, and in the end the Maswachuisit, the Akashneisit, and the
Naregannisit were forced to cede all of their lands to the Anglish
in return for an armistice. The Naquisit and Masquisit agreed not
to take up arms against Anglish people. The Anglish agreed not to
settle on Masquapaug at all, and to a lot of little details I don't

know about regarding the settlement on Naquipaug. But I know they didn't keep their promises there, once the coal seam was discovered. So far they've left Masquapaug alone, though. We don't have anything they want—or at least we didn't until Kasaqua."

"Well, it doesn't seem right that you should lack a torgar and associated ministry representatives, if you're a district of Lindmarden and are taxed as such," Marta said with a frown.

"If we have a torgar, I should very much like to meet him," I said. "As I am for the moment confined to this room for the sake of convenience and safety, could I perhaps petition you to take a trip to the library for me? I think I should like to finally lay hands on that book by Nordlund and another one . . . Something by Maurits-Jan van den Ouden. Frau Brinkerhoff recommended it to me, but I haven't had the time to look into it. I need to know the arguments that are made against my people if I'm to prove them wrong."

"It would be my great pleasure to go to the library in your stead," Marta said. "I'll be back as quickly as I may. While you read, I shall write letters. We'll put all this beastly nonsense behind us in no time at all, you'll see."

Marta smiled, and I smiled back, and not for the first time I wondered what life would have been like if the Anglish had never come to the shores of Markesland. It had been only us once: Masquisit and Naquisit, Maswachuisit, Akashneisit, and Naregannisit. People farther inland turned up in stories, like the Odwa and Wendat of the deep lakes. I'd never met any of those people, but they must have been real because they appeared in stories and in pennik novels about the brave Anglish settlers who were bringing civilization to the western frontier.

I hoped that the people in the west that I'd never met were having better luck at holding their lands against the settlers than we had.

ANEQUS WAS INTERVIEWED

The lichtbildmacher arrived the following morning, and I was dressed up in my school uniform and taken to the library along with Kasaqua to pose prettily in an assortment of mild and domestic scenes—Kasaqua in my lap while I read, her perched on my shoulder as I stood at the window, Marta and I conversing over needlework while both Kasaqua and Magnus lay sleeping on the floor. Magnus's presence made Kasaqua look a great deal smaller by comparison, which was probably the intention. The whole proceeding was overseen by Frau Brinkerhoff, and I came to understand that while it was going on, Frau Kuiper had called an assembly to address the other students.

After luncheon, Frau Kuiper called me to the library again to meet my interviewer. He was a smallish Vaskosish man in a brown tweed suit and a round-topped hat. He rose as I entered and offered his hand expectantly, and he shook mine quite vigorously when I offered it in turn. Frau Kuiper seemed poised to introduce us formally, but he spoke before she could.

"Luki Urdiroz, miss, *Vastergot Gazette*. May I say it's a pleasure to meet you, a great pleasure."

"Lovely to meet you, Herr Urdiroz," I said, only to be interrupted.

"Oh no, it's Mr. Urdiroz, not Herr. Herr Urdiroz is my father—fine man, my father, fine man. So I'm sure you won't find me rude for taking notes while we talk, because that's the point of this whole endeavor, right, miss? Good. Please, have a seat, have a seat."

He sat at the table opposite me, poised with a notepad and a wax pencil.

"Well, as you two seem to have acquainted yourselves amiably, I'll be in my office if I'm needed. Mr. Urdiroz, please come and see me there before you leave."

"Yes, ma'am. Thank you very much," he said, tipping his hat. After she'd gone, he turned to me and said, "So I've been absolutely dying to ask you, what made you decide to pursue a life as a dragoneer in the first place? Did it have anything to do with Mr. Knecht and his fantastic acquisition of a dragon last year? That must have been a great inspiration to your people."

"It didn't at all," I answered. "I didn't know anything at all about Mr. Knecht or his dragon until after Kasaqua had chosen me. And I didn't precisely *choose* to become a dragoneer. We hatched Kasaqua according to our own traditions, giving her a free choice at her hatching of anyone in the village. She chose me."

"Interesting! So you folks out on the islands have your own way of doing things? I suppose you'd have to, now, wouldn't you? And how is it that you folks came by a dragon egg exactly? Herr Stafn's colorful essay says the circumstances are poorly understood."

"I don't see why. I explained the situation very clearly to Captain Einarsson—he's the academy's representative to the Ministry of Dragon Affairs—when I first arrived. Kasaqua's mother laid the egg on the highest point of Slipstone Island, which is the last spit of dry land between here and Old Anglesland. I saw her briefly, and never interacted with her at all. But she seemed very sad, and it's well-documented that dragons whose dragoneers have died quite often pine to death not long after. The last I saw of Kasaqua's mother, she was flying out over the open ocean. I went to Slipstone Island the following day to mark the passing of a dragon, because that's significant to my people, and I discovered the egg. I brought it to our town meeting hall. There was nothing at all clandestine about the proceedings; if our representative to the ministry or our torgar failed to notice the presence of a dragon egg, it was only by lack of interest in Masquapaug in general. I'm not even sure if Masquapaug *has* a torgar, or who he is if we do have one—we've never met anyone of the sort. We contacted the academy straightaway after Kasaqua had hatched."

"Tell me, do you think of yourself first as a nackie, or as a citizen of Lindmarden?"

"I'm not sure that I understand the question," I said carefully. "I consider myself as myself, who I am to my family and to my community. Citizenship has never much factored into it. On Masquapaug, our only ties to Lindmarden are by way of tax collectors, and I only liminally understand taxation because I've never had enough of an income to get anyone's attention, nor did I ever expect to. My father pays taxes on his whaling income, but we generally deal very little in Anglish money, and thus in Anglish affairs."

"I must say you're terribly well spoken, miss," he said, and somehow it felt more like an insult than a compliment. "I've been told by Frau Kuiper that you're quite the accomplished scholar. What's your favorite academic subject?"

"In terms of preference, I quite enjoy natural philosophy. In terms of practicality, it's important that I excel at skiltakraft. I like to hope that I'll perform sufficiently well in both—though I've only been attending classes for a couple of weeks, so it's rather too soon to tell. I spend a good deal of my time reading, both for coursework and for pleasure, though I wouldn't have marked myself especially scholarly if someone else hadn't said so first."

"What kind of reading do you most enjoy doing, when it's not your coursework?"

"I'm a great follower of pennik novels," I said. "We don't get periodicals on the island, but I've recently begun reading the adventures of Sybille Stosch, as recommended by a new friend here at the academy."

"Well, we all need to indulge in our guilty pleasures now and again," he said with a wry smile, as if reading pennik novels and adventure serials was something I ought to be ashamed of. "You mentioned skiltakraft earlier. As I understand it, that's a terribly important sort of thing for a dragoneer to know. You think you've got a good handle on the subject?"

"I understand the underlying principles of skiltakraft as it relates to minglinglore and the transmutation of athers. Kasaqua is still quite young, but I'm confident that I'll be able to shape her breath effectively when the time comes."

"What do you hope to achieve with your dragon, when you've completed your education? What sort of career have you got planned?"

"I never expected to have anything but a simple life, and I don't see why Kasaqua choosing me should change that. I intend, when my education is complete, to go back to Masquapaug and to utilize Kasaqua's talents to assist my community—to produce zurfni to enrich the soil, or to draw water from the air in a dry growing season. Our blacksmiths are always in want of quality isen, as it can't be mined on the island, and I've read that isen can be derived from seawater with dragon's breath. I've entertained the idea that perhaps someday I could master the skilta that would allow me to produce strahlendstone, which is much desired by tinkers for the powering of tatkraftish devices. A tatkraftish gristmill could be of great use to my people, for example. We currently grind most of our corn by hand milling. Altogether, I'd like to have a life of good health and good comfort, for myself and my loved ones. Professor Ulfar has suggested that I might write and publish some treatises of natural philosophy. Kasaqua's breed isn't well described or documented in any of the available lore, and my observations of her growth and behavior might be of interest to those who make comparative studies of dragons."

"I understand that you're going to turn sixteen quite soon," he said. "Do you intend to have a formal announcement and season, now or after your education has been completed?"

I felt my cheeks flush at the suggestion. *Sævinsdottir's Guide* made much of the importance of the social season and of a girl's coming out at the age of sixteen or thereabouts.

"It's been my understanding that the primary purpose of the social season is the arrangement of suitable marriages," I said, trying to smile prettily but probably not managing it. "I'm not sure that participation in the social season would be the best use of my time."

"Oh, you might well be surprised, miss," he said with that same wry smile. "You are, after all, a very handsome woman, and a dragoneer at that."

I frowned uncomfortably and cleared my throat. "Well, in any case, at the moment I'm dedicating all of my time and attention to my education so that I may, while Kasaqua is still young, become the best possible dragoneer that I may be."

"Very prudent, I'm sure," Mr. Urdiroz said, apparently *finally* catching my mood. "Do you have any personal statements that you'd like to direct to the general readership of the *Vastergot Gazette?*"

"Only that I'm not as exceptional as everyone seems to think I am, and neither is Theod. We on the islands are quite ordinary people with quite ordinary lives. We farm and fish and mind our own affairs, as we have since the beginning of time. For a while, due to unfortunate circumstances, we did not have dragons—and we keenly felt the lack of them. Now, by providence, we shall have dragons again. Our stories and songs go back into mythic times, just as yours do, and they make much mention of dragons. This is nothing radical or progressive; it's a return to the old ways."

"That's a terribly interesting way of looking at the situation, Miss Anequs," he said, raising his eyebrows. "And I think that's as good a conclusion to the interview as I'm likely to get. Thank you very much for your time, and I do hope that we'll have occasion to speak again sometime in the future."

He stood and offered his hand, and shook my hand hard enough to rattle my bones before making his way to Frau Kuiper's office, leaving Kasaqua and me in the library.

I wondered if I'd be allowed to take dinner in the dining hall today.

ANEQUS BECAME A SUBJECT OF PUBLIC ATTENTION

I learned from Sander that Frau Kuiper's address to the students had largely consisted of warnings that there would be no tolerance of harassment of any student, without expressly mentioning Theod or me by name. That *any* violent or antagonistic behavior, anything that might upset a dragoneer to the point of inspiring action in their dragon, was a mark of unfitness to command a dragon and that the consequences could be as dire as expulsion from the academy or even destruction of a student's dragon.

The week progressed without much fanfare; the general attitude of the student body seemed somber and frightened, with a distinct edge of resentment toward me and Theod any time we entered a room. I attended my classes and spent most of my time reading. None of my classmates spoke to me at all, which I didn't particularly mind.

The interviews appeared in the *Vastergot Gazette* on Saturday, the twenty-fourth of September.

I'd never had a lichtbild taken of myself before—I didn't know if any lichtbildmacher had ever been to Masquapaug, in fact. I sent a telegram to Niquiat, telling him to buy a copy of the *Gazette* for Mother. I was very interested to read Theod's half of the interview; he hadn't been asked precisely the same questions that I had. His part of the article included a summary of the circumstances leading to Theod's binding with Copper and the subsequent moot. Interestingly, Theod had answered the question "Do you think of yourself first as a nackie or as a citizen of Lindmarden?" with a firm assertion of citizenship above anything else. He'd cited dragon husbandry as his favorite academic subject, and neatly skirted questions about skiltakraft.

Mr. Urdiroz did not seem to have been at all concerned with Theod's marriage prospects or reading habits, and something about that rankled just a bit, though I couldn't have explained why.

I was expressly told by Frau Brinkerhoff that I should not leave the school grounds that weekend, that time should be given for the general public to become aware of the interviews, for them to undo any ill feeling toward Theod and me that Herr Stafn's editorial might have inspired. Marta did not go away for the weekend, either, so I had to forgo my Sunday morning with Liberty. I took a long constitutional with Kasaqua and worked on the sorts of drills that Professor Mesman had prescribed. She very much enjoyed playing at fetch-and-carry once she understood the game. She did, however, become distracted quite easily. More than once I'd thrown the knotted rope and she'd returned with a freshly killed field mouse. I always praised her regardless.

On Monday, the twenty-sixth of September, I received three letters.

I was already familiar with the workings of the mail room because of my correspondence home and with Niquiat, but for the first time I'd received letters from parties unknown to me. One was sealed in gold wax, and the paper smelled faintly of rose water. When I opened it, it read:

To Miss Anequs Aponakwesdottir,

Will you favor us with your company for luncheon at the estate of Professor Tindra Brahe on Saturday, the fifth of November? Also invited are Frau Karina Kuiper, Mr. Theod Knecht, Herr Vidar Graversen, and Frau Lysa Mølgaard. We hope you will join us in conversation on the subjects of natural philosophy and folkreckoning. We will be assembling at one o'clock. Kindly respond if you are able to attend.

Yours ever sincerely,
Professor Tindra Brahe

I'd have to confer with Frau Brinkerhoff as to the correct course of action regarding invitation to luncheon from someone I'd never met. I didn't particularly want to go, but it seemed like the kind of social nicety that might well be required of me by the rules of Anglish society. The second letter was . . . strange. It was a piece of brown paper, thrice folded and sealed with an oily wax that had bled a greasy halo around the seal. The text within was inexpertly written in a large, bold hand.

Est. Miss Anequs,

I do hope that you will ~~ees~~ excuse the rudeness of my sending you this letter not having been introducd to you first. I wish you to know that your story has affected me v. strongly.
    My name is Ingrid Hakansdottir. I am 10 years-old and I am half nackie by my mother. I do not know much about being a nackie. Mother says that her grandmother was a daughter of the king of narry-gannet-sit. I have seen your

picture with your dragon in the Vastergot Gazette. You are very beautiful and very daring. It says in the article that you read Sybille Stosch, and I read Sybille Stosch too!

My favorite color is purple. What is your favorite color? My favorite books is The Erelore of Friedgr and Margund. What is your favorite book? My favorite time of year is winter because I love sledding. What is your favorite time of year?

My older brother Aksel is in love with you but he will not write a letter to tell you so.

I wish to become a dragoneer some-day and also I wish to visit Mask Island and I wish that I could meet you. I hope that you will respond to this letter. I can be got at the following address:

Miss Ingrid Hakansdottir
701 N Center Street 4th
Vastergot, New Anglesland

Yours sinserely,
Ingrid Hakansdottir

I returned to my room immediately to pen a response.

Dear Miss Hakansdottir,

I am terribly pleased to make the acquaintance of a descendant of the king of the Naregannisit! I have only just begun to read Sybille Stosch, but I am enjoying it very much; her adventures are quite engaging. My favorite color is red, my favorite book is <u>The Katermann Papers</u> because I enjoy intriguing mysteries, and my favorite time of year is autumn because it's when my father returns from sea and because I especially enjoy harvest foods and games. How old is your brother? I have three siblings—brother Niquiat aged 17, brother Sigoskwe aged 10, and sister Sakewa aged 8. I wish you the very best of luck in someday becoming a dragoneer, and perhaps someday when I am not living at school, I shall invite you to come and visit me and my family on Masquapaug.

Sincerely yours,
Anequs

I'd also received a letter from Mother, telling me all about what was happening on the island in my absence; the corn harvest and the dance following it, Sigoskwe having great success at snaring rabbits, Sakewa losing a baby tooth. I wrote back, telling my family about my adventures with Niquiat and Liberty, and about my classes and new acquaintances. By the time I'd finished that, it was time for luncheon. I'd have to ask Frau Kuiper about Professor Tindra Brahe's letter following my afternoon class.

AUTUMN CAME

Frau Kuiper enthusiastically endorsed the gathering at Professor Tindra Brahe's in November, and informed me that arrangements would be made for our attendance. But the gathering was soon driven from my mind because, at the end of September, everyone started to talk about Valkyrjafax and the fact that there was going to be a dance. It certainly occupied all of Marta's thoughts, and she lectured to Sander and Theod and me about it over dinner on Monday evening.

"The rite of the Valkyrja will be performed at sunset, and the ball will follow," Marta said. "They shore up the numbers of young ladies by having the boys invite sisters and cousins and all. We're going to have to have you outfitted in an evening gown, Anequs—none of the dresses that you have will do at all."

"And where am I supposed to get the money for a ball gown? That's asking rather more than train fare," I said, raising my eyebrows at her.

Marta turned to Theod.

"What did you do last year, for the ball? I don't remember seeing you, but we hadn't yet been acquainted, and in any case I spent most of the night comparing dance cards with Emmeline and Kerstin."

"I didn't attend the ball last year," Theod said, looking at his plate. "I don't own anything that would be suitable for the ballroom, nor am I versed in dancing. I joined Henkjan and the lads from the dragonhall for applejack and dice. It was a lovely time."

Marta stared for a moment, a look of polite incomprehension on her face, then delicately took a sip from her glass and dabbed at her lips with a napkin before she continued.

"Well. We shall have to talk to Fraus Kuiper and Brinkerhoff about the necessity of outfitting both of you for the ball, then. It's one thing for a man to choose not to attend, but it would be shamefully remiss for one of the only two female students not to be in attendance. I'm certain that my own seamstress could be persuaded to extend herself in an act of charity. I shall make the appointment, and both of you shall have to come and join me at Sjokliffheim in Estervall this Saturday."

"Miss Hagan, that isn't at all necessary," Theod said, looking slightly panicked.

"Nonsense," Marta said, flitting her fan. "I shall send a telegram to my father this very evening, and it shall all be arranged."

Sander wrote something in his tablet and slid it across the table to Marta. Marta read it and said, "Oh, that's all right. To be honest, I think that my father might take umbrage to my inviting a young man home anyway." She looked at Theod and me. "Sander won't be able to join us, as his mother has requested his company at their home this coming Saturday."

"If your father would take umbrage at you inviting a young man home, where does that leave me?" Theod asked.

"Oh, well." Marta blushed, closing Sander's tablet and sliding it back across the table to him. "It's rather different, with you, isn't it? It's not . . . The social implications aren't . . ." She glanced at me as if I could help her, but I only stared.

This coming Saturday was Liberty's salon; I had hoped to attend it with her. But there was no polite way for me to decline Marta's invitation on those grounds; Liberty and I weren't supposed to be seeing each other at all.

We spent the rest of the meal discussing the particulars of our classes and our progress therein. Sander was very animated on the subject of skiltakraft, favoring us with a number of diagrams drawn on his tablet. Marta fretted about the essay she had to write for erelore, and ended up reciting to us a very brief summary of the Vaskoslandish War, which had drawn the present border between Lindmarden and Berri Vaskos. We finished with dinner and the feeding of our dragons, and parted company with Theod and Sander for the evening. Back in our room, Marta went on at great length about what was currently fashionable in evening attire. She spent the better part of the evening trying on various dresses from her wardrobe, while I politely pretended interest and tried to complete a workbook of natural philosophy.

On Friday afternoon, Frau Brinkerhoff found me after the morning session of class and asked me to join her in her office, to "discuss my funds." She was very surprised to learn that I still had four of the fifteen marka she'd given me upon my arrival at school. My most expensive single purchase had been the corset and petticoat from Jenni's. Most of my money had been spent on postage, telegrams, and train fare—I'd been able to stretch it, at times, by Niquiat offering to pay my way when he could. Frau Brinkerhoff commended me on my thrift and good sense, and gave me *four* five-marka coins, telling me they were meant to last until the beginning of November.

The next morning, the first of October, Marta's father arrived in an automotor-carriage.

I'd never actually seen an automotor before, not close enough for it to matter. The front of it was low-slung, a long and narrow housing for the engine perched between yard-wide wheels clad in rubber. Behind that was the pilot's seat, and on a stage behind and slightly above was the passenger compartment, with two benches that faced each other, one forward and one backward. There was a folded mass of waxed canvas at the back, which could probably be drawn over the top of the compartments, but the weather was very fine and the pilot and passenger seats were open to the air just now. The rear wheels were twice as large as the front ones. Hitched to the rear of the carriage there was an open-sided horse trailer for Copper and Magnus to ride in. Kasaqua had been deemed small enough to be allowed to take a place at our feet in the passenger compartment, if only just.

"You'll find wrappers and goggles in compartments under the seats. You'll want to cover up, so as not to ruin your school clothes with the dust of the road," Marta's father warned in a jolly voice as he came walking down a little set of stairs that he'd deployed from the passenger compartment. He was wearing a brown canvas overcoat and a pair of dusty goggles himself, and he refrained from embracing Marta, though I could see that he wanted to.

"The pilot is my right hand, Herr Otterlo," Marta's father said, indicating him. "I'm very pleased to invite you to visit Sjokliffheim. Have either of you ever ridden in an automotor before?"

"Once, when I was transported here from New Linvik," Theod answered smoothly, "but it wasn't nearly as fine as this one."

I glanced at Theod in surprise, because he'd never spoken of his journey from New Linvik before. He wasn't looking at me. He was watching as one of the young men from the dragonhall led Copper—fully tacked and looking quite regal—into the horse trailer. Another was following with Magnus, who was trying to pull away and join Marta.

"Young man, if you'll go first and assist the ladies, I'll bring up the rear and disengage the stairs," Marta's father said, clapping Theod on the shoulder, which made him startle and stiffen.

Theod ascended the stairs and held out his hand to pull Marta up. I followed.

Theod's hand was dry and callused under mine, his grip firm and sure as he pulled me up into the passenger compartment. I met his eye for just a moment while he was holding my hand, and I felt something tighten in my belly the same way it had when Liberty had met my eyes while taking my measurements.

We donned the offered wrappers and goggles, and took our seats. I was seated beside Marta, facing the same direction as the driver. Theod took a seat beside Marta's father, facing us.

"I'm afraid that automotor travel isn't especially conducive to pleasant conversation," Marta's father said as the pilot started the engine, which was terrifically loud and rumbling, forcing him to continue at a shout, "but it's very bracing!"

The automotor proceeded at a modest pace down the road away from the school, but when we pulled onto the cobbled road that ran away from the train station it sped along, making the wind whip through my hair. I laughed, watching the scenery slipping by. I'd never gone this fast across land; we were *sailing*. Kasaqua put her foreclaws up on the edge of the compartment and stuck her head out, facing into the wind.

I wondered if this was what flying was like.

We arrived in Estervall before noon. Estervall was on the coast, and the car slowed considerably as it took a winding path along the edge of a high cliff that looked out over the ocean. Marta said something that I couldn't understand, but she was pointing, and I followed her gaze to a huge building of whitewashed brick perched near the edge of the cliff.

That was my first sight of Sjokliffheim.

ANEQUS VISITED NEW PLACES

The automotor stopped at the apex of a long, curving road that connected to a paved path leading to the front door. Copper was brought along with the auto to the dragonhall by the carriage house, but Magnus was released to join us and seemed entirely thrilled about being here, gamboling around like an excited puppy. Kasaqua joined him, pouncing and feinting as they chased across the grass, and both Marta and I giggled at their energetic joy.

Marta's house was cavernous. It had a front hall, and a grand parlor, and a main dining room, which we passed through with quickness. All of the walls were papered in flowery patterns and gay colors. All of the ceilings were whitewashed, all of the floors carpeted. The gaslight sconces were made of sparkling cut glass, and there was no soot on the walls above them. I'd seen water-color plates of rooms that looked like this, in magazines, but I'd never seen the reality.

We were introduced to the housekeeper, and Marta's father made a boisterous show of inviting Theod to join him in the trophy room for refreshment and a game of cards while he waited for Herr Otterlo to finish putting the auto away. Meanwhile, I was ushered up a massive carpeted staircase to Marta's private suite. She had a small parlor attached to her bedroom, with a washroom of her own beyond. From her parlor, I could see a wide lawn behind the house and a slate path that wound its way between fading rosebushes toward the cliffs. I could see the ocean beyond. It was a breathtaking view, and I felt an immediate and painful stab of homesickness. Marta didn't seem to notice.

"I've told Frau Rehn to have luncheon brought to us up here so we can talk about dresses. Papa's valet will see to Theod; it's always so much easier for a gentleman to dress, anyway. My seamstress should be here around two in the afternoon to deliver my gown and take your measurements." She proceeded to select a half dozen magazines from a stack on a shelf and spread them out before me.

"I'm going to be wearing a dress of apple-green silk taffeta with gold trimmings. This being an autumn ball, rich colors are much preferred, which is to your advantage because you've quite a dark and ruddy complexion. You'd look very well in ocher or bronze, I think, and your hair dressed with pheasant feathers and yellow chrysanthemums—something like this."

She thumbed through one of the magazines until she found the plate she was seeking and held it out for my inspection. It showed four young women in evening finery, watercolor paint over ink to show the colors. One of them was wearing a deep yellow dress with a cascade of ruffles.

"You're somewhat thick-waisted, so a dress that has some detailing at the hips would suit your figure best. Perhaps a draped overskirt? You'll certainly want puffed sleeves, because you've got lovely shoulders and a very delicate collarbone, and a draping sleeve will widen your profile above the waist and make you look more slender. You're going to need a proper hooped petticoat, for a ball gown. I've got several, so there's no reason you shouldn't borrow one of mine. They're quite forgiving in the waist. And you'll need a dress corset. The one you wear beneath your uniform won't do *at all* for an evening dress, and neither will the one I've seen you wear with your country dresses. I don't think any of my dress corsets will properly fit you, but you could try one on to get the idea—we'll just leave the laces well open at the back."

This led to me standing in Marta's dressing room, modeling her underpinnings. The corset was all silk and whalebone, embroidered along the top and bottom edges in pale blue floss, much more supple than my uniform corset but more structured than the one I'd bought from Jenni. It was a different sort of shape as well—it did quite startling things to my bustline, and drew my waist in at least a couple of inches, widening my hips in turn. Marta declared it a smashing success and demanded that I try one of her petticoats, too. Rather than cords, the petticoat had hoops of whalebone sewn into the seams of each of its tiers. I understood now how Dagny had achieved her supernaturally voluminous skirts. I looked at myself in Marta's absurdly huge threefold mirror. The effect was something like an overturned wineglass. Kasaqua walked around me and then nosed underneath the hem to locate my vanished feet. She was able to entirely conceal herself. Magnus rose from his spot beside Marta's bed, sniffing at my hem to see where Kasaqua had disappeared. When Kasaqua shot a paw out from under the edge and touched his nose, he startled back with a honking cry.

"The dragons will of course be relegated to the dragonhall or our rooms for the evening, to avoid such missteps," Marta said with a giggle, summoning Magnus to her side and consoling him with petting.

"Have you been to many dances?" I asked, shooing Kasaqua away from my feet and unfastening the petticoat. "I'm afraid this is yet another of those Anglish things for which I don't know the correct protocol."

"I attended my first real dance when I was twelve, at Frau Sveirda's School for Girls," Marta said fondly. "You'll be given a dance card, which outlines which songs will be played and in what order. Young men will petition you for the privilege of joining you in certain dances. It's best not to try and fill your dance card too quickly at the beginning of the evening, in case you meet someone you'd really like to keep dancing with. It's terribly improper to dance more than two sets with the same young man on the same evening, though. The purpose of dances is to mingle and socialize with young men of the appropriate social class."

"I don't know the steps of Anglish dances," I said, frowning.

"Oh my, that's right, you never went to primary school! We shall have to remedy this *very* quickly. I'm certain that I can teach you a passable waltz, and a tanz, in the space of a couple of afternoons. Springar and polka can be a bit more challenging, and if there's a zwiefacher on the program you might try to make an excuse to sit it out—take refreshment or a promenade or something. The better part of most dancing is really allowing your partner to lead you and keeping your steps fluid and dainty."

"You learned how to dance . . . at school?" I asked, tilting my head because I couldn't see how dancing would fit into the kinds of lessons that we'd been having at Kuiper's.

"Dancing gracefully is a very important skill for a young lady to have," Marta said primly. "After luncheon, but before my seamstress arrives, I was wondering if you'd like to take a promenade with me in the rose garden. The roses haven't quite passed, and the sea air is so lovely at this time of year."

By the time I'd finished putting my school uniform back on, the maids had brought us luncheon. There was tea, and cucumbers with dill, and some kind of squash soup that had been run through a mill. Theod, it seemed, was dining with Herr Hagan.

The weather was absolutely beautiful outside, and I was very happy to walk through Marta's rose garden, listening to her talk about the names of all the different varieties and how I really must come and see it in May or June, when it was at its best. Kasaqua chased after bumblebees, and Magnus chased after Kasaqua, showers of petals falling in their wake. I kept glancing past the edge of the garden, to the path that ran along the cliffside, and the ocean beyond. It had been more than a month since I'd been on a beach or smelled salt air.

I didn't especially want to be dressed up in silk and made to dance Anglish dances with Anglish boys who were very certainly not of "the appropriate level of society" as far as I was concerned.

I wanted to go home.

We came to an archway that was absolutely resplendent with pink-white blossoms and fat scarlet rosehips. Marta closed her eyes and leaned in, reveling in their fragrance. When she leaned back, she looked . . . sad.

"My mother always loved the rose garden so much," Marta said, cradling a blossom in her hand. "I miss her."

"I'm so sorry, Marta," I said, feeling helpless. It was different than Liberty telling me about how she'd lost her parents, somehow; Liberty was more matter-of-fact about it.

"You've got a large family, haven't you?" Marta asked. "I've met your brother Niquiat, and you mentioned another brother and a sister, and your parents are both still with you, and a grandmother . . ."

"Grandma who lives with us is my mother's mother—Grandpa, my mother's father, passed on a few years ago. My mother has two brothers; the older one is a whaler like my father, and the younger one lives on Masquapaug and has two sons and a daughter. I know the daughter best—my cousin Mishona, the drumsinger. She's four years older than me and used to do older-sister sorts of things with me and my friend Hekua, since neither of us had older sisters of our own and she had no younger ones. My father has a younger sister who has two girls and a boy. They used to live with my father's mother, before she passed on, but now they live with great auntie Mamisashquee and her husband because they have no children of their own to help them. My father had an older brother, but he and their father were killed in 1825. We don't speak much about them."

"The Nack Island uprising," Marta murmured. "I'd never considered . . ."

"How did you lose your mother?" I asked, hoping to change the subject.

"She became consumptive when I was ten," Marta said, letting her hand fall away. Several of the flower's petals came away with it, fluttering delicately to the ground. "She died when I was twelve. She never got to know that I actually went through with my mad-girl dream of becoming a dragoneer, so I don't know what she'd think of me now. She always wanted me to be a proper young lady. To marry well."

"I'm sure your mother is very proud of you," I said firmly. "It's a great honor to be chosen by a dragon. It marks you as a very special sort of person, who will accomplish important things for your people."

"Is that what your people think of you?" Marta said, smiling sadly. "That you're going to do great things for them?"

She turned to look at me, and for a moment her eyes met mine and I felt . . . hollow. Because that's what my people ought to have thought of me, and maybe some of them did, but the reality was that everyone was terribly worried about what the return of dragons to Masquapaug might mean—for us, and for the Anglish.

The maid called us then, telling us that Marta's seamstress had arrived, and we went inside to meet her without saying anything else.

AND LEARNED OF ANGLISH CUSTOMS

For the following three Saturdays, Marta conscripted Sander to be my partner as she taught me how to waltz and tanz and polka. We utilized an empty lecture hall, and Marta's Victrola. Anglish dancing involved quite a lot of spinning around and around each other, often at frankly dizzying speeds. There didn't seem to be much point to all of it—it wasn't at all like many of the dances back home that told stories or called to spirits—but it was a great deal of fun. Sander was stiff and awkward, constantly staring at his own feet. We stepped on each other's toes a great deal, but we laughed through it while Marta crossly reminded us that this was a very serious endeavor.

Niquiat became eighteen on the thirteenth of October, and I was permitted to visit with him in the city for the occasion. The two of us, and Strida and Zhina and Ekaitz, attended the same pennik opera I'd visited in the first week of September. Kasaqua was the size of a wolverine by now, though, and was very much more *noticed* than she'd been before. A great number of people wanted to pet her—it was apparently very good luck to touch a dragon—and she enjoyed the attention immensely.

My dress was delivered on Monday the twenty-fourth, four days before Friday's dance. Marta made me try it on in the gap between morning class and luncheon, and spent a long time fussing with my hair and cooing at me in the washroom mirror. I stood still and allowed it, feeling very much like a paper doll. She repeatedly commented about how *striking* my complexion was and how well the bronze taffeta complemented it. I had to admit that it looked very well on; Marta was right about the color suiting me. It didn't make me look washed out, as I had been afraid it might. The cut was *very* fashionable, and the boned petticoat made the skirt feel practically weightless. The puffed sleeves had starched internal supports, and the combination of large off-the-shoulder sleeves and an impossibly full skirt made my waist look very slender. It came with a pair of silk dancing slippers that were laced up with ribbon—they had thin, supple soles and felt more similar to moccasins than any other Anglish shoes I'd ever worn.

Much to Marta's disappointment across the two successive evenings, my hair could not be persuaded—either through hot isen, or waxy pomade, or prayer to Rune's Fingerbones and Enki's Teeth and Joden's Eye and Fyra's Tits—to hold a curl. She had to make herself content with a complicated array of braids in the Anglish style.

On Friday, classes were suspended. Our dragons were fed after luncheon rather than after dinner, and were seen safely away into our rooms or to their stalls in the dragonhall. Kasaqua was terribly cross and hurt about being shut up in my room with only Magnus for company, because she sensed that something of interest was happening to which she was not party. It made me feel *itchy*, somehow, at the back of my mind. I wondered if all the other dragoneers felt it, too, and how they managed if they did. From my observations these two months, it seemed to me that Anglish breeds of dragon were more generally docile and even-tempered than Kasaqua was.

Marta spent twice as long on her own dressing and hair as she had on mine. I had to admit that she did look enchanting in her green gown, her hair done up in a cascading mass of curls dressed with gold ribbons and a crown of gilt leaves. She'd outlined her eyes with a sort of black wax, making them look huge and liquid, like a doe's eyes. She offered to do the same for me, but I declined. With my luck I'd manage to smear it all across my face.

The sun was touching the horizon on the lawn behind the dragonhall when the bell rang to call us to assembly, and Marta giddily took my hand and led me into the fray.

There were more than two hundred people gathered on the lawn. Half of them were our classmates, but the other half were unfamiliar young women. I let Marta draw me through the crowd, because she seemed to have some idea of what was going on. I spied Niklas and Dagny, and Sander standing with Lisbet and their mother. Marta brought us to the edge of the crowd, which was arrayed in a narrow arc along some imaginary line.

A bell rang, and everyone fell silent, looking away into the field.

At one end of the field, Frau Kuiper was standing beside Gerhard, and at the other end Captain Einarsson was standing with his ferocious silberdrache. He was holding a burning torch and some kind of narrow-ended container on a chain. She was holding a silver goblet and a dagger. Between them, in the middle of the field from the far side, Frau Brinkerhoff and a number of the maids appeared, all dressed in white; Liberty wasn't among them. In fact, all of them seemed to be upstairs maids. They'd come from the road that led out to the farms, and they appeared as a procession with Frau Brinkerhoff at the head.

She was leading a white horse that was done up in very fancy tack with gold ribbon and bells. It was pulling a little wagon, and for a moment I thought there was a second horse, but as it came into better view I saw that it was only a sculpture.

They'd built a horse from bundles of wicker and straw. It was just slightly bigger than a real horse, standing on three legs with the fourth drawn up, its head held at a proud angle. The mane and tail were made of drawn flax, very cleverly done, and they blew slightly in the wind. It was wearing a wreath of wheat sheaves around its neck, and around its feet were piled garlands of sunflowers and chrysanthemums. The wagon itself seemed to be full of apples, at least a half dozen bushels of them. The whole cart was decked with ribbons and streamers, positively glowing in the last light of sunset.

"We're very lucky here at the academy," Frau Brinkerhoff said, her voice carrying across the field. "It's not everyone who has their own Valkyre to perform the rite."

Frau Kuiper laughed aloud—a harsh and braying laugh—but she moved from her place at Gerhard's side and strode purposefully toward the horse with the silver cup in one hand and the knife in the other. I watched with some alarm as she used the dagger to make a shallow cut low on the horse's neck, gathering the flowing blood into the cup. The horse jerked and stamped a little, but Frau Brinkerhoff was holding it firmly by the bridle, hushing and petting it while this proceeded, and the whole operation was completed in less than a minute. Frau Kuiper held the cup and the dagger aloft, and said, "For the glory of the Valkyrja, and of Fyra their mistress, we offer this sacrifice."

Frau Brinkerhoff led the white horse away, while Frau Kuiper dipped her fingers into the blood and used them to paint strange symbols onto the straw horse's head and neck and flanks—I recognized them as atheric figures, parts of a skilta.

"They say that there are still people back in the old country who sacrifice the *real* horse," Marta whispered conspiratorially, "but that seems terribly cruel and uncivilized, don't you think, when it's only a bit of blood that's needed?"

I could only nod mutely, watching as the maids moved to stack the piles of prepared firewood into the wagon around the straw horse. When they'd finished and moved away, standing in a circle around the wagon, Captain Einarsson came striding across the field. He did something to the bottom of his container, and something began spilling from the bottom of it in a fine column like sand through an hourglass. He began to walk a purposeful pattern around the cart, moving from one maid to another—drawing the lines of another skilta, I realized—an enormous one that centered on the wagon. When he finished, coming back to the point he'd started, he stoppered the bottom of the container again and shouted something in a language I didn't know. Possibly old Norse; some of the words seemed similar to ones I'd been learning in folklore.

From the dark of the road beyond the field, there was a sound of horns and bells. Another procession appeared, this one composed of the men who worked at the dragonhall, leading a wagon pulled by two oxen. It was just as bedecked as the horse cart had been, but its cargo was a rack of barrels with taps. They moved it to sit behind the wagon, at the point where many of the skilta's lines converged—the place where the final product of the transmuted inputs would be deposited.

Frau Kuiper and Captain Einarsson moved to stand at opposite edges of the circle, and all of the maids and dragonhall workers took three steps backward. Frau Kuiper and Captain Einarsson moved in tandem, producing brass whistles and blowing the same notes on them. Gerhard came to Frau Kuiper's side, and Captain Einarsson's dragon to his, and in unison they each shouted another word of probably old Norse.

Both dragons together loosed breath at the cart. A great pillar of flame rose up from it, and a gust of wind that smelled of burning apples and herbs. The fire diminished, over the course of a minute or so, to merely a bonfire. At some signal that I didn't catch, a cheer rose up through the gathered crowd. The young men came back and began unloading the barrels, each of them requiring four men to carry. They were bringing them in the direction of the kitchens.

"What happens now?" I asked Marta quietly.

"Now we make pleasant conversation for a while, until the opening of the ballroom is announced," Marta said into my ear, linking arms with me and drawing me toward Sander and his family. Everyone else seemed to be leaving the arc, too, moving toward the school or gathering with other guests on the lawn, so I allowed Marta to lead me.

"You're perfectly capable of speaking, Sander," Sander's mother was saying as she fussed with the creases of his neckcloth. "I won't have you scribbling away all night. It's rude."

Sander looked very distressed, blank-faced and pale, standing stiffly, hardly even breathing.

"Mother, must you?" Lisbet said sweetly, laying a hand on her mother's arm to still it. She noticed us first and made a dainty little throat-clearing noise as she nodded in our direction. The other two turned to look at us.

"Frau Jansen, you're looking very well," Marta said, dipping her head deferentially.

"Marta, dear, how lovely you look this evening," Sander's mother said, smiling and batting her eyes. "Lisbet, this is Anequs Aponakwesdottir, one of the academy's scholarship students."

"We met, briefly, when we visited to situate Sander here at school," Lisbet said, offering a warm and genuine smile. "Sander's mentioned you in his letters. You're in skiltakraft class together?"

"Yes," I said, just a bit surprised that this young woman seemed to know something of me when I knew practically nothing of her. Sander didn't converse much on the topic of family.

"Has Marta told you that she and I were in primary school together? Oh, we simply *must* sit and chat for a while before the dancing begins."

"Anequs . . . dance card," Sander said, tapping his hand against his thigh and looking resolutely at the ground.

His mother turned to him and sighed wearily before saying, "Sander, darling, we've spoken about blurting things."

"Are you asking me to dance, Sander?" I asked, looking at him. He glanced up, meeting my eyes for a split second and extending his hand. I gave him my dance card, and he visibly relaxed.

"Sander has been kind enough to assist Marta in teaching me how to perform Anglish dances," I said to his mother while he wrote on the card with its attached pencil. He handed it back to me. On the third line, beside the neatly printed heading announcing *Polka: "Boiled Sugar Candy"* he'd written, *Sander Jansen seeks the pleasure of your company*—*Thank You*.

"I shall be very happy to dance the 'Boiled Sugar Candy Polka' with you, Sander," I said, smiling at him and dipping my head. I glanced back at his mother, who looked absolutely stunned.

"Mother, if it's quite all right with you," Lisbet said, "I'd love to introduce Marta and Sander and Anequs to some girls who are here from my school. I believe that the chaperones are gathering in the foreroom with Fraus Kuiper and Brinkerhoff, for refreshment."

"We promise that we'll take the dearest care of Lisbet, ma'am," Marta added, smiling.

It was clear from her expression that Frau Jansen had been talked into a corner of polite behavior that compelled her to allow her children to come along with Marta and me.

"Well, I suppose the entire point of a dance is to mingle," she said tightly. "Do be sure not to get too carried away, Lisbet, and if Sander—"

"Mother, everything is well in hand," Lisbet said with a dazzling smile, taking Sander's arm.

We parted company with Frau Jansen, moving toward a group of young women who were chatting and laughing in the distance.

AND THE SOCIETY OF LADIES AND GENTLEMEN

Lisbet brought us to Annetta, Bergitte, and Saskia. I'd met all of them on the same occasion I'd met Lisbet—the four of them had brothers currently in attendance at Kuiper's. We were seated in velvet chairs that had been placed in artful clusters all around the main hall. All of the other girls were sitting with their hands folded in their laps, dance cards readily on display. I followed suit.

"Sander's letters to Lisbet have been telling us the most *delicious* stories about you," Saskia said. "You have a brother who lives in the cannery district?"

"Yes, Niquiat. Marta, Sander, and Theod joined me on an outing to meet with him in the city early in September, and it was a lovely time."

"Marta, you haven't!" Lisbet said, grinning.

"I *have*," Marta said. "Anequs, Sander, Theod, and I went down into the cannery district, and we had coffee at a Kindah coffeehouse, and shopped in the most charming little bookstore. Her brother is very witty. A matter of social precedent drew me away from that party, I'm afraid, but if Miss Anequs would be so kind as to invite me again on such an outing, I'd surely accept."

"And you're allowed to just . . . come and go as you please?" Bergitte asked, something longing in her voice. "Oh that's not fair at all, I want to go to a boys' school!" And she pouted. She managed to make pouting look pretty.

"You . . . aren't allowed to come and go as you please?" I asked, feeling faintly horrified.

"Well, of course not!" Saskia said with a tinkling laugh. "We must be properly chaperoned any time we leave the school, and all social engagements must be arranged beforehand and approved of by our headmistress or our parents. It's frightfully tedious."

"Where *is* your other nackie pupil, by the by?" Bergitte asked, gazing at the young men who were milling around the room, occasionally stopping to talk to groups of seated young women. "I've been searching for him among the gentlemen, but I haven't seen him. I was so hoping that he could be convinced to ask me to dance. My mother would absolutely faint at the news that I'd danced with a nackie."

There was something about the way she said it that annoyed me. I didn't think there was malice in what she'd said, but the implication that dancing with Theod would be, of itself, some kind of scandalous act rankled.

"I haven't seen Theod tonight, either," I said. "I suppose that we could go look for him—"

Marta turned to me wide-eyed and shook her head slightly. I might have asked her why not, if Annetta hadn't spoken.

"A lady's place is to wait patiently to be adored," she said, sounding as if she were reciting from a book. "A lady does not parade herself about, seeking attention. Gentlemen of quality naturally abhor such brazen behavior."

"Are there gentlemen of quality here?" I asked, looking around. "I only see my classmates. Oh, and Sander, of course, but he's already asked me to dance."

They all laughed nervously, as if I'd said something quite forbidden. Marta fanned herself with her dance card, the gilding on the front glittering in the light of the gas lamps.

Niklas Sørensen walked over to us, flanked by a couple of first-year students with whom I was only passingly familiar.

"Miss Hagan," he said, bowing to Marta, "it's come to my attention that the first dance of the evening will be the 'Leaves in Autumn Waltz.' Would you afford me the pleasure of joining me in it?"

"I'd be most delighted, Mr. Sørensen," Marta said, her cheeks going very pink as she handed him her dance card. He signed it with a flourish, and Marta giggled. Beside me, Sander sighed.

"You know, you could ask her to dance," I whispered to him, while Marta and Niklas were still chatting away about how lovely the decorations were.

"Miss Hagan is a lovely girl," Sander mumbled, looking at his hands, which were laced together so tightly that his knuckles had gone perfectly white.

"Where's your tablet gotten to?" I asked. Sander shook his head.

"You must appear as a presentable gentleman you will not shame this family," he said, all in a rush. I frowned and made a decision.

"Marta, do excuse me for a moment, I need to go and ask Frau Brinkerhoff a question."

"We'll be right here waiting for you, unless you're not back when they announce entry to the ballroom," Marta said.

I swept through the main hall and into the foreroom, where the professors and parents were gathered in groups, sipping from cut glass cups. I spied Frau Brinkerhoff and Frau Kuiper . . . but they were talking to Frau Jansen. That path was closed to me, then. I had half a mind to simply go to my room and come back with a sheaf of paper, but then I spied Professor Ulfar.

His crab-chair had been polished to a mirror shine, all of its joined components glittering and casting bright cascades of light on the walls and floor around him. He'd traded his usual blue coat for the same kind of trim black jacket that every single gentleman seemed to be wearing, though he still had his medals in a row across the left side of his breast. He was talking to several fourth-year students, laughing at something someone had said.

I walked over, trying to affect the kind of pleasant and placid smile that the other girls seemed to find so natural.

"Good evening, Professor Ulfar, you're looking very well," I said, dipping a curtsy.

"Miss Anequs, don't you look lovely! But what brings you out here to the foreroom? Shouldn't you be sitting in the main hall while young men fight one another for the privilege of filling your dance card?"

I laughed, while the young men who'd been talking to him looked at one another awkwardly, as if they were wondering if they'd be expected to ask me to dance. That wasn't something I desired any more than they did, so I quickly turned to the subject at hand.

"I know that you're in the habit of keeping small notebooks on your person to take field notes. I was wondering if you happened to have one handy? If not I'll have to go all the way back to my room, and I'm certain that I'd be missed."

"Oh, have you found something of philosophical interest that demands you take notes?" he asked, brightening, as he rummaged with his left hand in the little leather case that stood ever at the ready beside the velvet-cushioned seat of his chair.

"One might say that. This is, of course, the first Anglish ball that I've ever been privileged to attend," I replied.

Professor Ulfar handed me a little notebook bound in brown cardstock, the sort that he had dozens of.

"Thank you very much, Professor, this will be perfect," I said, meeting his eyes as I took it from him. He smiled at me, canting his head a bit.

"I do hope that you have a lovely evening, Miss Anequs. I'd be very interested in hearing of your observations and opinions—at a later time, of course."

"Thank you. I hope that you have a lovely evening as well, Professor."

I was returning to where I'd left Sander and Marta and the others when I noticed Theod.

He was standing against the wall near the doorway between the foreroom and the main hall, with his hands folded behind his back. A footman's stance. He looked very polished in the suit that Marta's father had bought for him, tall and slim and square-shouldered. He also looked absolutely miserable.

Propriety be damned, I walked over to him.

"Dance the opening set with me," I said quietly, offering my dance card. He looked at it as if it might bite him.

"Anequs, this isn't—"

"It's not a request, Theod," I said, glaring at him. "The whole school is watching. We've got to put on a good show. Sander is dancing the third set with me, but no one's asked for my hand in the opening set and no one's likely to, and if I'm not dancing in the opening set *it will be noticed*. I'll leave you alone for the rest of the night, if you want, and you can go on pretending to be part of the furniture, but I need you to dance the opening set with me."

"I don't know how to waltz," Theod said desperately.

"It's a simple three-count dance. I can lead, if you like," I said.

"Women do not lead when dancing," Theod hissed through his teeth.

"Anglish women don't," I said, "but we're neither of us Anglish, are we?"

"Do you have any idea how people will talk?"

"They'll talk regardless, Theod. Let's give them something to say."

The fourth-year boys who'd been talking to Professor Ulfar came walking through just then, one of them pausing to glance at us. Under the sudden scrutiny, Theod took the dance card from me and quickly scribbled his name on the first line.

"I shall be delighted to join you in the 'Leaves in Autumn Waltz,' Mr. Knecht," I said loudly as I took the card back, smiling radiantly at him. "I did promise Marta that I'd return to her directly, though, and I'm sure she's wondering where I am. She's introduced me to the most delightful group of young ladies from Vígsteinnsdottir's Academy. Perhaps you'll pay us a call before the dancing begins?"

"I would be most honored, Miss Anequs," Theod said, smiling with his mouth but looking as if he wanted to murder me with his eyes. I smiled back at him and turned with enough swiftness that my skirt swished in my wake.

"There she is!" Marta said as I returned to the group, pointing at me with her dance card. "We'd wondered if you'd gotten lost. What kept you so long?"

"Mr. Knecht asked me to dance the first set with him," I said, sitting down and smoothing my skirt.

"I'm jealous!" Bergitte said with a titter of laughter, "but I suppose it's to be expected, since you two are of a kind and all. Would you put in a good word for me with him?"

"I certainly will," I said, smiling thinly before I turned to Sander.

"Professor Ulfar sends his regards for the evening," I said, handing him the notebook.

Sander's eyes positively lit up as he took it. After a moment's thought I detached the pencil from my dance card and handed him that as well. I certainly wasn't going to need it, since I had no intention of dancing with anyone other than Theod and Sander, and both of them had already made their claims. Sander kissed my hand, and I felt my cheeks flush a bit as I pulled back. I glanced to see if the others had noticed, but they all seemed engaged in speculation about a group of young men who were standing some distance off, making furtive glances at our party. When I turned back to Sander, he was already writing on the first page. He was writing enough to have *filled* the first page. He underlined something quite forcefully, then his head snapped up and he said, "Marta. Read it."

Marta startled at hearing her name practically barked, and looked somewhat taken aback when Sander thrust the notebook in her direction. She offered a brittle smile as she gingerly took it from him and began reading. Whatever he'd written made her expression soften and her cheeks go pink. When she looked back up, she was gazing at him as if no one else were present.

"Oh, Sander . . . yes, of course, I'd be happy to dance the 'Sunlight on the Sea Waltz' with you," she said, handing the notebook and her dance card to him. Sander signed it quickly and then laughed aloud, eyes closed, drumming his hands on his thighs. His obvious enthusiasm made Marta giggle, and when he'd composed himself he glanced at her and looked down at his hands before asking, "Would-you-take-refreshment-with-me-dear-lady," all in a rush, as if he'd practiced it.

"I wouldn't want Anequs to feel abandoned," Marta said, looking at me with the same sort of guilt she'd had when she'd run off with Dagny and Joreid at the gardens.

"Don't worry about Anequs, Marta, we'll take the very best care of her. Besides, the ballroom should be opening any minute now," Lisbet said before I could say anything.

I looked at her sidelong for a moment, but I nodded at Marta and said, "Go ahead. I'm sure Theod will be along to collect me in a moment anyway."

Marta took Sander's arm, and they went off together to the foreroom.

"That was very kind of you," Lisbet said quietly, gaining my attention. "Giving Sander the notebook, I mean."

"I can't begin to understand why he doesn't have his tablet with him," I said. "I've seldom seen him without it—he writes so eloquently."

"Mother's here," Lisbet said, pursing her lips. "Mother disapproves of anything that marks Sander as . . . odd. She's holding the tablet hostage against his good performance tonight. It's worse, since Father passed on . . ."

"That seems . . . unkind," I said, trying to keep my words judicious. Sander had never mentioned his father, except in the past tense, and I'd never asked. I felt slightly ashamed for having never asked.

"I want to thank you, truly, for being a friend to my brother. He's not an easy soul to understand, but he's such a dear creature if one even attempts to know him. He's been so terribly *happy* to have friends at school. The boys at his primary school were very cruel to him, you understand. Children often are."

"Are they?" I asked, frowning. Children in my experience were not, but then, given what I'd been told about how the Anglish brought up their children . . .

Lisbet looked slightly confused for a moment, then recovered herself.

"I have to thank you a second time for bringing Marta around, because I can only presume that that's your influence. She's always been polite to my brother, but she's never really known him. She and I have been friends for years, you understand, but I've been to her home far more often than she's been to mine. Mother prefers us not to take calls at home if she can avoid it at all, and Sander is so often asked to stay in his room for fear that he'll do or say something to cause embarrassment."

"I'd like to confess to having no comprehension at all of the Anglish preoccupation with social rules and manners," I said. "No one has explained anything to me about what this dance is even about—or even whether or not Anglish dances are about things! I don't know what Valkyrjafax is or why we should be dancing for it, or what all that business outside was with the horse and the straw horse and the bonfire . . ."

Lisbet looked mildly surprised for a moment, then asked, "No one's ever told you stories about the gods at all, have they? I suppose that your folk, like the Vaskosish and the Kindah, worship another set of gods entirely?"

"Something like that . . . though I don't think that we talk about our spirits and mythic figures quite the same way you talk about your gods. They've always felt like a very different sort of thing, to me, and I haven't really tried to pursue a greater knowledge of them aside from what's needed in my erelore and folklore classes."

"Would you like me to tell you the story of Valkyrjafax?" Lisbet asked.

"If you wouldn't mind, yes," I said.

Lisbet shifted slightly, straightening up, placing her hands parallel on her lap and looking at the space between them much the way Strida had looked at her hands on the table at Haddir's.

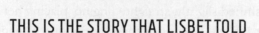

THIS IS THE STORY THAT LISBET TOLD

It was Sveni Alderaxe who stole the secret of mead-making for mankind.

In the ancient days before mankind had learned to work a forge, before Sigur Windtooth had conquered dragons for mankind, Joden and Fyra would rise to hunt at the turning of the first frost in the summerlands. His steed was the great lyndwyrm, a dragon beyond all mortal reckoning. Her steed was Hestejarl, the king of all horses. With them rode Fyra's Valkyrja and Joden's Skoggejan, and all together they rode across the sky with spears and bows of godly make, hunting the souls of men to serve them in Valhalya.

In those days, the Valkyrja—who were fierce, wild women who would take no husbands—would gain children by enjoying the charms of mortal men. What daughters they bore were raised among them to become Valkyrja themselves, but what sons they bore were left by night on the hearthstones of men's fasts. It's said by some that Sigur Windtooth, who slew the great lyndwyrm, was Valkyrja-born.

Sveni Alderaxe was a well-made man, broad in the shoulder and square in the jaw, his teeth straight and his hair golden. He lived in a great barrow-hall called Berni's Fast with many of his kin, and of them all he was the strongest and the fairest. Sveni went one day from Berni's Fast into the woods to select a tree to build a ship from. He had to travel far from Berni's Fast, because all the forest close by had been cut for wood long ago.

So off Sveni went, riding on the back of a mammoth, and he took with him a skin of sheep's milk to keep his strength up as he traveled. It was a day and a night and a day again before he came to the great dark wood, and his skin was quite empty by the time he began the work of felling an enormous tree.

Now, Sveni didn't know that the tree he'd selected was just then serving as a perch for a Valkyre who'd taken the form of an owl to come and have a pleasant sleep in the world of men, as Valkyrja are known to sometimes do. The strike of Sveni's axe awakened her, and when she looked down to see what had disturbed her sleep, she found Sveni quite pleasing! So she swooped down and changed into her true form: a naked woman with a cloak of owl feathers draped across her shoulders. She invited him to join her in her bower, and she led him to a clearing full of wildflowers where they lay together. When they were both quite exhausted from their sporting, she produced a pitcher of good mead and offered a cup to him, saying, "You have served me very well, young man! Drink this cup of mead, for those who drink of mead cannot be taken by the riders of the hunt, you know, by Fyra's decree."

But Sveni was clever, and he said to her, "I'm happy to take of your mead, my lady, but only if you drink as I drink! I would not want to become a drunken fool before you—unless you join in! And I must dress first. Among my people we never, ever drink in a state of undress."

She told him that this was agreeable, and while he dressed he fixed his drinking skin beneath his tunic, with the mouth hidden beneath his beard. They clicked their cups and she drank, but he only pretended to drink and instead poured the mead into his drinking skin. He said to her, "This is the finest thing I've ever tasted! What is it?"

She said to him, because she was merry with the mead and saw no harm in telling him secrets when the mead would make him forget anyway, "This is mead, made from honey and apples. It is what we Valkyrja drink when we ride a-hunting with Fyra. Here, young man, you must have another cup. It will make your tongue skilled at songs and stories."

They clicked their cups and she drank, and he poured the second cup into his skin as he had the first, and he asked her, "How is this wonderful drink made from honey and apples?"

She said to him, because she was merry with the mead and saw no harm in telling him secrets when the mead would make him forget them anyway, "Apples are crushed in a press, and the juice boiled with honey. When it's cool, the barm of beer is added, and it's sealed in casks. A certain figure is carved into the lid of the cask, and a prayer is said to Fyra over the cask each day. Through her blessing, the mixture becomes mead. But here, you must have another cup. It will help you stay young and hale."

They clicked their cups and she drank, and he poured the third cup into his skin as he had the first and second, and he asked her, "Could you show me this figure, and how to carve it?"

Because she was merry with the mead and saw no harm in telling him secrets when the mead would make him forget them anyway, she showed him how to draw the figure, and what words to say to Fyra to gain her blessing. Then, her head heavy with three cups of mead, the Valkyre lay down and fell fast asleep.

Sveni stole away quietly and found his mammoth grazing at the edge of the trees. He poured three drops of mead onto a handful of hay and fed it to his mammoth, which then had enough vigor to carry him back to Berni's Fast in a single night! He shared the mead around with all of his kin, and all of them became young and hale, with tongues skilled at songs and stories, and immune to the predations of the gods' hunt. Sveni was cheered as a great hero, one whose name shall never be forgotten.

Now that mankind knows the secret of making mead, the souls of men are not so often taken by Joden and Fyra in their winter hunts, and that is why it's important to make merry at the turning of the first frost, and to drink plenty of mead through the dark winter.

THE DANCING BEGAN

L isbet had just finished her story, and a group of boys had begun to approach us with their attention centering especially on Saskia, when a bell rang three times. Lisbet and the others stood, and I followed suit.

"The ballroom has been opened," Lisbet said. "If you're going to be dancing in the opening set, you should find your dance partner."

I didn't have to find Theod, because he found me. He understood the rules of the game.

All of the tables had been removed from the dining hall. At the head of the room, perched on a stage and surrounded by screens to direct the sound, there was a string quartet playing a simple tune that repeated over and over. There was a lichtbildmacher arranging his equipment on the left-hand side of the room. I took Theod's arm and joined him on the dance floor as the music quieted, stopped, and started again as the "Leaves in Autumn Waltz."

I had intended to make this a performance, to lead Theod in a competent waltz under the watchful eyes of the students and professors, to show that we could indeed be just as civilized as the Anglish, playing by their rules. But my plans fell apart when Theod took my hand and pulled me close as the music began, gazing into my eyes with a dark and desperate uncertainty.

I hadn't realized, in my practice with Sander, how frightfully intimate this dance could be. Waltzing required a closeness that I wasn't used to, with all of Theod pressed close to all of me, making me acutely aware of the heat of his body, and his breath, and the tension in his muscles. Sander had been perfunctory. His movements had been precise, almost mechanical, his whole demeanor polite and jovial. Theod was all tension and swiftness and strength. His right hand clasped my left and held it aloft. His left hand pressed at the small of my back, warm and utterly implacable. I guided him through the turns with a delicate push of the hand that clasped mine and pull of the hand that rested on his shoulder, counting the music in my head. He yielded to me, following the steps I led him through, letting me melt into the music and pull him along. I found my rhythm, twirling and twirling around him, around the other dancers, pretty leaves blown by the music's wind.

There was a sudden flash as the lichtbildmacher captured a moment. Theod nearly paused, but I pulled him into a turn to keep him from faltering.

I looked at him, and he was looking at me, his dark eyes falling into mine. There was *awe* on his face. The music came to its crest, and with three quick twirls I brought us to a stop just as silence fell. My heart was hammering, blood pounding in my ears, and I wanted more than anything to lean forward and kiss Theod. But that wouldn't have been proper at all, and it wasn't the kind of scene that I wanted to make.

A moment later, the band began again with the soft, looping tune that was played between sets.

"Would you like to take some refreshment with me?" Theod asked, sounding as breathless as I felt.

"Yes. Yes, I would," I answered, yielding to him and letting him lead me off the dance floor.

ANEQUS LEFT IT BEHIND

There was a decided theme among the offerings, and I was beginning to get the impression that this was an apple harvest and wheat harvest celebration before it was anything else. Several kinds of ciders were on offer, some harder than others, and all of them sweetly spiced. There were also several sorts of beer, and bread, and cake, and roasted apples. There were roasted chestnuts and hickory nuts, and little pieces of toast with swirls of orange paste that turned out to be roasted winter squash of some kind. There wasn't any corn, which seemed practically blasphemous for any kind of celebration in October, but the Anglish could be very strange.

"Do you plan to go on dancing?" Theod asked me once we were safely tucked in a corner with our cups of spiced cider.

"I've agreed to the third dance with Sander, but I doubt that anyone else is going to ask me. Why do you ask? Would you like another dance?" I took a sip and looked into my cup as I said, "I wouldn't mind another dance with you."

"I want to show you something. After your dance with Sander, come find me. I'll be in the main hall. You should go back to your flock of girls now. I'm sure they'll want to talk about the first dance and who danced with whom and all that. It's an important part of these proceedings, I understand."

He took my hand and kissed my knuckles, and then he bowed and walked away. I was left standing there, feeling flushed and dizzy. I drained my cup in one long, horribly unladylike gulp and went to find Marta.

The conversation was empty and pleasant, the girls chattering about whom they had danced with and would dance with while I politely pretended interest. I sat out during the second dance, watching as Lisbet and Sander took the floor, and then it was my own turn to dance with Sander.

Sander's dancing was as pleasantly and mildly accurate as it had been when I'd been learning. We both smiled, twirling our way through a bouncy polka. When it was over, he wrote me a note telling me that he was also dancing the "Thirty-Seven Blackbirds Springar" with Marta and that he'd never danced two sets with anyone before, except Lisbet. I was very happy for him.

Having finished my dance with Sander, I went to find Theod.

"So, what was it that you wanted to show me?" I asked quietly as I sidled up beside him. He'd taken his station against the wall near the door again, a place from which the entirety of both the main hall and the foreroom could be seen.

"Would you like to see what I did last year while all of this nonsense was going on?" he asked, his voice just as quiet.

"You said that you joined the lads from the dragonhall for applejack and dice," I said.

"Exactly. We've made our appearance and had a lichtbild taken. Let's slip away while everyone's distracted and spend time with people who are more of our own sort."

I didn't say to him that there weren't any people of our sort present here. I allowed him to take my arm and sweep me across the main hall, into one of the servants' corridors and down the

stairs beyond. Negotiating the steep stairway in a hooped petticoat was troublesome; we couldn't fit down them side by side. I
ended up hiking my skirts up quite indecently, so it was just as well
that Theod had taken the lead.

We had to leave through the kitchen, through the back entrance where deliveries were taken. The maids and the men from
the dragonhall were assembled on the back lawn in couples and
groups. One man had a fiddle, and another was playing an empty
tin pail like a drum. One of the women was singing in a joyful,
braying voice. It was a jauntier sort of music than what was being
played in the main hall, something like a polka but with a more
driving rhythm. Couples were dancing together in the crackling
light of a bonfire—dances that looked significantly more animated than the ones Marta had taught me. I wouldn't have been
able to do them in the silk gown that I was wearing.

I spotted Liberty sitting on a bale of hay off to the side, watching the dancers. She was drinking something from a jam jar. I
waved at her as we approached, and she looked absolutely stunned,
rising to her feet and setting her jar aside.

"Miss Anequs, Mr. Knecht, whatever are you *doing* out here?"
she said, dipping a quick curtsy.

"Leave off of that, Libby," another of the girls said. "If they're
out here with us, they've given up their right to be scraped at for
the night. The nackie boy spends more of his time with Henkjan
and the lads than he does with the posh ones anywise. Don't know
half of nothin' about the girl, though."

Hallmaster Henkjan came sauntering over to us.

"You're dressed too fine for the likes of us," he said amiably,
raising the jar and taking a sip before handing it to Theod.

"Wasn't my choice, Henkjan, but I think I clean up nicely. To
the glory of the Valkyrja and all that," Theod said, raising the jar
and taking a sip of his own. He handed it to me next, and I felt the
expectant gaze of Liberty and the hall keeper. I raised it up before
tipping it back and taking a generous swallow.

It was not cider.

Whatever it was burned its way down my throat with a fierceness like rum, and I had to swallow several times and hold my breath to avoid coughing. I forced a smile, handing the jar back. Henkjan clapped Theod on the back, laughing heartily.

"The bird's all right, lad! Come on; I've got a pair of dice burning a hole in my pocket."

"The girls and I need a fourth for a ladies' four-in-hand," Liberty said, touching my elbow. "Would you like to dance?"

"I don't know the steps of a four-in-hand," I confessed.

"Oh, it's *easy*, I'm sure you'll catch on dead quick," she said with a grin, taking me by the hand. I glanced back toward Theod, but he was already joining a group of men who'd set up a dicing circle between four bales of hay.

I didn't know most of the girls. Most of the upstairs maids weren't in evidence at all; these were the understairs maids, those from the kitchen and laundry.

The strong spirit I'd drunk from the jam jar had me feeling warm and dizzy, and I stepped on Liberty's foot more than once as she led me through the steps of a four-in-hand, which was met with raucous laughter by all involved parties. The jar went around again between sets, and I found that it didn't burn quite as much the second time.

Liberty and I had our elbows linked together, and she pulled me into a swinging turn, but I misstepped and my foot came down on the hem of my absurdly wide skirt. There was an awful tearing noise, and I looked down to see a length of the pretty gold lace that was supposed to be on the hem of my dress trailing along the ground in the hay. I stared at it dumbly.

"I can mend it!" Liberty said quickly, looking at me in horror. "No one has to know!"

"It's only a dress, Liberty," I said with a bubble of laughter. "There's hardly any harm done."

"What will you tell Miss Hagan, though?" Liberty pressed.

"Come on, let's just run to my room quickly, and I'll have it done up and then we can come back to the dancing."

She took me by the hand, and I followed her in through the servants' hall, all the way to her room. She lit a little kerosene lamp, and the room took on a soft glow. The room I found myself in reminded me a bit of Niquiat's flat; there were six beds with just enough space between them to walk. It was markedly cleaner, though. We were quite alone, she and I; everyone else who might have been sleeping here was apparently seeking revelry elsewhere.

"Come on, let's get you out of that so I can fix it," Liberty said, deft fingers working at the silk ribbons that laced my gown shut. In the dim, golden light her skin was absolutely glowing, a fine sheen of sweat glistening on her brow from our exertions in dancing. She was so incomprehensibly beautiful. She looked up at me suddenly, catching my eyes with an unreadable expression, her hands still tangled in the laces of my bodice.

So I leaned forward and kissed her. I'd never kissed anyone before, not like this, but I wanted to kiss Liberty. I couldn't think of a single reason not to, like I had earlier with Theod. She made a surprised little noise in the back of her throat, almost birdlike; one of her hands moved to my shoulder. For a moment I was afraid that she would push me away.

She didn't push me away.

Her lips were so much softer than I'd ever have guessed. Her hand, where it rested on the bared cusp of my shoulder, was callused and firm and far warmer than I could account for. It was moving downward by slow, tentative increments, curling its way over my shoulder to the small of my back. When the kiss ended, we stood there regarding each other. She had one hand around my waist and another tangled in the laces of my bodice. I had both of my hands on her hips. I couldn't precisely remember how they'd gotten there, but they felt completely natural.

I could still feel her breath on my lips, could still taste the cloying sweetness of the liquor. My own lips felt bruised, swollen. Terribly aware and wanting.

"We'll need to be getting back to the others, miss," Liberty said softly. "It seems you've gotten a bit giddy with spirits."

And just like that the moment was broken, and Liberty was easing me out of my dress, and I was sitting on her bed in my petticoat and underpinnings, and she was stitching up my hem.

"It's not because I'm giddy with spirits, you know," I said, lying back on her bed and staring up at the swirling plaster of the ceiling. "I really do fancy you."

"Proper young ladies are not tribades," Liberty said primly.

"I don't know what that means, but I do know that I'm not a proper young lady and I've got no intention of ever being one—not like Marta is. You should come to Masquapaug, Liberty. You'd like it there. No one has to be a proper young lady there."

"I might like it, if ever I went, but I'm still indentured, remember? Come on, up with you, let's get this dress back on and go find the others before they presume something scandalous has happened."

"Something scandalous *has* happened, hasn't it?" I said with a giggle, leaning up on my elbows. Liberty snorted and rolled her eyes at me, offering a hand to help me up. I felt a confused sort of disappointment at being ushered back to the gathering, unsure if it was because Liberty didn't fancy me or because her fancying me would be quite forbidden because I was a student and she was a maid. I wanted to say more about it, wanted to sit and talk with her, but I couldn't seem to put anything into words at all—so perhaps the spirits had affected me more than I'd realized.

Instead, I just pouted a little, and let her lead me back to the dancing.

THE END OF THE TERM APPROACHED

There was frost on the grass on the morning after the dance when I took Kasaqua to the dragonhall for her morning meal. November was almost here. Sometime in the next fortnight, the whalers would return. My family back in Masquapaug were very certainly making preparations for the whalers' returning dance. I should have been there, helping, but here I was, far from home, worrying about end-of-term examinations.

There were six more weeks until the end of the term, then I'd be home for Nikkomo.

I wouldn't be home to welcome my father back from the sea, though. I'd always been there to welcome Father home before. What was he going to think when he saw that I wasn't there?

I tried very hard to put it from my mind, because being home-sick and maudlin wasn't going to help me at all in my exams. I was entirely confident in natural philosophy, a bit less so in anglereck-oning, reservedly optimistic about folklore and erelore, and abso-lutely *dreading* the examination in skiltakraft.

The whole school was uncharacteristically quiet in the aftermath of the dance. Many of the students—Marta and Sander included—had gone home with their families for the rest of the Valkyrjafax celebrations. I was informed that there would be horsemeat on offer for Sunday night's meal for the ones who'd stayed, but there would also be cold roast beef as well in deference to the dozen or so Vaskosish students in attendance; Vaskosmen didn't celebrate Valkyrjafax, and they didn't eat horsemeat. No one asked Theod or me if there was anything *we'd* especially like to have served or not served in the dining hall with regard to holidays.

Theod was already at the dragonhall when I got there, talking with a couple of the young men he'd been dicing with last night. He looked different with them than he did when I saw him in class or the library. More at ease, more carefree in his demeanor. One of the other men saw me before Theod did, and he pointed at me and elbowed Theod in the ribs, saying something to him that I couldn't hear. Theod straightened up, folding his hands behind his back, dipping his head fractionally as I approached with Kasaqua at my heels.

"And yourself, Mr. Knecht," I said, canting my head right back. "Can I be so rude as to bother you about coursework and the upcoming examinations, after the dragons have been fed?"

"I suppose you can," he said, nodding to the others. "I'll talk to you later, lads?"

The others quietly wandered away, back to whatever tasks Theod had pulled them from in the first place. We each retrieved pails of mashed pumpkin and turnips with blood and offal for our dragons, and sat down on a couple of the hay bales still strewn about from last night's revelries.

"I'd have thought you'd be home for the next few days, like most of the other students," Theod said.

"Getting home, for me, is an all-day affair of trains and ferries, which all require money," I replied. "And the ferry directly to Masquapaug only runs on Tuesday and Friday, so if I wanted to, I'd have to take a ferry to Naquipaug and paddle across the channel."

"Your brother in the city, at least—"

"Valkyrjafax means less than nothing to me; we don't celebrate any such thing back home. This weekend isn't any kind of special occasion for Niquiat and me," I said. "I'm more worried about the end of the term, which is why I wanted to come talk to you. You'll already have gone through two sets of end-of-term examinations, being a year ahead of me. I'm doing well in natural philosophy, and I think I'm going to be all right with erelore and folklore, but every single assignment that I've handed in to Professor Ezel has come back to me covered in red wax about how unsatisfactory my efforts are. I have a good idea of what's going to be on the examination, and I'm certain that I'm going to fail it. What can I do?"

"You can fail it," he said with a shrug. "I did, and life went on. I've come to the conclusion that I'm always going to be completely useless at skiltakraft, which just means that Copper and I don't have a career ahead of us producing athers. If he proves a decent flyer, I might be allowed to make a messenger and courier of him. I don't expect I'll ever be allowed to actually perform skiltakraft."

"And that's perfectly all right with you?" I asked, looking at him sidelong.

"I was going to be a footman, and that was if I was lucky. I spent most of my life learning how to do that kind of thing. I know how to lay a table, how to tend a door, how to clean and keep good silver and porcelain, how to manage a coatroom and polish shoes and do simple mending of a gentleman's clothes. When I was younger, I did scullery tasks and fetched wood and coal and water, swept and dusted, shook out rugs and things. I'd have been *useful* to a proper household. I was *good* at that kind of thing. I'm not at all good at pretending to be a scholar. I can only just read; I get lost if there's a lot of words I don't know in a text. I'm absolutely useless at anglereckoning and al-jabr. I still don't know as much erelore as would suffice for a primary school. My presence here is, and has always been, a farce. I'm a servant, not a scholar. Frau Kuiper took pity on my situation and had the kindness to bring me here, so I'm in her debt. I'll go along with her plan to treat me as a student until she's satisfied that it's not going to work and just lets me become one of the dragonhall keepers under Henkjan. I'm well enough apt at the care and keeping of dragons. You ought to think more about what you'll do with the rest of your life now that you're a drag-oneer than about foolish things like academic examinations. No one is ever going to judge you by your school records, not when you're a filthy savage nackie. You could get a whole string of superlative marks, and they wouldn't matter to anyone."

"They'd matter to me," I said, glaring at him. "Or . . . No, it's not the marks. It's knowing the things I'd need to know to *get* the superlative marks. I don't give half a damn what Professor Ezel thinks of me, but I want to be competent at skiltakraft."

"Why?"

"Because—" I sighed through my nose, trying to think of how to explain, because I didn't understand why he didn't un-derstand. "Dragons aren't exactly animals, not the way we look at it. It's . . . All right, there are crows, and then there's Crow. There are whales, and then there's Whale. But all dragons—at least all *our* dragons—are Nampeshiwe. They're attached to an-other world in a way most animals aren't. When Anglish folk talk about Halya and Valhalya? We talk about the land west of the sunset. That's where dragons are from. They existed before the sun caught fire and will go on existing after the sun burns out. The person who becomes a dragon's companion is Nampeshi-weisit. It's not the same thing as a dragoneer. 'Isit' means be-longing to something, being a part of something. I'm Masquisit because I belong to Masquapaug and it belongs to me; it's what I *am*. When Kasaqua chose me, it changed the kind of person I am and the kind of things that I'm going to do for my people. I mean . . . didn't it feel that way for you, when Copper chose you? Didn't you feel it in your bone marrow?"

"I don't know that I'd say it that way, but I do know what you mean," Theod said, not looking at me. He was watching Copper, who had upended his pail and was holding it still with one foot so he could lick the bottom of it. "Not about the whole 'isit' part, you've lost me with that, but Copper and I . . . I can feel what he feels. I know if he's hurt or hungry or angry or frightened. When he's happy, it's like there's a steady warmth inside me."

"In Masquisit, the word we use for witskraft is 'musquetu.' It means 'medicine,' but it also means 'change' and it means certain kinds of work . . . Pine bark tea and coneflower root are musquetu. The corn-planting dance and the whalers' returning dance are musquetu. Dragons' breath is shapeless musquetu—pure, unworked. It comes to us, through them, straight from the land west of the sunset. It's sacred."

"That's nackie heathenry," Theod said. "That kind of talk will have people calling you an ignorant savage."

"As if saying that a dragon's breath reduces whatever it touches to its component athers is really any different from saying that the shapeless medicine of a dragon's breath is change. Truth is truth is truth. A dragon can breathe in a way that changes whatever it touches from one kind of thing to another kind of thing. It needs shaping, or else it just rends everything to ash and wind—kolfni and vetna. Kasaqua is going to grow up, and her breath is going to become more powerful and more dangerous, and I'm going to need to be able to shape it."

"That's more like sense than anything I've ever heard come out of Professor Ezel's mouth on the subject," Theod said. "I've never been able to make sense of the names of athers and their number of motes and their symbols and all that. I know that pure water breaks apart into vetna and stiksna, and that vetna and stiksna both burn, and that you can collect the parts of water into two different vessels if you can draw the right skiltas. If you mix them back together, you don't get water again. You get combustive air. But none of it means anything to me because I can't even draw the symbols for all the athers from memory."

"My brother's friend Zhina, from the tinker shop, wanted to know if Kasaqua could transmute strahlendstone. Professor Ezel's never said anything about strahlendstone, but it's on the chart on the wall of the laboratory, so I can tell you that it's got eighty-eight motes."

"The rest of the symbols for known athers are covered in the second half of the class; you'll take it in spring."

"Do you have the textbook for it?" I asked. "The second half of the class, I mean."

"There's a copy in the library."

"Want to come to the library with me, and we'll see if we can put together what we each know and maybe make half an ounce of sense from it?"

"I don't think it will do much good," he said, sighing heavily.

"Well . . . what else were you going to do today? I'm not bad at anglereckoning, if you'd like to compare notes on that, too. We're in the same class, not that you've ever said so much as hello to me in it."

"We're in the same class because I've taken Anglereckoning Two twice already and failed it both times. Anglereckoning One was mostly shapes and sums, and I got on with it well enough, but I've come to the end of my intelligence in that subject. This is my third round of this exact same class."

"I'd think that's more Professor Nazari's failing than yours, then," I said. Theod sucked air through his teeth, tensing the way he did anytime anyone said something disparaging about a professor, as if it were blasphemy.

"I'll let you try to talk at me about anglereckoning and skiltakraft if you and Kasaqua will join Copper and me for a walk around the grounds," he said. "It's what I usually do on Saturdays. If you follow the path behind the flight field for a mile or so past the pastures, there's a little stretch of forest and a pond . . ."

"Why, Mr. Knecht, are you inviting me on a constitutional? Without a chaperone? Whatever will people *say*?" I said, pretending to be scandalized. He stiffened again, stammering apologetic nonsense for a moment, before I laughed and said, "I'd love to."

AND SHE HAD A FRANK DISCUSSION WITH LIBERTY

Liberty did not appear at my door for our weekly chat. I waited fifteen minutes past her usual arrival time, and when she didn't show any signs of appearing, I decided to be bold and go and try to find her. I'd been to the servants' quarters the evening before last, after all, and nothing catastrophic had happened.

The servants' stairs were narrower and steeper than either the front or back stairs, and the air in the underpart of the school was very warm and close—it smelled like cooking and spent kerosene, a familiar, companionable smell. I hadn't really noticed it the other night. I came to a room where two maids were sitting at a long table, playing a hand of cards. One of them looked up at me, startled. I recognized her. . . . Hilde, that was Hilde, one of the laundry maids. I couldn't remember the name of the girl opposite her, but she'd been in the dancing circle with us.

"Is there something you need, miss?" Hilde asked, looking me up and down, gaze stopping at my feet to stare at Kasaqua.

"I was looking for Liberty, actually," I said.

"She's in the back quarters, fussing with her hair," the other maid said, pointing toward a door at the opposite end of the room.

I found Liberty seated at a little wooden table tucked against the far wall, the same place she'd sat while doing up my hem. Half her head was in small braids, the other half made a fluffy halo of tight curls. There was a small mirror hanging on the wall that Liberty was facing; she caught my reflection in it, and when our eyes met she looked positively startled.

"Anequs!" she said, turning to look at me. "I hadn't thought—"

"You didn't come up to sew with me, even though Marta's away," I said. I tried not to make it sound like an accusation.

"You shouldn't be here," she interrupted. "You shouldn't be in the maids' quarters at all, and we oughtn't be alone together. There could be . . . rumors. I think perhaps you've gotten the wrong sort of idea about my place and your place here, and I think I've encouraged it when I shouldn't have, because I quite enjoy your company."

"If this is going to be about how we're not supposed to be friends because I'm a student and you're a maid again—"

"It might be better if we don't spend so much time together," Liberty insisted, cutting me off again. "People have begun to notice, and some of the other maids are frightful gossips . . . It could get me sent back to the Society for Friendless Girls."

"How exactly could spending time with me get you sent back? Nothing has happened thus far."

"There are already rumors about me, in the upstairs maids' quarters. About my being a tribade, on account of not mooning over boys. It is known that I've refused to step out with two different lads from the dragonhall. So far I've been able to claim that I'm putting romantic notions aside until my indenture is paid off, but if they have reason to think I'm carrying on with you . . . That kind of thing is *not done*. Anequs, being a tribade is *unlawful*—it's congress outside of marriage. You could be brought before a moot and be charged with immoral behavior and be jailed. The Ministry of Dragon Affairs could declare you morally unfit as a dragoneer, and demand that Kasaqua be removed from you."

I suddenly felt cold and horrible inside, and Kasaqua must have noticed, because she came and pressed her head up under my hand, crooning softly. I slid my fingers along her hackles, not sure if I was trying to soothe her or myself. The Anglish made casual habit of *killing* dragons if they felt justified, but the idea of Kasaqua being taken away—being kept away from her while she pined for me—was worse, somehow.

"I take it that your people regard such behavior—two women carrying on together—rather differently?" Liberty ventured.

"It's not at all uncommon on the islands for a woman to have a wife," I said. "Is that what tribade means? Two women loving each other?"

"Two women loving each other physically," Liberty clarified. "So when you kissed me . . ."

"I kissed you because I fancy you," I said. "I didn't think it was any kind of complicated, though I see now that it is. I don't understand why the Anglish have to complicate their lives so awfully much with rules that make no sense! If I'd met you back home, I'd have been looking to court with you. You'd accept me or you'd reject me, and no one would think it strange either way."

Liberty closed her eyes, sighing wistfully.

"I've known since I was twelve or thirteen that I have no interest at all in young men, and an unacceptable interest in young women."

"I think I've got an interest in both," I confessed. "I very much wanted to kiss Theod when we were waltzing at the dance, but I didn't because I knew that it would make a scene."

"Mr. Knecht would be a far more sensible object of your affections," Liberty said. "Both of you are dragoneers and thus of

equal social station, and you're of the same race, and most importantly of all *he's a man*. It wouldn't be . . . *immoral* . . . for you to
pursue him, or he you."

"I don't see why I shouldn't be allowed to pursue you both," I
said stubbornly.

"Well, it's not as if you could marry both of us, even if marriage between women is allowed among your people," Liberty
scoffed.

"Why not?" I asked.

"It's possible to have more than one husband or wife among
your people?" she asked in return, sounding a bit startled.

"I don't see how it's so strange," I said. "Until I came here,
everything I knew about Anglish customs came out of novels.
There are *so* many novels with plots that revolve around one of
the characters falling in love with the wrong person—they're married, or engaged to be married, and they fall in love with someone
else. Everything always becomes very dramatic; characters running away to sea or committing murder for love or whatever.
They've always seemed so *stupid* to me! If all parties were being
grown-up about these affairs, they'd sit down together and have a
talk. Either the first marriage or engagement would be dissolved,
or the third party would be added to it."

"That wouldn't make for a very interesting novel," Liberty said
with an aborted giggle. "And you say 'dissolved' as if a divorce
isn't something damningly shameful . . ."

"It . . . isn't?" I said, frowning.

Liberty hemmed at that, cocking her head a bit.

"Among the Anglish, there's no greater shame that a man can
suffer than having his wife declare an intent to divorce him and
offer evidence of grounds to do so. It would mean that he's had
congress outside of marriage, or that he's behaved in a way that
shames his family. If a man decides to divorce his wife . . . Well, if
a man has reason to believe that his wife has been engaging in
congress outside of their marriage, he has the right to challenge

her lover to holmgang—single combat to the death. If he won, he'd also have the right to divorce his wife. In any case, I can't imagine people being that sensible about strongly emotional matters like love and jealousy and betrayal and all that."

"Well, I imagine it can be quite fraught for the parties involved at the time, but the point is that everyone in all the involved families comes together to try and help them solve things amiably. When a couple separates they have to go on being neighbors, even if they can't be friends, and if they've got children they've still got to be parents to them."

"So among your people, if a man decides to forsake his wife to run off with some other woman . . ."

"Everyone in his family would shame him about being an ass if he did such a thing, and the woman's family would do the same to her. Their mothers would probably drag them by their ears to the meetinghouse and have them explain themselves to the sachem and the council and each other's families. The man's wife would be within rights to put him out of her house for such behavior. But that kind of thing almost never happens. A married man who fell in love with another woman would talk about it with his wife!"

"And she wouldn't be jealous or angry?" Liberty asked skeptically.

"She might well be," I said, "but she might as easily be glad at the prospect of adding a second wife to their marriage. A household operates more smoothly with more women in it—a woman and her mother, or a woman and her grown daughters, or a woman and her sisters or cousins, or a woman and her wife. My mother and father don't have any other husbands or wives, but it's only because they never wanted to—they're a love match. My mother jokes, sometimes, how she should get herself a wife because Father is away for half the year. How he should go find one for her."

"And what if he actually did?" Liberty asked.

"Then she'd come to live with us, and I'd regard her like an aunt or an older cousin," I said, shrugging. "If a second wife had come into their marriage when I was very young, I'd regard her as a second mother. I'm not sure if my mother could ever fall in love with another woman, though . . . I can't imagine her loving anyone but my father. But a whaler married to two wives who are in love with each other is very common, because then the wives aren't as terribly lonesome when the whaler is away. Come to that, a good number of whalers have husbands who go to sea with them, for the same reason."

"That's another thing you must never say to anyone!" Liberty cautioned, the color draining from her face. "It's even worse for two men to be discovered as . . . intimately engaged . . . than it is for two women. Such an accusation made of a man is grounds for a holmgang."

"And the Anglish have the nerve to call *my* people savage and wild and all that nonsense, when they can't think of any better way to solve a fight than to kill one another over it?" I said, frowning.

"For what it's worth, I think from everything you've told me that your people are far more sensible about the whole thing. I should very much like to go and visit this island of yours," Liberty said with another sigh. "But at present, I'm indentured, and I can't go anywhere without the express permission of my mistress."

"Who's your mistress?"

"Frau Brinkerhoff, officially."

"Frau Brinkerhoff has always seemed quite reasonable to me," I said thoughtfully. "How much debt are you in? Is there any other means of repaying it? I know that Marta is forever saying that it's rude to talk about money . . ."

"My weekly wages are ten marka, two of which are taken for my room and board. My debt, when I began, was two thousand marka. If I put every marka of my pay back toward my debt and never went into the city or bought anything for myself, I'd have been able to pay myself to freedom in five years. I try to be as mean as I can with my money, but I can't keep myself presentable without pressing oil for my hair, and I like to have my own mending supplies beyond those that are provided for my office, and I think I'd go half-mad if I didn't go out into the city sometimes to be with other black folk . . . I'm still in just over a thousand marka of debt. It will be two or three years yet before I'm paid off, depending on how careful I am with my coin."

"And there's no way for you to earn extra money to free yourself more expeditiously?"

"Frau Brinkerhoff bought my contract for two thousand marka with the presumption that I'd be working here for five years. The law allows me to pay my debt by any means available to me, as quickly as I can, but there's some employers that would feel cheated out of the years of service they'd have had if I was only paying my debt by my wages. If I'm able to buy my way out of service early, she'll have to acquire another girl to replace me and have her trained up and all. I was hired on at fourteen, and that year one of the other indentured maids wasn't making any progress at all on her debt, and it turned out she was carrying on with a young man in Vastergot. She came into a delicate condition because of it, and arranged for him to pay the rest of her debt. Frau Brinkerhoff was *very* cross about it. Buying out of your contract early is the sort of thing that'll have a mistress giving you bad letters of recommendation . . . but I don't really intend to seek work as a maid when I've finished this contract. I think I've got enough skill to be a proper seamstress. Do you think you'd have use for a seamstress on your island?"

"We're always in want of women with skill," I answered. "Allow me to extend to you a personal invitation, open and ongoing, whenever you're able to oblige us with your company."

"I might just take you up on that offer, when I've paid off my debt. And at that time, if you're still interested, I might well be open to courting. But I do hope you understand that I cannot accept such affections from you here and now."

"I do," I said with a sigh, "though I won't pretend not to be frustrated about it. Not with you, with the situation that society here has put the both of us in."

She offered a sad smile in return.

"I really do need to finish up with my hair—you ought to go back upstairs. Coming down here for any reason at all is likely to start rumors."

"Will you still come to sew and chat with me next Sunday?" I asked. "I promise not to do or say anything untoward. I've got to go to a luncheon with some scholars next Saturday, and I'm sure to have a lot to say about it afterward. If anyone asks, you can say that I was reading improving lore aloud to you—I've read in Marta's magazines that reading improving lore to one's servants is *precisely* the sort of thing that a lady of quality ought to do."

Liberty giggled again, looking back toward the door and biting her lip to stifle it.

"Yes, I'll come up next week," she said. "But get out of here now!"

I dropped a deep curtsy and said, "As you wish, miss."

She rolled her eyes as I departed, Kasaqua scampering a few steps behind me.

ANEQUS AND THEOD TOOK LUNCHEON WITH SCHOLARS

Classes resumed on Monday morning as usual. Frau Brinker-hoff once again called me to her office to discuss my funds, and gave me another twenty marka—five marka a week—to last the month of November. In all of October, I'd only spent three marka—penniks and five-penniks at a time for postage and telegrams. In addition to my letters home and to Niquiat, I was developing a regular correspondence with Ingrid Hakansdottir, who remained full of questions.

On the morning of Saturday, the fifth of November, Theod and I were escorted from the school grounds to the Vastergot estate of Tindra Brahe; Frau Kuiper accompanied us. Theod and I both wore our school uniforms. She wore her full dress uniform, the one she'd worn on her first visit to Masquapaug, including her brace of pistols. I wondered why she felt that she needed them, but decided not to ask.

I was allowed to bring Kasaqua with me—she'd grown to the size of a young wolverine, too big to perch on my shoulder but still small enough to sprawl across my lap if I was in a chair that could accommodate her. Theod was not allowed to bring Copper, on the grounds of his being too large—the size of a large horse now.

Tindra Brahe's residence was a tall, narrow townhouse made of whitewashed brick, facing an open square adjacent to the public gardens. It wasn't nearly as imposing as Marta's house had been. Frau Kuiper led the way, and we were greeted at the door by a black woman of middle years who wore a plain gray dress. We were not introduced to her, nor she to us. She offered to take our coats and escorted us to the sitting room.

It was very much like Marta's private parlor: a circle of low silk-cushioned chairs surrounding an oval table laid with a tea service and fruit and pastries. Two women and a man were seated already, and one of the women rose as we entered, meeting Frau Kuiper by the parlor's entrance. She was very tall, and the pale green day dress that she wore was very square across the shoulders. It made her look . . . formidable—not entirely different than the effect of Frau Kuiper's uniform. She was probably somewhere between thirty and forty years of age. Her hair was dark, her eyes pale, and she had a pair of spectacles perched on her nose that were attached to her collar by a delicate silver chain.

"Karina, darling, how lovely of you to come," she said, offering a brilliant smile. "And these must be your pupils?"

"Tindra, I'd like to present to you Mr. Theod Knecht and Miss Anequs of Mask Island," Frau Kuiper said smoothly, dipping her head in a way that would naturally lead the other woman's gaze to Theod and me. I was very glad that she hadn't introduced me as "Aponakwesdottir."

"A great pleasure to meet you, Frau Brahe," I said, offering a formal curtsy.

"Please, come have a seat," Frau Brahe said. "Allow me to introduce the three of you to Herr Vidar Graversen and his sister, Frau Lysa Mølgaard. Frau Mølgaard's husband is, as I understand it, a military acquaintance of Frau Kuiper's. Herr Graversen is a professor of natural philosophy at the King's Academy in New Linvik, lately here in Vastergot visiting family."

If I'd had to guess, I'd have placed Herr Graversen as the elder and Frau Mølgaard the younger. They were both round-faced and pink, with Frau Mølgaard tending to plumpness, and both were probably between forty and fifty years of age.

"A great pleasure to meet both of you," Herr Graversen said, nodding.

"Please help yourself to refreshments," Frau Brahe said, taking a seat. "Did you have a pleasant journey? The weather can be so fickle at this time of year."

"It's a bit brisk outside, but the sun is shining, and we're all of stout constitutions," Frau Kuiper answered. "Herr Graversen, Anequs here is quite the adept at natural philosophy."

"Does your academy's library subscribe to *The Lindmarden Journal of Natural Philosophy*?" Herr Graversen asked. "There's a most fascinating article this month by the naturalist Roland Hellwig concerning feral dragons of the deep lakes region. I understand that your dragon, Miss Anequs, is of a breed endemic to this land?"

He was looking not at me but at Kasaqua, who'd elected to take a position at my feet.

"I don't know if we do subscribe, and in any case I haven't sought that periodical out because I've been quite busy with my studies," I answered. "But I most certainly will, upon your recommendation."

"What was the name of your dragon's breed again?" Frau Brahe asked.

"Kasaqua is a Nampeshiwe, ma'am," I said, "and yes, sir, she's as endemic to this land as Theod and I."

"Yes, that's it! Most of my studies concerning the endemic people of Lindmarden have been upon those who previously frequented the mainland, the Massy-chooseit and Narry-gannet," Frau Brahe replied.

"Maswachuisit and Naregannisit," I agreed. Frau Brahe looked mildly surprised.

"As I understand it, all of you natively speak languages that stem from a common root?"

"Masquisit and Naquisit share a great deal of commonality, and if you speak one you can generally make yourself understood in the other," I said uncertainly. "I don't have a working knowledge of the original languages of the mainland, I'm afraid. I'd only ever been as far inland as Catchnet before coming to the school, and I've never met anyone who speaks Akashneisit. I don't know if anyone does anymore."

"May I ask what your studies *are*, precisely, ma'am?" Theod asked.

"The study of peoples and how they live is properly known as folkreckoning," Frau Brahe answered. "It's a field that borrows from erelore and folklore, originally conceived by the ancient masters in Tyskland but much expanded in the modern age by explorers and frontiersmen coming into contact with previously unknown peoples. I am a dedicated folkreckoner. I rather fell in love with the subject as a child, reading Emanuel Nordlund's stories of his time among your people in an age before much Anglish influence. Have either of you read his works?"

Theod shook his head, pouring himself a cup of tea, so I answered.

"I'm beginning to. I'm pushing through *The Savage Peoples of New Linvik* when I have time, though it's not an especially easy read. The spelling choices he makes are . . . interesting. And his appendix of useful phrases is either exceedingly out of date or else patently wrong in quite a lot of places, concerning 'the language of the islands,' as he terms it."

Frau Brahe laughed prettily, taking a sip of tea before saying, "Well, you must understand that Nordlund was forging new ground in the transliteration of the words into Anglish script. Your people had no script of any kind before we introduced it to you."

"Not in the sense of an alphabet, no," I said, "but we have traditional songs and stories stretching back into antiquity, and a great deal of history is recorded in images. The temple columns on Slipstone Island tell the story of how Masquasup the Giant threw Masquapaug up from the bottom of the sea on the first morning after the sun caught fire."

"Do your people put much faith in such stories?" Frau Mølgaard asked.

"Do yours put much faith in the story of Enki stealing the secret of writing from Joden to give to humankind, or in Joden having learned it from a great wolf, who learned it from chewing on the roots of the world tree?" I asked in return.

Frau Mølgaard looked just a bit startled, but recovered quickly, selecting a pastry before saying, "I suppose I see your point; that which is lost to the depths of time can only be a matter of faith, I suppose."

"Except that which is supported by observable, physical evidence," Herr Graversen said. "We know, factually, that there was a long winter—possibly the one spoken of in legend as being a thousand years long—because evidence of the ice rivers' passage has been wrought upon the stones of the world for anyone to see."

"Do your people's legends have anything to say about the long winter?" Frau Brahe asked, looking to me and to Theod but focusing back on me.

"Most of the stories that I know concern figures from the time before the sun caught fire—which may well reference the long winter. I understand that we lost a great deal of our lore during the great dying."

"Great dying? That sounds terribly ominous," Frau Mølgaard said.

"The common vermutun among those who study the natural philosophy of Lindmarden," Herr Graversen said, "is that it was once a great deal more *peopled* than it was when Stafn Whitebeard led his settling expeditions to Vastergot and New Linvik, and that in those distant times the people had command of dragons."

"That's not a vermutun; it's plain truth," I said, staring at him. "The great dying is as recent as my great-great-grandmother's childhood. We still have things from that time—paintings and carvings and such. It's common knowledge. Something like eight of ten people died. They thought that the world was ending."

"Stories about the end of the world are common in the folklore of many people; the difference between folklore and erelore is observable evidence. Surely if such a calamity had actually occurred—"

"There used to be a city on Masquapaug with as many people as Vastergot, before the dying," I said, my voice rising in pitch just a bit. "We have *ruins* of it on Slipstone Island, and on Beachy Hill and near Great Sweet Pond. I'm sure there are ruins on Naquipaug as well, and there must have been ruins here on the mainland, too, before they were plowed under and paved over. If they've been ignored or taken to bits for the stone, it can only have been deliberate."

Everyone was staring at me now, a cool silence taking over once I'd stopped talking. I'd made a social misstep—become too emotional or something. Ladies were supposed to be calm and moderate, civilized people objective in their opinions. I set my jaw, swallowed hard, and took a sip of tea. It was bitter.

"I think I should very much like to see these ruins," Frau Brahe said roundly, after a long tense moment had passed. "Though as I understand it, travel to Mask Island is only allowable by direct invitation from local governances."

"In accordance with the New Linvik treaty of 1757," I said. "You'd need a letter of invitation from Sachem Tanaquish."

I did not say that she'd also have been allowed to visit if she was someone's personal houseguest, because I did not want to be pressed into having to invite her out of politeness.

"And without such an invitation, I shall never see the ruins or report upon them to relevant journals of folkreckoning," she said, very obviously pressing.

"Perhaps you would be so kind as to provide me with your calling card, ma'am," I said, smiling with gritted teeth, "and I could see if such an invitation might be arranged at a future date."

Tindra Brahe smiled at me, but something about it made me feel cold.

Herr Graversen and Frau Mølgaard excused themselves shortly afterward, thanking us all for a "bracing" afternoon of conversation. Herr Graversen said that he'd send a letter as to which journals our institution subscribed to and would sponsor subscriptions to any critical ones that we were missing. Shortly after that, Frau Kuiper excused our party, and in a flurry of genial goodbyes we were packed into the carriage and taken back to school.

I didn't have the impression, from Frau Kuiper's dissatisfied frown and distant gaze, that I had performed to expectations.

SHE RECEIVED A VISITOR

I visited with Liberty on Sunday and told her all about my tea with Frau Brahe and her associates. I went to my classes as usual on Monday, and chatted with Theod about his opinions on the scholars while we fed Kasaqua and Copper—though he was largely without opinions on that subject. On Tuesday morning I sat through another of Professor Ezel's lectures on skiltakraft, making notes to myself about which bits I'd need to seek further information from in books. Any advances I was currently making in skiltakraft were currently due to my work with Theod, not anything that happened in class.

On Tuesday afternoon, I was sitting with Theod in Professor Ibarra's erelore lesson in the library when there was a knock at the door. He frowned and rose to answer it. Frau Brinkerhoff was standing there, pink-faced and flustered.

"Please excuse me for the interruption, Professor Ibarra," she said, "but I've come to collect Anequs. She's wanted in the front hall."

"Frau—" Professor Ibarra began, only for Frau Brinkerhoff to interrupt, in a voice like wrought isen.

"She is wanted immediately."

I was reasonably certain that Frau Brinkerhoff outranked Professor Ibarra. I knew that Frau Kuiper did, and Frau Brinkerhoff seemed to have quite a lot of pull with her. I stood and gathered my notes and dipped a curtsy before turning to join Frau Brinkerhoff, Kasaqua following at my heel. She, at least, was excited at this development because she had been very bored and restless in class.

When Frau Brinkerhoff had closed the door behind us, I asked, "What's going on? Have I done something wrong?"

"Your father is here, and I need you to talk some sense into him, because he's got it in his head that he's going to take you and your dragon back to that little island of yours immediately."

"My father . . ." I whispered, my breath catching in my throat. Kasaqua made a little trilling noise of question or concern. We'd come to the end of the corridor, and as we made the turn into the main hall I saw him. He was pacing back and forth in front of Frau Kuiper, half shouting at her. I'd never considered Frau Kuiper a small woman, but my father was a very big man. She was facing him, her hands on her hips, reaching for pistols that weren't there just now.

Would she have shot him if she'd had them?

I didn't want to think about that. So instead I called, "Father!" and he wheeled around to look at me like a startled bird.

I ran to him and he ran to me, and when we met in the middle of the room he scooped me up and spun me in a circle before pulling me into a tight hug. He smelled like oil and soot and *home*. It was a long moment before he put me down. Kasaqua was prancing around both of us, making little noises of inquiry.

Father gazed down at Kasaqua with a kind of quiet awe on his face. She was a more impressive creature now than she'd been upon her hatching. Her crest of rust-brown feathers had fully grown out, and her mustard-yellow skin had warmed to golden.

The speckles were starting to fade, and her wingleather had taken a red-orange hue at the leading edge. She might have the sunset brilliance of her mother one day.

"She really is a Nampeshiwe," Father breathed, crouching and extending his hand toward her. She sniffed it for a moment, then pushed her head up under his hand to demand petting. Father looked at me and said, "My daughter has become Nampeshi-weisit."

"Father, what are you *doing* here?" I asked, bewildered, as I watched him standing back up. He looked worn out, with hollows under his eyes. He was wearing corduroy trousers and a calico shirt with the sleeves rolled up, his whaler's tattoos on open display. Half his head was shaved, and he had a new tattoo curling along his scalp, high above his ear. A pair of clasping hands over a line of breaking waves. He'd saved someone from drowning.

"I've come to take you home, where you belong," he said.

"I'm coming home in five weeks," I said. "I'll be there for Nik-komo. I've got classes until then, and examinations—"

"I came to take you home, and I'm *going* to take you home," Father said, setting his jaw.

"What you fail to understand about the situation, Mr. Apon-akwe—" Frau Brinkerhoff said diplomatically, coming to stand beside Frau Kuiper.

"I've heard enough out of you," Father growled, glaring at both of them.

"Father, stop!" I blurted, gaze darting from them to him and back again. "I'll go with you today, but I'll come back on the Fri-day ferry, if that makes everyone happy. I'll come back and finish my classes and take my exams, but if my father wants me to come home for a few days to welcome him back from the sea, that's his right because he's my father and I'm his daughter and nobody asked *him* about any of this back in August. I'm not a ward, like Theod. I've got a family missing me. I haven't seen my mother or my younger siblings in almost three months!"

There was silence for a long moment after that, my heart hammering against my breastbone. I hadn't exactly meant to say any of what I'd just said, but all of it was true.

"That . . . might be an agreeable compromise," Frau Kuiper said evenly. "There is precedent for parents coming to collect their children in times of family crisis. Your professors will be informed of the circumstances. You will, of course, be required to make up any assignments you miss and will be responsible for anything covered in the lectures that you do not attend."

"Of course, Frau Kuiper," I said, nodding. "I would be very appreciative if someone could explain the situation to Miss Hagan and Mr. Knecht and Mr. Jansen; they'll be worried otherwise."

Frau Brinkerhoff's expression softened slightly. "Of course, dear," she said.

Frau Kuiper hadn't softened at all when she said, "You should go and collect anything you'll need from your room. Your father can remain here while you do."

I nodded again, and said to Father, "I'll be right back. I'll tell you everything on the way back to the train station. Please don't be angry at Fraus Kuiper and Brinkerhoff; they've done nothing wrong."

I hitched up my skirts and ran to my room, not giving half a damn about proper comportment. I stuffed my skiltakraft textbook and all of my notes into my rucksack and rushed back, Kasaqua bounding after me in great excitement the whole way because she was very aware that something interesting was happening. I managed to smooth myself into something like orderly poise as I descended the stairs, nodding to Fraus Kuiper and Brinkerhoff before taking Father's hand and letting him lead me out of the school, toward home.

AND MADE A REQUEST

Father had insisted on carrying my rucksack for me as soon as he realized that I was carrying one. He hadn't really noticed at first, because he'd been paying attention to Kasaqua. As we walked down the road to the train station, I explained everything that had happened—my seeing Kasaqua's mother on Slipstone Island, climbing the mound to the ruins and finding the egg, the hatching and Niquiat and Frau Kuiper and the school. Father listened with quiet attentiveness, never interrupting. When I finished, having told him about Marta and Sander and Theod and Liberty, about my professors and my classes and journeys into the city, he asked, "And this is making you happy, Chipmunk? Being here, far from home?"

"It's something that I need to see through, whether I'm happy or not," I said. "But . . . it's not terrible. I'd rather be back at home, most days, but I'm not suffering. It's not forever."

"How long do you plan to stay here, among these people?"

"Until I'm sure that I can shape Kasaqua's breath safely, and until I've learned to ride her when she flies. These people can teach me those things. It's customary, for the Anglish, to attend a secondary school for four years, but I really don't think that I will. I'll know when Kasaqua and I are ready. I haven't told that to Frau Kuiper yet, and probably no one should. They think I'm doing my best to do everything they want me to."

Father made a low humming noise, looking off at the train station in the distance.

"We should go see Niquiat before we go back home," I said. "The train from school into Vastergot stops on the half hour, but the train from Vastergot to Catchnet only comes on the hour, so we'll have time to drop into the coffee shop where he spends time to see if he's there. He might come with us, if you asked him to."

"Niquiat is a grown man, and he made the decision to leave home," Father said. "He knew my feelings about it, and he decided to leave anyway. There's no more to be said on the subject."

"Niquiat is your son, and my brother. He's still Masquisit, even if he's living in Vastergot, and he should be home with family during the whalers' returning dance. Besides, you should see his workshop. You might understand better, if you did."

"You and I should go *home*. Your mother's already angry with me for coming to get you. She thought that I should send a telegram first and wait for a reply, but the dance is tomorrow. There wouldn't have been time."

"Imagine how happy she'll be if you've got both of us with you when you come back!" I pressed. "We have to pass through Vastergot anyway, to get the train to Catchnet. It's not a long walk to Niquiat's workshop, or to Haddir's."

"Anequs . . ."

"Please?" I said, planting my feet and looking up at him. Kasaqua made a little protesting noise, coming to butt her head against his ankle.

"You're as stubborn as your mother when you set your mind

on something, you know that?" Father finally said with a sigh. "Fine. Show me what my son's been doing."

It was half past two when we pulled into the train station in Vastergot. The next train to Catchnet left at three, which would put us in Catchnet with just enough time to get on the evening ferry, which departed Catchnet at four. We didn't have much time to find Niquiat and convince him to come with us. I took father to Haddir's first, because it was the friendliest place that I knew in Vastergot.

Niquiat wasn't there, but Jorgen and Zhina were.

"Hey, it's Niquiat's sister the dragoneer!" Jorgen called as soon as we'd come through the door. He was waving us over. "Your brother took a late shift at the cannery; come and have coffee with us. Who's this with you?"

"Jorgen, Zhina, this is my father, Aponakwe," I said as I moved to sit next to Zhina. Father probably wouldn't have approved of me sitting next to Jorgen. "Father, this is Jorgen—a master tinker—and Zhina, his chief apprentice. Niquiat is part of their co-op."

Father eyed both of them critically and didn't say hello. Jorgen, at least, wasn't put off in the slightest.

"Pleasure to meet you, Mr. Aponakwe. Your son is brilliant, but you probably know that," he said, pushing the pot of coffee toward us. "He's still working on a self-stabilizing engine reciprocator that uses its own spinning to steady the lodestone cachet—"

"I don't know anything about that kind of thing," Father said. "When you see my son, tell him that I came here looking for him. My daughter and I would like him to come home, if only for a few days. Anequs, you seem to know these people. If I give them travel fare, can they be trusted to give it to him?"

"You're being *unbearably* rude, Father," I said, glaring. "But yes. They can."

Father reached into his pocket and pulled out two five-marka coins, laying them on the table with a dull clink. They were like the ones that Frau Brinkerhoff had given me three of. I didn't know what fifteen marka had meant to her, or what ten marka meant to Zhina and Jorgen for that matter, but for Father it was most of a week's pay.

"Tell him that I'll want to be paid back," Father said, "seeing that he has a job that pays Anglish coin and all."

"I'll tell him," Jorgen said, shrugging. "Is it rude to ask if something happened? If there's a tragedy, I offer condolences."

"Nothing bad happened," I said quickly. "It's just that the whalers have returned and there's a dance about it. I'm going home for it, and I want Niquiat to come home, too. I'll be going back to school on Friday morning. It would be good if he came home, because then he could escort me back and I wouldn't have to make any leg of the journey alone."

"I'll let him know," Zhina said, meeting my eyes for a moment. She seemed to understand better than Jorgen the kind of thorny mess I was trying to untangle. Niquiat might have talked to her about it before. She was the one who picked up the coins, not Jorgen.

"We should go back to the train station, Anequs," Father said. "We need to catch the one leaving at three."

"Nice to have met you, Mr. Aponakwe, sir," Zhina said, canting her head politely.

Father didn't return the nicety. He just got up and left.

So I got up and followed him.

AND RETURNED TO MASQUAPAUG

The ferry that departed Catchnet at four came to dock on Masquapaug at five-thirty. It would leave again at seven and not come back until seven-thirty on Friday morning.

Mother and Sigoskwe and Sakewa were all waiting for us at the dock, Sakewa asleep in Mother's lap, Sigoskwe sitting a little way down the bench, carving something by the light of the lantern that sat between them. He saw us before the others did and shot to his feet.

"Father's back and he's got Anequs and she's got her dragon!" he shouted, folding his knife and stuffing it and the carving into his pocket.

Sakewa made a complaining noise as Mother woke her and made her move so she could stand, and then I was there and she was embracing me and I couldn't even breathe.

We walked back home together, Sakewa hoisted up on Father's back, and I told them everything I'd told Father—except for the beginning parts that they already knew. I didn't make any mention of Niquiat, or even say that Father and I had gone looking for him. He'd come or he wouldn't. Sigoskwe kept marveling at how big Kasaqua had gotten in just a couple of months, and Sakewa complained about how they'd had to wait *all day* at the dock for us, though Mother said it had only been the last hour or so.

There was a pot of sobaheg waiting on the coals when we got home, Grandma stirring it slowly. I went to her and wrapped myself around her and didn't say anything at all. Nothing needed saying. I was *home.*

I fell asleep in my own bed that night for the first time since August, Kasaqua curled against my belly and my old calico quilt drawn over us both, and I didn't ever want to leave again.

I woke up to Sakewa's face half an inch from my own.

"She's awake!" she squealed, much too loud for how early it was. "Come on, you need to get dressed and we need to go to the meetinghouse because everyone's there and Great Auntie Mamisashquee and Auntie Shanuckee and all our cousins from Naquipaug came and you weren't here but I wove you a sash anyway, get up!"

I had a bowl of na'samp with maple syrup and a handful of hickory nuts on top, and a cup of black coffee that was nothing like the coffee at Haddir's, but tasted like home. Having finished that, I felt far more able to get dressed and go about a day that promised to be . . . a lot. The house was full of chatter and action: Sigoskwe following Father around with constant questions about his journey, Mother helping Grandma put her hair up, Sakewa showing me all the finger-weaving she'd done in the last two months, Kasaqua getting underfoot.

My dancing dress was packed away in oilskin and camphor paper in the roof beams, having last been worn for the corn-planting dance last spring. It was pale brown buckskin with a yoke of quahog shell and oyster shell beads. Grandma had begun it for me when I'd become a woman two years ago. It wouldn't fit me for much longer, and we'd put it away for Sakewa to wear once she became a woman herself. I'd gotten a bit taller, but not much wider since last I'd worn it. It fit snugly, sliding on like a second skin, and no one asked me to wear stays or petticoats underneath it.

I braided Sakewa's hair, and she braided mine. As if nothing had changed at all.

We went together to the meetinghouse, Father and Mother leading with Grandma on Father's arm, Kasaqua at my heel and Sakewa and Sigoskwe behind me.

Sachem Tanaquish was blessing the dance circle when we arrived. Grandma went to sit with a group of other elders, and Sakewa scampered over to meet her friends. Mother went to join the other whalers' wives in preparing the feast—roasted corn and squash, and smoked whale meat, and all kind of sundries like roasted nuts and cranberry jam and sweet corn cakes. Father spotted Auntie Shanuckee sitting with Great Auntie Mamisashquee and went over to them. I might have joined him, because I hadn't seen my aunt or great aunt since last year, but someone shouted "Anequs!" across the breadth of the meetinghouse.

Hekua was standing there with a half dozen other girls my age, waving me over. I went to join them.

"We saw your picture has been in the *Vastergot Gazette twice!*" Hekua exclaimed as soon as I was close enough to hear. "The second time you were in a silk gown and you were dancing with a young man. He was *handsome*. You need to tell us everything!"

"Well, first of all, his name is Theod Knecht," I began, as we all found somewhere to sit together.

I talked about what I'd been doing at school, and my friends talked about the things I'd missed in the village. Mishona was going to marry Ashaquiat in the spring. Minanneka had a baby boy at the end of September. Rumor had it that Seseque, who'd come back safe from his first whale trip, was planning to give Hekua a carved whale tooth after the first dance.

"Are you going to accept it, if he does?" I asked, deliberately *not* looking over my shoulder to where the group of young whalers was gathered.

"I don't know! He's handsome and I get along with his sisters, but he's going to be gone for eight months of the year for most of his life probably, and I don't know if I want to court that sort of man, and Mother says I'm too young to be formally courting anyway . . ."

I drew in close, pulling Hekua's face near mine, and whispered, "I kissed a girl at school. We can't formally court, for lots of reasons, but *I think that she fancies me, too.*"

Hekua made a little high-pitched noise at the back of her throat and opened her eyes very wide, clapping her hand over her mouth. A moment later she regained her composure and asked, "What's her name? What's she look like? How'd you meet her? Is she a dragoneer, too?"

"Her name is Liberty. She's black-folkish, and she has the prettiest eyes. She's a maid at the school—indentured! So no one can find out that Liberty and I are sweet on each other."

"Indentured? Oh, that's awful!" Hekua gasped. "What's her debt?"

"A little over a thousand marka, but she says she'll have it paid off by the time she's twenty. She takes in extra work when she can, to make money to pay it down faster. She's a good seamstress. We've been spending time together on Sunday mornings."

"Well, maybe if she's not going to be indentured for very much longer, you can court her later? And what about Theod? Are you courting *him*?"

"I don't . . . he's different," I said, wrinkling my nose. "He's so formal and prickly, it's hard to even get him to smile. I don't know what he'd do if I kissed him, though I wanted to at the dance— I really, *really* wanted to."

"So why didn't you?"

"Because we were in the middle of a whole ballroom of people and it wouldn't have been *proper*. That's absolutely the worst thing about living among the Anglish: all the *rules* they have about how one is supposed to behave that don't make any sense at all. I wish I'd brought that awful book that Marta loaned me, so you could see and laugh with me. I'll bring it for Nikkomo. I've got to at least pretend that I know all the rules and care about them, because otherwise I'm not civilized and I'm just proving right all the awful things they think about me already."

"Someone thinks badly of you? Who? Why?"

"A lot of the boys at school," I said with a groan. "Some of the professors, too. I just . . . There's this boy called Ivar Stafn and he's a monster, and I slapped him because of it, and Frau Kuiper—she's the one who came on the dragon that day back in July, the one with the pistols—she took me aside and gave me a whole speech about how I've got to be a good representative of my race. But Theod has taken that kind of talk very much to heart. It's like . . . he wants to *be* Anglish."

"But he's not, though. He's Naquisit, you said."

"I know that and you know that and everyone else in the world knows that. But I think he's been brought up trying to have people not notice. He'd never spent any time around other nackies at all until he met me."

"Well, that's awful, too! Your school term ends in December, doesn't it? You should invite him here for Nikkomo."

I felt a quick flash of shame at the fact that I hadn't considered at all what Theod did during the winter recess. If all of the students went home to their families from the middle of December to the middle of January, and Theod didn't have a home to go to . . . did he just stay at the school? Did the hall lads and the maids stay? Did the professors? Was he just there all by himself? Had he been there all by himself for all of summer as well? It was too awful to comprehend.

"I don't know if it would be allowed," I said after a long moment, "but that's a very good idea, Hekua. I'm very certainly going to ask about it at the next opportunity."

Hekua beamed at me, and I might have said something else if Sachem Tanaquish hadn't started beating on the hand drum he was carrying to signify that the first dance would begin soon.

"I've got to go join Mother and the other whalers' families," I apologized. "I'll find you again after the dance, all right?"

"Of course. I heard that Noskeekwash is going to tell a story about your father. I mean, we've all seen the new tattoo."

"I know! He hasn't even said anything about it yet; I think he didn't want to rob Noskeekwash of the story. I'll see you after!"

And with that I went across the meetinghouse to where Mother and Sigoskwe and Sakewa were already assembled around the rim of the dance circle with the other whalers' wives and children and parents.

Sachem Tanaquish walked the circle first with a bowl of burning tobacco and juniper, stopping at each of the four directions to offer thanks to creation, to the earth, to the sun, to the moon. When he came back around to the entrance at the east, he set down the bowl and picked up his hand drum, setting the rhythm that the great drum would follow.

The whalers took up their positions in line to enter it from the east, moving south to west to north, the youngest men first and the older ones behind them. Father was toward the middle of the group; he winked at me as he went by. They formed a double ring around the fire; young men in the middle and older ones on the outside, protecting them. They all sang together, the song about Whale and how Masquasup the Giant had taught humankind the way to hunt him. They moved together, two rings of men weaving in and out, toward and away from the fire. Kasaqua, standing at my heel, was watching them with rapt attention. I was afraid she might think it was a game and pounce in, ruining the gravity of the dance, but she was absolutely still. She saw something that I wasn't seeing. I knew that, without having a reason to know it, and it was important. What the dancers were doing was *important*. It was ringing inside of me with each drumbeat, something pulsing behind my eyes and in my breastbone.

All I could do was breathe, and wish that the dragons of Masquapaug hadn't all died two hundred years ago, because then there'd have been someone to explain this to me—what this feeling was, and what I was supposed to do with it.

But they had. So I'd just have to work it out for myself.

ANEQUS GATHERED HER FAMILY AROUND HER

After the first dance, informal dances began; young men showing off their skill, inviting young women into the circle. Seseque invited Hekua to dance with him. In the gathering circle, where people were sitting down with food from the feast, individual whalers started coming forward to tell stories of perils and heroic deeds that happened during their journey. When I sat down beside Father, with Kasaqua draping herself across my lap and pointedly watching every single morsel of food as it moved from my plate to my mouth, Noskeekwash stood.

He told the story of how my father had dived under the waves and untangled his ankle from a length of rope that was pulling him down when one of the whaleboats was overturned by a great whale—how cold and biting the waters of the north were, how strong my father had been when he'd pulled him back to the surface.

But Father wasn't looking at Noskeekwash as he told the story. He was looking at Kasaqua.

He was trying not to stare, and I was trying not to stare at him staring. It was a good story Noskeekwash was telling, and we were both rude to not pay attention. But the heroism of whalers in the face of peril was something we all knew about already. Father hadn't been around in that time from July into August when Kasaqua had scrambled all around the village at my heel or ridden on my shoulder.

In the last few months, dragons had become normal to me. Every student at Kuiper's had a dragon, and most of the professors as well. How had I so quickly forgotten that feeling I'd first had when I'd seen her mother, that something of incalculable importance was happening just because a dragon was present?

Kasaqua, sprawled across my lap, didn't seem to have any idea of her own relevance.

"When I didn't see you on the pier with your mother and the others, the first thing I thought was that something terrible had happened to you," Father said softly. I turned to look at him, but he wasn't looking at me. He was looking down at his hands. "Sigoskwe is the one who said you'd become Nampeshiweisit, before anyone else told me anything. He was so excited to have me know. Then your mother told me you'd gone off to Vastergot to some Anglish school and that you wouldn't be back for five weeks and . . . I couldn't. I couldn't let it be that way. I knew that I had to see you, had to hear it from you that you were safe and happy and well."

"I'm sorry that there wasn't any way for me to tell you, when you were still at sea—"

"And then I find you, exactly where everyone said you'd gone, and you're walking around the corner in your starched school uniform and I'm thinking to myself: 'She's grown up. She's a woman, and Nampeshiweisit, and nothing is the same anymore.' But then you ran and hugged me."

"Father . . ."

"And it was like every time you've met me on the pier since

you were old enough to walk. Even last year, when I came home to less family than I was expecting. Do you remember what you said to me then?"

"I said that I'd always be here waiting for you," I said, feeling a catch at the back of my throat, because I'd made a promise and I'd broken it.

"When your brother left us . . . I half expected your mother to say he'd gone off with a girl to live with her family. That wouldn't have hurt so badly. I knew that Niquiat wasn't going to be a whaler. I knew it years ago. He's a different kind of person. I didn't want to believe it, but I knew it. But you . . . you've always been . . . what you should be. A firstborn daughter. I thought I knew what to expect with you."

"I thought I knew what to expect with me, too. But then Nampeshiwe's mother paid us a call, and everything is different now."

"I don't know that it is. We'll all of us have to see what comes of this. But . . . Anequs, you're kind and you're clever and you're diligent. You always have been. All my children are clever, and you must get it from your mother, because you certainly didn't get it from me. I'm sure that sometime very soon I'll get around to being very proud of you for having been chosen by the first dragon born on Masquapaug in two hundred years. If I was a better man, pride would have been my first thought. But I can only be what I am, and I can't pretend that this doesn't make me fearful. Gaining the attention of the Anglish . . . I've lost too much family that way, Chipmunk. I don't want to lose you, too."

"You're not going to lose me, Father," I said. "I'll go to school on Friday and I'll come back for Nikkomo and I'll go to school in January and I'll come back for Strawberry Thanksgiving. That's how it will be for a while. You go to sea for seven or eight months at a time, and you always come home. I'll always come home, too. I promise."

Father opened his mouth to say something else, but his gaze

shifted suddenly, fixed somewhere across the room. I tried to follow it, to see what he was seeing.

Niquiat was standing in the doorway, looking around. Looking for us.

I saw the moment that he met Father's eyes. How his face changed. It made my throat tighten, the way his face changed.

Niquiat came over and nodded at Father and took a ten-marka coin out of his pocket.

"You came," Father said, as Niquiat put the coin into his hand.

"I came," Niquiat said back, sitting down at Father's other side. "Had to paddle across from Naquipaug, but I came."

The whalers' wives were gathering at the entrance of the circle for the second formal dance. Niquiat was watching Mother, so I watched her, too.

Anything that needed saying could be said later.

AND HAD A REVELATION

On the day after the whalers' returning dance, it was traditional that the children of whalers employ themselves in something useful or entertain themselves in some way that kept them far from the house until sunset, so that whalers' wives could welcome whalers home in their own way.

Sakewa and a whole gang of children her age and younger had taken dominion of the dance circle and were using it to play ringtoss. Niquiat was among them, carrying Sakewa on his shoulders. Kasaqua, to their delight as much as her own, was making a nuisance of herself by intercepting the rings in flight. She kept bringing them to me, trying to get me to join the game.

I was trying, again, to make sense of skiltakraft. Hekua was sitting with me, working on a basket that she was weaving. Sigoskwe had come to join us, perched like an owl on an overturned barrel, looking over the arc of notes and diagrams I'd spread in front of me.

"This is the kind of thing you're learning at school?" Hekua asked, looking at all of my inexpert scribbles.

"This is the kind of thing I'm trying to learn, anyway," I said with a sigh. "I've got other lessons, too—anglereckoning and folklore and natural philosophy and dragon husbandry—but I'm doing well enough in all those things. This is the subject that's giving me the worst time, and is far and away the most important for me to learn, and the professor is a beast and he hates me and that doesn't help at all! I wish Professor Ulfar taught skiltakraft; he's kind, and he makes sense when he talks. I can't make sense of even half of what Professor Ezel says, and I'm not allowed to ask questions. The book isn't much better."

"Well, explain what you *do* understand," Sigoskwe suggested. "Then when you get to a part you can't explain, you know that's the part you *don't* understand—right?"

"Right," I said, because that was how teaching ought to be. "So a skilta is like . . . a map? A drawing that one makes to shape a dragon's breath." I turned one of my workbooks to a new page and fished around in my satchel for a stick of black wax. "You put the things you want the dragon's breath to transform into the middle of a skilta, or at specific points around the middle, and then you draw the lines of power indicating the athers that you want to produce. Athers are the purest thing that something can be. The more motes an ather has, the less pure it is . . . only that's not quite right? Vetna has one mote."

I made a single dot on the paper.

"Kolfni has six motes."

I drew the six-pointed star that represented kolfni.

"Kolfni is what charcoal and lampblack are made from. Because of the way it's shaped, it has four places that other athers want to clasp onto. Vetna and kolfni can join together in long chains; earth coal is made of chains of kolfni and vetna, and that's why it burns. Vetna can also clasp onto stiksna—that's what water is made of."

I drew the complicated triple star that meant "water" in a skilta.

"But you can use a dragon's breath to break it apart, and get vetna and stiksna again."

I drew the three stars separately, a little way apart from one another.

"Once they're apart, they don't want to be water again; you have to recombine them with fire. I'm . . . confused about how that works. You can take stiksna out of air, too, and then you're left with mostly zurfni. Zurfni has seven motes—"

I'd laid out the motes and was drawing the lines that connected them in their proper order. I closed my eyes for a moment, and my hand slipped. When I looked at the ruined figure, I saw that instead of a straight line between the two motes, I'd drawn a curve.

I'd drawn a curve because a curve felt more *right*.

"That doesn't look like the other ones," Sigoskwe said uncertainly.

"No, no, I broke it, but . . . Wait a moment!"

I picked up a new piece of paper and laid the motes out again, connecting all of them with curving lines this time. What I was left with didn't look like a star; it looked like a flower. It felt like something I'd seen before, but I couldn't remember where.

"It's prettier that way, with the swooping lines instead of the straight ones," Sigoskwe said.

"But it's wrong that way, or at least Professor Ezel would say so. But there's something about it . . ."

I made a row of my misshapen skiltas—vetna, kolfni, zurfni, stiksna, brinesna, sindle, pospor, saffle, kalisna, limesna . . . Isen wasn't drawn as a star, because it had twenty-six motes. But if it was . . . if the motes were laid out in the same way and looped together with a long, curving line . . . I drew isen, kessel, and spelter. Spelter had thirty motes, and the flower figure it made was dizzying. Turning and turning.

Like a dance.

The lines of saffle and kalisna were so numerous that they made concentric circles, framing the emptiness at the center where the components to be transmuted would be placed. I traced one of the mote paths on the kalisna skilta with a fingertip, arcing gently from mote to mote, and found myself humming a spring-time song. I *knew* this path. I'd danced it.

I drew a threefold figure with the flower-star of zurfni drawn directly on top of a figure of pospor, linking and interweaving like the two rings of men in the whalers' dance. In the middle, I drew the figure for kalisna at about half the size of the other two. I chose a mote and traced the path I'd drawn for it, and realized that what I'd drawn was the corn-planting dance. Seven girls would stand at the mote points of zurfni with baskets of fresh mussels. Fifteen boys would stand at the mote points of pospor with bas-kets of bleached bone, and nineteen old women would stand at the points of kalisna, closest to the fire, with baskets of wood ashes. They'd follow the curving paths I'd drawn between the motes, around and around. This is what it would look like from above . . . to something flying.

To a dragon.

All of the stories about Nampeshiwe and Nampeshiweisit had to do with dancing.

My people knew nothing of skiltakraft, despite being the com-panions of dragons since the beginning of time. The two facts slipped together in my mind and fastened like a knot.

The corn-planting dance was meant to make the earth of the fields rich. I'd learned in natural philosophy that abundant zurfni in tilled earth was good for green leaves. Abundant pospor and kalisna caused plants to bloom and set fruit.

The corn-planting dance was a skilta.

"Sigoskwe, do you know where Grandma is right now?"

"I think she's having coffee with Sachem Tanaquish and some other elders at his house, why?"

"Because I've just realized something about musquetu and skiltakraft . . ." I said, my voice faint because my mind was spinning around itself. "I think I need to go talk to elders about it. I need to bring Kasaqua."

I left the meetinghouse with Hekua and Sigoskwe and Niquiat, and a whole procession of children following us.

My great aunt Mamisashquee was there with Grandma and Sachem Tanaquish and a half dozen others, gathered around a fire outside the sachem's house, talking and laughing. I didn't know all of them, so some must have come from Naquipaug for the whalers' returning dance, like Great Auntie had. They went quiet as we approached, possibly because we'd come as such a crowd. But this seemed important enough to merit a grand procession. I took the lead, with Kasaqua bounding after me, and when I reached the elders, I canted my head respectfully.

"I hope that all of you are well today," I said. "I'm Anequs, daughter of Chagoma and Aponakwe," I said, being formal and polite for the benefit of the elders who might not know me . . . which was stupid, because of course they already knew who I was. I had Kasaqua walking at my side, and who else could I possibly be? But it felt right to be respectful. "I've come to ask you questions about dancing."

I tried to explain what I'd just realized about dancing and skiltas. Sachem Tanaquish's house wasn't far from the shore, and when words eventually failed we all went together down to the plane of hard-packed sand just above the wave line, and I used a stout piece of driftwood to scratch out skiltas much larger than I'd ever been able to draw on paper. Niquiat stood close to Grandma, an arm around the small of her back to keep her steady on the sand, quietly describing everything I was doing.

"The fire would be here," I said, laying a little bundle of driftwood sticks to mark the spot, "and . . . Sakewa, you and those other girls come stand on these spots. Sigoskwe, you and the boys stand on these ones," I continued as I laid out the motes for zurfni and pospor. "And we don't actually have enough elders to do this properly and I think you all need to be that far back to see this the way it's meant to be seen anyway, so if some of you others want to come and pretend to be elders for a few minutes, I need nineteen of you on these spots."

I stepped back to where the elders were standing, looking at the massive skilta I'd scratched into the stand and the children ready to follow its traces.

"Does everyone here know the corn-planting dance at least a little?" I called to the children. They collectively answered back in a generally positive way. "Look at the lines I've drawn, and follow them to the next spot."

It wasn't at all as flowing or graceful as a dance, but the children all moved together, shuffling across the sand, adding their footprints to the traced lines. Most of the girls knew enough to spin without being told to when they came to the lines of convergence, feet sweeping across the sand to add little swirls that didn't have any analog in a drawn skilta but which, like the curved lines, felt important and right now that I saw them. The boys stamped their feet at the proper intervals, as if they were packing the whole structure of the skilta dance down, driving it into the sand.

Kasaqua was watching, still except for the flickering tip of her tail.

The elders were watching, murmuring softly to one another.

Sachem Tanaquish had tears in his eyes.

"You see, don't you?" I asked, turning to the gathering of elders. "If you could, I'd like your help in drawing figures like this"—I held up the corn-planting-dance skilta that I'd drawn onto paper with black wax—"of every formal dance that any of you can remember. Old dances that we don't often do anymore. Because I think that this is what Crow taught the people at the beginning of time. This is how to shape the unbroken medicine of a dragon's breath."

"I knew that the Anglish couldn't teach you to be a Nampeshiweisit," Grandma said with a crack of dry laughter. "I knew it! Daughter of my daughter, you're going to teach us all how to dance with dragons again."

Everyone was looking at me. The elders. The children, who'd gone solemn and silent because they knew that Tradition was happening. My brothers and my sister.

Kasaqua.

"Yes," I said, into a stillness broken only by the lapping waves, "I will."

AND REJOICED WITH HER LOVED ONES

That afternoon, when Mother and Father were ready to have company again, Grandma and Mother and Father and Niquiat and Sigoskwe and Sakewa and I all went into the forest on the south side of Great Sweet Pond to gather late-fallen nuts. Chestnuts and walnuts and hickory nuts had begun their season in September, just as I was leaving for school, but they'd keep falling from the trees until we got heavy snow. It had been a family tradition for years for us all to go nut-gathering together after the whalers' returning dance.

Kasaqua was the new addition, and she certainly kept things interesting.

There were maple seeds falling with every breath of wind through autumn leaves, spinning in tight circles like fluttering insects, and Kasaqua took great joy in leaping at them as they did. She ate a few, and apparently found them to her liking. She pounced and bounded, making the newly fallen leaves crackle underfoot, flaring her little wings to sweep them into the air in great clouds. Her excitement at being out and about in the forest filled me up inside with a kind of dizzy joy. The air was crisp, just the warm side of frost, and all of us made plumes of steam as we breathed. The sun came in golden shafts through the leaves, and we spent the time talking about everything and nothing. The food at school and how awful it was. Niquiat's engine tinkering and Zhina's airship plans. Sigoskwe and his friends organizing a hunt for next week, for small game: possum and squirrel and turkey. The new book Sakewa had gotten from one of her friends in trade for a finger-woven sash, and how we all should read it. Mother planning what we should cook when Great Auntie Mamisashquee and Auntie Shanuckee came for dinner tomorrow. On Tuesday, the family would be going for the annual shopping trip to Catchnet.

We *didn't* talk about how Niquiat and I would be leaving on the morning ferry tomorrow.

Kasaqua took off running and came back a few minutes later with a squirrel, which she messily devoured while sitting under a hickory tree, watching us. Sigoskwe claimed the tail from her leavings, because it was an especially fine one.

We went back home late in the afternoon with gather-baskets full to bursting, and spent the rest of the evening sorting them and shelling the ones that weren't dry enough to be put by in their shells. Kasaqua sampled some of the nutshells that we were letting fall to a drop cloth on the floor, and did *not* find them to her liking.

Mother and Sakewa made a blue squash stuffed with smoked turkey and wild mushrooms and juniper berries, and Niquiat and I toasted nuts to make a boiled-honey dressing.

Father sat by the fire with Grandma, telling the story of how Crow had stolen fire from the sun and brought it to humankind, which had always been one of my favorites. He did a harsh, braying voice for Crow, and a booming one for the sun.

When the story was done, Father said how proud he was that we had a Nampeshiweisit in the family who was slyly tricking knowledge out of the Anglish. I hadn't really thought of it that way until he said it, but he wasn't wrong. I had become like Crow, venturing to dangerous and unknown lands to bring fire back to my people. I wondered, as we sat together in one another's company, what we were going to burn with it.

After dinner, we played hop-peg and hubbub. I tried to explain the skilta revelation I'd had to Mother and Father, sketching skiltas with a piece of charcoal. Sakewa read to us from her new novel until she couldn't keep her eyes open anymore, and Grandma tucked her into bed.

I sat up watching the fire with Mother and Father and Niquiat, talking quietly about everything and nothing, long after everyone else fell asleep.

I spent the earliest part of the morning packing my rucksack and another bag besides. I had a much better idea of what I wanted and needed at school now. A couple of cattail mats and my old calico quilt, my duck-feather pillow and a winter rabbit skin that Sigoskwe had tanned for me. A few of my favorite pennik novels. A hop-peg board and all its little wooden pieces, because Marta might like it and Sander certainly would, and Theod should be taught to play if he was going to come visit during the winter recess. Mother packed me a handbasket with candied nuts and corn cakes, jars of smoked eel paste and cranberry preserves, dry-smoked venison and rabbit.

There was no way for me to make it back in time for my Friday classes—the ferry would leave Masquapaug at nine and arrive in Catchnet at ten-thirty, and the train would leave at eleven, and we'd arrive in Vastergot around noontime. If I got on the train to school at twelve-thirty, I'd be there around one. Which would still make me late for the afternoon session.

So there wasn't really a reason for me not to have lunch with Niquiat in the city and take a later train back to school. We met with Zhina and Strida and Ekaitz at Haddir's, and we took lunch at the Naquisit street vendor Niquiat had brought me to on my outing with my schoolmates.

"You could come visit for Nikkomo, too," I said to Niquiat. "Please say you will? I'll be going home on the afternoon of Friday the sixteenth. I'll be coming back to school on the thirteenth of January. Please say you'll come home for at least part of the break?"

"Not making you promises that I don't know if I can keep, Chipmunk," Niquiat said with a sigh. "Nikkomo is the same day as Jule this year, on the twenty-first. Zhina's folk have a holiday on the twenty-third that I don't remember the name of, but there's a midnight feast and she wants me to go with her to it and meet her father. I hope it goes over better than when she met mine."

"I'm sorry he was so rude. I brought him to Haddir's because I thought you might be there, and if Jorgen and Zhina hadn't been there to tell us that you were working, I'd have gone to the workshop next. I probably should have gone to the workshop first; I wanted him to see it."

"He wouldn't understand even if he saw it," Niquiat said sourly.

"If you're going to a holiday feast with Zhina, you should invite her to Nikkomo. Father will be in a better mood having been home for a month, and she can meet Mother and Sigoskwe and Sakewa."

Niquiat snorted. "Mother will want to know if I'm courting her."

"Are you?" I asked.

Niquiat swatted me with his hat, which I took to mean yes.

I went back to school on the three-thirty train, arriving at four, feeling a kind of peace and confidence that I hadn't even been wholly aware of lacking. I felt much better about the prospect of end-of-term examinations, having spent time back home.

ANEQUS RETURNED TO SCHOOL AND
CONVERSED WITH THEOD

Upon arriving back at school, I went to my room and un-packed all of my things, hanging my clothes in the wardrobe and remaking my bed. I made my way to Frau Brinkerhoff's office to let her know that I'd returned, and she suggested that I might stop at the dragonhall because Theod had asked after me while I was gone.

He was trimming Copper's claws when I found him; he put down his brush and file and scrambled to his feet when I walked in.

"You're back!" he said, looking more genuinely pleased than I'd ever seen him before. Something about that made me flush a bit, that he should be so happy just from seeing me. Kasaqua made a little trilling sound and bounded over to touch her nose with Copper's.

"I spent the last few days on Masquapaug," I said. "I don't know if anyone told you. My father came for me, and I left with him and attended the whalers' homecoming dance. I'm sorry that I didn't tell you more properly before leaving. There wasn't much time, not if we were going to catch the ferry home."

"It's not my business what you do with your time," he said, his expression closing up to its usual guarded blank. "I'm glad to see you're well, and I hope you had a good time with your family."

"If I'd had a moment to give it thought, I'd have invited you to come with me," I said. "Where do you go when the school is in a long recess, Theod?"

"I stay here," he said softly. "Fraus Kuiper and Brinkerhoff live here throughout the year; so does Professor Ulfar. They leave to visit their families, but they arrange for at least one of them to be in attendance at the school at all times. It's . . . quiet, during recesses. Some of the staff remain; I spent last Jule with Hallmaster Henkjan. He and his wife live very nearby, and were kind enough to invite me for dinner. We had roasted pork and cheese and mulled wine, and we stayed up until sunrise singing Jule songs. He gave me a carving he'd made of Copper, a very good likeness. I didn't have anything to give him."

"Would you like to come to Masquapaug for the winter recess?" I asked. "You could stay with my family."

Theod blinked at me, his face going utterly blank—stony, even. It hurt to see him close up that way, to know that I'd made him look that way by asking a question. He turned away from me, looking at Copper instead.

"Frau Kuiper would never allow it," he said, his voice just the slightest bit uncertain.

"Why does Frau Kuiper need to *allow* it?"

"You haven't learned anything from your time here, have you?" Theod said, making a noise in the back of his throat that was half scoff and half sob. "Frau Kuiper is responsible for my behavior and that of Copper. Other people are depending on us to be on our best behavior, for us to be *good* and *civilized* nackies. To set an example for our people as to how they can better themselves. But you resist being elevated at every turn, and you're trying to drag me down with you—"

"You don't know anything about your own people," I said.

"I don't *have* any people, Anequs," Theod said, something sharp creeping into his voice. "I'm an orphan."

"You know, it's very likely that you still have living family on Naquipaug, and that's something that you ought to look into. Father's originally from Naquipaug. He might have known your parents. I didn't think to ask him when I saw him, because there was so much else to talk about—"

"If I wanted to seek out any remainders of my family, I could have done so by now with folkreckoning records," Theod said, his face hardening.

I crossed my arms and stared at him.

"You can't have it both ways. You can't sob about being an orphan with no people and then refuse to look into your people. If you want to go through your whole life pretending that you're not a nackie, that's your affair and not mine, but it's not ever going to work out for you. Everyone else will always judge you as one."

"Do you honestly think that I'm too stupid to know that? That I'm not acutely aware of the fact that I am judged first by my race and second by the fact that my parents were seditious murderers and third by the fact that I'm an undeserving dragon thief vying for a place above my station? All I have in this world is my good reputation, Anequs."

"Your good reputation isn't going to take care of you, now or ever," I said. "Your family would."

"And how exactly would they manage that?" he demanded, glaring at me. "*If* I've any family on Nack Island, they can only be destitute."

"It's not about money. On Masquapaug and on Naquipaug, we take care of one another. Theod, you could have a *home* to go to."

"The academy is and always will be my home, because this is where Copper is, and he's the closest thing to family that I've ever had," Theod said. "I'm hopeless at skiltakraft, which means that I will never be allowed license as a dragoneer; Copper is technically owned in trust by the academy, in Frau Kuiper's name. It's pointless for me to look beyond the school; I don't have a future beyond it."

"Well, of course you don't, if you refuse to reach for one!" I snapped. "You've decided that you're useless at skiltakraft just because Professor Ezel is a beast who doesn't *want* you to learn anything. I've seen your work, when we study together. You're not as bad as you think you are. If you've really got your heart set on being a dragonhallmaster like Henkjan, you can come and be master of the hall that we're going to eventually build for Kasaqua."

"Such a thing would never be allowed," Theod said.

"Allowed by whom, and why not?"

"By society in general, because we would be out of suitable supervision. Frau Kuiper has been allowed to make pets of us because she has a flawless record of military service and is rather a darling of the jarl, and of the high king and queen. If she hadn't intervened on my behalf two years ago, I would have been quite friendless in the whole affair. Copper would have been killed, or sent to a bestiary to be used as a breeder. I would have been held accountable for the cost of his egg and would be indentured now, probably to the meanest employment that Herr Mahler could find for me. Intervening on my behalf set the precedent that allowed Frau Kuiper to intervene on your behalf. It might have turned out much worse for you. You and your whole village might have been hanged for treason, hiding a dragon."

"But none of that happened," I said. "Might-have-beens are useless. If being a darling of jarls and kings is what needs to happen to secure my freedom and Kasaqua's, then I'll endeavor to become a darling of jarls and kings."

"If you want to be the darling of jarls and kings, you'll have to be a lady and a scholar, and marry a gentleman of good breeding, and comport yourself prettily."

"Like Halya I will," I said with a snort. "Frau Kuiper didn't."

"She's a dedicated handmaiden of Fyra," Theod said.

"And I'm a Nampeshiweisit," I said. "And you're a dragoneer.

And we're both of us nackies, and have a natural right to be among our own kind, seeing to our own needs and attending our own desires."

"No one has ever given half a damn about the natural rights of nackies."

"Then someone ought to *make* them give a damn," I said.

"Those are the kinds of words that will get you arrested and hanged," Theod snapped.

"Let them try," I said. "I'm *not* friendless, and I've made no special effort to stay below anyone's notice. Masquapaug has been too long without dragons. The only two nackies who have them ought to be standing together against anyone who wants to stand against us. You ought to come and meet your family, Theod."

"My family are murderers, Anequs. There's a reason they were hanged. Your people might not be savages, but mine certainly were. Savage behavior must be met with firm reprisal," Theod said.

"It was the Anglish who were savage at Naquipaug," I said forcefully, hissing through my teeth. "They found out that Naquipaug had coal, and when the Naquisit wouldn't sell them the land, they started poisoning wells and burning farms, trying to drive everyone off the island. Sachem Peyaunatam and some of his elder council went into their steading to seek an accord with them, and *they were murdered.*"

"Where did you hear this?" Theod said, staring at me wide-eyed.

"Everyone on Masquapaug knows it. There are still people alive who remember it. My *father* is from Naquipaug, and he lost most of his family. If he hadn't been at sea when it happened, he'd have been old enough to have been in the war party that tried to drive the Anglish off the island."

"The nackies killed women and children in their beds," Theod ground out. "They painted themselves with the blood of the people they murdered."

"The Anglish turned dragonfire on whole villages! They poisoned corn silos with arsen! How many women and children died then?"

"The arsen poisonings were a tragic misunderstanding," Theod said. "The poisoned corn was meant to deal with the rat infestation, to stop the spread of rat-catcher's yellows—"

"That's a lie. It was a war, and the Naquisit lost it. That doesn't mean they were wrong to fight. It doesn't make them murderers any more than the Anglish. Naquipaug belonged to the Naquisit, and it was stolen from them."

"That's *not* what happened," Theod said, shaking his head. "That's not what I was told—"

"Who told you, Theod? What do they think of you, and what do they want you to think of yourself? Frau Kuiper has plainly said to me that she expects you and me to prove that our people can be 'civilized,' and from what I understand, that means 'made Anglish.' I'm not interested in pretending to be Anglish or pretending to be just like the other students. But I'm going to smile and nod and watch and learn, and when I go back to Masquapaug, I'm going to know more about the Anglish than anyone there has ever known before, and I'm going to be riding a dragon when I tell them what I've learned. What happened to Naquipaug won't happen to Masquapaug."

"They'll kill you," Theod said, swallowing. "They'll kill your dragon, and they'll kill you, and they'll kill everyone you've ever loved."

"Then I'll die defending my people. Like your parents did."

Theod was silent for a very long time. He stood with his back to me, looking down the hallway.

"Please go away, Anequs. I think I'd much prefer to be alone for a while."

"You'll think on what I've said?" I asked. He turned to stare at me, his eyes cold and hollow.

"Go," he said.

So I did.

WINTER CAME

It was Sakewa's birthday on the twenty-eighth of November, and I had enough money set aside from my allowance from Frau Brinkerhoff that I felt confident in taking a trip into the city with Liberty on Saturday the twenty-sixth to visit Jenni and purchase several rolls of colorful cotton cord from her. Sakewa loved to finger-weave, and having a whole rainbow of colors would delight her. When I told Frau Brinkerhoff what the parcel was and who it was for, she didn't even charge me parcel postage.

It snowed on the first of December—not the sort of frosty dusting that we'd been getting since the middle of November that melted as soon as the sun hit it, but proper ground-coating snow that turned the whole world sparkling and white. I donned my boiled wool cloak and took Kasaqua outside into it before breakfast, feeling a dizzy, buoyant joy as she pranced and leaped and dug furrows in the fascinating new material. I threw snowballs for her, and she was very cross when she couldn't find them. I took her back inside when the tips of my fingers began going numb, making a mental note to pack a pair of mittens when I came back from winter recess.

Theod had been studiously avoiding me for the past three weeks. Even in the classes that we shared, he spoke to me only as much as the subject matter required. He didn't take meals in the dining hall at all. The looks he gave me any time I tried to start a conversation made it clear that such attempts were unwelcome— not precisely angry but blank and lost. Haunted.

After our anglereckoning lesson on Monday the fifth, Theod stopped me in the hallway as we left the classroom.

"Anequs, will you do me the kindness of joining me in the library? I've given a lot of thought to what you said the last time we spoke, and I'd very much like to have a conversation with you."

The library was largely deserted, and it wasn't at all difficult to find a quiet table couched by a couple of shelves. Kasaqua fretted a bit, wanting to go outside, because going outside was what was supposed to happen after sitting in class for two hours. I had to imagine that Copper was wondering where Theod was, and that Theod was acutely aware of that. There had to be a reason he'd asked me here and not to the dragonhall.

"I'd like to apologize to you, for how I've treated you these past three weeks. I was deeply affected by the things you said— about potential remainders of my family, and your suggestion that I visit Masquapaug. I . . . I spoke with Frau Kuiper about it. She was far more amenable to the idea than I'd ever have anticipated. Because of the laws regarding Copper's wardship, and the fact that I haven't passed the relevant examinations in skiltakraft, I wouldn't be allowed out of her auspices for more than fourteen days, but . . ."

"But you'd like to visit Masquapaug for fourteen days during the recess?" I asked.

"If your invitation still stands, yes. I understand if it doesn't, given how absolutely boorish I've been these past weeks. I felt that I was too emotionally affected to converse civilly, and the best thing I could think to do about that was to absent myself as much as I was able. It's occurred to me that it was not, perhaps, the best way to manage the situation."

There was a palpable anxiety and shame in his words, and I didn't really think about what I was doing before I found myself reacting. I reached across the table, taking his face in my hands, running my thumbs along his cheeks. He sucked a harsh breath through his teeth when I did, and I realized how forward I was being and pulled back immediately.

"I'm sorry, that's . . . it's a Maquisit thing, but it's a Naquisit thing too, the face holding. It's—"

He closed his eyes and took a breath and asked, "How can I find out if I've got family on Naquipaug?"

"We could ask my father," I said. "He grew up on Naquipaug, lived there until . . . until 1825."

"I would very much appreciate it if you'd introduce me to your father," he said, shuddering, sighing deeply, as if that had been a very hard thing to say—as if saying it had torn something from him.

"I would be delighted, Theod. If you'd be kind enough to travel with me to Naquipaug, it would save a lot of trouble with arranging a chaperone for the journey. I'll send my family a telegram and we'll work out a plan of action. That said, would you like to accompany me to the dragonhall? Kasaqua is absolutely cross with me now about being delayed."

"Yes, absolutely," he said. "Copper's practically frantic—I can feel him pacing in his box. My being so emotionally affected has been quite hard on him."

Theod pushed away from the table, and I rose as well. Kasaqua made an excited little trill, leaping to her feet and scampering toward the door, looking back at both of us expectantly.

We walked together to the dragonhall in silence that was, unlike the silence for the last three weeks, wholly warm and companionable.

SHE LEARNED OF OTHER ANGLISH CUSTOMS

ander was absent from skiltakraft class the following day. It worried me only a little, because I knew that he'd been home for the weekend. He arrived at our usual luncheon table with something tucked under his arm and an absolutely giddy gleam in his eyes. He set his parcel down without first going to get food and immediately took out his tablet and began writing. It was obviously of some importance to him, so I read it as soon as he put it in front of me.

Neither of us will be here for Jule, so I wanted to give you this before the end of the term.

I looked up from the tablet, and he was pushing the parcel toward me. It was wrapped in glossy colored paper with a stamped pattern of snowflakes.

"Open it," he said, looking at the parcel as he put it in my hands.

It took me a moment or two of turning the parcel over to find the seam, because it had been very neatly folded to make the pattern stamped on the paper line up. I peeled the paper back carefully, not wanting to tear it. I found myself holding a brand-new leather-bound book; it still smelled like the printing ink. The cover was embossed with gold letters: *Sybille Stosch, A Girl's Own Story* and below it in slightly smaller letters, *Omnibus Edition 1836–1840.*

"This is the backlog of all the Sybille Stosch stories? With her beginnings and all?" I asked, opening the front cover gingerly because I didn't want to crack the fresh binding.

Sander wrote on his tablet, *I thought you might like to read them, because then you could talk about them with Marta and me. I know you've read a few of the early ones. The omnibus edition only comes out every four years, but I have the stories from 1840 to the present cut out and pressed into a remembrance book at home. I can bring it after the winter recess and you could get caught up.*

"Thank you very much, Sander, this is very thoughtful," I said. "Though I'm not sure what it's got to do with Jule?"

It's a Jule present. Do your people not give Jule presents?

"My people don't celebrate Jule; we celebrate Nikkomo, which I gather is a different sort of thing. I don't really know much about Jule, since I've never known anyone who celebrates it. Are gifts customary? I haven't gotten anyone anything . . ."

"It's better to give than to receive blessed Jule and blessed Fyra her gift is the sun," Sander said, all in a rush, his cheeks going a bit pink. He bit his lip and took his tablet back and began writing again.

Jule is supposed to be about celebrating how Fyra argued with Joden when he decided to smother the world in ice; she convinced him to bring back the sun. But really it's mostly about being with family and feasting and wassailing and giving gifts. On the first night of Jule you kill a boar and you're supposed to pour its blood on the roots of an ash tree, but no one does that anymore. I think in some country places where they keep livestock near people they might still say oaths over a boar before they kill it; in my family we've always just said oaths over a ham wrapped in waxed paper before giving it to the cook.

"Oaths?" I asked.

Just normal sorts of things like how you'll be diligent in the new year to come and that—he started writing, but then looked up and said, "Marta!"

Marta had already gotten food and was approaching the table with a look of polite interest.

"I bought a book!" Sander said, pointing at the book. "Blessed Jule for Anequs."

"Oh . . . are we exchanging gifts?" Marta said, her eyebrows rising. "I hadn't planned . . . but of course we absolutely should! Oh, I'll have to send Papa a telegram! There are still fifteen days before Jule, after all, and that's plenty of time to make arrangements. Of course both of you must come to the party; Papa always hosts a party on the second or third night of Jule."

"I'll be on Masquapaug at Jule," I said firmly. "And it's the twenty-first this year, isn't it?"

"Jule always begins on the twenty-first of December," Marta said, as if I should have known that.

"Nikkomo is also on the twenty-first this year. It isn't always. Nikkomo happens on whatever night is the longest night, so it's the twenty-first some years and the twentieth others."

"Well, that doesn't matter so much, I don't think. You'll do Nik-homo on the twenty-first and then you can still come to my party on the twenty-third. Oh, and of course dear Lisbet must come, Sander. I'll send both of you formal invitations, but you can tell her to be expecting one if you like."

"I'm telling you now that I won't be able to come, so there's no point in sending me an invitation," I said. "I'm very sorry, and I'm sure it will be a lovely time, but it's important to me to be with my family. Besides, traveling from the island is a great deal of trouble, and I've got nothing to wear to an event like that anyway unless you want me to wear the same dress I wore on Valkyrjafax."

"Well, I could certainly arrange for my seamstress to make you another dress—"

"Marta, I'm flattered to have been invited, but *no*."

She blinked at me with absolute incomprehension.

"But it would be such a wonderful chance for you to see and be seen by selected members of society! I'm arranging to invite Lisbet's school acquaintances who were introduced to us at Valkyrjafax, and there will be a number of eligible young men there—"

"Why would I care about eligible young men?"

"Well, this is the sort of event that could help you eventually become . . . well situated in life. And besides that, it's going to be ever so much fun! You've gotten so good at dancing, and so many people in my father's acquaintance are absolutely dying to meet you in light of the editorial and the interviews and the article concerning Valkyrjafax. You and Theod are becoming figures of public interest—"

"*I* don't especially want to meet *them*," I said. "I've read enough of your etiquette book to know that 'well situated in life' is a polite way to say 'married to a man of good character who has a good income,' and I have absolutely no intention of marrying any Anglish man. I didn't especially enjoy the Valkyrjafax ball, and I have no desire to repeat such an experience unless it's absolutely necessary—especially not when the alternative is being with my family in the days directly following Nikkomo!"

"I'm sure that you don't intend to give insult," Marta said, frowning, "but this is *not* the appropriate way to decline an invitation."

"Ugh, fine, send me a card inviting me and I'll send you a card expressing my regrets and we'll both have wasted ink and paper if that's the way you'd like to do this. Sander, thank you very much for the book. Marta, thank you for your invitation, even though I must decline. I doubt that I'll be able to arrange gifts for either of you before the end of the term, but I'll be sure to bring you each back something thoughtful from Masquapaug. I'm afraid, for the moment, that I must absent myself. I have erelore this afternoon, and I need to catch up on my reading. I'll see you at dinner."

I finished my luncheon as quickly as I could and left them to their own devices.

On Saturday the tenth, I visited Niquiat at the tinker co-op. When I arrived, Jorgen and Strida were pawing through a cartload of junk and scrap that Strida had bought by the pound from a local junkyard. Zhina and Niquiat were sorting things as they were handed them. Kasaqua spent a little while looking around and sniffing at things, but eventually settled herself near Strida's forge, curled up like a cat. There were all sorts of things that I recognized and all sorts of things that I didn't: part of a Victrola, the detached head of an automaton horse, broken clocks and windup contraptions, and tangled masses of copper wire. They all seemed very excited about it. It was a higher class of discards than they were usually able to afford.

"Marta wanted to invite me to a fancy party at her father's house and I had to tell her no at least half a dozen times and I think she's still pouting about it," I complained, lending a hand to put things onto shelves and into bins as I was told. "Sander gave me a present for Jule, which means that it's only polite for me to give him one, and I know that Marta intends to give me one, so I've got to get something for her, too, and I have no idea what Marta could possibly want that she can't just buy for herself."

"The idea is to get her something that shows you're thinking about her and that you know the kind of things that would make her happy," Strida said. "It doesn't matter if it's something she could get anywhere; it matters that *you* got it. Fancy chocolates always go over well, or little paper boxes with pretty pictures pasted on that you cut out of magazines. Pressed flowers, hair ribbons, perfumes, soaps—that kind of thing. That's what everyone always got me when I was younger, when what I really wanted was goggles or a cutting torch or a nice set of socket wrenches. Marta seems like the kind of person who'd actually want the little girlish treasures."

"I should probably get some books about Anglish gods and

holidays and all that, so I can be more knowledgeable about this sort of thing in the future," I said with a sigh. "I'd probably be better in folklore, too, because all the stories seem to presume that I already know all the gods and goddesses and heroes and all that. Professor Ibarra keeps pointing out that I've missed obvious references and callbacks to other stories and what they imply about characters and events, and that this or that *obviously* symbolizes the approval or disapproval of whichever god. It's awful, and I don't even *care* about any of it!"

"So your folks don't believe in a whole pack of bickering gods?" Zhina asked, looking up from the thing she was drawing. "Niquiat was telling me you have a feast on the night of solstice, and I'm still not sure if I want to go because it's sort of the opposite of what I properly should be doing that night. But then again, acquiring higher knowledge is one of the cardinal virtues, and so are charity and love, and your Nikkomo's kind of about that, yeah?"

"On the long night, we all come together with the best of what we have in our stores and share it out equally among ourselves so that no one wants in winter," I said with a shrug. "It can really matter to some people, in a bad harvest year. No one on Masquapaug starves unless all of us are starving together."

"See, you and Zhina here have the same kind of faith, I think," Strida said, smiling. "One that's about how you act and being good and all. Us, we're about erelore. The stories of gods and heroes and how things came to be as they are, pleasing the gods so they look favorably on mankind. Any of you heathens know the story of Jule?"

"Sander said it was something about Fyra and Joden?" I answered.

"So it goes like this," Strida said, putting both hands on the edge of the cart and leaning forward a little. "Joden—the king of Valhalya—learned the secret of writing and runes and skilta and all that by feeding his left hand and eye to Hrothvitnir, the great she-wolf that makes her den in the roots of the world tree. He kept this knowledge only for the gods for most of time, but then Enki the mad god tricked him into giving it to people, because Enki had made a bet with his wife, Rune—but that's a whole other story. Anyway, Joden was so angry about it that he decided to smother the world in ice. For a thousand years, there was no summer. We know this bit is true because of natural philosophy; you can see what the rivers of ice did to the land. Anyway, Fyra, Joden's wife, she likes people because she thinks we're valorous and entertaining and we offer her blood and flesh and fruit and wine. She didn't want all of us to die smothered under ice. Now, Fyra and Joden are both powerful witskrafters, and they had a bloody battle for many days and nights, and Fyra won—because of course she did, she's the queen of battle and has the Valkyrja for handmaidens—and she made Joden give the sun back. So on the first night of Jule we give blood sacrifice to Fyra and swear oaths to her, and we light bonfires and wassail and stay up all night waiting for the sun to come back, because once it didn't for a thousand years. And when it comes back, we're all so happy that we sing and drink and feast and give each other gifts. Jule is nine days long, and there's a reason for that, but I can't remember except that nine is a lucky number. The tenth day is Last Day and the one after that is First Day. So that's Jule. What's your folks' feast day about, Zhina?"

"The solstice—the longest night—marks Madyem Gaanbar, the midyear," Zhina said. "We fast from the time the sun goes down on the solstice to the time it comes up the next morning, reflecting on our works in the year and if we've been true to the virtues. Then there's a feast that goes on for five days. Back in Kindah, it's a whole-city kind of thing and it happens in the street with pavilions, but there's only a little quarter of Kindah folks here in Vastergot, and it's very cold here at the midyear, so we take turns hosting at our homes."

"You folks believe that there's just one god, right?" Jorgen asked.

"There's one creator and he's had many prophets," Zhina said.

"Everything, including spirits and other powerful beings, are his creation. We understand that what you call gods were and maybe still are real, and that they're important in your part of the world, but they—like everything else—were made by the one creator, the everlasting flame who warms and lights creation. Can we *stop* talking about religion now? It always makes my teeth itch."

As she said it, she put something down on the table in front of her that caught my eye.

"Is that a sewing machine?" I asked.

"Well, it's most of one. If it's in the junk pile, it means it doesn't work anymore," Jorgen said. "We see things like this, time to time, and take them apart for their workings. They're useful for fiddly little clockworks inside. Why, do you need a sewing machine for actually sewing?"

"Liberty might," I said, hopping off the stool to edge around the table and take a closer look. Zhina pushed it toward me.

It seemed to be all in one piece, the black lacquered body of it made in two halves fastened together with bolts and screws shaped like butterflies. The needle was broken, its point snapped off, but the needle housing seemed to be fine. I tried to turn the crank and found it absolutely stuck.

The butterfly screws turned when I held them between my thumb and knuckle and really put muscle to it, and when I'd gotten them all out and set them carefully aside, the whole thing came apart as easily as an oyster. I immediately saw the problem; the whole of its insides were a wretched tangle of cotton thread. Niquiat came to look over my shoulder.

"If you want to save it, you're going to need tweezers and hooks and scissors and probably a torch," he said.

"You've got all that here, haven't you?" I asked.

"You thinking of joining the co-op, Chipmunk? I'll cover your first week's dues."

I glanced at him, not quite sure if he was serious. He walked over to one of the crowded shelves and selected a rolled-up bit of leatherwork. When he brought it back and unrolled it, it proved to be full of little hand tools: hooks and pliers and screwdrivers and tweezers.

"If you want to take the trouble to fix the thing, you can have it," Strida said. "Cost me maybe a few penniks, so I don't mind. Tell me a story and we'll call it even."

I picked up one of the little pairs of pliers and began attacking the tangle of thread, and while I did, I told the story of Requeiska and the Hurricane.

By the time I had to go back to school, carrying the sewing machine and the roll of hand tools with me, I'd gotten the crank to move again.

AND COMPLETED HER END-OF-TERM EXAMINATIONS

Examinations began on the twelfth of December.

My first examination was in natural philosophy, for which I was very glad. It involved moving around the room to observe the various stations that Professor Ulfar had set up. At one station we had to identify four white powders by various means—dissolving them in water and in vinegar, observing their texture and their scent, things like that—and explain how we'd reached our conclusions. At another, we had to use fiddly glassware to measure out an exact number of drops of water into a marked vial. Professor Ulfar moved among us, asking questions and offering suggestions, marking our progress in one of his little cardbound notebooks.

Monday afternoon brought my anglereckoning examination, which was exactly what I'd expected it to be: a straightforward list of questions. I didn't encounter anything that I didn't know how to proceed with.

Tuesday morning, however, was my examination in skiltakraft by Professor Ezel. I was reasonably confident in my understanding of the subject matter now, because of the study I'd been putting in with Theod. My realization concerning skiltas and dances made it a great deal easier to memorize the correct figures; to keep track of the motes by imagining them as separate dancers. I knew Professor Ezel's low opinion of me, though, and that he would probably judge anything I did very harshly.

I didn't go to breakfast with Marta, instead electing to eat some of the candied nuts and dried cranberries I'd brought back from Masquapaug and spend every moment I could going over my textbooks and notes. Kasaqua stalked around the room, annoyed or anxious or something. She squawked at me crossly when I left her to go to class; I'd been told in advance that dragons were to be quartered during this examination, as there would be no physical component to it.

I was the first to arrive in Professor Ezel's laboratory, giving myself ample time because I knew that he'd dearly have loved to lock me out of the room as tardy and fail me without even letting me try. He was seated at his desk when I entered.

"Disregard your normal seating; you will be seated alphabetically for the duration of the examination. Come to the front of the room. Find your place."

There was a card that said *Aponakwesdottir, Anequs* sitting on the frontmost right-hand desk, next to a card that said *Frederik Anderssen*. Frederik had never said even one word to me, which made him preferable to a good number of young men I might have had to sit beside, but I'd have much preferred Sander. I expected that the fact that I'd have much preferred Sander was among the reasons for the change of seating today.

That, and the fact that Professor Ezel probably expected me to attempt to cheat.

I knew in the cores of all of my bones that it was important for Professor Ezel not to know about my revelation concerning dancing and skiltakraft. Better that he think me a dull-witted savage without hope of improvement than have him and who knew how many other Anglish people nosing around, wanting to come to Masquapaug to watch us dance and working out how it was done. No one had said it, but I had the decided feeling that Captain Einarsson expected that I'd never excel in skiltakraft, meaning that no one would ever have to worry about me passing the examinations of the ministry and thus being free to go and do as I liked with Kasaqua without Frau Kuiper's oversight. Theod seemed disconcertingly content with the idea of living the rest of his life here at the academy, and perhaps they'd expected the same of me—that Masquapaug was someplace I'd be happy to leave, that I'd want to come here and become Anglish and be a society lady like Marta.

I was going to have to show them otherwise.

When the rest of the students silently filed in and the door was locked and Professor Ezel put the paper in front of me, I found to my abject relief that there was nothing on it that I didn't know! All of my study, much of it wholly independent of this class and including books from the library that had not been assigned to me, seemed to have had the desired effect—I understood the principles of skiltakraft.

On the top of the first page was written: *Below are two templates of the chart of athers. Complete the first one with the names and number of motes, and the second with the symbols of each ather.*

I'd spent enough time staring at the copy of the chart that was generally present on the wall to have committed all its details to memory. I glanced at the spot where it normally hung. It had been taken down. Professor Ezel noticed me glancing. He met my eyes for a bare moment, and his mouth twitched into a smug and unpleasant smile. I looked back down at my paper.

The first time I'd been asked to do this, I'd had no idea what I was doing and I'd been working with thick ink and a tin-nibbed pen. This time I had significantly better ink, and a quill that I'd cut myself to my own preferences, and three months of ceaseless practice.

I glanced at the clock standing against the far wall.

I filled the charts in twenty minutes.

Other questions on the exam were, similarly, exactly the kind of thing I'd been studying for in my textbook and Theod's textbook and the books available in the library: the atheric diagrams of water, salt, sugar, alcohol, borax, smothering air, blasting powder, yellow vitriol, rust, coal gas, saltpeter, tatkrafted air, quartz, rusts of kessel, spelter, and zan.

I was aware, as I carefully and precisely drew each figure that was asked for, that other students were walking past me to put their completed examinations on Professor Ezel's desk. I couldn't help glancing at the clock now and again, but I didn't allow myself to rush. I would finish or I wouldn't, but what work I did I was determined to do correctly.

I finished drawing the rust of zan two minutes before the period would have ended. I was the last student left in the classroom when I walked up to Professor Ezel's desk and laid my completed examination on the stack. I didn't look at him. I dipped a curtsy and left.

Sander was waiting for me in the hallway outside the classroom, his back to the wall, worrying at his little ball of clay. He tucked it into his little waxed-cloth bag and put it in his pocket as I approached.

"I did well, did you do well?" he asked.

"I think I *did*! There was nothing that I didn't know how to answer, at least. He's probably still going to cover the paper in red about my execution, though. When we take the examinations for the ministry, who judges them? Is it him, for skiltakraft?"

Sander took out his tablet to answer me.

I think that because Captain Einarsson is the school's representative, he'll be conducting the ministry examinations of flight and skiltakraft. But that won't be until spring of next year for you probably, and longer for me because Inga is a velikolepni and they're slow to flight.

"I've noticed that Inga is the only velikolepni present at the school. Is it an especially rare breed?"

Inga's egg was made available to me as a favor from one of Frau Kuiper's associates. Frau Brinkerhoff arranged it. She's my great aunt—my grandmother's younger sister. You knew that, didn't you? It seems everyone knows it. I don't make much mention of it because I don't want to be accused of favoritism. There are already enough people who think I don't deserve to be here and don't deserve to be Inga's dragoneer without giving them a reason to think I've been given an unfair advantage.

"I can't see how you've been given more advantage than anyone else here; everyone seems to come from a well-off family from what I can tell, except Theod and me, and we're under Frau Kuiper's charge."

Do you want to join me at the dragonhall? I'm going to practice tacking procedures for the husbandry examination this afternoon.

"I'm reasonably certain that I've mastered Kasaqua's tack, but I'll join you anyway. Marta's sure to be fretting about whichever of her exams she just had if I go back to our room, and I'd much prefer your company."

Sander smiled and nodded, tucking his tablet away into his jacket pocket, and we proceeded together to the dragonhall.

AND PRESENTED A GIFT TO A FRIEND

I spent Wednesday afternoon finishing repairs on the sewing machine. I'd pulled enough thread out of it to weave a handkerchief from, and after retightening some of its interior screws and polishing all the inner workings with machine oil and replacing the smashed vial of strahlendstone with a fresh one supplied by Niquiat (or more correctly, supplied by Zhina), I found that it operated quite smoothly. I had no idea where to obtain a needle for it, or spools and bobbins of the correct size, so I couldn't actually test its operation. I could only hope it was in working order.

On Thursday morning, my erelore examination proceeded without special difficulty or interest; it was just a long list of questions about the dates of significant events and a few short essays on their causes and effects. When I'd completed the exam, Professor Ibarra gave me a list of texts that he expected me to read over the winter recess for my directed study.

I stopped by the mail room after the exam and found that Ingrid Hakansdottir sent me a card that had been signed by at least a dozen people. Upon conferring with Marta about the correct response I sent a letter back wishing her and her whole neighborhood a blessed Jule and an abundant Nikkomo.

After luncheon, I made the excuse of having popped the stitches of one of my shoe buttons to give me reason to visit the laundry and convey to Hilde that Liberty simply must come and meet me at my room to repair it. I spent the better part of an hour waiting for her there, wondering if she'd received my message at all. Kasaqua was pacing the room all the while, feeling my unease.

It was nearly two o'clock when she knocked on the door.

"I'm glad you're here!" I said as she came in, giving me an odd look.

"I can't stay long, mind you, I've got duties today. But Adeline said that Hilde seemed to think it was something urgent."

"I'm leaving for home tomorrow, and I won't be back for a month, and Sander got me a Jule present, which is how I learned Jule presents are even a done thing and . . . well . . . I got this for you," I said, carefully setting the package on the table. I'd made a carton out of cardstock. I had no idea where one went about getting the fancy printed paper that Sander's gift had come wrapped in, but there was an endless supply of plain brown paper in Professor Ulfar's laboratory. Liberty stared at the package, blinking a couple of times and looking up at me and then back down, her brow furrowing.

"I'm sorry if I'm doing it wrong; I've never celebrated Jule before," I faltered. "I just . . . I gathered that it's customary to give gifts to your friends? Sander got me a gift, and I'm going to make gifts for Sander and Marta over the recess, and I invited Theod to come celebrate Nikkomo and . . . I got you this."

"No one gets Jule gifts for servants," Liberty said through her teeth.

"Would you at least open it? Please?" I asked.

Liberty took a long moment to stare at me before she moved

to very gingerly peel back the paper. She folded the sides of the carton down, and there sat the sewing machine in all its lacquered glory.

"It's a sewing machine . . ." Liberty whispered. "I don't have a treadle table to gear it into, though . . ."

"No, it's tatkraftish, it doesn't need a treadle; you have to wind it up like a clock. There's a lodestone cachet and a coil of copper wire inside that feeds to a little vial of strahlendstone that can store the tatkraft. You can see it glowing in this little window here, so you know if it needs winding. It's got a gearbox, and you can shift the gears to adjust how slowly or quickly you'd like it to stitch. It needs a new needle, and I didn't know where to get spools and bobbins, but it—"

"This must have cost a fortune," Liberty said, looking up at me. "Just the cost of the strahlendstone . . . I can't accept this."

"It didn't, really! It was broken, someone had thrown it away as scrap, and my brother helped me fix it. He gave me the vial of strahlendstone, too. I just thought . . . You spend so much of your time sewing, I thought you might like it."

Liberty looked up at me, her eyes full of tears.

"No one gets presents for servants, and this is so much, and you're just . . ."

"I'm sorry if I'm doing it wrong," I said. "I thought you'd like it."

Liberty stepped around the edge of the table and pulled me into an embrace. She was trembling.

"Thank you," she said, her voice muffled against my shoulder. "Thank you."

Yet all I could think was that Liberty smelled like almond oil and soap, and that she was warm and shivering. I tentatively wrapped my arms around her and hugged her back, not sure if that was allowed in the unspoken bounds of "we are *not* courting each other."

"No one's given me anything even half this nice since before my parents died," Liberty said, right against my ear. "I'll have to think of something to do for you in return, when you come back in January."

"You don't have to," I said quickly, letting her pull away a bit. "It's not . . . We don't do Jule presents, my people. I didn't get you something expecting you to get me something. I just . . . It was there, and I thought it could be useful to you. I was thinking of you, and thought it was something you might like."

"I do. You don't understand how much I do. I really do have to get back to my work, but . . . We can write each other, over the recess, can't we?"

"Of course we can!" I said, smiling brightly, feeling a strange little flutter in my belly.

"You're not like anyone else I've ever met, Anequs, do you know that?" she asked suddenly, her face twisting into an expression that I couldn't quite decipher. It made my mouth go quite dry, though.

"Thank you?" I ventured.

She smiled, but it was a painful sort of smile.

"I have to go. Thank you again, Anequs."

I didn't want her to go. I wanted to take her back to Masquapaug with me and introduce her to my family and sing and dance and walk along the beach and just . . . everything.

But I just smiled and nodded as she folded the sewing machine back up into its carton and took it back to her room downstairs.

ANEQUS AND THEOD WENT TO MASQUAPAUG

On Friday morning, Theod had his husbandry examination with Professor Mesman. Sander had already departed the previous night, and Marta had made the room intolerable with her frenzied packing, so I elected to take a constitutional with Kasaqua around the grounds. It had snowed again last night, just a couple of inches, making everything fresh and sparkling. Lacking mittens, I was carrying a rolled-up blanket as a makeshift muffler. Kasaqua seemed entirely unbothered by the snow; I'd learned in dragon husbandry that she was able to warm herself from within by means of a poorly understood atheric process. It meant that steam rose from beneath her folded wings if she stood still long enough, just as it billowed out from her mouth and mine as we breathed.

The crown of Kasaqua's head stood level with my hip now, and the tips of her wings crossed just above the base of her tail when she had them folded. In the last two weeks she'd developed a pair of knobby growths on the curve of her skull, equally spaced between her ears and eyes, just in front of the first feathers of her mane. They were covered in velvety down, less like a deer's velvet and more like a baby bird. She liked me to run my fingers over them, leaning in and crooning any time I did. She was tawny gold all over now, her spots and speckles almost entirely faded except for the black markings on her face and ears. Her wingleather was paler than the rest of her, creamy yellow shading to orange and red along the leading edge.

At the rate she was growing, I might be able to ride her by next autumn. Sometime in the next couple of years, she'd be able to fly. What would it be like then, to not have to worry about trains or ferries or even canoes, to be able to fly from one place to another without a care for roads or forests or bodies of water or impassible rocks? I knew from reading and from overhearing casual conversation that most any dragon could make New Linvik in a couple of hours, and quicker breeds in less time than that. Kasaqua's conformation was somewhat like a bjalladreki, and somewhat like an arin or an akhari, though she was longer in the body than any of those breeds. The midsize breeds from across the eastern ocean were generally wolfish in conformation; Kasaqua was much more like an outsize wolverine or raccoon in her proportions and gait. Based on the shape of her wings, she was probably going to be quick and agile in the air.

I didn't have observations and illustrations and notes about behavior concerning Kasaqua as I did with other breeds of dragon, because she'd come to us from someplace beyond the western frontier. Someplace the Anglish had never been, or at least had never taken hold.

What was it like to live someplace the Anglish had never been to?

Someday not far in the future, I was going to be able to fly on Kasaqua, and I wasn't planning to ask anyone's permission to go looking for answers to questions like that.

Marta's father came to collect her in his automotor shortly before luncheon, and I said my goodbyes to her. She complained again that I really ought to come to her Jule party and that I was missing a great social opportunity and all that. Having the room to myself once she was gone was plain relief.

Theod and I met for luncheon, parted to get our satchels from our rooms, and announced our departure to Frau Brinkerhoff. Frau Kuiper happened to also be in her office when we stopped by, and she wished us well—and reminded Theod that he was to be back at the school on the thirtieth. If he was not, she'd be forced to come to investigate the cause of the delay.

We both had satchels full of books and papers, work to complete while on recess. Theod had a suitcase as well. I didn't, being perfectly content to spend the recess wearing clothes that I'd left at home in November. Copper's tack was equipped with satchels, and he made no complaints about serving as a packhorse for us. We caught the one o'clock train into Vastergot. Copper *did* mind—loudly and plaintively—being relegated to a horse box while the rest of the party proceeded to the passenger car. There was really nothing to be done about that, given his size.

We arrived at Vastergot station around one-thirty, transferred trains without great trouble, and arrived in Catchnet around three-thirty. There was a little more to-do than usual because we had to disembark Copper, which involved engaging a ramp because the platform here wasn't elevated—passengers were expected to use the stairs.

A gang of raggedy-looking children had gathered at the platform, waiting to see what was being carried in the horse box. They were a mixed lot of nackie and black and Anglish children, and seemed to share a similar level of general poverty. They evidently hadn't expected a dragon, because as Theod led Copper down the ramp there was a chorus of excitement and surprise.

It became immediately apparent that I'd spent far more time among people with Kasaqua than Theod had ever spent among

people with Copper. Kasaqua was excited at the prospect of attention, her wings slightly flared. Theod seemed absolutely
alarmed, as if he expected to be attacked, and I watched his face
shut down to the careful blankness he often maintained at school.
Copper put his head on Theod's shoulder and made an anxious
whining sound.

I put myself and Kasaqua between Theod and the children,
greeting them warmly as I put my hand on Kasaqua's hackles and
tried to impress upon her a need for restraint.

"You're them, ent you? Theod and Anequs?" one of the tallest
children asked: a boy in grease-stained corduroys and a faded and
much-patched calico shirt. He was nackie, but not of island stock—
he had a mainlander look. "We've seen you in the weekly, and ent
no other nackies got dragons so you've got to be them."

"Yes, you're right—very pleased to meet all of you. I'm Anequs, this is Kasaqua, he's Theod, that's Copper. We've got to get
to the docks, though, if we're to arrive in time to make the four
o'clock ferry to Masquapaug."

"Can I pet your dragon? Mama said it's good luck," a different
child asked: a black girl, somewhat younger than the boy who'd
spoken first. I nodded, and she approached timidly. Kasaqua
obligingly sank to the ground, her forelegs splayed far apart, her
tail thumping up and down. She made a pleased crooning sound
when the little girl carefully combed her fingers through the crown
of her mane. The girl grinned.

The lot of them followed Theod and me to the docks, barking
questions the whole way that I answered as best I could. We made
quite the procession, all together, and people on the street about
their work paused to watch us pass. I could see them whispering
to one another, some of them pointing. The children watched and
waved as we paid our fare and boarded the ferry.

We arrived on Masquapaug at half past five.

THEY SPOKE TO HER FATHER ABOUT A PAINFUL TIME

My family was waiting for us at the dock, and so were some of Sigoskwe's and Sakewa's friends. We were met with cheers as we stepped onto shore. The ferryman looked vaguely disapproving of the commotion as he walked into Mr. Aroztegui's office with a parcel of letters. I made introductions to everyone regarding Theod, and we proceeded to the village with the children making a great fuss about the dragons. Copper stayed very close to Theod, but Kasaqua had a great deal of fun running forward and back along the trail, chasing the children who were chasing her. When we got to our house, I introduced Theod to Grandma, and Father suggested that the rest of the children go home.

He had to make the suggestion several times.

In preparation for hosting Theod and Copper, Father had erected a three-sided shelter with its back to the wind, floored with a thick layer of bundled straw and hung with plain cattail mats. It was big enough to comfortably hold Copper and Kasaqua at the same time. Kasaqua probably could have fit inside our house, but she'd trip over herself and likely knock things around with her wings and tail. Copper couldn't have fit through our doorway at all.

We had dinner together—corn cakes and sobaheg and roasted chestnuts. Everyone wanted stories about school; whether I was doing well and what I'd learned. Theod was mostly silent, answering in the greatest possible brevity when directly asked questions.

It wasn't until after Sakewa and Sigoskwe had gone to bed that I asked quietly, "Father . . . can we talk about Naquipaug?"

"You know well enough that it's not a happy story, Chipmunk," Father said with a weary sigh, staring into the fire. "Why are you asking about it?"

"Theod's parents were hanged in 1825. He might still have some family there."

Theod jerked his head and looked at me, something painful and betrayed in his eyes, as if I wasn't supposed to have mentioned that.

"I was still courting your mother then," Father said. "Hadn't quite decided if I was going to move to Masquapaug to marry her. Niquiat had been born in October, which was making the choice easier, but things weren't well on Naquipaug, and hadn't been since the Anglish settlers found the seam of coal. They'd already taken most of the east coast of the island by then, building houses and fencing in fields. I knew that my leaving would loosen my family's claim on our land, because the Anglish reckon that land passes father to son instead of mother to daughter. Shanuckee was going to have the house and land from Mother, and Motuck-quas had no inclination to marry. We talked about trying to get your mother to come and live with us, in fact, to keep our land claim. I left in the beginning of April to go to the north sea, and when I came back in November, half my family was dead."

"They waited for the whalers to leave, so there wouldn't be as many men," I said softly, making it clear for Theod.

Father hummed agreement, then said, "Shanuckee and Mami-sashquee could tell you more, since they were there when everything happened. They're coming for Nikkomo."

"Theod's mother was spared from hanging because she was with child," I said. "She was taken to New Linvik prison. Someone must know who she was—"

"Nepinnae," Father said, stopping in his tracks for a moment, looking stricken. "Theod is Nepinnae and Menukkis's child. I *knew* them; they'd both been childhood friends of mine. Menukkis was one of the loudest voices on the council by the time everything started happening. His father had died of a fever, and some Anglish people had begun building a house on one of his mother's fallow fields despite being shown land deeds and maps and all. He and a small party of others burned it down while it was only half-built. The corn silo was poisoned not long after that, and then a war band raided one of their farms for untainted corn and a lot of people ended up dead . . ."

"Did Nepinnae and Menukkis have any family who survived the massacre?" I asked.

"Only a hundred or so people survived in South Village; the corn silo was emptied after the poison was discovered and was still standing empty on the night the Anglish came, and a lot of elders and children were hidden there. I know that Nepinnae had a younger sister. I don't know if she was one of the lucky ones who was hiding there that night."

"But we could find out," I pressed.

"We could find out," Father agreed. "I'll send a telegram to Shanuckee in the morning. No one ever told anyone on Naquipaug what became of Nepinnae's child, I don't think. Nothing else was heard about her at all, after she was taken away. I don't know if anyone asked, and I don't know if the Anglish would have answered if anyone did. I think it was widely accepted that she'd miscarried, or that the baby hadn't survived long after birth. Everything was so awful after that—the thanegards posted in North Village, and Naquisit people entirely barred from Nack

Port and everything. I never went back to live on Naquipaug after I learned that Father and Motuckquas had been killed. Shanuckee stayed to look after Mother. I went to Masquapaug and married Chagoma."

After a few moments of thoughtful silence, Theod said, "I lived in the Mahler household from the age of six to the age of sixteen. It was the only home I'd ever known; I remember hardly anything about the orphanage. I'd thought I had friends there, with the Mahlers, but not a soul asked after me when I was taken to jail or when I was taken to the school or any time after that. I sent a few letters, at the beginning. No one wrote back. I didn't send more."

"It was wrong for you to be taken from your family," Father said, his voice bitter. "The Anglish didn't have any right. They should have given you back. You should have grown up on Naquipaug."

"I'd never have been chosen by Copper if I hadn't been a houseboy in Isbrand Mahler's house. I can't be sad about a life I never had."

"You have a right to be, if you want to," I said.

"That's just it; I'm not sure if I want to. How can I know if I should be angry or sad about something if I've got no idea what I've missed? I've never had a family, just . . . employment. I've never even known my parents' names."

"Your father was named Menukkis," Father said. "Your mother was Nepinnae. He was a boatwright. She was an eldest daughter, and a weaver. We were children together; I went to Naquipaug for their wedding feast. It was held a couple of weeks before the whalers' departing. Nepinnae was already with child. You."

Theod looked hollow and haunted at the revelation, his mouth pressed into a thin line, his eyes wide and shining.

Father sighed deeply and said, "I'm going to bed—you two be sure not to stay up too late. I'm sure every child in the village will be on your heels in the morning wanting to see the dragons."

He got up and left Theod and me sitting by the fire.

Theod was quiet for a few more moments before he said, "No one ever told me my parents' names, or that they'd ever been anything but murderers. I've spent most of my life hating them, because I've always been told that I should. What do you think they'd have named me, if they'd gotten the chance? Knecht means 'Jarl's servant,' more or less, did you know that? Lots of the orphans in the orphanage were named Knecht. Don't know why they chose Theod, though, whoever it is who named me."

"I don't know what your parents might have named you. I don't know what you were like as a child," I said. "Names can change, anyway, if there's a reason. Lots of people take a new name if something changes about who they are. If you wanted a new name, you could have one."

Theod made a noise. A cough, or a sob, or a bark of laughter. Something like that.

"Everything is so simple for you, isn't it? You always have an answer ready for anything."

"I don't," I said. "I just . . . When a problem is presented to me, I look for ways to solve it. If that means I've got answers, then all to the better."

"See, there you go with a ready answer again," he said. We were quiet for a while, and then I asked, "If you knew that you could pass your examinations and you could live anywhere in the world, where would you want to live?"

"I don't know, Anequs," Theod replied, sounding tired. "I *don't* have an answer for everything."

I got up and went to find Mother and Grandma, because I got the distinct impression that Theod didn't want to talk anymore just now.

FAMILIES WERE REUNITED

I spent all of Saturday showing Theod the island and introducing him to people. We had coffee with Grandma and Sachem Tanaquish, and visited Mishona's household, and paddled out to Slipstone Island so I could show him where I'd found Kasaqua's egg.

So I could show him the ruins.

On Sunday morning, Father received a telegram from Aunt Shanuckee. Nepinnae's sister *was* alive, and so was her mother, and the whole family was going to paddle over and stay in the village through Nikkomo! We didn't have room for so many guests in our house, but there was plenty of room in the meetinghouse for Nikkomo visitors to stay.

They arrived late on Sunday afternoon. Theod and I were entertaining a whole gang of children down by the shoreline when Father came to find us, to tell us, and to walk with us back to the meetinghouse.

The meetinghouse was already very busy, even though the Nikkomo feast wasn't until Wednesday, because lots of people had family from off the island come to stay. There was a group of older children outside who'd built snow walls and were heartily engaged in a snowball fight. Kasaqua was elated to join immediately, Copper somewhat more reluctant, looking at Theod with concern in his golden eyes and whining very softly.

Inside, the central fire had been lit and groups of people were hanging about in twos and threes—chatting, drinking coffee and tea. I saw Auntie Shanuckee and Great Auntie Mamisashquee standing with . . . well, presumably Theod's people.

Theod stopped and stood absolutely still, blank-faced and staring, as if someone were holding a knife to his throat.

Father didn't seem to notice that Theod and I had stopped walking over to where they were standing. I put a hand on the middle of Theod's back and marched him along. Theod's family, noticing our approach, lined themselves up neatly for introductions. Without taking my hand off Theod's back—because I was honestly afraid that he'd bolt if I did—I nodded deference to his grandmother. Father made formal introductions.

"Theod Knecht, this is your grandmother, Wuskuwhani—Nepinnae's mother. Your aunt, Wampsikuk. Wampsikuk's husband, Kuhaukis. Their children, your cousins, Qunnis, Wunnepan, and Ommishqua. Everyone, this is Theod Knecht, son of Nepinnae and Menukkis."

Wuskuwhani stepped forward, taking Theod's face in her hands, running her thumbs along his cheekbones.

"You have her eyes," she said softly. "My daughter's, I mean."

Theod swallowed audibly, his gaze darting to meet mine as if he wanted rescuing. "I'm very pleased to meet all of you," he said, stiff and formal, his voice half-strangled. "I'm sorry that I've never met any of you before . . ."

"They took you away and hid you from us," Wampsikuk said, with venom in her voice. "They hanged both my brothers and took Nepinnae away and we *never heard from her again*. It's against the law to put a woman to death when she's with child, so they locked her up in some stinking hole until she wasn't anymore, and then they hanged her anyway. We didn't know you'd been born alive. You should have been sent home to Mother and me—to your mother's family. I don't know if there are things about that in the treaty, but there damned well should be!"

"I'm sorry," Theod said, his voice cracking. "I didn't know. I didn't . . . I didn't try to find you. You didn't try to find me and I didn't try to find you and I've been an orphan all my life and I don't deserve . . . I shouldn't . . . They told me my parents were murderers. I didn't want . . ."

Wampsikuk came forward and wrapped herself around Theod, and he sobbed.

"We should let them have some time to themselves," Father said from behind me.

I didn't want to leave, but it seemed like the polite thing to do. I took Father's hand, and together we walked back home.

TOGETHER, THEY CELEBRATED NIKKOMO

Theod stayed that night at the meetinghouse with his people, and spent all of Monday with them as well. On Tuesday, Niquiat and Zhina arrived on the morning ferry—which meant they must have spent the night in Catchnet because the ferry departed there at six in the morning to be here for seven-thirty. Nobody commented on that, but Mother and Father shared a *look* when they arrived together at our door at a quarter to eight.

Sigoskwe and Sakewa were introduced to Zhina as we made breakfast together. They each had a lot of questions for her about minglinglore and tinkering and tatkraft, once she told them that she was a tinker's assistant. Mother and Father had questions about who Zhina's people were and where she was from. Mother didn't outright ask if she and Niquiat were courting, which would have been rude, but a lot of her questions were asked in ways that invited Niquiat and Zhina to tell us whether they were courting.

Neither of them gave us a real answer, which was clearly driving Mother to distraction.

We spent the afternoon preparing for Nikkomo, packing boxes and crates full of the best things from our stores—ground corn and acorn flour, smoked meat and salt fish, nuts and canned fruit, lard and rendered seal fat. Things that would keep until spring-time.

"So what are you doing with all of this?" Zhina asked as we were sitting around the fire afterward, crowded by the stack of boxes.

"It all goes to the meetinghouse, to a shared pantry there," I answered. "Some of it gets used for the Nikkomo feast, but most of it will go on being in the pantry for anyone who needs it."

"Ashaquiat shot a skunk pig last week, and he's going to bring it to the feast," Sigoskwe said. "December is the best time for skunk pigs because they're still fat from fall chestnuts and things."

"Pigs are unclean animals," Zhina said, wrinkling her nose. "My people don't eat them."

"How is a pig unclean?" Sakewa asked. "In one of the novels I read, there was a princess from Indusland, and she didn't eat any animals at all, not even fish."

Zhina hummed agreement and said, "Lots of folks from In-dusland are dharmists and think it's wrong to ever hurt any animal for any reason. I follow masadayassa—we don't eat pigs because pigs eat carrion, and will eat of their own dead if they get the chance. Animals that eat dead flesh are unclean . . . come to think of it, animals that eat flesh at all are unclean, mostly, I think. Cows and deer and turkeys only eat plants, so they're clean animals. Ducks and geese are fine, but you can only trust chickens if you know how they've been raised, because chickens will eat dead flesh if it's given to them. Squirrels are clean animals, but rats are unclean. There's a lot of different scripture about fish, but gener-ally it's acceptable to eat any fish that doesn't have sharp teeth. Oh, and you're not supposed to eat bulls because they're sacred—

a bull once saved the life of the great prophet Zarthu. If you want to eat a male cow you need to render it a steer when it's still a little calf."

"But why can't you eat things that eat things?" Sakewa asked.

"Because the wisdom of the prophets forbids it," Zhina said with a shrug. "Besides, I've seen pigs. I'm not especially keen on eating them."

"But they're *good*, though," Sigoskwe insisted. "If you don't eat pigs does that mean you don't eat lard, either? What do you fry things in?"

"What about seals?" Sakewa asked. "They only eat fish, so can you eat seals?"

"So, Anequs has mentioned that these kinds of things often involve dancing," Zhina said sweetly, smiling with all of her teeth. "Are there any special Nikkomo dances that I should know about?"

"There's the gale-driving dance," Father answered, and we proceeded to talk about dancing and gatherings and house building and plans for springtime. Zhina sketched a diagram of her planned airship, which the children found terribly exciting.

On Wednesday, the day before the long night, Theod and I joined Sigoskwe and Sakewa and Niquiat and Zhina in carting boxes to the meetinghouse. Sachem Tanaquish was taking account of what was being added to the pantry. This hadn't been a particularly spare year; the harvest and hunting had been good. There was no doubt about the pantry lasting until the first spring harvests.

The cooking pit outside the meetinghouse had been lit, and the fine fat skunk pig that Ashaquiat had shot was spitted above it, presided over by Mishona and her mother and Ashaquiat's mother, who were openly discussing plans for the wedding feast in spring. At other, smaller fires there were haunches of venison and whole turkeys roasting, and pots of boiling fat where corn cakes were being fried, apples and pumpkins being roasted in the ashes, and crocks of baked beans. Every family had its own small fire arranged in a loose ring around the meetinghouse, and everyone spent time visiting everyone else's fires, sampling their hospitality and enjoying good conversation. The sun was already hanging low in the sky, casting golden light across the ice-crusted snow that rivaled the orange-red glow of the fires.

When the sun set and most everyone had finished eating, when what was left of the food was put by, a circle was drawn, and the drumsingers began.

There were informal dances, some for girls and some for boys and some for both. Niquiat dragged Theod into a young men's social, insisting on teaching him the steps. I watched, laughing, until Hekua pulled me aside to demand information on Theod— particularly whether or not I was courting him or intended to in the future.

"I'm not courting him, but I can't say I haven't thought about it," I whispered, watching Theod inexpertly following Niquiat's instructions.

"He's so handsome, though!" Hekua said. "*And* he's a dragoneer! Besides, aren't you already courting that girl at your school?"

"Liberty has made it very clear that she and I are not courting, just now, because of circumstances," I said. "Besides, I thought you were courting Seseque?"

"I'm not *married* to him," Hekua replied, giving me a sly look. "And if there was an eligible young dragoneer available for courting . . ."

"You're awful," I said, grinning. "Want to dance with me for the young women's social?"

"Of course! And you need to teach me that Anglish dance you were talking about, the one with four . . ."

"Four-in-hand," I said. "We'd need two more girls."

"Well let's see if we can't pry Mishona away from Ashaquiat for five minutes . . ."

I danced with Hekua, and then we pulled Mishona and Zhina

into the four-in-hand lesson, and I danced with Niquiat, then sat out and watched Niquiat and Zhina dancing together in a couples' dance. I helped myself to more corn cakes and cider, and threw snowballs for Kasaqua, who had made herself a delightful nuisance and distraction, running from fire to fire to beg for whatever anyone would give her, with a group of children in constant pursuit.

It was probably close to midnight when I found Theod again, though I didn't have a watch on me to check. Lots of the younger children had already fallen asleep; half the village returned to their homes. Father was still talking with Auntie Shanuckee, and Mother was at Uncle Mequeche's fire talking about Mishona's wedding. Theod was sitting on a bench by a fire, drinking something from a wooden cup, watching Copper pounce and roll under the attention of a half dozen children—his cousins included. The present game seemed to be throwing snowballs as high in the air as anyone could and seeing how high Copper could or would jump for them. Kasaqua, seeing the game, immediately bounded over to join in.

I sat down beside Theod.

"You've ruined me for school, you know," he said, his voice wistful. "They invited me to come live with them, if I want—my family, I mean. I tried to explain the situation with Copper and his installment at the school's dragonhall, but I don't think they understand—or maybe they just don't care? I've never even *been* to Naquipaug."

"I've only been a couple of times myself, and never to Nack Port," I said. "Usually family comes here instead of us going there. Father's asked Auntie Shanuckee and her family to come and live with us here on Masquapaug, but they're staying on principle. Those who leave lose all rights to their land, according to the treaty of 1825."

"I wonder if I could get permission to visit for a week or two over the summer recess? If I did, would you come with me?"

"To Naquipaug? Yes, of course, if your family would have me," I answered with a smile.

"Do you *really* think you could teach me how to do skiltakraft properly?" he asked. "Well enough to pass the ministry exam on it, I mean? I know damned well that Ezel never will, but I think that maybe . . . the way you explain things . . . if I could pass the proficiency exam I could be given the same dispensation as all the other students to bring their dragons home for the whole of summer recess . . ."

I took a breath and considered. I hadn't told Theod about my revelation over the Whalers' Return, because I hadn't known if I could trust him to understand why it had to be kept from the Anglish—and from Professor Ezel especially. But something seemed fundamentally different about Theod, having spent several days on Masquapaug and having met his family. I decided to trust him, because I thought that he finally understood that *he was one of us.*

"If I tell you something, can you promise me that you'll keep it secret from everyone at school? Particularly from Professor Ezel, and Fraus Kuiper and Brinkerhoff, and Captain Einarsson?"

He looked at me over the edge of his cup, halting mid-sip. His eyes were suddenly very wary. I didn't say anything else, just met his eyes and kept looking until he looked away, setting the cup aside.

"Yes," he finally said. "For you, I could."

"When I was here for the whalers' returning dance back in November, I worked out something about skiltakraft and formal dances, and how our people practiced witskraft before the Anglish came here."

I tried to sketch the skilta for kolfni in the snow with my finger, but there was a crust of ice over the snow, and it quickly proved more trouble than it was worth. I stood back up and crossed my arms, then turned to Theod and offered a hand to help him up.

"Let's go over there where the snow's flat, and I'll show you on a bigger scale. You stand here. Now, watch—"

I sketched out where the motes ought to be in my mind and started a shuffling crow-hop to make an unbroken line in the snow connecting them, passing close to Theod each time. He followed me with his gaze, turning on the spot I'd put him, looking slightly confused. I came back to the point I'd started, standing in front of him, slightly breathless.

"All right," I said. "What have I just drawn?"

He looked at the snow tracks, his brow furrowed, and I watched realization come into his eyes.

"Kolfni," he said, eyebrows going up.

"Exactly. There are formal dances that we do at certain occasions and times of year, and I think all of them are actually skiltas. I worked out the corn-planting dance; I think it transmutes kalisna, zurfni, and pospor from the offerings into the soil. I haven't had enough time to look into other formal dances because I've spent so much time studying for my final examinations, but I think all of them are skiltas. They're meant to be viewed from above, from a flying dragon's point of view. In stories, people can do dances that push back hurricanes and break great stones and move soil like it's water and . . . and I always thought it was just the kind of thing that happens in stories, before—like talking to the sea and having it talk back, or people turning into animals and animals into people—but now I think some of it might actually be real. I think the gale-driving dance can, in some way, literally drive off bad storms. It might be the sort of thing our ancestors could do, before we lost our dragons to the great dying."

"And you don't want to tell anyone about this because . . ."

"The treaty we signed with the Anglish doesn't allow us to have *pistols* here on the island, Theod. What do you think they'd do if they knew we could turn hurricanes?"

"You have a point. But this isn't something you're going to be able to hide forever, if it's true."

"I don't plan to hide it forever—just long enough for me to get a good handle on it. I need time and space to study this, to practice, without anyone meddling. Understanding how the dances work has helped me understand the underpinnings of skiltakraft. I think I could teach you this, and then you'd understand skiltakraft better . . ."

He put his hands on my shoulders, looking at me with his eyes very wide.

"You're amazing," he said, sounding breathless.

Then he leaned in and kissed me.

To my credit, I didn't startle and pull back. I relaxed as his arms folded around me, drawing us together, reminding me of the Valkyrjafax dance. Whatever he'd been drinking had left his mouth sharp and sweet; something alcoholic. He broke the kiss before I did, drawing back fractionally, his breath warm against my lips. I gradually became aware of a crowd of children whooping and shouting some distance away. Theod looked that way, and then I did, still holding each other.

Copper was flying.

ANEQUS HAD A FRANK CONVERSATION WITH THEOD

I slept until the middle of the following afternoon—most everyone who'd stayed up to see the dawn did. We went to the meetinghouse for luncheon to say our goodbyes to people who were returning to Naquipaug. Through the day most of the Naquipaug residents—Theod's family, my aunt and her family, and several others—went back across the sound by canoe. Theod was going to Naquipaug to visit his family's home, just for a few days, because he had to be back at school for the thirtieth.

Father decided to go as well, to visit at Aunt Shanuckee's home—the one he'd grown up in—because he hadn't been back in several years. I walked with both of them down to the canoe launch, and hugged Father and wished them a safe journey, and Theod gave me a look. When he got back, we'd definitely have to have a talk about last night's kiss.

On Friday, Niquiat and Zhina went back to Vastergot to be at the last few days of Zhina's family's feast. I spent the next couple of days on pleasant pastimes. I strung a beaded watch-chain for Sander—smooth beads and knobby ones that turned freely on a waxed cord, something he could fidget with. I visited with Hekua and Mishona and all my other friends, and went ice fishing with Sigoskwe and Sakewa on Great Sweet Pond. Kasaqua was very interested in ice fishing, sitting at the edge of the hole and reaching in with one foreclaw until she was shoulder deep. She actually managed to pull up a trout that way, and was terribly proud of herself as she ate it.

A new coat of snow fell on Sunday morning, and we went sledding and built a dragon out of snow with icicles for spines and teeth. We drank hot cider and ate succotash and told stories by the fire. I carved an oyster shell pendant for Marta as I listened.

On Monday, Father and Theod returned from Naquipaug. Theod looked markedly different, and it took a moment to realize that it was his clothing. I'd seen Theod in his school uniform, and in the formal suit he'd worn to the ball. I'd never seen him dressed like a nackie. He was wearing corduroy trousers and a calico shirt and a waxed canvas coat. None of it was new—the trousers had patches at both knees bordered with fancy embroidery, and the coat was frayed at the button edge. They were clothes that had been worn by other people before—by men in his family, probably.

I tried not to let on how affected I was about seeing Theod dressed like that. Like any other young man in our community. Like the kind of young man I might have courted.

I thought of the kiss, and something tightened in my belly.

When we got home, Mother suggested rather strongly that perhaps Theod and I should find something to do with ourselves for a few hours *out of the house*, because she wanted to welcome Father home after his visit. Grandma was having coffee with the other elders, and Sigoskwe and Sakewa were out playing.

I took Theod to the stony ridge that overlooked Great Sweet Pond, where a huge weeping beech made a natural shelter. There were children ice-skating on the pond, and both Copper and Kasaqua joined them. Kasaqua had great fun chasing and sliding across the ice, and Copper made short flights from one bank to the other.

"Did you have a good time on Naquipaug?" I asked, once we were comfortably situated.

"It's . . . different there," he said thoughtfully. "People are more guarded, I think. Did you know that in what used to be South Village, nobody older than fourteen or younger than fifty survived?"

"I knew that there were only a hundred-odd survivors, but I don't think I've ever had it explained to me exactly that way, no. I know that most of the people who survived were in hiding. That anyone fit to fight did, and that everyone who fought but wasn't killed in the battle was hanged."

He made a humming sound of agreement, drawing his knees up and slinging his arms around them, one hand holding the other wrist. Very poignantly not looking at me, as if he was afraid to.

"Your cousin is getting married in the spring, I heard," he said after an awkward silence.

"Mishona, yes," I said. "She's my mother's brother's daughter, the closest I had to a bigger sister growing up."

"She seems young to be marrying," Theod said. "I've heard it said that young marriages are often unhappy ones. The arrangement of marriages is a principal source of gossip among the staff of great houses."

"Well, she and Ashaquiat have been formally courting since she was sixteen and he was seventeen, and they were childhood sweethearts for years before that," I said. "If they learn, after marrying, that they don't suit each other for some reason, they could just unmarry in the future. It's not shameful among our people the way it is for the Anglish."

There was another silence before he said, his voice low and quiet, "Your father asked me if I was courting you, when we were paddling back from Naquipaug."

"Oh?" I asked, glancing at him and then quickly away again. "And what did you tell him?"

"I said that I didn't know anything at all about courting. I was raised to be a servant, and servants seldom marry. I told him that you'd have to lead if there was going to be . . . anything. Between us, I mean. That if we were to court—"

"And what did he say about that?" I asked.

"He said that I was a good man," Theod said, sounding absolutely bewildered. "He didn't say any more on the subject after that, and now I don't know what to think—"

I leaned in and kissed him on the cheek, and he stopped stammering. His breath hitched, and he turned his head to face me.

"Anequs," he said, "I think that I'm in love with you."

I sucked a breath through my teeth and swallowed hard, looking away from him, feeling my cheeks grow hot.

"I think," I said, carefully, "that you and I should—for the moment—focus on our studies. That if we court, it needs to be something that the school and all its people know absolutely nothing about. They wouldn't approve at all."

Theod's face fell, and he took a shaking breath before saying, "I shouldn't have said anything, this isn't at all appropriate and I've been much too forward—"

"I'm very fond of you, Theod," I said. "And I liked it very much when you kissed me the other night. I wanted to kiss you at the ball, but it would have made a scene. I just mean . . ."

"No, I understand," he said, though his voice sounded broken.

"After you've passed your skiltakraft exam, when you come to live on Naquipaug this summer with your family, we can talk more seriously about courting," I said.

"But what if—"

"*When* you pass your exam, which you *will* because I'm going to teach you, then you'll be allowed to take Copper home from May until September. You'll join us for Strawberry Thanksgiving, and the corn-planting dance, and the longest day. You'll be here for clambakes and bonfires and canoe races and all the other summer things. And then, if you still want to, we'll start courting formally. I should warn you that I'm not going to be the only one interested in you, though; Hekua has already asked if we're courting. There are lots of girls like me—"

"There are no girls like you, Anequs," Theod said. I felt my breath catch, because he was looking at me like I was the most important person in the world. I looked away, feeling terribly flustered by the intensity of that look.

I might have said more, but Sigoskwe called my name from down at the pond's edge. He was standing with Kasaqua and Copper, who were looking expectantly in our direction.

"Anequs! Theod! You got a *telegram*, and you've *got* to come open it! It says it's from some kind of nackie association in Catchnet!"

I laughed, though I wasn't exactly sure why. Everything was so *much*, and it bubbled out of me like a pot of soup boiling over. Theod stood before I did, offering me a hand up, and we went down the path together to see what was so terribly exciting about this telegram.

ANEQUS AND THEOD RECEIVED AN INVITATION

The telegram was trifolded and fixed with a pin. According to Mr. Aroztegui, it had arrived around nine in the morning. I thanked him, and we went to the meetinghouse to read it because it wasn't yet noon and Mother and Father had suggested that we not come back to the house until luncheon. I unpinned the telegram, putting the pin through the turn of my shirt collar for safekeeping. The telegram read:

```
TO: ANEQUS APONAKWESDOTTIR THEOD KNECHT
FROM: CONF. OF FIRST PEOPLE OF AKASHNET

WE INVITE YOU TO JOIN US AS GUESTS OF
HONOR FOR MIDWINTER FEAST TOMORROW
TUESDAY 27 AT WAREHOUSE 120 MERCHANT
STREET FROM 10AM TO 8PM
TWO WAY FARE PREVIOUSLY ARRANGED
```

"They want us to come for their midwinter feast, these folks on the mainland," I said to Theod and Sigoskwe and everyone else who'd come to hear what news was so urgent that it was worth sending a telegram over. "It's tomorrow."

We told Mother and Father over luncheon, and then we told Sachem Tanaquish and asked his opinion on the matter. Our people hadn't had much to do with nackies in Catchnet even before the massacre of 1825 on Nack—though there were a handful of young men who'd married mainland girls and gone to live with them, and a few mainland men who'd married onto the islands. The sachem thought it was a good idea, overall, that Theod and I and our dragons should go and share a feast with our mainland neighbors.

We packed a basket of corn cakes and a jar of jam, and a crock of succotash, and a haunch of dry-smoked venison; turning up to a feast without food would have been rude. We took the morning ferry across the sound, arriving at half past ten. There was a group waiting for us at the docks; I recognized several of the children who'd followed us from the train station when we'd first arrived.

"I told you they'd come if we sent a telegram!" said the boy who'd recognized us. He was looking up at a man who seemed to be between thirty and forty.

"Hello!" I called, waving as we disembarked. "Good to see you again. I'm afraid we didn't catch your name last time because we were in quite a hurry."

"I'm Viggo, and this is my pa. He's on the council!"

"Kjell Nishattucag," the man said, nodding at us. "Very glad to have you here; I've been saying for ages that we mainlanders ought to get more friendly with you islanders, then Viggo came home last week talking about how he and his friends had seen the two of you heading to the ferry docks, and here we are. Come on, I'll introduce you to the rest of the council."

I'd never been to Catchnet at Jule; there were candles lit in all the windows, even though it was daytime, and red and gold ribbons hanging from many windowsills, and branches of pine and holly over doorways.

We walked together down Main Street to Merchant Street, to the same gawking and pointing from people in windows and doorways. Several Anglish men gave us grim, hard looks as we passed—as if we had no business being here. Viggo chatted the whole way, throwing a long list of names at us mostly. When we arrived at the warehouse that had *120* written in bold script above the doorway, Kjell invited us inside.

It was just like the meetinghouse. There were boxes and crates lined up against the walls, forming a long bench around the central circle. There were a couple of tables at the back, piled with feast foods. We added the food we'd brought, and were led to a short dais at the entrance of the dance circle where several people were waiting. Kjell made introductions.

"Lise Nokehick, my mother, speaking for Akashneisit. Alrik Mowashuck, speaking for Maswachuisit. Mokumannit Aestridsson, speaking for Naregannisit. We welcome you, Anequs Aponakwesdottir and Theod Knecht, and your dragons—what are their names?"

"This is Kasaqua," I said, nodding to where she was standing at my heel.

I looked to Theod, and he said, "This is Copper."

Lise took half a step forward, putting herself in front of the others, and said, "We, together, represent the confederation of the first people of Akashnet. We've put aside the differences between our bands and have joined together to try and hang on to our ways in the face of the Anglish invasion. The return of dragons to the islands seemed an opportune time to make a pleasant invitation in hopes of overcoming old enmities and kindling a friendship with our islander cousins."

"Thank you very much for inviting us!" I said. "I'm sure that Sachem Tanaquish would be open to lending what support we can to our mainlander cousins."

This seemed to please them very much, and after introductions were completed, Viggo practically dragged us over to the feasting table.

There were dances, but no one asked either Theod or me to dance. We were instead ushered to the table set up on the dais, and people came to introduce themselves and thank us for coming. Kasaqua was pleased by the attention, presenting herself for petting, while Copper stayed stubbornly at Theod's side. Many people had questions about life on the islands, and of course only I could answer, and only for Masquapaug. In the middle of the afternoon, an Anglish-looking man with a camera turned up and asked if he might take some lichtbilds of us and our dragons. Lise explained that he was someone's husband's cousin, and a professional lichtbildmacher, and we happily agreed.

AND SOME TRULY ALARMING CORRESPONDENCE

We returned to Masquapaug on the afternoon ferry, arriving at five-thirty. We'd been feasted enough that neither of us was terribly interested in dinner, but we stayed up for a while playing hubbub and talking about our day in Catchnet.

On Wednesday, Theod and I visited with Sachem Tanaquish and told him the names of the leaders of the confederation of the first people of Akashnet and how they'd like us to join them in their efforts to preserve the old ways. He said that he'd send a letter to Sachem Wompinottomak on Naquipaug and get his opinions before taking any kind of action. I considered the matter largely out of my hands at that point; I'd just been the receiver and the bearer of invitations. The real possibility of a formal alliance of any kind was a matter for the elders.

On the morning of Friday the thirtieth, when the ferry arrived from Catchnet at seven-thirty, there was a letter from the mainland addressed to Theod and me. Mishona had been waiting at the docks, because she was expecting correspondence from her mother's family about the upcoming wedding. There hadn't been any letters for her family, but she brought us the one that'd come for us and had coffee and chatted a bit before going home.

The letter was sealed in red wax, and when I opened it, I saw that it had been written in red ink as well.

To the filthy skræling thieves,

I have been a dragoneer for thirty-five years, having graduated from the King's Academy of New Linvik in the year seven. My ancestors came to Vaster Hold with Stafn Whitebeard himself. I served in the jarl of Vastergot's guard, under Jarl Kjeld Niklasson, and was a member of the band that put down the Nack Island uprising. I am not alone in my opinions. <u>Filthy and degenerate skrælings cannot be allowed the honor of association with dragons; it is an insult to all dragoneers.</u>

I have written several strong letters to the Ministry of Dragon Affairs complaining of the bad judgment that has led to your installation at Kuiper's Academy. Skrælings have no place in a modern society and when a worthy jarl is once again chosen, your kind will again be declared nithings and it will be permissible to kill you on sight, as it was in my grandfather's time.

We demand that both of you relinquish your dragons to a collection and exile yourselves back to Mask Island, or there will be a purging of skrælings in this hold and others; your dragons will be shot and you will be hanged as an example to the rest of your kind.

<u>We are coming for you,</u>
A Proud Citizen of Lindmarden

I felt cold in the pit of my stomach, reading the words over again to be sure of what I was looking at. Kasaqua made a crooning noise of concern, and I ran my hand through her hackles without looking at her. Father, who was sitting by the hearth and mending a leather coat, must have seen my expression because he asked, "Anequs, what's wrong?"

I swallowed hard, unable to find my voice, and walked over to hand him the letter. Theod was saying something, but I couldn't understand his words over the roaring in my ears. I looked around at my family; Grandma and Sakewa had been working on some beading together, Sigoskwe had been reading a book, Mother was visiting with Uncle Mequeche . . .

Some Anglishman with a dragon, under no one's say-so but his own, could easily come here and burn down the village and kill everyone I loved, and how would we stop him?

"I need to go back to school," I said.

"What?" Father said, looking back down at the letter and back up at me.

"You said you don't have to go back until January thirteenth!" Sakewa protested.

"What's going on?" Grandma asked, evidently realizing that something was very wrong.

"Neither of you is going anywhere until we call a council and contact the thanegards about this. This is some Anglishman, which means it's their duty to—"

"Father. You don't understand," I said, taking a breath. "I have to go back to the school because at the school there are something like a hundred other dragons, including dragons that are trained fighters. If I'm here, everyone here is in danger. If I'm there, then that's where whoever it is who wants to kill me will have to come find me. I'd rather they came and found me at school and had to fight Frau Kuiper, for everyone's sake. I have to go back. I have to go back *today*, when the ferry leaves at nine. Every day I'm here is a day that everyone's in danger, and if I don't go today, I won't be able to go until Tuesday, and who knows what might happen by then?"

"You can't—" Father started, looking appalled at the suggestion.

But Grandma interrupted him, saying, "You daughter is right, Aponakwe. Pitting one group of Anglishmen against another is a safer bet than trying to defend ourselves if a dragoneer comes here—" She cut off, turning her face toward Sakewa, who was looking pale and frightened. She sighed heavily and continued, "What could we do against even one fully grown dragon, Aponakwe?"

There was no more argument after that. Father took the letter to show Sachem Tanaquish, and I packed my things, and Sigoskwe went to get Mother from Uncle Mequeche's house. Inside of an hour I was saying my goodbyes to everyone who'd come to the meetinghouse—dozens of people, everyone who'd gotten wind from Sachem Tanaquish that something was wrong. The letter was copied down word for word and signed by the sachem and by Mr. Aroztegui as witnesses to its accuracy. Theod and I took the original copy to show Frau Kuiper.

Father came with us, all the way to the school, because he wanted to see for himself that I was situated in a safe place and that Frau Kuiper understood the gravity of the situation. None of us had much to say during the journey. Theod insisted on staying with Copper in the horse box, despite the ticket collector's protests. The man finally agreed when Copper growled at him, deep and menacing, flaring his wings slightly and baring his teeth. Father and Kasaqua and I were put into the passenger car directly adjacent, and no one else was seated in that car at all.

There were thanegards waiting for us when we arrived at Vastergot station. Three of them, surrounding the platform where Copper would disembark; someone must have contacted them from a telegraph station at one of the earlier stops. The ticket collector was talking to the one on the left, pointing at us, looking cross. Father put himself between us and the thanegard that approached us.

"We've had a report that there was a disturbance concerning an aggressive dragon and a group of intractable nackies aboard this train," the thanegard said sternly, looking at all of us.

"Then it seems there's been a misunderstanding," Father said, keeping his voice even. "This is my daughter and her classmate. I'm escorting them back to Kuiper's Academy, because they've received a threatening letter. Understandably, neither of them wished to be separated from their dragons, and Theod was quite willing to stay with his dragon in the horse box. The ticket collector, that gentleman over there, was adamant that he wasn't allowed to do so, and became quite terse. The dragon growled at him, because he saw his dragoneer being berated. That was the entirety of any incident."

"I'm sure you'll understand that it's in the public interest for us to detain you until this can be confirmed with a representative from the academy," the thanegard said. "It would be in everyone's best interest for you to come along quietly."

Father looked over his shoulder at Theod and at me. I nodded. He sighed.

"All right," Father said, sounding slightly defeated. It *hurt* to hear him sound like that, a tight pain behind my breastbone and a pricking in the corners of my eyes.

We were walked to the thanegards' hall, which wasn't at all far from the station.

"Your dragons will be brought to the stables—"

"I will not be separated from Copper," Theod said, with more conviction than he usually had for anything at all.

"Nor I from Kasaqua," I said in solidarity.

The thanegard sighed through his nose, giving us all a hard look.

"Your dragons will be taken to the stables, and if you refuse to be separated from them, then so will you."

"That's perfectly all right," Theod said.

And that was how Theod and Copper, and Father and Kasaqua

and I, came to be *locked into* adjacent stalls in the stable behind the thanegards' hall. Each stall had a door of isen slats that stretched from floor to ceiling—something I'd never seen in a stable before—and they'd closed those doors behind them and locked them with a set of formidable-looking brass keys before leaving us. There was a man posted at the door with a rifle. The rifle was slung at his side, just now, and he was smoking a pipe, staring at us evenly.

"We haven't done anything wrong," I said softly.

"I spent two nights in New Linvik Jail, waiting for my case to be brought before the moot," Theod said. He was standing with his eyes closed, leaning against Copper, running his hand up and down his neck in a smooth pattern. It wasn't entirely clear who was comforting whom. "They put Copper in a cage down in the kennels, with the hounds; he was small enough for it then. They put me in a cell upstairs. Copper cried for me the entire time. I was too far away to actually hear him, but I *felt* it."

"And nobody at all said anything in your favor?" Father asked, not looking away from the man with the rifle. "The cruelty shouldn't surprise me, given the things I've seen."

"I'd stolen him, in the eyes of the law," Theod said, with a bark of bitter laughter. "Better he should have gone feral than be harnessed by a nackie ward with no attachments. There was an hour between Copper choosing me and the thanegards arriving to take us away, and Herr Mahler spent every minute of it railing at me, cursing the fact that he'd ever accepted me as a ward of service."

A long silence followed. I sat down on a bale of hay, Kasaqua planting herself at my feet, sitting at attention, full of nervous energy. Theod went on standing beside Copper. Father took to pacing at the front of the stall.

It felt like an eternity that we stayed there in the cold, locked in like animals, but it was probably only a few hours that we were imprisoned.

Then Frau Kuiper arrived.

BATTLE PLANS WERE LAID

I didn't get to see Frau Kuiper's arrival or the discussion she had with the thanegards; I only knew that she arrived at the stables in a scarlet rage and demanded that we be released.

"What, by *sweet Fyra's milky tits*, did you think you were doing?" she said, her voice tightly controlled as the man who'd been posted by the door unlocked the stalls and let us out.

"We didn't do anything!" I protested, only for her to reach into the breast of her jacket and pull out a newspaper. It was folded to expose a particular article, which included a picture of Theod and me standing with the representatives of the confederation.

"Do you have any idea who these people are? I demand to know what circumstances led to this lichtbild being taken. You two had permission to be on Mask Island, not anywhere else. You have openly defied me—"

"You will not speak that way to my daughter," Father said with an air of warning in his tone.

She turned to him, glaring, and said, "Mr. Aponakwe, it would be in your best interest to return to Mask Island. These young people and their dragons will be returning to the academy with me, and their dragons will not be leaving again."

"You have no right—" Father said, only for her to interrupt.

"I have every right. These dragons are my legal wards, and so is this young man! I am responsible for any misconduct on their part, and that is the charge by which all of you have been detained. You are all exceedingly lucky that the ticket-taker has chosen not to pursue this unto a hearing before a moot. There's been no expense spared in the attempt to teach these children civil and rational behavior, and yet I turn my back upon them for a fortnight and find them appearing publicly with known rabble-rousers—"

"Frau Kuiper," I said, keeping my voice as even as possible, "we were invited to a midwinter celebration. We attended. If that article you're holding says anything other than that, it's lies, and I'd like to pursue the author on grounds of libel. Theod and I are both here, now, because we have received a letter that directly threatens our lives, the lives of our dragons, and the lives of our families. I'd like to pursue that, too. We were coming directly to you and would have arrived at the academy already if we hadn't been detained. Copper growled a bit at a man who was shouting at Theod."

"What?" she asked, narrowing her eyes, directing all of her attention on me. I felt very much like a chipmunk that had noticed an owl's appraisal, under that gaze. "We clearly need to have this conversation at the school. Captain Einarsson is waiting for us. Mr. Aponakwe, go home; you are likely to be arrested if you go anywhere else. I assure you, these young people will be in the most capable of hands."

Father turned to me, coming close enough to put his hands on my shoulders as he levelly met my gaze.

"Do you still want to go back to the school? Because if you

want to come home right now, nothing in this world will stop me from bringing you there."

"I *have* to go back to the school, Father. I can't bring danger home."

Father closed his eyes and nodded, then pulled me into a tight hug.

"I trust you to know the right thing to do," he said. "The Nampeshiwe chose you for a reason. Be safe, and come home when you can."

"I will," I said.

And that was the end of the conversation. Theod and I and the dragons went with Frau Kuiper, and Father walked back toward the train station—in the company of a thanegard.

I could only hope that he'd get home safely.

Theod and I came to be seated opposite Frau Kuiper, Frau Brinkerhoff, and Captain Einarsson in the room on the second floor with all the windows along one side—the same room I'd been interviewed in upon my arrival at school in September. Copper and Kasaqua had both been put into Henkjan's care. Kasaqua was very unhappy about being separated from me, because she knew that I did not want her to be. I wished, in fact, that she was still small enough for me to gather up into my arms.

Frau Kuiper had just read the letter we'd received on Masquapaug aloud to the others.

"If this 'proud citizen' really is a former jarl's guard who served under Kjeld Niklasson, it should be a relatively simple matter to have all former holders of that office questioned," Frau Brinkerhoff said, her voice steely.

"I very much doubt that the ministry will be willing to launch an investigation that calls the integrity of dragoneers into suspicion," Captain Einarsson said. "Not over the matter of a letter that may well have been written on a whim."

"Two of my students have received explicit threats on their lives and the lives of their dragons," Frau Kuiper replied angrily.

"Regardless of your opinions, Captain, the law is very clear. As per the treaty of New Linvik, all persons residing on the outlying islands are citizens of Lindmarden and subject to its laws. That would imply that they're also subject to legal protections. I want the author of this letter found, and I want him brought before a moot. Threats of this kind cannot be tolerated—especially if they can be legitimated as coming from a dragoneer. A man in command of a dragon has the means to make good on any level of threat."

"I will report this to the ministry," Captain Einarsson said, "but I cannot guarantee that they'll be as quick to action as you'd like. It was my understanding that we were gathered here to discuss these students' infraction during the winter recess."

"That matter also requires further investigation," Frau Kuiper said, looking to Theod and me. "This article, which appeared in the Thursday edition of this week's *Catchnet Daily Local*, implies that the presence of dragons commanded by nackies has emboldened warsome actions among a particularly vocal group of nackies in Catchnet. That there are talks of some kind of alliance between the island nackies and the mainland ones. That there may be an uprising in the making, of the kind there was on Nack Island in 1825."

"The confederation of first peoples of Akashnet invited us to join them for their midwinter celebration," I said. "We were glad to join them, and to talk about friendship between their people and ours because we are *cousins*. Dragons have absolutely nothing to do with it."

"I very much doubt that," Captain Einarsson said. "In any case, it's clear that these students cannot be trusted to act with proper forethought. It is imperative that the dragons to which they're bonded be confined to the academy's grounds indefinitely."

"You two will also be confined to the school's grounds until such time as the threats in this letter have been thoroughly investigated," Frau Kuiper said. "I want to know where each of you is at every moment of the day."

"Would it be permissible for us to receive visitors here, if we're not to leave school grounds?" I asked. "My brother lives in Vastergot. As far as I know, he hasn't heard anything about any of this. The letter came on this morning's ferry."

"This is an institution of learning, not a social club—" Captain Einarsson began, only to be cut off by Frau Brinkerhoff.

"There is no policy specifically forbidding students from entertaining day guests on school grounds. I would strongly discourage such things on days with classes in session, as guests could be a distraction and a nuisance, but on the weekend I can see no reason why day guests should not be allowed. Do you agree, Karina?"

"Social gatherings under the supervision of the school would be ideal, at least until this matter is settled," Frau Kuiper agreed. "I do expect to be informed of any visits that you arrange at least a day in advance of the arrangement, however."

"Of course, ma'am," I said.

"Our next course of action will be endeavoring to improve the general public's perception of the two of you as upstanding citizens. You must become well known to the people of Lindmarden, and you must have flawless reputations. Powerful people have decided to be your enemies, and so you will require powerful allies. Hallmaster Henkjan and his trusted associates have been informed of potential threats and will react swiftly to any intruders onto the grounds. You may not remove your dragons from the dragonhall for any reason whatsoever without informing him of your intentions and your whereabouts."

I looked at Theod. He had that practiced blank look on his face again, still as a statue. His hands were balled into fists on his thighs, and he was trembling slightly.

"In your absence, I've received correspondence on your behalf," Frau Brinkerhoff said. "Theod, you have been invited to trail riding and rabbit hunting at the Sørensen estate. Anequs, you have been invited to tea at the Jansens' townhome. These are important social connections, and you *will* attend these functions. The families of your classmates are generally well connected in society, and you would do well to spend time with them socially. In the meantime, you should continue to make gracious replies to any letters sent to you in good faith—and I expect you to bring your replies to me for review before you send them. Any invitations that you receive or extend must be reported to me directly. There will be no secret or clandestine correspondence of any kind."

"Yes, ma'am," Theod said quietly. "Thank you, ma'am."

"You are dismissed," Frau Kuiper said. "I would strongly suggest that both of you remain in the company of others as often as you're able. Anequs should as much as possible attach herself to Miss Hagan, when she returns on the fifteenth of January. Theod . . ." She puzzled for a moment, her mouth drawn into a thin line. "Theod should report to Hallmaster Henkjan."

I didn't think of Marta as a friend, exactly, but she was a natural match for me because we shared a room and were the only two female students in attendance. I'd have much rather attached myself to Sander, but there were evidently social complications about that. Theod didn't have any friends among the students to attach himself to, apart from me.

That we attach ourselves to each other in solidarity was evidently not a notion worth mentioning.

"For now, both of you will go to your rooms and stay there until further notice," Frau Kuiper finished. "And I do mean your room in the young men's quarters, Mr. Knecht, not your dragon's box and not in any part of the dragonhall workers' quarters."

"Ma'am—" Theod started, looking alarmed.

"I will accept no argument from either of you," she said. Theod swallowed and nodded.

We left the meeting room and walked in different directions. I returned to my room and sat heavily on the edge of my bed, re-sisting the urge to scream and cry and *bite* something—though the latter urge was probably Kasaqua's desire bleeding into my own.

If I was allowed to extend invitations to have day guests at the school, I was going to invite Niquiat and Zhina as soon as could possibly be arranged. Then I was going to invite Ingrid Hakans-dottir, and her brother, too, and damn it to Halya if I wasn't going to invite every single nackie in Vastergot. I'd have to send Sachem Tanaquish a letter asking him to inquire as to whether there was any group in Vastergot like the confederation of first peoples in Akashnet, and if we couldn't extend friendship to them as well.

I was going to make sure that the Anglish understood that we had never gone anywhere. That despite their best efforts, we were still living here among them on the lands where we'd always lived.

I was going to show them just how many of us there were.

ANEQUS RECEIVED A GIFT,
AND CLARIFIED HER INTENTIONS

When I opened my wardrobe to hang up my cape, there was a calico day dress hanging there that I'd never seen before. It was a gold-and-cream stripe, with pinstripes of black, and all the seams were beautifully matched. The bodice was decorated, on either side of the button placket, with pin tucks that did interesting things to the stripes. The cuffs and hem were decorated with double rows of black binding. A scrap of brown paper was pinned to the collar. I had to bring it out into the light to read it.

> Blessed Jule, Anequs!
> —With all my love, Liberty

On the reverse side it said, in much hastier writing,

> I used the measurements from the beginning of the term, presuming that you'll be wearing the corset and petticoat

you got from Miss Jenni. Please let me know if anything
needs adjustment. The machine sews beautifully.

It was a lovelier dress than any I'd have been able to afford in a
shop—nicer than my Catchnet shopping dress—but not at all the
kind of thing that Marta wore. It was a dress I could actually wear
out into the city without feeling ridiculous, the way I'd felt in the
ball gown.

Except that I didn't know when I'd next be allowed to go out
into the city. I didn't know when I'd be able to go home and show
such a dress to Hekua and Mishona and everyone else.

I closed the wardrobe and rested my forehead against its cool
surface for a moment, and I heard a knock at the door. When I
answered it, I was quite surprised to find Frau Kuiper there.

"Hello again, Miss Anequs. There was a matter that I wanted
to speak to you about privately. Please have a seat," she said, indicating the group of leather chairs. She chose a spot opposite me.
It felt wrong for her to be here, in my room, sitting where Liberty
sat when we visited together—like a violation of privacy or something. It shouldn't have, because Frau Kuiper was the headmistress of the school and had a right to be anywhere at all within it.
Perhaps her coming here was a means of reminding me that this
was *her* place and not in any way my own.

"Professor Ezel had some very vocal concerns about your
performance on your end-of-term examination," she said, once
we were both seated.

"Did he?" I asked, making a great effort to keep my voice cool
and impassive. "What concerns did he bring to you?"

"He baldly accused you of cheating," Frau Kuiper said archly,
"though he couldn't explain a mechanism by which you'd accomplished it."

"He made me sit in the front row for the duration of the examination," I said evenly. "There's no way I could have cheated;
he watched everything that I did."

"Which is what he reported to me, with enraged bafflement. It would seem that you've acquired knowledge that's beyond the scope of his first-year curriculum."

"How would he know that, ma'am, if I've only completed the first-year examination?" I asked, narrowing my eyes.

"Because he adds several questions to the exam that pertain to knowledge present in the later chapters of your textbook that are not part of the assigned curriculum in order to measure who is or isn't reading ahead," she said.

"Theod and I have been studying together. I've been looking at his textbooks as well as mine, and at other books in the library; no one told me that I shouldn't."

"I'd thought as much. You seem to have great initiative, as a scholar; Professor Ulfar has spoken very highly of you. Interestingly, Mr. Knecht's understanding of skiltakraft seems to have also improved markedly. He was not academically accomplished in his first year, but he performed better on his own end-of-term exam—something else that Professor Ezel couldn't credit. It wasn't a passing grade, mind you, but it was much better than his previous efforts."

"I haven't found Professor Ezel's lessons especially helpful in my understanding of skiltakraft, ma'am," I said evenly. "I've been trying to make up the gaps in my understanding by whatever means I can."

"Which is the conclusion that I reached when I asked to see your assignments and your examination, but it's good to hear it from you as well. Professor Ezel remained skeptical that you could have achieved such understanding by independent study, which led me to question his teaching methods. He said that you don't ask questions in class."

"He forbade me from speaking at all on the first day, and especially from asking questions," I said, anger creeping into my voice despite my best efforts. "He told me that I was being *tolerated*, and that I would fail like Theod had failed."

"And you didn't bring this to my attention earlier in the year?" Frau Kuiper asked, clear disapproval in her voice.

"Why would I have, ma'am?" I asked. "You never gave me any indication that I should report to you on the behavior of your professors."

"You must have known that his conditions were unreasonable—"

"Why must I have known?" I interrupted, folding my arms. "I haven't attended an Anglish school before. Professor Ulfar is the only professor who seems to really invite questions and conversation in his class. Professor Ezel made his disapproval of me *very* clear. I presumed that you were aware."

"I . . . see," she said, sighing. "Well, that does leave us in a bit of a quandary as to how we should place you in the coming term. You've earned a place in Professor Ezel's class, but given your performance this term, I think that might actually be a waste of your time and his. You scored the second highest on the examination, after Mr. Jansen. Do you think you would benefit more from attending Professor Ezel's lectures or from pursuing independent study with Mr. Knecht?"

"I would much rather study with Mr. Knecht, if you're giving me the choice, ma'am."

"Then I'll mark you down for independent study. I'll also tell Professor Ezel that I have spoken with you and have found his accusations to be unfounded. You will, of course, still be expected to complete the same examination at the end of the term that Professor Ezel will be giving to the students that attend his lectures."

"Of course, ma'am," I said, nodding.

"Do you understand that satisfactory completion of the examination at the end of this term is required, not only by the academy but by the Ministry of Dragon Affairs, for dragons to be allowed to leave the auspices of this dragonhall for any period longer than fourteen days?"

"That was not made clear to me at the beginning of the term, ma'am, but I've come to understand it. I feel that a disservice was done to me when I first came here; presumptions were made about my familiarity with Anglish ways and institutions. No one properly explained what it meant that Kasaqua was to be associated with this dragonhall, or what that wardship entailed. No one at all has presented me with any documents concerning what the laws are regarding dragons and their quartering. I'm having to piece everything together from bits and snatches. You accused Theod and me this afternoon of openly defying you by making a day trip to Catchnet, but you never told either of us that such a thing was forbidden! Expectations of me have never been made entirely clear."

She gazed at me pensively for a long moment, then said, "It's quite possible that we have done you a disservice. Your situation has, from the beginning, been rather different than Mr. Knecht's, but I will admit that I considered you as being very similar to him. I certainly hadn't anticipated your desire to travel into Vastergot and back to Mask Island as often as you do."

"Quite a lot of other students go home on the weekend. Marta has been away more often than she's been here. All of the other students went home for the entirety of the winter recess. I presume that means that all of the other first-year students passed their end-of-term examinations for the first term?"

"Many of the young men here are themselves the sons of dragoneers. Their fathers necessarily associate with other dragonhalls, and can take responsibility for their sons' dragons during recesses."

"May I ask what you did expect of me, back in September, ma'am? If you didn't expect me to want to visit with my family and spend time at home?"

"I had expected that you would be quite happy to leave your former life behind and immerse yourself in the society of dragoneers. I had hoped that you and Miss Hagan would become friends, and that you would associate yourself with her social peers—something that proved quite impossible for Mr. Knecht because of his personal social failings and vulgar upbringing. I feel that I've been remiss in allowing him to find a comfortable place among the staff. He is and will continue to be a dragoneer, and I have not properly impressed that fact to the rest of the student body—that you, and he, are their peers and must be recognized as such."

"Ma'am," I said, leveling my gaze at her, "I am not a peer of any of the young men at this school. I am not a peer of Marta's friends, or of the sisters of other students. I am a Masquisit woman, a native of Masquapaug. Kasaqua is a dragon native to the land that you call North Markesland. I am not a dragoneer, I am a Nampeshiweisit. When I've learned all that I can learn here, ma'am, I am going to go home. My goal is to do what I need to do for Kasaqua to be allowed to come with me, permanently. My second goal, now, is to help Theod accomplish whatever he has to to achieve the same end. Over the recess, we were able to reunite Theod with the remainders of his family—his grandmother, his aunt, his young cousins. They want him to come home, too."

"Your answers to the interview did allude to that," Frau Kuiper said with a weary sigh. "I had hoped that you might be swayed from such a course by exposure to civilization."

"There is nothing uncivilized about my people, ma'am," I said coldly.

"I'm afraid that you will find, Miss Anequs, that opinions to the contrary will put you through a great deal of trouble and pain. I don't think that you understand the hornets' nest you two have thrown a stone at by appearing in public with the likes of Machman Aestridsson."

"Mokumannit, ma'am. He's the speaker for the Naregannisit in the confederation."

"The Narry-gannet people are acknowledged as generally quarrelsome and insular, causing strife in Catchnet Thede. Svend

Jespersen, the thane of Catchnet, has had to censure the party several times. They are not people that you should associate with if you wish to maintain a good reputation."

"Ma'am, respectfully, I think that you and I have very different ideas about what constitutes a good reputation," I said.

She sighed again, rising and standing over me.

"That, Miss Anequs, is precisely what I'm afraid of."

She took her leave without saying anything else, and I was very glad when the door shut behind her.

SHE MADE AN INTERESTING OBSERVATION

Dinner was brought to me in my room by one of the kitchen maids—Elsa, whom Liberty had specifically warned me against speaking to because she loved nothing more than to report misconduct of any kind to the cook. I read, and paced, and fretted about Kasaqua. She wanted me and didn't understand why she was locked in. I wondered what the consequences would be if I simply marched myself over to the dragonhall and collected her and brought her back with me. She was still small enough that there was no *practical* reason that she should be stabled like a horse. There was no practical reason that I should be confined to my room, either. To my knowledge, there weren't any students in attendance just now apart from Theod and me.

I found that sleep was impossible.

It was just past sunrise when I gave up on sleeping entirely and decided to read instead. I went to the window seat to read by the new morning light rather than bother with lighting a lamp.

Gerhard was standing at the head of the flight field, tacked and ready. Frau Kuiper was standing at his shoulder, talking to Frau Brinkerhoff. I couldn't tell what they were saying, but Frau Brinkerhoff looked unhappy. Frau Kuiper was holding Frau Brinkerhoff's hands, stroking the backs of them with her thumbs. She lifted one hand to stroke Frau Brinkerhoff's hair, then leaned in to kiss her. They embraced briefly, and then Frau Kuiper pulled back and said something else, shaking her head at Frau Brinkerhoff, who looked a bit grim.

Frau Kuiper mounted up on Gerhard and spurred him into flight. Frau Brinkerhoff stood there in the field until he disappeared along the tree line, then turned and walked back toward the school.

Well . . . that was something worth knowing, that Frau Kuiper and Frau Brinkerhoff kissed. I knew immediately that it was something I wasn't supposed to know about; they couldn't have expected anyone to be awake and sitting at a window at this hour.

Liberty had made it very clear to me that women courting women was something that the Anglish considered wicked. If Fraus Kuiper and Brinkerhoff were tribades, they could be brought before a moot and charged with immoral behavior. The ministry could declare Frau Kuiper morally unfit as a dragoneer and demand that Gerhard be removed from her, and very likely put to death.

Several things began to make a bit more sense about Fraus Kuiper and Brinkerhoff—their attitudes and demeanor. I tucked the knowledge of what I'd seen away in my mind and wondered what Frau Kuiper would think if I told her that, among my people, she and Frau Brinkerhoff would be easily accepted as wives, and what that meant about the civility of my people and hers.

I was allowed to collect Kasaqua from the dragonhall after Frau Kuiper returned, which was shortly after luncheon. I spent the remainder of the afternoon playing in the snow with her, until we were both quite exhausted from running and chasing. She flopped down on the floor beside my bed once we were inside. She was longer than the bed now, from nose to tail. She hadn't been, before the recess.

How long would it be before she was too large to be welcomed indoors and had to be installed in the dragonhall permanently? Having spent a night apart from her, I understood much better why Theod often elected to sleep in Copper's box with him.

I hadn't talked to Theod since we'd been detained. I didn't know if I was supposed to talk to him without some other chaperone being present. I knew that he'd been made to stay in his assigned quarters last night, and that Copper had not been in his box when I'd collected Kasaqua.

I didn't know how to find out more about what was presently expected of me without presenting myself to Frau Kuiper, which was something I didn't feel particularly inclined to do.

I decided to go to the library and read for a while, taking Kasaqua with me. I left a note on the door of my quarters detailing exactly where I could be found, in case anyone came looking. I didn't want to be accused of going anywhere that I wasn't supposed to be.

LIBERTY WELCOMED HER BACK

I was appreciative beyond words when Liberty arrived at my door
with her sewing basket on Sunday morning. I hugged her tightly
as soon as she'd set her basket down, and she allowed it.

"I'd heard you were back from the gossip in the kitchens;
that you're in some kind of trouble but nobody knows just
what," she said carefully, pulling away to look at me with great
worry. "Weren't you supposed to be off on your island until the
fifteenth or so?"

"Someone sent Theod and me a death threat—threatening my
whole village, in fact. Threatening the dragons. Then Copper
growled at a ticket collector on the train who was giving Theod a
hard time, and the thanegards detained us, and my father with us,
and Frau Kuiper was *so* angry about it. They let my father go, in
the end, but I haven't heard from him. I've been told to stay right
here in this room, and I swear I'm going *mad*."

"That's awful," Liberty said, looking stricken. "Surely Frau

Kuiper is doing something about it, though? Launching an investigation?"

"She and Captain Einarsson are reporting it to the ministry and the thanegards, and Frau Kuiper thinks it shouldn't be terribly hard to find out who wrote it, because the author identifies himself as a former jarl's guard. But the idea of someone coming to Masquapaug with a fully grown dragon to do violence . . ."

"Well, I do hope that I can help the 'going mad' bit by distracting you with pleasant conversation," Liberty said, attempting to smile. "And perhaps you should get out your beadwork to have something to do with your hands. I've always found that doing something with my hands settles my mind."

Liberty talked about the last fortnight, and the celebration of Jule among the servants. She told me about how wonderfully the sewing machine worked, and I thanked her for the lovely dress she'd made me. Then, after looking around as if to make sure that no one could possibly be listening in on us, she leaned toward me and said quietly, "I went to visit with Jenni yesterday, and she has agreed that I can make gloves and handkerchiefs on commission. The sewing machine you gave me makes mending anything at all quicker, so I've been able to make time for piecework. The girls who share my room are helping me keep it secret, in exchange for my taking on some of their mending duties. The machine's too loud to use in the early or late hours, but I can usually carve out half an hour in the middle of the day if I shift my other duties around. I've made forty marka, thus far, on top of my wages! My exact debt right now, according to Frau Brinkerhoff's ledger, is one thousand and forty-six marka. I could have my debt paid off in a year, if no one catches me and puts a stop to it!"

"If your debt's paid off by this time next year, you could come to Masquapaug for Nikkomo and see if you like it well enough to want to move there permanently," I said with excitement. "I'm sure you will, though, and my friends have been wanting to meet you."

"You've spoken to your friends about me?" she asked, sounding mildly surprised.

"Yes, of course," I said, smiling. "You're one of the pleasantest people here, and I enjoy your company very much. You know so much about the erelore of fashion and about the social workings of the school . . . I fear I'd be quite lost if I had only Marta to rely on to explain Anglish behavior to me."

Liberty flushed and looked away, but she was smiling, and the thrill I got from having made her smile distracted me a bit from my many troubles. Kasaqua, who'd been perched in the window seat looking outward, seemed to take notice of us at last. She jumped down and padded over, rubbing herself against Liberty's knees. Liberty smiled fondly and scratched her behind the ears. That pleased Kasaqua very much, and I felt it beneath my breastbone.

Liberty and I chatted and worked on embroidery and beadwork; I showed her how to do herringbone stitch as a tube, and found that she was quite right about the calmative powers of working with one's hands.

I felt much better, overall, by the time we parted ways for luncheon.

THE OTHER STUDENTS RETURNED

The rest of the recess passed quietly. I received a telegram from Father, Theod and I resumed taking meals in the dining hall, and we spent time in the library studying. I worked on needlepoint and beadwork with Liberty. I read the entirety of the *Sybille Stosch* omnibus that Sander had given me.

On Sunday, the fifteenth of January, the rest of the students returned. I was informed that the same sort of smörgåsbord luncheon was going to be held that there'd been at the beginning of the first term, allowing the parents of returning students to politely socialize.

Liberty was unable to come visit with me, because Marta arrived directly after breakfast in her father's automotor with her trunk full of effects.

"Did you have a good recess?" she said as she began unpacking. "You were dreadfully missed at my party, I'll have you know. Lisbet and Sander came, and I danced with Sander, and the Sørensens were there, and Papa even invited that captain of his, and his family. I can't remember any of their names, because names among your people are all so complicated, but they were all perfectly polite. Oh, and I've gotten you a Jule present, but I'm afraid it's nothing terribly exciting. Magnus learned to fly over the recess, and he's thirteen inches taller at the shoulder!"

"That's wonderful," I said. "Does that mean he'll have to be quartered in the dragonhall now?"

"Yes, he will, the poor thing, and he's ever so upset about it. We're to have our own hall at Estervall, of course, did I tell you? Papa's going to be interviewing potential dragonhallmasters all week, and he intends for me to visit again on Saturday to meet any that he finds satisfactory; I'm to have final say! I've never gotten to have final say on the hiring of any of the help before. Anyway, this certainly means that I'll be placed into flight this term. We'll be getting our course assignments after luncheon. When did you arrive? I'd thought that I'd be back before you, since you have to worry about trains and ferries and all that."

"The ferry only runs to Masquapaug on Tuesday and Friday," I said. "The latest I could have come back would have been this past Friday. But I've been back since the thirtieth, because Theod and I received a very threatening letter. At home. They threatened my family. My whole village."

Marta stopped still, putting down the little glass bottle of something or other that she'd been unpacking. She turned to look at me as if she was waiting for me to tell her it was a joke.

"What are Frau Kuiper and Captain Einarsson doing about it?" she asked, after a long moment of frigid silence.

"I'm not entirely sure yet," I said. "Theod and I and our dragons are being confined to school grounds indefinitely, until things are solved. We'll only be allowed to go on previously arranged outings, and we're not to be seen at all in the city. Frau Jansen apparently wants me to come and have tea with Lisbet and Sander; she sent a letter to Frau Kuiper to arrange it. Theod's been invited to trail riding and rabbit hunting at the Sørensen estate."

"You really ought to have come to my Jule party, Anequs,"

Marta lamented. "You could have made very excellent connections. I really will send a telegram to Papa and tell him that he simply must pen a letter to the editor of the *Estervall Gazette* praising his captains and their sailors."

I understood far better now how such a thing might actually be of use than I had the first time she'd suggested it, back when Thane Stafn had penned his editorial. How the attitudes of the Anglish concerning nackies being dragoneers were terribly important.

Marta's father did write a letter to the editor of the *Estervall Gazette*, which was reprinted a week later in the *Vastergot Weekly Review*. Frau Kuiper and Captain Einarsson also arranged for dragoneers of their acquaintance, including a member of the current jarl's guard, to pen opinion pieces regarding "nackies being allowed to become dragoneers," as they put it. In the second week of February, Captain Einarsson wrote an article detailing the process by which dragon eggs were licensed and bought and sold, how dragoneers were educated and winnowed, and what happened to those that did not prove capable. It was a more thorough explanation of the subject than I'd heard from anyone else about the whole affair, and I made sure to send a telegram to Mother and Father letting them know that they should secure a copy to keep.

The answer to the question of "what happens to a dragon that's bonded itself to a dragoneer lacking sufficient intelligence, skill, and good character" was almost always "the dragon is put to death."

I would not, under any circumstances whatsoever, allow that to happen to Kasaqua.

ANEQUS TOOK TEA AT THE JANSENS' TOWNHOME

O n Saturday the eleventh of February, a carriage arrived to escort Sander and me to the Jansen home. Both of our dragons remained at the school—Kasaqua because she was big enough to be trouble for a carriage and Inga for reasons that Sander was somewhat evasive about. We spent the journey conversing in notes about the latest serials; he was trying to convince me that I ought to be reading *Berthold Büchner, Boy Adventurer* because Berthold had lately traveled into the west and was having dealings with wild savages, and I might have enlightening commentary on that. I kept trying to demur on the grounds that I still wasn't caught up with *Sybille Stosch*, who never left New Linvik and spent her time solving mysteries, crimes, and scandals. I had a feeling that, while I probably would have a great deal of commentary, I would not at all enjoy the depiction of "wild savages of the west" in *Berthold Büchner*.

The Jansen household was well outside the center of town, on a street lined by wrought-isen fences and young birch trees. Sander closed his tablet and tucked it into his breast pocket with a sigh as we walked up the stone steps to the house.

Sander took my coat with a small bow and momentarily disappeared with it, leaving me standing in a little chamber with two tall windows and a low table with an arrangement of flowers on it. I wondered absently if they had a housemaid, but it wouldn't have been polite to ask. Sander returned and led me into a tea parlor not at all unlike the one where Theod and I had visited with scholars in the first term, where Lisbet and her mother were already seated. Frau Jansen's gaze went directly to Sander, plainly scanning him for flaws as he led me to my seat. When I was seated, her appraising gaze went to me. She had an overly practiced smile.

"I do hope you won't find me remiss in not having invited you previously," Frau Jansen said. "I'm not accustomed to Sander being at a school that has female pupils. I understand that you and Marta spent some time with Lisbet during the festivities at Valkyrjafax?"

"Yes, along with some other girls from her school. They were all very charming and informative about the customs of Anglish evening dances; it was the first I'd ever been to."

"Is your society quite different, on your little island?" she asked, pouring tea for each of us in turn. "What sort of events do you have, that young people may become acquainted with one another?"

"Well, as it's a village of a thousand people, it's rather hard for young people of similar ages *not* to be acquainted with one another," I said. "We don't really have exclusive events; dances and gatherings involve the entire village. The niceties of conversation and who should talk to whom are somewhat different when there are no strangers."

"Well, that's very interesting indeed," she said. "I suppose, then, that your people don't have anything resembling a season, or coming out into society?"

"No, ma'am, we don't," I said.

"Lisbet will be coming out this season," she said mildly.

"It's been my understanding that it was typical for a lady to come out at the age of sixteen; have I misunderstood?" I asked. Lisbet was, if I was recalling correctly, seventeen or maybe even eighteen by now. I didn't know when her birthday was.

"Oh, no, sixteen *is* the traditional age," Frau Jansen said, "but we decided to wait until Lisbet had completed at least two years of secondary school, to best hone her accomplishments."

"Sander's mentioned in his letters home that you're quite an accomplished scholar, Anequs," Lisbet said. "What other things have you studied?"

"I'm afraid I haven't studied the traditional ladies' suite of accomplishments," I said. "I don't know how to paint watercolors or play the concertina or anything—that's what 'accomplishments' generally means, from what I've read? I've mostly been studying scholarly subjects: anglereckoning, erelore, natural philosophy, that sort of thing. What have you studied at your school?"

"We've studied conversation, wordlore and letter writing, floral arrangement and decorating, dulcimer, harpsichord, needlework, sketching, and watercolor," Lisbet said crisply, not sounding especially proud or enthused.

"I should very much like to hear you play sometime," I said, sipping my tea. "I'm not terribly familiar with either harpsichord or dulcimer; I've only heard wax cylinder recordings."

"Perhaps you'd like to join us for a recital some evening?" Frau Jansen suggested.

"That would be lovely, ma'am," I said. "My afternoon session of class concludes at three o'clock each day."

"I can't imagine that your school does much to provide suitable outings for ladies, given that it's only you and Miss Hagan," Lisbet said. "Though I believe you mentioned traveling into the city with Marta for shopping and sightseeing?"

"During the first term, we were generally left to make our own arrangements; certain social developments this term have kept me from leaving the grounds. Thank you very much for inviting me into your home."

"Have you spoken to Karina about having outings arranged?" Frau Jansen asked.

"I haven't, ma'am," I said. "I wouldn't have considered it something worthy of her time. She chaperoned an outing in the first term for Mr. Knecht and me; we visited with some folkreckoning scholars."

"Well, that seems quite educational, if not especially diverting. She and Elsie have, of course, had to design their program to cater to the needs of young men first. It's exceedingly uncommon for a young woman to pursue a career in dragoneering. I imagine that Miss Hagan will have a rather difficult season when she chooses to come out, unless she plans to exclusively pursue connections to other young dragoneers."

"We should invite Marta to our next gathering, if you're curious about that, Mother," Lisbet said, smiling sweetly. "As the sole heir to her father's fortune, I doubt that she'll lack for suitors of good quality, dragon or no. I don't believe that she personally aspires to be a Valkyre."

"Marta is lovely," Sander said, drumming his fingers on the table for a moment before pressing both hands onto the tablecloth as if to still them. Frau Jansen looked at him as if he'd just shouted vile blasphemy, then looked away again.

"I understand that you and Marta and Sander are all close acquaintances at school?" she asked, looking back to me almost fervently. "He does often mention you in his letters."

"Yes. We often dine together, and we share some classes. Sander and I were both in skiltakraft last term, but he's gone on to Skiltakraft Two while I've taken up an independent study on the subject with Mr. Knecht."

"Such things have always seemed dreadfully technical to me," Frau Jansen said with a pretty little laugh, "but our Sander has always been so clever at the drawing of figures. It seemed a natural field for him to pursue, and an athermacher can arrange for orders to be made by third parties without much cause for direct interactions with their patrons, which would suit Sander's . . . particular needs."

"Sander and I haven't greatly discussed our future careers," I said.

"Your interview in the paper said that you intend to go back to your island and pursue farming?" Lisbet asked.

"Yes, that's always been the plan. Athermaching is something I hope to excel at eventually, though not in quantity or for profit. Just to have the materials."

"Sander is going to become an athermacher; he will operate out of our home. We're having a laboratory fitted in one of the upstairs rooms—"

"I will have a house," Sander said, staring down at his hands as they pressed against the table. "Inga will make athers. I will sell athers. I will have a house, Mother."

"Sander, darling—"

"Sander darling we have talked about this before you mustn't blurt things you must be still you must you mustn't you must you mustn't you must you mustn't you must you mustn't—" He paused with his mouth open for a long moment, making a little catching noise at the back of his throat. He balled his hands into fists and drummed them on the table and said, "Anequs is my friend."

He glanced up briefly, brilliant blue eyes flashing at his mother and then right back down. Frau Jansen had gone very pale.

"Lisbet, if you would be so kind as to see your brother up to his room, as it would seem that he is unwell at the moment—"

"Go to your room Sander," Sander blurted, scowling down at his hands. "You mustn't fidget you mustn't scribble you will not shame this family go to your room really whatever are we going to *do* with him Emile go to your room what will people what will people say about us go to your room what will people say you will not shame this family go to your room go to your room go to your room go to your room." He was breathing hard through gritted teeth, and he looked up and met his mother's gaze directly. "Go to *your* room. Mother."

A cold and fragile silence filled the room, and Sander reached into his breast pocket to retrieve his tablet.

"What have I said, darling, about scribbling at the table?" Frau Jansen said tightly.

Sander took a deep breath and said, "Go to your room, Mother," without looking up.

"Lisbet, I do believe I'm feeling a bit faint," Frau Jansen said tightly. "Would you be so kind as to arrange a carriage to take Miss Anequs back to school? I'm afraid we must conclude this visit a bit earlier than expected."

"Mother, please," Lisbet said. "Perhaps you *ought* to retire for a bit. You are looking very pale."

"I hope that you better understand now why we can't often have guests for tea, darling," Frau Jansen said. "Our home is not fit for company."

"There's nothing wrong with our home, Mother," Lisbet said. "Sander and Anequs are very good friends, and she is quite accustomed to him speaking through his tablet. There wouldn't have been a scene if you hadn't insisted on his keeping it out of sight."

"It is my responsibility to think of both your futures, darling. If your brother cannot make a good presentation, how do you expect to marry well?"

"I will *not* marry any man who has unkind things to say about Sander!" Lisbet said. "We are being utterly terrible hosts to our guest. You should retire to your sitting room, Mother. We're not going to have any more tea gatherings like this—but only because they are clearly too great a strain upon your constitution."

Lisbet and her mother stared at each other icily for longer than could possibly have been polite, and then Frau Jansen said, "If that's what you think is best, darling."

She rose and swept away from the table, moving with a swift and brittle grace. Lisbet went with her.

Sander tapped on the table twice with his needle, catching my attention. I looked at him, and he slid the tablet toward me. On it he'd written, *I'm terribly sorry that you've seen me lose my composure. My mother can have that effect upon me. This was an ill-advised gathering. The three of you would have gotten on better without my company, or you and Lisbet and I without Mother. Lisbet would like to be your friend, but Mother forbade all correspondence until recently. Don't show this to either of them, please. It would embarrass Lisbet.*

I closed the tablet when I'd finished reading it and pushed the button on the spine that would erase the words. Sander, watching my hands, smiled. He took it up again and wrote,

Mother doesn't want me to ever leave home. If she'd had her way, she'd have shut me up in an attic room when I was a little child and never let me out. Father didn't let her. But Father died two years ago from sudden failure of his heart. Mother's had no one to check her since.

"Why would she ever want to do such a horrid thing?" I asked.

It is commonly done with children who are disappointments. Simple, or sickly, or mad. I wasn't an easy child; more than one governess left us because I would scream and hit and bite when I couldn't make others understand me. They had a very hard time keeping me in clothes, because everything itched and chafed and felt terrible against my skin. I would say words, but they wouldn't be the right words. I'd mean "I want to leave" but I'd say "put your coat on" over and over, like you saw earlier, until I'd break down in tears. It's still like that with me sometimes, where my voice just gets stuck and I can only say one thing. Lisbet could usually understand me, more than anyone else. She could guess what I'd meant to say.

"But your mother . . ."

She sent Lisbet away for primary school, so she wouldn't be <u>tainted</u> by me. Mother and Father hired a governess, Miss Keitl, she was the one who made me do the lines | | | | | | |. She would hit me with a yardstick if I did any-thing she considered misbehaving. She taught me how to read and write. As far as I'm concerned, it's the only good she ever did. I got older, got better at behaving, learned that certain kinds of fidgeting can help me <u>think</u>. Father *bought me my tablet, on her advice. Every day, all day, for four years, Miss Keitl made herself my everything. She charged my parents quite a lot of money to do it. It's why we're in trouble now—that and the purchase of Inga's egg. We aren't rich anymore, not like Mother thinks we ought to be. We can't give Lisbet the dowry she ought to have.*

"What's a dowry?"

The money that a woman brings to her marriage.

"Ah."

When I was twelve, Father thought I behaved well enough to be sent to primary school. <u>They'd</u> starve me or lock me in closets or beat me if I didn't behave. Eventually I learned just not to speak at all, if I could avoid it. Keep my eyes down, keep below notice, read and do anglereckoning and draw figures, because I'm clever at that. It was Frau Brinkerhoff's idea that I should become a dragoneer. An athermacher. It was all arranged with Inga's dam's dragoneer and the bank, and all a year before Father passed. I'm sure that Mother would have stopped it if she'd had the power. I love Inga, and I wouldn't mind being an athermacher or a minglinglorist, but I don't want to live with my mother ever again. Lisbet has said that I can live in her house, when she gets married, but that depends on her finding a husband who'd tolerate that. I want a house of my own. I want I DON'T WANT to have to answer to people who don't bother to understand me. Mother thinks I'm simple, and that it would be best to keep me out of sight.

"Is it unkind of me to say that I think your mother's a beast?"

It is unkind, but you're not wrong.

"What are you going to do?"

I'm going to study hard and become proficient at skiltakraft and make athers. A lot of money can be made by the sale of certain athers to the right sorts of people, and I'm sure Frau Brinkerhoff will help me find someone who'll buy from me. It will take time, but eventually I should be able to support myself.

"But until you've become skilled enough to shape Inga's breath . . ."

I shall have to continue to tolerate Mother. According to Father's will, I stand to inherit his estate when I become twenty. But that's four years on, and until then my mother is the singular controller of our finances.

"I wish there was something more I could do to help. I wish I'd said something to your mother just now."

It's better that you didn't. She wouldn't let me continue being your friend if you had, and I've had few enough friends in my life. I shouldn't like to lose you.

"You won't, as long as I've got anything to say about it," I said, smiling.

Lisbet was a bit pink-faced when she rejoined us a minute later, but her voice was utterly genial and composed. Their mother was not mentioned again, and the three of us had a lovely luncheon.

AND LEARNED OF SPRINGTIME CUSTOMS

On the first day of March, there was a frightful storm—a gale of snow and sleet that beat against the windows with a pelting hiss. All outdoor activities, including flight lessons and dragon husbandry, were canceled. I sat in the library listening to the sound of sleet against the big windows, and Kasaqua stood with her foreclaws on the windowsill and stared out at it. She wanted very much to go outside. I tried to put that fact out of my mind as I committed useless facts of erelore and landreckoning to memory.

After my morning study, but before luncheon, I visited the mail room to find that I'd received another letter from Ingrid Hakansdottir. Again it was written on brown paper and sealed with . . . probably the drips of a tallow candle, from the texture of it and the greasy stain. It read:

Est. Miss Anequs,

I planted some tulips for Fyrafax but right now they're just little green leaves. I know how to make flower crowns and my mother is going to teach me how to bake honeycake this year. Do you celebrate Fyrafax on Mask Island? My friend Astrid says that nackies don't believe in the gods or ever go to temple, but my mother does and she's a nackie so I think Astrid is wrong.

I hope that you will respond to this letter.

Yours with great esteem,
Ingrid Hakansdottir

I penned a response explaining that we didn't celebrate Fyrafax, but that the first thaw was the best time to find early spring greens—ramps, fiddleheads, cress, spruce tips, and that sort of thing. It was the time of year for shad bakes; I asked if she'd ever had cedar-plank shad baked over a smoky fire.

I joined Marta and Sander for luncheon after leaving the mail room. Theod wasn't in evidence, and it wouldn't have surprised me at all to learn that he was in the dragonhall with Copper, taking lunch with Henkjan and the hall lads; I wouldn't have wanted to cross the field in this weather for the sake of the luncheon offerings in the dining hall, either.

There was a new dish available today, along with the cold cuts of meat and boiled eggs: fresh cabbage chopped finely with some kind of white sauce. I took some, if only because it departed from the pickled cabbage that had been on offer all winter.

"Afternoon, Marta, Sander," I said, taking my seat. "Could someone please tell me more about Fyrafax, like when it is and what its traditions are? We don't celebrate any such thing on the islands, and my young admirer, Miss Hakansdottir, has lately asked me about it."

"It's the first of May, the beginning of summer," Marta said.

"The beginning of summer is in the third week of June," I said, looking at her sidelong. "The longest day is an event fixed by the stars. It's when we celebrate the strawberry harvest."

"No, that's midsummer, Jodenfax," Marta said, shaking her head. "Fyrafax is about the blooming of the land into springtime.

It's all flowers and milk and honeycakes, short mead for children and meddyglyn for adults."

"What's meddyglyn?" I asked.

"It's like mead, but with herbs, and often fortified with distilled spirits," Marta answered. "Typically one takes it as a cordial, mixed with water and honey."

Sander tapped on the cover of his tablet with his needle to get my attention, sliding the tablet across the table to me.

Jule is about Fyra bringing back the sun after the long night; Runefax, which is at the beginning of April, is about the melting of the ice. When Joden froze the world, Rune was imprisoned beneath a shield of ice and the land was as dry as it was cold. There's not much fuss made about Runefax by anybody but sailors and fishermen, I don't think, because she's the goddess of the sea and is prone to being tricksome and nasty. Fyrafax is about how the sun, which has been growing in strength ever since Jule, has healed the land and made it fruitful. It's especially good luck for children to be born at this time of year, and it's when the culling of the suckling lambs happens, so there's always lamb dishes and new cheese.

I passed the tablet to Marta after I'd finished reading it.

"Weather permitting, it's traditional to have outdoor parties—especially children's parties. Fyrafax is something of a children's holiday, really—a celebration of innocence and youth and all. Little girls in white dresses with flowers braided into their hair, winding ribbons around a maypole."

I'd seen watercolor plates of that exact sort of scene many times on the end pages of magazines, and I nodded understanding.

"The beginning of May is when we have the corn-planting dance back home," I said. "But it's not a set date; it's when the frost is over and the land is ready."

"I suppose that's sensible," Marta said. "Have you asked Frau Kuiper about inviting your younger siblings to the Fyrafax festivities? I should so like to meet them, and students were encouraged last year to invite younger siblings to round out the number of children present."

"I haven't, but I will this afternoon," I said. "What was it like last year?"

"Pleasant, but not especially diverting," Marta said. "Annetta and Saskia came, each chaperoning their younger sisters, but I think that Saskia's sister will have turned thirteen over the winter, which makes her a bit too grown for this sort of celebration. It's children between the ages of six and twelve that are most desired. Younger ones have nursery parties and decorate eggs and make paper garlands and flower crowns and things like that. The first time I went to a garden party for Fyrafax was at the Sørensen estate; I was six and Dagny was eight, playing hostess for the first time. I think I recall Lisbet being there, or certainly at another of the gatherings Dagny hosted. I never saw you there, though, Sander . . ."

Sander picked up his tablet and jotted something quickly, sliding it back to her.

"Oh, I see," Marta said, looking a bit embarrassed. She slid the tablet to me.

I wasn't allowed to attend children's parties, or parties in general. I'm not going to be at the school's gathering, I'm afraid. Mother has asked that I be home for the weekend and I can't put her off.

"Do you think I'd be allowed to invite other children of my acquaintance?" I asked thoughtfully. "Frau Kuiper has insisted that Theod and I must become known and well liked by the people of Vastergot, and Ingrid Hakansdottir is exactly the sort of age to enjoy this kind of gathering."

"Well, it wouldn't hurt to ask," Marta said doubtfully, "but I don't think such a thing has been done before."

"Lots of things concerning Theod and me haven't been done before, it seems," I said with a smile.

I went to Frau Brinkerhoff's office after my afternoon class had finished. Frau Kuiper was the one I was supposed to petition about having guests on school grounds, but Frau Brinkerhoff seemed slightly more sentimental than Frau Kuiper, and more likely to agree to my inviting a crowd.

"Frau Brinkerhoff?" I asked, peeking in through her doorway, which was only partially open.

"Oh, Miss Anequs, how lovely to see you! Did you need something?"

"Nothing, really, it's only that I've been talking about Fyrafax with Marta and Sander, and Marta mentioned that last year's students were asked to invite their younger siblings for the festivities. I've got a younger sister and a younger brother, both under twelve years of age. Theod has cousins aged five, eight, and eleven."

"I'm sure it would be delightful to have your siblings and Mr. Knecht's cousins visit us, but would they be traveling alone all the way from Mask Island?"

"Theod's cousins live on Nack," I said. "As there's still plenty of time to plan, I'm sure I could arrange for my older brother to escort them. Would he be welcomed at the festivities as well, as a chaperone?"

"Well, he has visited the grounds before, so I can't see why not," Frau Brinkerhoff said pensively.

"And also . . . I know this might be straining a bit, but I've been in correspondence with a little girl named Ingrid Hakansdottir, who is apparently a great admirer of me as a dragoneer and aspires to be one herself someday. She's ten years old. Would it be permissible for me to invite her as well?"

Frau Brinkerhoff frowned and looked thoughtful for a moment, then said, "I'll have to talk to Karina about that. This child, she's a citizen of Vastergot?"

"Yes, ma'am," I said.

"This might be an ideal sort of opportunity for you to become more well known to the general citizenry, if this girl is the right sort of person. We shall have to look into her and her connections. Come and see me again on Friday and you'll have your answer."

"Thank you very much, ma'am," I said, smiling. "I should so like to offer an invitation to her—and if she wishes to be a dragoneer, it would be very thrilling for her to see dragons at close quarters. Perhaps she'll even be a student here one day."

Frau Brinkerhoff hemmed slightly, writing something down, then said, "If there's nothing else, dear, I really do have to balance these accounts."

"Of course, ma'am. Have a good day."

I ducked back out of her office with a smile on my face. I'd been seen with the wrong sort of nackies over the winter recess; surely visiting with the right sort would improve the public's opinion. If I was going to become known to the people of Vastergot, I was going to be sure that it was the nackie folk of Vastergot who knew me first and best.

NIQUIAT VISITED, WITH SOME EXCITING NEWS

The following Saturday, Niquiat and Zhina came to the school for luncheon. Sander was visiting at home, and Theod was on his gentlemanly trail hunt at the Sørensen estate, but I convinced Marta to join us. She and I walked to the station together to meet Niquiat and Zhina. It had snowed yesterday, then rained, then frozen overnight, leaving a brittle crust of ice over everything. Marta and I were obliged to move very carefully down the gravel path, but Magnus and Kasaqua bounded playfully all around us. Kasaqua was still light enough to be able to skitter across the ice without breaking it, despite her size. She was making a game of spreading her wings against the wind and letting it blow her backward, sailing across the slick snowbanks. Magnus was making a game of taking short flights to and from us.

Marta fretted the whole way to the station.

"I'm not sure if Dagny's being deliberately unkind or if it's simply an oversight that I didn't receive an invitation to the tea party she's holding in parallel with Niklas's hunting party. I shall have to host an event soon at Sjokliffheim and be very sure to invite her, thus pointing out her slight. You *will* come, if invited, won't you?"

"I'm sure you could talk to Frau Kuiper about including such a function in her campaign to make Theod and me figures of public esteem," I said, knowing that it was exactly the sort of thing that Fraus Kuiper and Brinkerhoff would want me to attend. "I'd need another dress, though, unless this one is suitable for a garden party."

I was wearing the dress that Liberty had made for me, it being by far the nicest day dress that I owned. I'd paired it with my seal-skin cape and mittens, for warmth, and in my opinion the dappled brown and gray of the sealskin complemented the black and gold of the dress well. Marta, though, looked me up and down critically.

"You'll need a formal spring dress anyway, for the social at Fyrafax," she said. "Your measurements haven't changed significantly from October, I don't think, so I'll have my seamstress put something together."

Niquiat and Zhina met us on the path before Marta had a chance to say more.

"We think we've cracked the Shiang-Gang engine!" Niquiat said as soon as he was close enough for it to be polite.

"You did? What was it that wasn't working?" I asked.

"Some of the inlays in the original needed to be filled with gold," Niquiat said.

"Gold? As in actual gold?" I asked.

"Not much; hair-fine wire," Zhina said. "A wedding ring gave us enough to work with for the original engine and for the reproduction we built."

"Do I want to know where you got a wedding ring?" I asked.

"Ekaitz got it," Zhina said with a shrug. "We didn't ask from where."

"I'm afraid I've gotten a bit lost," Marta said, offering a pleasant smile.

"Oh, sorry. You visited the tinker co-op with us the one time, remember? They've been working on restoring a scrapped engine that came from a shipwreck; it's probably from Shiang-Gang originally."

"Oh. How . . . diverting," Marta said.

"We've got diagrams and whatnot, once we get near a table to lay them out on."

We chatted about inconsequential happenings in the city as we walked back up the path to the school, and situated ourselves in the dining hall. Niquiat reported that the question of nackies and our place in society had become a common topic in local pub talk, at least in the cannery district. One of the venues he'd frequented, the one where we'd seen Ekaitz's cousin play, had started to refuse admittance to nackies. The presence of nackies was distracting and tended to invite quarrels that the proprietors didn't want to deal with. Marta was scandalized by the injustice of it, and managed to make her shock and rage look pretty.

It was quite early for luncheon, and we had the dining hall entirely to ourselves. Niquiat produced a roll of papers from his satchel and laid them out, using salt and pepper shakers as paperweights.

"These are some drawings we made of what was on the main engine disc. Does any of this look familiar?" Many of the pages just had imperfectly drawn skiltas on them—flowery-looking skiltas with bent lines, not wholly unlike the dance skiltas I'd drawn.

"They're clearly skiltas," I said, turning one of the pages around. The skilta was asymmetrical, but it didn't look like it was intended to be that way.

"I wonder why they're all bowed out like this?" Marta asked, frowning. "The lines ought to be straight, but apart from that, this one looks like it's for containment, or direction."

"Here, we've got a drawing of the whole disc," Zhina said. "It's sort of bowl-shaped, if that matters, but very shallow. About the size of a dinner plate. Isen on the outside, brass on the inside. All the skiltas are on the brass side, and some are meant to be inlaid with gold."

"There's probably a layer of lood between the brass and isen," Marta said. "Lood can give the athers produced by a skilta direction to travel in by blocking their path."

"We'd have to cut into it to find out, and we haven't wanted to do that since we've got just the one to work from," Niquiat said. "This is the best picture we've been able to make of it."

The drawing was on brown paper, true to life size, laid out in a half dozen colors of wax and ink.

"This circle here in the center is a cup, it's where the fuel goes—we presume coal because there's a Shiangish word etched there and Zhina says it's the word for coal; she knows because she's seen it printed on crates in her father's shipments. There's a housing above the cup—they sort of nest together—and it's got a soft isen spindle wrapped all around with a coil of copper wire— yards and yards of it. Each end of the wire has a little screw-node on it, a beginning and end point for the flow of tatkraft. There are sort of spoon-shaped bits that connect to an array of cogs that turn a lodestone cachet around the spindle. The cogs have the lodestone cachet going at fifty revolutions for every one of the spoon-wheel. You can turn it by hand, with the one we built, and it generates a sad little bit of tatkraft, but getting it really going has to do with the skilta disc and the coal."

I was arranging the individual pages of skiltas in a ring around the top-down drawing of the disc, working out which ones overlapped with which other ones.

"You've got the colors all wrong, this isn't how the associations go," I said, folding two of the pages so I could slot them against each other and work out how the patterns would overlap. "Look here, Marta, coal is made mostly of kolfni, right?"

"Right . . . but it's the bits in between the motes that let it hold tatkraft—the vetna, zurfni, stiksna, and saffle," she said. "Professor Ezel is always on about how purities and impurities in base components can make the difference between a skilta that works and one that explodes into ash and wind."

"These skiltas here would transmute the coal into its constituent parts, and these ones here are all about channeling," I said, turning the picture around. "It pulls water and smothering air out of the coal, leaving pure kolfni and saffle behind. All these other skiltas are about channeling the air, using the water . . . It would make a sort of spinning ring of hot and cold air, I think?"

"And that would turn the spoon-wheel, like a windmill," Niquiat said, his eyes lighting up.

"But we'd need a dragon's breath to make the skiltas go," Zhina said. She looked from me to Marta to me again expectantly.

"This is far past the level I'd be comfortable loosing Kasaqua's breath on. There are so many layers of transmutation, and tripping on any of them could cause an explosion or produce a deadly waste or something," I said. "It probably wouldn't go amiss to find an actually decent skiltakraft practitioner who could advise on it before we attempted to power any of the skiltas. Certainly not Ezel or Einarsson, because they both hate me, but surely there are other dragoneers elsewhere who might be willing to assist?"

"Without taking the credit for it?" Niquiat said skeptically.

"Point," I said. "Still, I think I'll ask Fraus Kuiper and Brinkerhoff if they can't arrange some kind of social gathering for Theod and me involving other dragoneers who aren't our classmates. I've been curious as to what most dragoneers do with their careers, because if the academy is producing twenty-odd graduates every year, they can't *all* be joining the dragonthede or the jarl's guard, can they? Particularly any women who've been among them."

"In my first year, when I roomed with Emmeline and Kerstin," Marta said, "they both mentioned that there'd been a girl named Dynah in attendance the previous year. She was from one of the small towns in the northwest, in Runestung Hold—not far from the border of the contested lands. I could write to Emmeline and Kerstin to see if either of them are still in contact with her. As I understand it, she went back to her town upon completion of her studies."

"I'll ask Frau Kuiper about her as well; if Emmeline and Kerstin don't have her contact information, then Frau Kuiper surely will, and any of them would be a suitable social connection, I think. Thank you, Marta."

"Well, now that all those arrangements are made, you want to show us what you folks here do for luncheon?" Niquiat said with a grin. I smiled back wryly, knowing that he and Zhina were going to be disappointed.

ANEQUS RECEIVED A VISITOR ONCE AGAIN

On the third day of April, I received a telegram from Masquapaug telling me that Father's ship would be departing for the north sea that coming Sunday, and that he wanted to visit me on Friday to say his goodbyes. After a quick back-and-forth of telegrams, Niquiat arranged to meet me at the Varmarden station to greet Father when he arrived. Frau Kuiper made it very clear that I was absolutely not, under any circumstances, to board the train—but that the station was practically part of the school grounds and thus walking to and from it would be acceptable.

The morning was cool, and the air smelled of thawing earth as I walked to the station. There were crocuses and squill poking their heads through the grass at the margins of the pastures, and I wondered if there were ramps growing near the pond at the end of the trail behind the flight field. I didn't have anywhere to cook them even if there were—students were not allowed in the kitchen—so it didn't especially matter.

It was the kind of weather to turn soil in.

Turning the soil was always the last thing Father helped us with before going back to sea. It was time for the first plantings of the year—peas and bush beans, turnips and beets, radishes, onions, cabbage, and spring squash. Things that could survive a light frost. Summer crops would go into the ground just as the radishes and turnips were ending: flint corn and winter squash and climbing beans. When it was time to harvest strawberries, we'd put sweet corn and tomatoes and peppers and eggplant into the ground, and the crops would take us right to the first frosts in winter.

My fingers itched with not being in the soil. Kasaqua noticed, and tried to help by taking a sudden interest in the digging of holes and trenches any time she was on a suitable patch of earth. I got a terrible scolding from Professor Mesman when she tore up a strip of turf outside the dragonhall; I was meant to control and curtail behavior like that. He'd muttered something about "denning" and it being the last thing the school needed.

Over the course of winter, Kasaqua's velvet-shrouded knobs had resolved themselves into a pair of two-pronged antlers, gracefully curved with points forward. The shedding of the velvety down had been a messy and, in fact, quite bloody process. She had the annoying habit of rubbing her antlers on anything conveniently the height of her bowed head—doorjambs, table edges, bedsteads—leaving scarlet stains and shreds of velvet on all, much to Marta's horror and lamentation. It also *itched*, and I spent as much time scratching my own head as she did hers.

She'd retained the dark markings on her face, ears, and neck, but they'd faded completely elsewhere, leaving her skin a markless tawny gold with a burnished sheen, her wingleather blending to brilliant scarlet on the leading edge. Her russet mane feathers began dropping out by ones and twos, and more richly red ones grew in their place, the quills veined brown-black and some of them barred at the base. I kept every dropped feather that I found, because dragon feathers seemed too precious to squander.

Kasaqua bounded up and down the path, sniffing at new green growth and pausing to scratch or dig when she saw fit, covering three times the distance I covered by the time I reached the station.

Niquiat was already there when I arrived, and I joined him in sitting on the sheltered bench while we waited for Father. I told Niquiat about my adventures in proper society, what an absolute beast Frau Jansen was. He told me about various things he'd done with Zhina in her quarter of the city, and about new happenings at the tinker co-op.

Father arrived.

He seemed surprised to see Niquiat sitting there with me, and not especially pleased.

"I expected to come here today to spend time with my oldest daughter," Father said, crossing his arms, looking hard at me. "I hadn't expected my oldest son, who left home against my wishes, to be part of this day."

"I asked him to come," I said, "because it would be bad luck if any of your children failed to wish you good travels before you leave for the north sea."

"My ship leaves from Nack the day after tomorrow," Father said, looking from me to Niquiat and back. "It's a shame that neither of you could come to the whalers' departing dance."

"I've been barred from leaving school grounds. And even if I wasn't, I'm not going to come home and bring danger while there's someone writing me death threats," I said, straightening my shoulders and trying to stand tall. "I asked Niquiat to meet us here because the two of you need to talk to each other, more than I need to talk to either of you."

Father sighed, glaring at me, then looked at Niquiat. They held each other's gaze for a long time—Father's eyes flinty, Niquiat's jaw set.

"Niquiat and his tinker friends have been working on an engine from Shiang-Gang," I said, when the silence became unbearable. "It will require a dragon's breath to activate the skiltas involved, but—"

"I don't know anything about that kind of nonsense," Father said, frowning.

"No one on the island does," Niquiat replied, his voice tight. "That's why I had to come to Vastergot to study it. If we're to keep up with the rest of the world—"

"And why should we concern ourselves with keeping up with the rest of the world?" Father interrupted. "Our people have lived on the islands since the beginning of time, and we've done it without the need of clockworks and engines and any other kind of Anglish nonsense. What's wrong with living the way our ancestors have always lived? We've kept our old ways more closely than any of our cousins on the mainland, or even on Naquipaug, because we don't willingly involve ourselves in Anglish affairs."

"Because the rest of the world is moving forward, Father!" Niquiat spat. "How did living like our ancestors always lived work out for us when the Anglish turned up on our doorstep with guns? What would it have been like if our people had already worked out gunpowder back when Stafn Whitebeard first beached a skiff on the shore of Naquipaug?"

"That's a different kind of thing," Father said. "But the Anglish have robbed us in so many ways, I can't condone giving up who we are to become more like them."

"I don't see you balking at using the ferry or the train, or at pocket watches or canned fish or any number of modern comforts and conveniences. We grind our corn in isen crank mills, but didn't our ancestors use mortars and pestles for that?"

"It's not the same—"

"What makes a hand-cranked mill better or purer or more traditional than the same mill with a tatkraftish engine fixed to it? Why is it all right to ride a train, but not for me to study how trains are crafted? Would you be angry if I'd taken up an apprenticeship with a blacksmith on Naquipaug? Or in Catchnet?"

"If you'd wanted to be a blacksmith, there would have been ways of making that happen."

"But I don't want to be a blacksmith, Father. I want to be an enginekrafter. I knew there wasn't anyone on Masquapaug, so I looked on Naquipaug and I looked in Catchnet and I looked all the way down the coast. Vastergot is the nearest place that's got people who can teach me. I'm here studying mechanics and enginekraft and minglinglore because *I want to bring it home*. Because I know what we could accomplish with a fully modern machine shop. I want to work out how to do things better, faster, more efficiently. I want to make our lives easier with machines. How much more land could we till with an automaton horse? How easy would it be to cross the sound if I could build a canoe with tatkraftish paddlewheels? What if we could build a machine that flies? I want to build machines that the Anglish haven't even thought of yet! I don't want to be more like them; I want them to take us seriously as a modern people with modern ideas."

Father stared back, sighing through his nose. His mouth remained a thin, hard line. I spoke before he did.

"I came to Vastergot to learn how to be a dragoneer, because there's no one back home who could teach me to be Nampeshiweisit. Niquiat came to Vastergot because there's no one back home who can teach him to be an enginekrafter. When we come home, we'll know enough to teach other people. The world is changing, Father. We're going to have to change with it."

"I wish that you would both come home," he said softly, turning away from us, looking to the field where Kasaqua was stalking and pouncing at sparrows. "But I suppose I can make myself content with the idea that you intend to, eventually. I'm from an older world than either of you. When I was your age, before everything happened on Naquipaug . . . No, that's not something I want to talk about now." He raked a hand through his hair, turning back to us. "Things are . . . different now. I suppose I should expect my children to be different, too. I always thought that my first son would be a whaler like me, that my first daughter would take care of me in my old age. Now my daughter is Nampeshiweisit, and my son . . . I don't even understand what he is. But so much of my life hasn't been the way I expected it to be. I shouldn't let myself be angry about this. I shouldn't let myself be afraid. I should have more courage. About you, and your futures."

Niquiat stepped forward and embraced him. "I never meant to hurt you, Father," he said, his voice muffled against Father's shoulder.

"I see that," Father replied.

I smiled a little, hoping that things would be better between them now.

They parted, and Niquiat scratched the back of his neck, looking down at the ground.

"So, are you going to tell us what we've been missing in the village?" I asked.

"Mostly preparing for the whalers' departure, this past week," Father said. "You know, Noskeekwash's oldest son is joining us for the first time this year, when we go to sea."

"Chequnnap?" I asked.

Father hummed agreement and said, "I was at their fire the other day, for chat and dice. Chequnnap asked about you."

"Oh? What did he ask?"

"He asked if I'd seen the article that you were in, and he showed me your picture that he'd cut out of it," Father said. "He asked if you were courting anyone."

"Did he now," I said, feeling my face flush. "I wonder why he wants to know."

Father looked at me sidelong and smiled. I could hear Niquiat stifling his laughter. I didn't look at him.

"You know why he wants to know," Father said.

"Well, I can tell you with certainty that I'm not planning on courting Chequnnap. So if that news somehow got back to him before he embarrassed us both by carving me a whale tooth or something . . . it would be good."

"My daughter the heartbreaker," Father mused. "I can't help

but notice that your schoolmate Theod is quite a handsome young man."

"Oh, you've noticed that?" I said, folding my arms and glaring at him. "Do you want me to find out if he's courting anyone?"

They both laughed at that, and it felt the same as it had felt when Niquiat and I were little children.

"So, I've heard it said that there are a hundred different dragons at your school," Father said, still breathless from laughing. "Shall we go see some?"

I grinned, slipping my hand into his. Niquiat smiled, and the three of us proceeded up the road that led back to the school.

SPRING CAME

In the last week of April, the school grounds erupted in daffodils and tulips. Marta, despite not formally "coming out" this year, was dreadfully excited about the beginning of the social season—and about Fyrafax festivities. She'd had a dress commissioned for me without even bothering to show me watercolor plates. I didn't even know about it until it arrived.

It was pale yellow satin with a cross-striped pattern worked into the weave of the cloth. It fit correctly and looked well enough on . . . but when I gazed at myself in the mirror while wearing it, I had that same disconnected sense that I'd had upon first dressing in my school uniform—that feeling that I didn't know who was looking back at me. I'd much rather have worn the dress that Liberty had made for me. I felt like the smartest version of myself in that dress—clean and pressed and well put together, but *myself*. I didn't feel like any version of myself at all in this dress; I felt like a paper doll that had been dressed up.

Marta knew more about what was proper for this sort of occasion, though, so I deferred to her wisdom on matters of fashion.

I'd sent my invitations to Sigoskwe and Sakewa, and Theod had sent his to his cousins. Only Qunnis and Wunnepan would attend, Ommishqua being judged too young to travel from the island. Niquiat had arranged to travel with them. I told them, in the invitation, to dress as if they were going shopping in Catchnet and for the girls to wear white if possible.

I'd also, having received permission from Fraus Kuiper and Brinkerhoff, invited Ingrid and told her to bring whatever chaperone she felt was appropriate. I'd sent the letter with four tenpennik coins folded inside it, for train fare. Ingrid's family didn't seem particularly flush with coin, from what I'd gathered in our correspondence.

Marta rose early on the morning of Fyrafax, and made me get up early as well, and spent a great deal of time fussing with her hair and mine. I was to wear a crown of daffodils, and she a crown of pink rosebuds that matched her dress.

The school didn't have a formal garden like the one behind Marta's house or the one in the middle of Vastergot, with winding paths and artful plantings and all. Still, when we walked out of the front entrance, I found that the flight field had been converted into a sort of outdoor ballroom. Tables had been placed against the rear wall of the dragonhall, all laid in white linen. In the middle of the field, a maypole had been erected. There were a number of children playing in the field—boys kicking a ball around, girls weaving flower crowns as they sat on a blanket on the grass. Some dozen or so dragons had been allowed out of their stalls and were lounging on the grass between the flight field and the main entrance. Kasaqua trilled interest at my side, and I placed a hand on her hackles to still her. Her hackles were level with my waist now. At the rate she was growing, she'd be large enough to bear my weight by summer. I'd have to ask Marta if there was any ladies' equivalent to the kind of trail riding and hunting parties that Theod had been attending lately.

I spied Theod standing with Copper on the far side of the field, talking to Professor Mesman. Both were dressed in the same sort of sharply pressed suits that the gentlemen had worn for the Valkyrjafax ball, though at Valkyrjafax the common color had been black and now all the gentlemen seemed to be dressed in pale tan.

"The whole point of a garden party, for adults, is to see and be seen by one's peers," Marta said conspiratorially. "Take refreshment, promenade, comment upon how darling the children are, and inquire about whom they're related to. You're forging social connections."

The people we were likely to see and be seen by on this venture, apart from the ones Theod and I had invited, were not in any way my peers, but I didn't have the heart to point that out to Marta.

"Quite a lot of matchmaking goes on at garden parties, too," Marta continued, glancing slyly at a group of our classmates. I noted that Niklas was among them. I scanned for Ivar, but thankfully he didn't seem to be present.

"I do not intend to make any matches," I said, frowning.

"Well, of course *you* don't," Marta said, giggling, "but it *is* the sort of thing that parties like this are for. And for little children to enjoy themselves and be introduced to one another, of course. Come on, let's see who's arrived. You're expecting guests, aren't you? Oh, and there will of course be a lichtbildmacher milling about. We simply *have* to have our picture taken together; you look so lovely and so well put together in that dress."

Pictures of me looking as Anglish as possible were probably something that Frau Kuiper would heartily approve of. I forced a smile and allowed Marta to lead me over to the refreshments.

I did not like meddyglyn. It was distinctly herbal and sharp in a way that reminded me of medicine, with a cloying sweetness that didn't quite mask its underlying bitterness. Aside from the meddyglyn there were boiled eggs that had been dyed in flowery colors, and a wide assortment of sweet pastries, cold cuts of lamb with an herbal sauce, and white cheeses. Marta and I were sampling a kind of sticky almond and honey pastry when I spied Niquiat coming up the pathway that led from the train station.

He had a crowd with him.

Zhina was in the lead, having an animated conversation with Sakewa. Theod's cousins trailed a step behind, talking to one another. Sigoskwe was talking to a nackie boy just older than him—maybe thirteen or fourteen years of age—whom I didn't know. A nackie girl of about ten was talking to Niquiat while he clearly pretended polite interest. Ingrid, I realized, and probably Aksel, by association. They'd come, and they'd met Niquiat at the station. Niquiat waved when he saw me, and Ingrid turned and locked her gaze on me and on Kasaqua. Her face absolutely lit up, and she squealed as she scampered toward us.

"I'm so terribly pleased to meet you!" she said, quite breathless, as she came to a halting stop in front of me. "I didn't know your dragon was so big; she looked much smaller in the pictures! May I pet her? Thank you very much for inviting me; I hope it's all right that I've brought Aksel to be my chaperone. You sent enough train fare for two people both ways!"

The rest of the party caught up a moment later, Sakewa running to embrace me, Sigoskwe rushing to pet and coo at Kasaqua. Aksel seemed slightly lost, standing a few paces back, looking on uncertainly. I took it upon myself to make formal introductions, though they'd almost certainly introduced themselves already between the station and the school.

"Niquiat, Zhina, you already know Sigoskwe and Sakewa, Qunnis and Wunnepan, and you've met Marta. Everyone, this is Miss Ingrid Hakansdottir, who's been in postal correspondence with me, and her brother, Aksel. Ingrid, Aksel; Niquiat, Sigoskwe, and Sakewa are all my siblings. Qunnis and Wunnepan are cousins of Mr. Theod Knecht. Zhina is a close friend of Niquiat who works in the same enginekrafting co-op. Miss Marta Hagan is my classmate, a fellow dragoneer."

"You didn't say you were enginekrafters," Aksel said, turning to Niquiat and Zhina with a sudden keen interest.

"Well, we only just met you all of five minutes ago." Niquiat chuckled. "You keen on machines?"

Which led to Aksel, Zhina, and Niquiat pulling away slightly to converse about gear ratios and laws of mechanical action. Marta touched my elbow and said quietly, "This is rather more people than were expected, isn't it?"

"Well, I didn't expect Zhina or Aksel, but I can't see how it should be a problem. Let's see if we can't pry Theod away from Professor Mesman and we can make introductions to him, too."

Marta hemmed, sounding wildly dissatisfied with that suggestion. "If you don't mind terribly, I had been planning to ask Niklas about Dagny; I've heard that she's gotten a spring cold, the poor thing. You're invited to join me, of course, but . . ."

I resisted the urge to roll my eyes at her.

"Oh, no, do go on ahead; I've got guests to entertain," I said in my best genial Anglish society voice. "I'm sure we'll have a chance to mingle properly later."

The morning proceeded quite pleasantly after Marta absented herself from our company. Ingrid was intensely curious about life on Masquapaug, and she inundated Sakewa, Sigoskwe, Niquiat, and me with questions. At some point, a couple of other little girls joined our party. I didn't catch their last names, but the younger one was called Hjana. Both were, presumably, younger sisters of my classmates. Sakewa gathered up the other girls and taught them all a hand-clapping song. Sigoskwe and Aksel eventually joined some other boys in their kickball game. Niquiat and Zhina tried meddyglyn, and both of them seemed to enjoy it a great deal more than I did. Theod demonstrated Copper's flight skills, to the breathless thrill of all the children. We enjoyed food and idle chat, and told one another stories.

None of us made a special effort to mingle with my classmates, and none of my classmates made a special effort to mingle with us—though Niklas did pull Theod aside for a bit to chat over cups of meddyglyn. Theod seemed unenthused by whatever they were talking about.

There was a great deal of staring and murmuring directed at our party, but the younger children didn't seem to share any antipathy. Sakewa explained basic finger-weaving to a group of avidly interested girls and demonstrated with grass stems. Ingrid taught her how to weave flower crowns in the Anglish fashion.

At some point the lichtbildmacher found our party and asked us all to pose together—Theod and me and Niquiat and Zhina in the back, and all six children in front, flanked on either side by Kasaqua and Copper.

Our party carried on, couched in the larger garden party, until late into the afternoon. Niquiat then escorted everyone back to the train station with many thanks for the enjoyable day and promises to write.

On Wednesday the third of May, there was an article in the *Vastergot Gazette* about Fyrafax celebrations in and around the city. There was a pleasant little paragraph about the academy, accompanied by the lichtbild that Marta and I had posed for, wherein she and I looked very much the watercolor scene. Below it, there was the lichtbild of us all together, as well as several other candid images of children playing together, and one of Theod speaking with Niklas.

On Saturday the sixth, a scathing and vitriolic editorial by "A true son of Vastergot" was published in the *Vastergot Weekly Review*. It posed that Kuiper's Academy was harboring not just two nackies but a whole *crowd* of them—most from the filthy slums of the cannery district. It went on to posit that it was criminally irresponsible to allow nackie children to mingle with Anglish ones, because it put the Anglish children at risk of the sorts of filthy diseases that were common to the slums. It suggested that any true sons of Vastergot who had sons enrolled at the academy should withdraw them immediately, and that they should write letters to their thane and to the jarl and to the high king himself about the travesty that was taking place.

On Sunday, the seventh, there was a massacre of nackies in the mill district. It had begun with the murder, at a mead hall, of Hakan Gilvertsson.

Ingrid and Aksel's father.

THE GRAVITY OF THE SITUATION WAS MADE VERY CLEAR

We learned about the massacre on Monday morning, when Theod and I were called to Frau Kuiper's office directly from breakfast—before our morning session of study. Fraus Kuiper and Brinkerhoff were there, as well as Captain Einarsson. He looked at Theod and me with such open and vile disdain as we entered that I momentarily froze like a deer that'd heard a noise before I could bring myself to sit.

Frau Kuiper slid a copy of the *Vastergot Daily Bulletin* across the desk toward us; the headline declared that six people were dead. I read aloud, in a shaking voice, that a brawl started in the mead hall when an unnamed man had insulted the wife and children of Hakan Gilvertsson. A holmgang had been declared, and the men had begun fighting, but soon other men had become involved. By the time the thanegards had arrived to put down the disturbance, one Anglish man and five nackies had been killed. Their names were listed, but I didn't recognize any of them other than Ingrid's father. A number of people were being detained, awaiting a moot and an investigation. The article ended with the prediction that no one would be charged with any wrongdoing.

But Ingrid's father and five nackie men were *dead*.

"I hope that you understand the role you've played in these events," Frau Kuiper said, her mouth a thin, hard line. "Neither of you will be having guests of nackish descent on the school grounds from now on."

"We didn't do anything wrong," I said, feeling as hollow as a scooped-out pumpkin as I looked at her. "I asked for permission, and I got it. Our guests were all well dressed and well behaved. No one did anything that the other children and guests didn't do."

"Neither of you is old enough to remember anything about the war, are you?" Frau Kuiper asked, still frowning. "You've never seen dragons willfully turned to violence and mayhem. Do you really know what they're capable of, in the hands of a competent dragoneer?"

"I know that unshaped dragon's breath can turn farms and fields and livestock and people into wind and ash," I said, "because it was done on Naquipaug."

Frau Kuiper's gaze slid away from mine, glancing at Theod. He was looking stiff and pale, his gaze fixed resolutely on the table before him.

"Do you have anything to say on the subject, Mr. Knecht?"

"No, ma'am," he said crisply.

"Are either of you aware of the fact that Thane Stafn, Ivar's father, is an open member of the Ravens of Joden, or the significance of that?"

"It's a political party, isn't it?" I asked. "Marta and I talked about it, a bit."

"The Freemensthede is focused, politically, on creating a modern society in the image of classical Tyskland: laws shaped by the will of the smallfolk, education and patronage of the arts and philosophies, innovation and freethinking. It is no great secret to

society that I am an open and outspoken member of the Freemensthede, as is our currently sitting jarl, Leiknir Joervarsson."

She glanced at Captain Einarsson, who snorted slightly.

"In contrast, the Eiriksthede is more politically bent to main-
taining social order: laws shaped by the council of thanes, the
founding of thedes and strongholds, competent city planning, the
judicious use of resources. The previous jarl of Vaster Hold, Kjeld
Niklasson, was a staunch Eiriksthedeman. There were many people who were very angry when the council of thanes put down
Niklasson in favor of Joervarsson at the althynge of 1836. There
will be another althynge on the first of January 1845—two years
from now. The Eiriksthede is working diligently to overturn the
decision, and put Niklasson or another Eiriksthedeman back into
the jarl's seat.

"Which brings us to the Ravens of Joden. They are primarily
driven by an adherence to the will of the gods as dictated by the
leids and sagas. Tradition, moral rectitude, piety, and social su-
premacy. They've been very angry since the treaty of Bloodwater—
in fact, they would much rather we were still at war with Berri
Vaskos. They hold that our cession of lands south of the Polvaara
was cowardly and shameful. They hold, too, that it is the godstrewth
right of Norsfolk to secure rule in the manner of our ancestors—
to go a-viking and raiding into the lands of lesser folk, slaughtering them or taking them as thralls as befits the situation. It was in
that manner that folk of Norsland, Swedeland, and Daneland
took possession of many of the southlands of the old world:
Finnland and western Russland, Anglesland and Frankland, Tyskland and Polland. All were gained through bloody and glorious
conquest. The Ravens would have us return to such things, to take
the south from the Vaskoslandish and the west from the Wapash-
neepee Rikesband with great violence—and never mind the cost
in lives."

I felt cold, listening to that. I had a sudden urge to go to
Kasaqua, whom I'd left eating her breakfast in the dragonhall. I
swallowed hard and tried to quell it.

"What does all of this have to do with Theod and me?" I asked, trying to keep my voice steady.

"The two of you stand at the crux of two very different ways of thinking, and represent different directions that society could take. In one world, the Freemensthede gets their way, and our people shine the light of civilization onto yours. We bring you progress and modernity, law and order, and improvement of the land through agriculture and industry. In the other world, the Eiriksthede and the Ravens of Joden get their way, and your people are wholly exterminated in our conquest of the lands south and west, allowed to exist only as thralls—if you are allowed to exist at all."

"I don't think that I like either of those worlds, ma'am," I said, keeping my gaze even. She looked at me sharply, as if she was deciding whether or not my response was intolerably insolent.

"Since the posted bill was discovered this morning, Captain Einarsson and I have been in telegram correspondence with the Ministry of Dragon Affairs and the Office of the Jarl. Tomorrow morning, the two of you and your dragons will be escorted to the jarl's palace at Vaster's Hill to be examined by the jarl and the Council of Thanes. You will do as you are told, speak when you are spoken to, and answer any questions asked of you in fullness and in truth. I will tolerate no indiscretions. I have posed that it's possible for nackies to become rational, civil people—to be worthy of commanding dragons, to have a place in the modern world. You will not prove me wrong. If you shame this institution, I will not hesitate to allow the Ravens of Joden to rip both of you apart—to have your dragons put to death and have you exiled to Nack and Mask Islands respectively. To, ultimately, have both islands razed by dragonfire and rebuilt in the Norslandish image. Do you understand?"

"Yes, ma'am," I said, my voice as crisp and cowed as Theod's so often was.

I took a breath and tried to convince myself that I wasn't afraid.

ANEQUS AND THEOD WERE BROUGHT
BEFORE THE JARL AND HIS COUNCIL

On Tuesday morning, we were taken to the jarl's palace by automotor carriage. It was a rather different kind than the one Marta's father owned: a stouter, more somber affair with a fully closed seating box of black-lacquered metal and smoked glass. Our dragons were expected to accompany us to the meeting, to be presented much as we ourselves were being presented. They were currently housed in a horse trailer in the back, equally enclosed, and Kasaqua was not at all happy about it. Her unease made knots in my belly . . . or possibly my unease was making her unhappy.

The jarl's palace was even grander and more sweeping than Marta's house in Estervall. I'd seen it from a great distance, of course; it was perched atop Vaster's Hill—an impressive edifice of tiered roofs and sweeping wings surrounding a central tower. I'd never had occasion to be anywhere near the exclusive and moneyed neighborhood of Vaster's Hill, though. Approaching it as it was meant to be approached was a rather different experience. We had to pass through several different guarded gates as we ascended the hill, and by the time we got to the stone wall and massive wrought-isen gates that marked the entrance to the grounds of the palace itself, the entrance was guarded by men in black-and-scarlet uniforms perched on the backs of fierce silberdraches.

We were expected to make the journey from the carriage house to the palace proper on foot, as a formal procession, Frau Kuiper and Captain Einarsson in the front, and Theod and me behind them, each leading our dragons by their tack-rings. Approaching the front door necessitated that we travel a wide gravel-paved path between a series of carved columns.

We were being watched. I couldn't see who was watching, but I could feel it.

The grand edifice of the palace was built from huge timbers and plaster, carved with complicated reliefs of knots and whirls, then painted in striking colors and inlaid with gleaming metal. The overall effect was dazzling and just a bit *too much*. It had a much older sort of feel than most of the buildings in Vastergot. According to my erelore studies, it had originally been built as Vaster's Hall by Vaster Stafn, and had been completed in the year 1650—a hundred years before Emanuel Nordlund had come to make his folkreckoning of Naquipaug. It occurred to me, looking at all its lavish detail and breathtaking grandness, that I didn't know the year in which the temple had been built on Slipstone Island, or when the ruins on Beachy Hill had been built. But I could imagine, from the ruins, that they might have been as *much* as this once.

We were brought to a receiving hall, and then down a long corridor, and finally into an expansive square room with a high ceiling. There were three wooden tables arranged in a U-shape, just far enough from the walls that the chairs could be comfortably pulled out and rearranged with enough space to walk behind them. There were men seated in all of the chairs, watching critically as we entered. There was a smaller, less ornate table placed at the open end of the u-shape, which formed a three-sided enclosure around it. The chairs were arranged such that those sitting at the small table would be facing the other tables. Directly opposite us, in the center of the table placed nearest the back wall, there was a high-backed chair carved in the image of a two-headed dragon.

The jarl of Vastergot was seated in it.

He rose as we entered, placing both of his hands on the table, and all the other seated figures rose as well. He was a tall man, probably between forty and fifty years of age, with curling blond hair pulled back in a complicated array of braids. He even had braids in his *beard*, woven with little golden beads. He was dressed in silk and velvet, and he had an absolutely excessive gold chain around his neck and a golden circlet on his brow. On either side of him were two pairs of men in the same kind of uniform that Captain Einarsson wore: stark black with a red dragon on the right breast. Beyond them, sitting at the two flanking tables, were five men dressed like typical Anglish gentry.

"I greet you, my esteemed guests," the jarl said, smiling with all of his teeth. "As you surely know, I'm Jarl Leiknir Joervarsson of Vaster Hold. You are Anequs Aponakwesdottir and Theod Knecht, of Mask and Nack Islands respectively, aren't you?"

I wasn't sure if I was supposed to answer and flashed a glance at Theod. He was taking a short bow. I made a polite curtsy, hoping that I wasn't unbearably rude in my delay.

"Allow me to introduce my thanes," the jarl said, gesturing to each of the seated gentry in turn. "Arjan Stafn of Vastergot, Svend Jespersen of Catchnet, Havard Authunsson of Estervall, Jorborg Eidsson of Varmarden, and Gustav Lindgren of Skaldstead." He then gestured broadly to the four men standing most immediately around him and said, "Allow me also to introduce the lieutenants of the Ministry of Dragon Affairs: Karste Vaernes, Orri Hedinnsson, Aleksanteri Turunen, and Maik Theiner. You of course are already well acquainted with their captain, Johan

Einarsson. And everyone here knows the esteemed Frau Karina Kuiper."

I couldn't help keeping my gaze on Thane Stafn, remembering the editorial he'd written that had started all of this awful attention. He was an older man with a neatly trimmed white beard and yellow hair going white at the temples. He had the same icy, colorless eyes as his son.

Kasaqua, sensing my mood, made a barely imperceptible growl low in her breast. I swallowed and willed her to be silent.

"Alek here is supposed to be the minister in charge of all the outlying islands," the jarl continued, looking at the second man to his left, "so imagine my surprise that he didn't know about your dragon at all, Miss Aponakwesdottir, until you were in the papers."

The man he was looking at stood motionless, tight-lipped and pale, gazing resolutely into the middle distance.

"Alek isn't going to be a minister anymore," the jarl said, with a thin smile. "Run along, Alek."

The man took an aborted bow, turned on his heel, and filed out to the left, passing behind half of the thanes.

"Now, let's all be seated, shall we?" Jarl Joervarsson said, smiling, taking his seat with a confident sort of leisure. Everyone else sat, again moving like a wave away from the jarl. Frau Kuiper took a step forward and pulled out the chair on the leftmost side of the table, glancing back at me with steely eyes. I sat, and she pulled out the chair beside me and sat as well. To the right of Frau Kuiper, Captain Einarsson sat, and on the rightmost side of the table sat Theod. Kasaqua took her place at my feet at the left side of the table, with Copper at the right. Glancing left and right, I felt very much boxed in.

I felt *imprisoned*.

"I've been meaning to drop by the academy ever since Thane Stafn here had that editorial published—without consulting me or the other thanes, might I add," the jarl said, looking hard at Thane Stafn. "Then lovely Karina here arranged for the interviews, and I thought, 'Oh I really need to make a trip there, maybe bring my boys, let them squeal at the dragons, get Heidi to have tea with Karina and Elsie,' and then the article was out about the Valkyrja-fax ball, and the both of you so well dressed, then Karina's send-ing me a telegram about how you've gotten threats made to yourselves and your dragons and your families and your homes, so we launch an investigation about all of this and who might have sent them. But there's always just one more thing that needs doing, isn't there? So I put it to the side and then there's an article about Fyrafax, and everything seems lovely, and then I wake up yester-day morning and get told that there's been murder in the streets and six of my citizens are dead. So that made me go ahead and clear my schedule for today and round up this lot, so we could invite you here to talk. It's painfully obvious that we haven't been paying enough attention to what's going on out on the islands since all the bad business on Nack a dozen years ago. When was it, precisely?"

"March and April of 1825, sir," the man most immediately to his left said.

"That's right," the jarl said, in a way that indicated that he was wholly aware of exactly when it had been. "When we were still under Kjeld Niklasson. I've had to clean up a lot of negligence left over by the dear Herr Niklasson, and there've been a lot of people who'd rather it not be cleaned up because they're comfortable with the mess. Still, the only way out of a mire is through it; I learned that when I was just a whelp . . . back on the banks of the Polvaara."

He paused for a long moment and nodded at Frau Kuiper. She nodded back.

He clapped both hands loudly against the table. Kasaqua star-tled, and I gritted my teeth.

"It is the appointed duty of a thane to gather information from the torgars beneath them, to be familiar with their positions among the smallfolk of their holdings. Thane Jespersen, the out-lying islands are subjects of Catchnet, aren't they?"

"They are, sir," Thane Jespersen replied. He was an old man, bald, with a long gray beard.

"Who's the torgar responsible for the islands?"

"That would be one Wilhelm Hasenjager, greatfather of the Hasenjager family, who principally own the coal mine on Nack Island."

"He didn't tell you that a dragon was hatched on Mask Island last summer?"

"He did not, sir, though I can't fault him," Thane Jespersen blustered. "The egg was not registered, its hatching not reported. The nackies on Mask Island were deceitful about the whole affair."

"How often does Herr Hasenjager go to Mask to hold votes?" the jarl asked.

"I don't believe that he has ever had occasion to visit Mask Island," Jespersen answered.

"Pretty shit torgar, then, isn't he?" the jarl asked, in a way that wasn't asking at all.

Jespersen remained silent, scowling.

"On the first of August, I will be taking a small delegation to Nack Island to view lands that are held in common good by Catchnet Thede, and thus by Vaster Hold. While I'm there, there will be held a thynge. I want all those chosen as representatives of Nack and Mask there—people who have the authority to make decisions on behalf of the nackies because the nackies have voted for them to have that authority. Unlike my predecessor, I intend to prevent unfortunate situations like what happened on Nack. I intend to know what you want, what you need, as citizens. I want to make it very clear to all the people in my hold that the folk of the outlying islands—nackie and Norslandish alike—are citizens of Vastergot, of Lindmarden, of Markesland."

"Sir, this goes too far," Thane Stafn said, slapping his hand against the table. Kasaqua startled visibly this time, snapping her head toward him, making an aborted hiss as her hackles rose.

"The fact that nackies are citizens was established in the 1757

Treaty of New Linvik," the jarl spat, rising from his chair. "Do you intend to contest the treaty, Thane Stafn? Would you like to tell High King Yngvarr that he has to give Narrow Island and Mana-hatta back? I understand that the formerly savage folk known as 'Lenni-lenni' make up a large part of the working class there, as nackies of Massy-chooseit and Narry-gannet do in my own hold. Do you intend to invalidate the treaty and invite them to riot in the streets, Thane Stafn?"

"They were put down at Nack, and they could just as easily be put down in our own cities, but you and the rest of the Enki-wroughten Freemensthede are bent on letting them have dragons. Nackies are banned from the ownership of repeating arms and small arms of any kind on Nack and Mask, because of their inherently deceitful and violent natures. How much more damage will they be capable of, when they decide to rebel again, if they have dragons?"

"May I ask a question?" I asked, feeling my heartbeat in my throat—afraid to look at Frau Kuiper because I knew she had to be seethingly angry at me for speaking out of turn when she had very specifically forbade me from doing exactly that. There was a cold silence after I spoke, and Thane Stafn stared at me in disbelief.

Jarl Joervarsson laughed.

"Well, I can see why a dragon picked you!" he barked, slapping his knee. "Go ahead, girl, ask what you want."

I swallowed hard and took a breath, turning my head to look at Thane Stafn directly.

"Sir, the events at Naquipaug in 1825 were reactive in nature. The settlers there seized lands that they had no right to in accordance with the treaty. They violated the treaty and committed several murders. *That* was the cause of what you're calling the rebellion. You seem very sure that my people are going to decide to rebel again, sir. Do you intend to take violent actions against us that we would have cause to react to?"

"How *dare* you—" Thane Stafn snarled, looking remarkably like Ivar had in the moment after I'd slapped him. Kasaqua rose to her feet, snarling right back at him. I stood, putting a hand on her hackles, and Frau Kuiper grabbed my other hand at the wrist, her grip like an isen band.

I glanced at her.

There was actual fear in her eyes.

That frightened me more than anything in all the previous proceedings had.

"I apologize if the question seems impertinent, sir," I said quickly. "It's only that Theod and I have both received numerous explicit and direct threats to our lives and the lives of our families, from parties either anonymous or identifying themselves as 'true sons of Vastergot.' I have never wanted to hurt anybody—"

"You assaulted my son, you savage little bitch," Thane Stafn interrupted.

"I slapped Ivar because he was asking about carnal congress with girls thirteen years of age, sir," I said, keeping my voice as calm and even as I could. "He suffered no lasting harm, and hopefully learned that there are consequences for speaking crassly to a woman."

There was a ripple of quiet laughter from the gathered men, but Frau Kuiper's grip on my wrist tightened to the point of pain. I willfully prevented myself from wincing and continued.

"Neither Theod nor I have any intention of turning our dragons toward violence against anyone," I said. "Not toward the Anglish settlers on Nack Island, and not to anyone else, anywhere. I want nothing more than to study the skiltakraft relevant to athermaching and to become proficient enough to produce useful materials for the people of my village. I do not have the spirit of a Valkyre sleeping in my soul. I've never killed anything fiercer than an aging rooster, and I don't ever intend to. Theod would tell you the same, though he's far too polite to interrupt his betters the way I am now."

Frau Kuiper's grip on my wrist loosened fractionally.

"I do believe I like this girl, Karina," the jarl said. "She's got fire. Anyway, I invited you here to answer questions that my thanes had for you. So, thanes, have at it; ask your questions."

"Catchnet Thede rests," Thane Jespersen said, knocking twice on the table. "No further questions."

"Skaldstead Thede rests," Thane Lindgren echoed, also knocking.

"Varmarden Thede rests," Thane Eidsson said, knocking rather more softly than the other two had.

"Estervall Thede has a question," Thane Authunsson said, a smile in his voice. Marta was from Estervall. This was the thane that Marta's father voted for. "One would think that Stafn or Jespersen would have more to ask, with Jespersen's thede being the one you came from and are presumably going back to, and Stafn's thede the one you're occupying in the interim—except isn't the school actually in Varmarden Thede, Frau Kuiper?"

"It is, Thane Authunsson," Frau Kuiper answered, finally releasing my wrist. I pulled it back and rubbed it with my other hand; I might well have bruises tomorrow.

"So it most properly falls under Thane Eidsson's thede, doesn't it?"

"It does, Thane Authunsson," Frau Kuiper answered.

"So, really, I've got to wonder what business of Thane Stafn's any of this is at all," Thane Authunsson said, "as the students in question neither originate from his thede nor reside there. But let's put that aside for a moment. We've heard from the young woman. What about the young man? What do you intend to do with that fine beast there? It looks big enough to be flying. Is it?"

"Yes, sir," Theod said quietly, after a moment's hesitation. "Copper can fly, and he can bear my weight while on the ground, but he cannot yet bear me into the air."

"Can he make athers?"

"Under the guidance of Professor Ezel, he's demonstrated the ability to rend wood and stone into ash," Theod said. "My skilta-kraft skills, at present, are not well honed enough for true ather-maching. I'm still studying. Sir."

"What do you hope to achieve with your dragon, son?" Thane Authunsson pressed. "What purpose do you intend to turn him to?"

"I don't think I'll ever have the skill to be terribly useful at athermaching," Theod said. "But I know enough about dragon husbandry that Professor Mesman and Hallmaster Henkjan agree that I might have a promising career as a dragonhallmaster. Copper is an akhari, a Kindah breed selected for stamina in the air. There are reports of akhari dragons flying from Kedar to Kindah in thirty hours. He could be useful as a messenger and courier—though there's less need of that now in the age of telegraph."

"Have you considered joining the dragonthede?" Thane Authunsson asked.

Theod shook his head, seeming to shudder a little. Copper, at his feet, made a small noise of concern. "I'm not a fighter, sir. If I were called into service by my jarl, I would of course answer, but only in defense of my country. I've never wanted the kind of life that being a soldier would give me."

"I'm sure that we're all aware of this young man's parentage and provenance," Thane Stafn said. "The product of murder-ers—"

"His father, Menukkis, was a boatwright," I said. I'd gotten away with interrupting this far, after all. I folded my hands behind my back to keep Frau Kuiper from grabbing my wrist again. "His mother, Nepinnae, was her mother's oldest daughter, and a tal-ented weaver. I met his grandmother, and his aunt and uncle and cousins, this past December. His younger cousin Qunnis, who is eleven, is apprenticing to be a scholar of folklore and erelore."

Thane Stafn looked like he was about to say something, but the jarl raised his hand, and Thane Stafn closed his mouth with an exasperated sigh.

"Is there a dragonhall on Nack Island for you to apprentice at, young man?" the jarl asked, looking at Theod.

"I've only visited Nack Island once, and didn't really leave my grandmother's home while I was there," Theod answered. "But to my knowledge, there isn't one."

"Then the building of a dragonhall and the assigning of an appropriate hallmaster for you to apprentice under will have to be discussed at the thynge in August," the jarl said.

"Sir, the island of Nack is within my thede," Thane Jespersen said, glaring at the jarl. "Surely it's within my right to contest the building of a dragonhall, even if it's built on land held in the common good."

"It is, Thane Jespersen," the jarl said evenly. "So long as you are thane of Catchnet. We are going to hold a thynge, and I expect all the torgars of your thede to be there. If they tell me that they love you well enough for you to go on being their thane, then you can protest whatever you want."

"You don't have the authority—" Thane Stafn began, only for the jarl to once again leap to his feet.

"By Joden's wolf-bitten eye I don't!" he barked. Then he spat on the floor, glaring at each of the thanes in turn. "Niklasson let the lot of you rule your thedes like jarls, like petty kings! I am not going to do that. You are thanes, and you answer to the people of your thede—landowners *and* smallfolk. Up, all of you."

With great hesitation and a lot of hateful staring, all five thanes rose to their feet.

"Does anyone here want to invoke holmgang? You, as the people-voted thanes of Vaster Hold, have the right to challenge me to single combat for the position of jarl. Does anyone want to do that?"

There was a long, chilly silence.

"Arjan?" he sneered, glaring challenge at Thane Stafn. "Svend?"

The silence remained.

"Then my declarations stand. You will return to your thedes and make them known to your people. Anequs Aponakwesdottir and Theod Knecht are citizens of Vaster Hold, and thus of Lindmarden. Threats made against them, or against their dragons, will be answered in light of that. There will be held a thynge on the first of August on Nack Island. I expect the four of you to be there," he said, gesturing broadly at our table. "And, of course, Thane Jespersen and *all* of your torgars. I will be sending an inquiry to each district of your thede, to be sure that each district has a people-chosen torgar to represent it. So I declare. This council is dismissed."

"Jarl Joervarsson—" Thane Stafn began.

"This. Council. Is. Dismissed. Go home, Arjan, and tell your flock of ravens what I've said."

"This isn't over," Thane Stafn said.

"No, it isn't," the jarl concurred. "But this council *is*."

The thanes all bowed and filed out the doors to either side of the chamber. The jarl sighed hugely after they'd gone, letting his head roll backward for a moment before regaining his composure and turning to us.

"Meanwhile, my esteemed guests, might I invite you to dine with me in my private gardens? I've had Heidi and her maids arranging everything while we've all been shouting at each other."

"We would be very pleased to accept, Jarl Joervarsson," Frau Kuiper answered. She stood, placing a hand on my shoulder, gripping it tightly.

I'd have to answer to her later for my behavior, but I didn't regret a single word of what I'd said.

THEY TOOK LUNCHEON WITH THE JARL AND HIS FAMILY, WHICH DID NOT GO AS PLANNED

The gardens of the jarl's palace were just as grand and ornate as the rest of it—low hedges cut into winding knotwork, fragrant herbs and flowers along every path. We came around a stand of lilacs to a wide lawn that sloped downward and revealed a breathtaking view of the city and the ocean beyond. We were led to a small pavilion where a smörgåsbord luncheon had been laid out, and we were introduced to the jarl's wife and sons. They seemed more interested in our dragons than in us, which suited me perfectly well. Kasaqua was still bristling with tension, and stretching her legs by playing at chase and catch with a couple of children was exactly what she needed. Copper, for his part, seemed reluctant to leave Theod's side. When Theod took his seat, Copper lay beside him and put his huge head in Theod's lap, crooning softly.

"I'd like to thank all of you for putting up with that nonsense," the jarl said, "and for giving me an excuse to call a thynge in

Catchnet Thede. Jespersen has been thane there for forty years without interruption. I haven't been able to prove that the vote tallies are ingenuine, but I'm certain they are. If I can see him replaced with a member of the Freemensthede, we'll have a three-fifths majority in the council and we can actually get some things *done* for a change."

"I do wish that Eidsson would grow a backbone and take a stance," Frau Kuiper said. "You could have a four-fifths majority if he'd formally declare."

"He's not willing to make an enemy of Stafn, and I can't really blame him, poor boy," the jarl said. "Varmarden is shouting distance from here, after all, and he's so afraid of tarnishing his father's legacy. He'll get better, I'm sure of it. Speaking of succession, Johan, have you got someone lined up to take Alek's spot?"

"I'm still deliberating. Your announcement yesterday took me blind, I'm afraid," Captain Einarsson said with plain irritation. "You do realize that his career has been utterly destroyed? He's planning to go to Runestung Hold now, to see if he can't scrape together a good name for himself with valorous conduct."

"His job is to know things. If he doesn't know things that he should know, then he's of no use to me at all. Whereabouts is he going, do you know?"

"Most of the open combat is occurring in the area of Rune's Falls, where lake Catch-It-Coming thunders down into lake Ox-wagon. The Hudden-seeonnee Rikesband in the area have lately been very helpful in pushing back the Wapash-neepee Rikesband; they're quite keen on having a railroad built on lands they consider their own, and are very game toward settlers. Have you ever traveled to the west holdings, sir?"

"I haven't," the jarl said. "Spent all my soldiering years on the south border, holding the Vaskoslandish back at the Polvaara."

I was able to distance myself a bit from the jarl and Captain Einarsson by turning my attention to the food. Theod joined me as I was arranging a plate.

"I can't believe you actually spoke to Thane Stafn," he said softly.

"Well, *someone* had to," I said, "and no one else seemed to be asking the kind of things that concerned me. I'm going to have to send a telegram to Sachem Tanaquish about what happened here today, about there being a thynge on Naquipaug in August."

"If there's a dragonhall built on Naquipaug, would Kasaqua be housed there?" Theod asked.

"I hadn't really considered her housing, in terms of Anglish law. Until she can fly, I fully intend to keep her at home. Once she can fly and bear my weight . . . Well, a canoe with strong paddlers can get from Masquapaug to Naquipaug in an hour or so in clear weather. I've no idea how quick a flight might be. It probably wouldn't be sensible to have two dragonhalls in such close proximity."

"I hadn't considered ever leaving the school, but if there's a hallmaster installed on Naquipaug who can take over the wardship—"

"Or you could just continue to master skiltakraft," I said, looking pointedly at him.

He sighed. "I'm going to eat, and then I'm going to see if I can get Copper to calm himself enough to play with the jarl's boys. I'm in this awful loop where he's worried because I'm worried and I'm worried because he's worried."

I nodded understanding. I already felt markedly better in all ways, now that Kasaqua was unwinding herself. Theod and I could discuss skiltakraft at length when we were safely back at school.

Two of the tables were butted together, forming a corner, and I was standing in it as I selected another of the fancy little cakes when the jarl walked up to me. I was quite unable to retreat without making a scene of it. I glanced around to see where Frau Kuiper was, because I was reasonably certain that I wasn't actually supposed to speak directly with the jarl. She was a dozen paces away, talking to Captain Einarsson and the jarl's wife, paying me no attention at all.

"Your dragon; I've not seen the breed before," the jarl said conversationally. "Einarsson has, though, in action on the border of Runestung Hold; that's what's got his back up about all this. The Huddens and the Kannons have dragons, several different breeds. And skiltakraft like we've never seen before."

"I'm afraid I don't know anything about that, sir," I said.

"It's a bad business, what happened on Nack. Blood on everyone's hands, by the end of it. Yngvarr and me and the other jarls of Lindmarden, we've all talked about Runestung Hold. About what we're even trying to do out there. About the official policies of Lindmarden, as a nation, regarding natives. What do you think?"

"I don't know that I'm qualified to give an opinion, sir," I said carefully. "I can tell you that we on Masquapaug have no interest in fighting anyone, but I don't think anyone would be especially pleased if Norsfolk decided they wanted to come and live on Masquapaug in numbers, the way they do on Naquipaug. We're more interested in keeping to our own affairs. We'd probably be open to trade, but we don't have anything that you want. It's why we've been below notice for so long. Naquipaug didn't have anything that anyone wanted, either, until the coal was uncovered."

"Like I said, a bad business," the jarl said, wincing. He looked like he was about to say something else, but his gaze shifted, looking past me. I turned to look and saw a man walking resolutely toward us, his face grim and nervous. He was dressed in black and scarlet, like one of the dragon ministry officers, but he had a red sash quite unlike anything I'd seen before. He was carrying a thick folio.

"That's one of Stafn's torgars," the jarl said, frowning. "I'm afraid you'll have to excuse me."

The jarl turned on his heel, the corner of the two tables necessitating that he stand indecently close to me for a moment before he took a step forward. He moved like the sort of man who was used to having people make way for him.

The messenger was only a half dozen paces away now, and I saw very clearly as he reached his right hand into his jacket and drew out a pistol.

Everything happened at once then.

The pistol made two loud pops in quick succession. There was a sudden fiery pain all along my side, at the bottom of my rib cage. I fell onto the grass, curling on myself, my hand flying to my side to find a burning ruin of torn fabric and hot metal. Kasaqua made a noise I'd never heard before—an anguished scream, like a puma or a redhawk. Everything swam for a moment, then seemed to sharpen and brighten. The connection between Kasaqua and me intensified suddenly, to the point that I couldn't tell what was me and what was her. We were one creature—a creature that couldn't seem to take a full breath, a creature that was running. There was screaming and shouting, frenetic action everywhere. The pistol popped loudly again, and there was a bright flash of pain in our wing. We tasted blood on our teeth because *bite his face throat neck and break and rip it loud bad hurt stop it stop it stop it!*

We were one creature that loosed a breath around the bad thing in our mouth, which crumbled to ash. We were one creature that was panting in a sudden stillness, bewildered and half-mad and in pain.

Over the course of several breaths, we became two again.

The blood and ash was in her mouth, not mine. The pain was in my side, not hers. She was standing over a scorched place in the grass, her teeth flashing scarlet and her eyes flashing gold as she hissed challenge at anyone who dared approach. There was a bleeding wound in the leather of her right wing. I ran my hand along my side, but I didn't seem to be bleeding. The bullet hadn't actually pierced me. It had hit me sidelong, glancing across my ribs, deflected by layers of canvas and steel. My lowest left rib might well be broken, but I wasn't dying. Theod appeared at my side just as I was collecting myself enough to try sitting up. He helped me to my feet. I pushed him away, staggering over to Kasaqua. I caught her head in my hands, stroking her face and her neck, panting and sobbing, wholly unable to stop myself.

By the time she and I were calm enough to think, the jarl's men had arrived. They found Frau Kuiper and Captain Einarsson flanking the jarl, who was sitting on the grass, holding a wadded mass of cloth against his right side. The cloth was red with blood. I felt slightly disconnected from the series of events that followed, because I would not be separated from Kasaqua, feeling the need to keep my hands on her even as the jarl's doctors coaxed me out of my jacket and blouse to examine my non-wound. Even as they stitched the rent place in Kasaqua's wingleather.

The jarl had been wounded beneath his ribs on the right— a dangerous place prone to bleeding and infection because of all the delicate internal workings there: kidney, liver, gut. He was still in great danger.

Kasaqua had, however, very effectively dispatched the attempted assassin.

We were all ushered inside and bade to sit down, and I was offered something to drink. There was a lot of talk that I didn't precisely follow. Witnesses, statements, investigations. I sat on a padded chair with a blanket draped around my shoulders, one hand clutching a cup of something hot, the other playing through Kasaqua's hackles.

Apparently, she and I were heroes. We had halted an assassination attempt on the jarl. She had been injured in the process, and I very nearly so. It was going to be in every newspaper by tomorrow morning.

I was going to need a new uniform jacket before I had my lichtbild taken.

I was going to have to send telegrams home as soon as possible.

THE SCHOLARLY YEAR CAME TO AN END

Jarl Joervarsson didn't die.

We had first arrived at the jarl's residence on the ninth of May, and Theod and I remained guests of the jarl—and under the explicit protection of the jarl's personal guard—until the twenty-second. It was much to Frau Kuiper's dismay, as we were missing weeks of classes. In the interim, quite a lot of things happened.

I was more thoroughly examined by a doctor, several hours after being shot at. The doctor determined that the two lowermost ribs on my left side were cracked. The whole area was bruised—red-purple fading to blue-black. My ribs had to be bound, and I was ordered to take seven days of bed rest, and three weeks of light activity thereafter. I was given a cup of tea with a dose of laudanum in it, which left me generally insensible for the better part of the following day. I determined that I did not like laudanum at all and refused it thereafter.

Frau Kuiper returned to the school on the tenth, to see to affairs regarding the end of the scholarly year. Captain Einarsson returned to the offices of the Ministry of Dragon Affairs, to manage the replacement of Lieutenant Turunen.

There was a telegraph on the grounds of the palace, and thus I was able to send messages home, and to Niquiat, and to Marta and Sander and Liberty. Everyone expressed great sympathy and worry in the letters they sent back.

Mother wanted me to come home as soon as possible.

Marta wanted to host a party in my honor—a celebration of my bravery and valor.

Sander was taking legal steps to formally disown his mother, that he might continue attending Kuiper's Academy despite her attempts to withdraw him; she'd apparently taken to heart the article that suggested that any true sons of Vastergot who had sons enrolled at the academy should withdraw them. Twenty-eight students were withdrawing from Kuiper's Academy of Natural Philosophy and Skiltakraft, bringing the total population of students from one hundred and four to just seventy-six. Those withdrawing included notable names like Ivar Stafn, son of the thane of Vastergot, Frederik Anderssen, younger brother of a sitting jarl's guard, and Niklas Sørensen of the vastly wealthy and influential Vastergot Sørensens. Frau Jansen was concerned that being associated with an academy so contentious might badly impact Sander's future. Lisbet agreed that it was wholly reasonable of him to seek independence from her. He was going to remain a guest of Frau Brinkerhoff through the summer recess.

Liberty wished me a swift recovery.

On the eleventh of May, an investigation was launched by the jarl's guard concerning the attempted assassination. The assassin, as it turned out, was Torgar Birning Svenisson, son of Sveni Audulfsson, the official wroughtthane of the Ravens of Joden Thede. In total, thirteen people were arrested in association with the conspiracy to assassinate the jarl—one of them a former jarl's guard who openly admitted to being responsible for the threatening letter written to Theod and me. His name was Otrygg Otryggsson. He was brought before a moot by the Ministry of Dragon Affairs and declared morally unfit for the position of dragoneer. His dragon was to be put to death on the morning of the twelfth. He was found dead in his prison cell on the evening of the eleventh, having hanged himself. He'd left a plea behind that his dragon be spared, as she would do no harm to anyone if he was not her dragoneer.

The dragon was put to death anyway.

Thane Stafn could not be proven to be involved with the conspiracy at all, but the jarl called a thynge on the fifteenth of May on the grounds that even suspicion of involvement invalidated him as a thane.

But the torgars of Vastergot Thede voted to keep Thane Stafn in power.

Jarl Joervarsson issued a formal statement affirming that all persons dwelling on the outlying islands were citizens of Lindmarden and that violent action taken against them would be addressed accordingly in the eyes of the law. The Anglish on Naquipaug responded with a petition to overturn the statement. The jarl responded to the petition by posting six officers of the dragonthede to steadwatch the margins of the land where Naquisit holdings and Anglish holding met. The Anglish on Naquisit quit their coal mine and declared that no coal would be mined or shipped from Nack Island until the statement was retracted.

Our classmates took their final examinations during the week of the fifteenth to the nineteenth.

Theod and I returned to the school on the twenty-third of May. The other students had mostly gone home for the summer recess. Professors Ulfar, Ibarra, and Nazari all declared that Theod and I should be exempted from our final examinations, with our placements in the autumn session of classes to be determined by our general performance in the year. Professor Nazari was very pleased with my anglereckoning skills. Professor Ibarra lamented that I'd need to be in directed studies for another year, at least, to be as proficient and knowledgeable as a young woman of my age should be. Professor Ulfar asked that I pen a few profiles of the natural philosophy of Mask Island during the recess.

Professor Mesman, however, insisted that Theod be tested in his flight proficiency.

Professor Ezel insisted that both of us be tested on our proficiency in skiltakraft, and that if we failed, our dragons must be quartered through the summer at the school's dragonhall, under the supervision of Hallmaster Henkjan and the authority of Frau Kuiper. Captain Einarsson agreed with him. Such measures typically only applied to dragons that could fly, but Kasaqua had demonstrated both an ability and a willingness to kill a man with her breath. I needed to prove that I was in command of her, that I had all the skiltakraft acumen that a first-year student could be expected to possess.

So it was that on the twenty-fourth of May, Theod and I came to be seated in Professor Ezel's laboratory, at opposite ends of the room. Frau Kuiper was also present, sitting at the back of the room, writing observations in a small notebook. I didn't think that she sat in on any of the other students' examinations. Perhaps it had to do with Professor Ezel's accusations of my having cheated on the first end-of-term exam. Perhaps she wanted to be present to see for herself.

When Professor Ezel put the exam in front of me, I put all other thoughts from my mind. If nothing else, I had to prove that I was worthy of Kasaqua. I could not allow myself to be declared morally insufficient or lacking in scholarly knowledge. Too much relied on my being Nampeshiweisit. And if I didn't perform well, I'd be a prisoner here until I did.

This wasn't the rote memorization of the test I'd taken in De-

cember. There were things asked of me that I'd never done before. It asked me to join several skiltas into a single one, asked me
to construct skiltas to achieve complex outcomes . . . But all of it
was quite logically laid out, one subject leading to the next, the
application of theory made into examples. Yes, it required things
from the second-year texts, and from library texts that hadn't been
assigned to me, but I'd read those books anyway. It required me to
understand what skiltakraft *was*.

And I did.

I was still writing when I heard Professor Ezel spit, from the
far corner of the room, "How, by Enki's Grinning Teeth, do you
know how to do *that*?"

I looked up and saw him leaning over Theod's shoulder.
Looming, really, everything about his position a tacit threat.
Theod was hunched, breathing heavily, his hand shaking. I couldn't
see his face. I hoped, for his sake, that he wasn't crying.

"Anequs taught me," Theod said, his voice so soft I could
hardly hear. I glanced at Frau Kuiper. She was looking at Theod—
and at Professor Ezel, too.

"Anequs, who was in my class for one term, and who has been
instructing you for less than one term, taught you what you
couldn't get through your thick skull in *three* terms in my class and
independent study over the summer recess?"

"Yes?" Theod ventured.

Professor Ezel whipped around, looking right at me, catching
me looking at him. He pointed at me as he strode over.

"You got away with this somehow in December because I
couldn't prove it, but you'll not get away with it again! How are
you accomplishing this?"

"Professor Ezel—" Frau Kuiper said sharply, rising to her
feet, but whatever she'd meant to say was lost behind his fury.

He loomed over me, a kind of frantic madness in his eyes.
"Where are you getting your answers?"

I would not be cowed by a tantrum. I'd been shot at and come through it; what was there that Professor Ezel could do to me? I took a breath and said, "I've studied."

"You've *studied*," he repeated with a sneer. "I'm to believe that you have somehow understood the deepest and most difficult principles of skiltakraft by *studying independently*?"

"Professor—" Frau Kuiper began again, but this time it was I who talked over her.

"I've studied with Sander, and I've studied with Marta, and I've studied with Theod, and I've studied on my own. I've read all the books in the library. I've practiced drawing skiltas until I got blisters from the quill. So yes, I've studied. Have a look at my answers to these questions. Give me more questions, if you like. I'm even willing to do a practicum, if given leave to have Kasaqua loose her breath onto skiltas I prepare. I know what I'm doing because I have worked at this, ceaselessly, since my first day here at the academy."

"Yet you elected to leave my class this term," he accused.

"I was given the choice, and you weren't helping," I said, keeping my gaze steady, staring into his icy eyes. "Your lectures were a waste of my time."

"Theod has never passed a single examination I have given him. He has always failed to grasp the foundational principles of skiltakraft."

"Then I suppose I'm a better teacher than you, Professor," I said.

He raised his hand as if he meant to strike me. But Frau Kuiper—who had appeared rather abruptly behind him—caught his wrist in her isen grip.

"You are dismissed, Professor," she said coldly. "The examinations will be delivered to you in your office when they're completed."

"Karina—"

"Reinhard."

Professor Ezel sucked a breath through his teeth and let it out as a short sigh through his nose. He straightened his jacket, tipped his head to Frau Kuiper, and stalked out of the classroom.

"You tolerate far too much impudence from these children, Karina," he said, over his shoulder.

Frau Kuiper did not reply.

I looked back down at my exam and completed it in silence.

SCHOLARLY SKILL WAS MEASURED

Frau Kuiper instructed me to go to the dragonhall after my exam and see to Kasaqua. Theod was taking his practicum—actually drawing skiltas and having Copper breathe on them. I'd be next.

The dragonhall was emptier now than I'd ever seen it; Gerhard was asleep in his stall, but Captain Einarsson's dragon, and Professor Ibarra's, had gone with their respective dragoneers to their summer lodgings. I knew, abstractly, that Hallmaster Henkjan was still somewhere on the grounds, but he wasn't immediately in evidence.

The place seemed hollow. Lonely.

I took Kasaqua to the meadow between the dragonhall and the main building. She wasn't particularly inclined to chase after sparrows or field mice today and merely sat quietly at my side.

It was half an hour or so before Theod came walking across the field, Copper tidily at heel, still fully tacked. Theod looked slightly dazed and sat down beside me heavily. Copper flopped down next to him, mindless of his tack.

"How did it go?" I asked.

Theod sighed, dragging his hand through his hair.

"Nothing exploded."

"Well, that's always a good sign," I said, trying to chuckle and not precisely succeeding.

We were both quiet for a moment, and then he asked, "How are your ribs?"

"Better than they were, and worse than they will be," I replied. "I don't recommend getting shot."

"When I saw you fall, that day . . . it was like the bottom dropped out of everything," Theod said quietly. "I know I haven't been an easy person to . . . to do anything at all with. I'm standoff-ish and I jump to all the worst conclusions without any evidence. I've spent my whole life set apart from everyone and everything, just trying to make myself useful to someone. Just trying not to make trouble, to not be a nuisance or a burden."

"Theod—" I said, but he kept talking right over me.

"But then you show up, and you do nothing *but* make trouble, and . . . it's worth it. I don't know if I've done well enough on my skiltakraft practical to be considered proficient, but I know that I've done so much better on it than I ever have before, and that's because of you."

"All I've ever tried to do is the right thing," I said. "If that's so very different from how things have been done before, then what's been done before was wrong."

Theod looked at me in a way that made something tighten in my throat. Looking like he might have something important to say. I bit my lip, because I very much wanted, in that moment, to kiss him.

Until Frau Kuiper cleared her throat loudly, drawing my attention away.

At the far end of the flight field there was a wide, shallow, bowl-shaped hollow of sandy soil that was kept free of grass by daily raking. The ground was damp, as if it had just rained. It hadn't just rained. It was also freshly raked.

Frau Kuiper said, "I have here two stoppered loodglas flasks. Your task is to fill one with vetna and the other with stiksna."

"Which will require me to produce water first," I said. "May I have a vessel to gather the water in?"

"No, you may not," Frau Kuiper said. "The drawing of water from air and the transmutation of water into vetna and stiksna can be done in a single figure, if you have the skill."

"Compound figures don't appear in any of the first-year texts and materials," I said.

"But do you have the knowledge and the skill?" Frau Kuiper pressed.

I sighed through my nose, realizing that I shouldn't have expected the test to be fair.

Frau Kuiper handed me a black, polished cane. She met my eyes as I took it from her, and I could tell that she was trying to communicate something to me, but I hadn't the slightest notion of what that was.

I marked out the motes of water-from-air, but I didn't connect the lines. I drew a skilta of containment and direction around the figure, and to either side I laid out the motes for vetna and stiksna, placing the flasks at the centers of them. I drew a containing circle around all of it, and Frau Kuiper asked, "Is there a reason you've drawn it clockwise?"

"Is there a reason I shouldn't have?" I countered, pausing.

"No, but drawing skiltas clockwise is in my experience a quirk of left-handed individuals, which you are not. I find it curious."

"There's a long tradition among my people of art forms moving east-south-west-north," I said evenly. "It's the direction that comes most naturally to me."

She made a mildly interested sound in her throat and gestured for me to continue. I completed the circle, then took a step back to make sure everything was in order before dragging the tip of the cane through the sandy soil and joining the motes with a single unbroken line that looped and swirled around and around an imaginary center an equal distance between the flasks. It took the better part of three minutes, but I managed to join the end to the beginning without stopping or lifting the cane from the sand.

Frau Kuiper examined my work, walking around its margins to see it from all angles, then said, "Now instruct your dragon to power the skilta you've drawn."

I closed my eyes and took a breath, then opened them again and looked to Kasaqua, meeting her gaze. Expressing to her, in thought, that what I'd drawn was a shaping device—like a dance— and that she should loose the fullness of her power upon it. I felt her understanding in return, and she stepped forward and exhaled shapeless medicine onto the skilta I'd drawn.

There was a faint sensation of wind, and the smell of tat-krafted air. A cloud of fog billowed out from the center of the skilta. It dissipated a moment later to show the two flasks standing where I'd set them, unbroken, apparently unchanged. Frau Kuiper walked over and picked up one, then the other. It felt profoundly wrong for her to be walking over the skilta I'd drawn, though I couldn't have explained why or how. I set my teeth and squared my shoulders.

"I'll want to examine these in the laboratory, but nothing went catastrophically wrong," she said, sounding mildly surprised. "In the meantime, I suggest that you find your dragon something to eat and allow her to spend some time running. Examinations typically make dragons restless and nervous because of the heightened emotions of the dragoneers."

"Thank you, ma'am," I said, taking a breath. I didn't feel restless or nervous at all, because Kasaqua felt . . . calm. Accomplished. Triumphant. It was a buoyant feeling, something that made me want to *fly*. We walked together to where Theod was sitting by the dragonhall. Copper was laid out on his back, belly up, Theod scratching his chest and belly with a stout-bristled brush.

"Would the two of you like to join Frau Brinkerhoff and me in our private dining room for dinner in two hours' time? I believe that we have much to discuss, in light of recent events."

It wasn't precisely an invitation, because I did not at all feel at liberty to refuse.

DELIBERATION WAS REACHED, AND PLANS LAID FOR THE FUTURE

I'd never given much thought to where Fraus Kuiper and Brinkerhoff took their meals, but their private dining room was adjacent to the kitchens, on the side opposite the students' dining hall. It was much, much smaller, and elegantly appointed. Maids brought food to us as we sat uncomfortably under Frau Kuiper's appraising gaze. Liberty wasn't among them—though I shouldn't have expected her to be, because she was a laundry maid and not a kitchen maid. I wondered where she was and what she did during the summer recess. There couldn't have been nearly as much work to be done, with so few students in residence. How much more time could she devote to making gloves and handkerchiefs?

How long would it take for her to amass enough money to buy her freedom?

I considered how I could arrange for Theod and Liberty to meet next term. If I was going to be courting both of them, they really ought to know each other.

"Well," Frau Kuiper said, catching my attention back, "it certainly has been an eventful year. Even Mr. Knecht's first year with us was not of such intense interest to the public as yours has been, Miss Anequs. I must say that was . . . unexpected."

"I never meant to make a spectacle of myself, ma'am," I said.

"I'm not sure that it could have been avoided," she said. "Nor that it should have been. Events larger than the two of you are shaping themselves even now. When each of you agreed to come here and be pupils of my academy, it was understood in the eyes of the law that I would be responsible for your actions and those of the dragons you command, until such time as you proved yourselves worthy and able dragoneers. Competency in skiltakraft is a part of that, as is competency in flight—but so, too, is the matter of personal character. There is a certain willfulness to be expected of dragoneers; it's a characteristic that dragons seem to favor when choosing."

"I have always endeavored to do whatever is asked of me to prove myself worthy of Copper," Theod said. I glanced at him, because he so seldom spoke unless in direct answer to a question.

"And so you have, as far as character goes," Frau Kuiper said thoughtfully. "But there's still the matter of knowledge, and of skill. When I was your age—"

"Karina," Frau Brinkerhoff said, her voice fondly chiding, "when you were their age, you were committing deceit against crown and country regarding your age and sex, all to be allowed to stand before a dragon egg. As I recall, it *did* make the papers."

Frau Kuiper turned to glare at her, and Frau Brinkerhoff smiled sweetly.

Someone knocked on the door.

"Come in," Frau Kuiper said, turning that way.

Professor Ezel entered, looking mildly startled to find Theod and me seated with Fraus Kuiper and Brinkerhoff. He sighed exasperation and came in anyway, closing the door behind him.

"Good evening, Professor Ezel," Frau Kuiper said. "Have you come to a conclusion regarding the examinations?"

"I would have preferred to speak to you in private confidence," Professor Ezel said, plainly irritated, "but I can see that I'll be denied the pleasure. As much as I might disagree with the qualifications of these students regarding their social fitness to be dragoneers, I cannot fault their skiltakraft performance. Which you have many times reminded me is the only rubric on which I am qualified to judge."

"They're proficient?"

"Demonstrably so, yes. Mr. Knecht, while his technique and base knowledge leave much to be desired, is as acceptably skilled at the work I'd expect from a second-year student. And Miss Anequs has the same level of skill—or possibly more so—though I cannot determine the source of her knowledge."

"Is it so difficult to believe that the girl might be *clever*, Reinhard?" Frau Brinkerhoff asked, looking at him with disapproval, and he sighed through his nose.

"Is it your professional opinion, as a professor of skiltakraft and a judge of its application," Frau Kuiper continued, "that these two students are capable of independent study? Can they be allowed the freedom to take their dragons from the grounds for summer recess?"

"As much as I am loath to say this . . . Yes, they can. I can provide no practical reason to retain them here."

I turned to Theod, smiling.

He wasn't smiling. He looked absolutely stunned.

"You are welcome to remain on the grounds of the school, Mr. Knecht, if that's your preference, but it is no longer legally required of you. Both of you are at liberty to go where you will, and to bring your dragons with you. I only ask—for your safety and my peace of mind—that you report your location to me periodically. It's certain that there are still people at large who present a very real threat to you and your dragons. I'll expect you both back here on the fourth of September, for the beginning of the autumn term."

"Of course, ma'am," I said, unable to stop grinning.

I was going to go *home*.

And I rather suspected that Theod was coming with me.

ANEQUS AND THEOD WENT HOME

At the dragonhall, after dinner, Theod and I stood together watching the sun set over the field.

"I got a telegram from my aunt and her family," Theod confirmed. "They want me to come stay with them for the summer."

"You should," I said. "You deserve a chance to get to know them, and for them to know you."

"They'd like me to invite you to visit, too," he said.

"That shouldn't be difficult to arrange," I said. "A sturdy canoe can make the crossing in an hour or so." I glanced at Kasaqua. She was certainly too big for my little one-seat canoe, the one I'd used to carry her egg back from Slipstone Island. "I might need a bigger boat for her, though, and someone to help paddle it."

"You don't lack for friends or family," Theod said.

"Neither do you," I replied. "But if you think it would be easier just to fly over and visit me . . ."

"I'll need to anyway, for skiltakraft lessons. Besides, I'm a hopeless dancer," he said.

"You're not," I said, elbowing him lightly. "I've seen you dance, remember?"

"I didn't mean that kind of dancing," he said, laughing, "I meant . . . the nackie kind."

"You know, since my brother left for Vastergot, there's been an empty pallet in my mother's house. If you wanted to come and stay with me . . ."

"Are you sure we wouldn't get in trouble for the sheer impropriety of sleeping under the same roof without a chaperone? There are going to be Anglishmen all over Nack, keeping track of my comings and goings because of the thynge and the building of a dragonhall and all that. My aunt said that there are already a pair of dragoneers in Nack Port, assigned there by order of the jarl."

"With my grandmother, mother, brother, and sister likewise sleeping under the same roof?" I asked, scoffing. "I don't think there could be any scandals."

Theod laughed. He looked quite good laughing.

"That said, if you *wanted* there to be scandals . . . Well, there are plenty of places on Masquapaug where two young people might find time and space to be alone together."

Theod looked at me, startled, his mouth partly open. It was my turn to laugh. I made a note to myself that as soon as Liberty was free, the three of us simply had to meet and have a long talk about courting. I had a feeling that Theod would choke at the idea of two women courting at all, not to mention the idea that I might like to court him and Liberty at the same time.

That I might like to marry both of them, eventually. If everything went well.

Maybe I'd bring it up at Mishona's wedding feast. I smiled to myself, considering. We walked together back toward the school as the sun went down. We both had packing to do.

On Friday morning, we went home.

To Masquapaug.

Together.

MONIQUILL BLACKGOOSE began writing science fiction and fantasy when she was twelve and hasn't stopped writing since. She is an enrolled member of the Seaconke Wampanoag Tribe, and a lineal descendant of Ousamequin Massasoit. She is an avid costumer and an active member of the steampunk community. She has blogged, essayed, and discussed extensively across many platforms the depictions of indigenous and indigenous-coded characters in science fiction and fantasy. Her works often explore themes of inequality in social and political power, consent, agency, and social revolution.

EXPLORE THE WORLDS OF DEL REY BOOKS

READ EXCERPTS
from hot new titles.

STAY UP-TO-DATE
on your favorite authors.

FIND OUT about exclusive
giveaways and sweepstakes.